Storm
AND THE MERMAID'S KNOT

MEGHAN RICHARDSON
AND
TINA VERDUZCO

LunaSea Publishing
ST. AUGUSTINE, FLORIDA

Published by LunaSea Publishing, Saint Augustine, FL 32080 USA
Visit us at LunaSeaPublishing.com

Cover artwork by Paul M. Archetko. Cover design by Dean Richardson
Typeset in EB Garamond and Gondola SD-Swash

SECOND EDITION

Library of Congress Cataloging-in-Publication-Data is available on file

HARDBACK ISBN: 978-0-9985495-0-7
TRADEPAPER ISBN: 978-0-9985495-1-4
EPUB ISBN: 978-0-9985495-2-1

WHAT READERS ARE SAYING...

A must have for a Summer Reading List! I just finished the book and thought it was amazing. - Melinda Bernholz

A Delight for All Ages...Although written for a young adult audience, it is a great read for more mature readers too. - Amazon Customer

Five Stars - Awesome for teen/tween's!! - Teresa A. Sibley

Delightful and Fun!! The book was absolutely delightful. The emotions of the characters are so spot-on, that even as a "not-so-young" adult, I absolutely connected to them... - Mary Williams

Fantastic! Awesome! Make sure you have time because once you pick this book up you won't want to put it down until the end! Really looking forward #2! - TauSupporter

Fabulous Read! Totally captured from the first page and couldn't put it down until I finished. Great girl power from Storm, her mother and grandmother. - M, New Bern, NC

******

Tell us what you think! Please visit:

LunaSeaPublishing.com or
Storm and the Mermaid's Knot-A Novel on Facebook

Dedication

For my three mers, Shannon, Jonathan, and Owen who remind me every day that in order to see you must first believe. ~Mom (Meghan)

For my mom, Ethel, who always believed in me and now will be able to read this book before she's dead and for Paul, for twenty amazing years and the constant reminder that magic is all around us. ~Tina

"The arrival of the Storm that Spring was more than a meteorological phenomenon. The legend behind the legend of the unseasonable tempest that caused destruction for days along the East Coast of the United States begins and ends in our tiny seaside town of St. Augustine Florida...

Clouds, pregnant with rain, grew into colossal mountains. For three days, the rains and winds were unrelenting. The downpour eased her transition into the world; the waves pounded the shores with each contraction until the howling wind finally cried with joy. Without being aware, as so often happens, we were all witnesses to the birth of a Storm; and this is where I agree with the weathermen because it really was a Storm like no other. While some say it was a onetime event and others say the Storm left us forever, I know the Storm will return. And for her, I will wait.

Be this the truth or be me a liar. And I tell you I ain't no liar."

— M. Humpphrey, Birth Of A Storm, Legends Behind the Legends of St. Augustine

Storm

AND THE MERMAID'S KNOT

Chapter One

"Come on Storm, it's not that bad."

"What? Oh," I mumbled and picked up my pace. Nana was already ten feet ahead of me in the parking garage lined with rows of rental cars. Sweat rolled down my arms and my clothes hung limply about my body. *Seriously? Not that bad? The temperature must be over 90 degrees in this stupid garage!* I shoved back a heavy ringlet of hair from my face...again. *I hate this.*

"Is sweat supposed to be running in rivulets down my arms and legs?" I called to Nana who was now fifteen feet ahead.

Nana's laughter echoed around me. It didn't help my mood.

"Rivulets?" She asked when I finally caught up to her. Her grey-green eyes twinkled with amusement.

"Yes, rivulets. Meaning a small brook or stream. See?" I held my very much not amused left arm up to show the disgustingly large, wet circle that ringed my underarm.

The wrinkles around Nana's eyes and mouth deepened as she laughed again. "Well, I'm glad that at least the Word of the Day Calendar is coming in handy. Just a touch farther, Dear, and we can stem those rivulets with some air conditioning." The whirring of her suitcase's wheels started again and before I even had my bags back in place I was ten paces behind her. "Humph," I grunted. *Whatever.*

My nana was a rare, Florida native. A descendant of some Lighthouse Keeper from the 1800's, she was born and raised in the tiny, historic, seaside town of St. Augustine. *Perhaps that explains her ease in this heat.* But then again, I'm technically a native, too. But far from growing up in St. Augustine, Dad, Nana and I barely escaped with our lives when a massive storm devastated the town. I don't remember it 'cause I was just a baby. My mom wasn't as lucky as we were.

"I'm dying here." I called weakly to Nana's backside. Nana's smooth, silver hair, tied low on her neck in a loose bun, mocked me with every cheerful bounce. *Seriously, I hate this.*

"I see the space up ahead," her voice drifted back, "G-5."

"I'm hot *and* tired, my shoulders hurt from my backpack, AND one of the stupid wheels on my stupid suitcase keeps rolling all crooked!" *I REALLY HATE THIS!*

"UGH!" I dropped my bag to the ground. It made a loud THUNK. I flapped my mass of sweat-drenched hair like a fan on my neck, sat down on my mountain of bags, and hung my head between my knees. "I hate this place and I hate you for bringing me here," I mumbled to Nana's back. A rumble of thunder emphasized my feelings. When I glanced at the open sides of the garage, the palm trees that had sparkled brightly with sun a moment before had dulled. I prepared for the next rumble of thunder but my ears were caught off guard by a deafening silence instead. *Uh oh.* I looked up sheepishly.

"Did you just stamp your foot and then sit down in a huff?" Nana had stopped.

A mumbled, "maybe," tripped out.

"These teenage moments are becoming more frequent Stormy. Get it together and stop acting like a spoiled child. I miss my Storm of old who was always up for adventure."

"She'd come back if we could just go back home," I whispered.

"Stop mumbling."

"I said, 'she'd.come. back. if. we. could. just. go. HOME!'"

Nana exhaled slowly through her nose. And when she spoke, her voice was unnaturally controlled. "Don't start that again. We're here for the summer whether you like it or not. That is your choice to make. So if you want to be miserable about it, so be it, but sitting on your bags in protest isn't going to get you to the car any faster."

Nana's bag began it's drone on the cement floor. With no choice but to follow, I grudgingly hoisted my back pack to my shoulders, straightened my roller bag for the hundredth time and trailed in her wake. I consoled my drained limbs by composing an entry for my blog about how my summer adventures were off to a swimmingly splendid start surrounded by air thicker than water, temperatures that rivaled the sun's, and a caregiver who mocked my discomfort. Dad and Nana were my only readers since neither of them would let me publish anything online because of an absurd fear about stalkers and perverts, and identity thieves, and probably even alien abductions. Everyone else I know has some kind of online account. Most of the kids at school have multiple. But not me. Nope, you aren't going to be able to find me in the cyber world. I feel so much safer. *Yeah right. How the heck do they expect me to communicate without the use of computers?*

"Here we are!" Nana chimed with what I considered an overly cheery voice.

"Finally!" I whined.

Nana unlocked the trunk. "Calm down, Stormy. It really isn't that hot."

"Tell that to my neck, armpits and knees! I'm dripping and feel all wobbly!" I felt the electric charge in the air before the lightning flashed. Thunder grumbled in response.

Nana's look, the one with the lifted eyebrow told me I 'had better change my tone.'

"Humph." I collapsed into the passenger seat.

"Here's some water." She handed me a small bottle she saved from the plane and I greedily emptied it in three large gulps. I had never been this thirsty and this drenched all at the same time before. Nana shifted her seat toward the steering wheel and adjusted the rear view mirror down to accommodate her petite frame while I pushed my seat all the way back to give my cramped legs space to stretch.

"How are the legs feeling, Stormy?" Nana asked as she focused on the side mirrors.

"Full of pins and needles, but I'll live." The past few months I'd been having really bad growing pains in my joints.

Nana brought the car to life and I relaxed into my promised air conditioned comfort.

"Ahhh." The popping in my knees felt wonderful as I stretched.

"Aren't you a little excited to be here? The course starts Monday. I really think you'll love it not to mention getting to know the town where you were born," Nana said as we spiraled down through the levels of the garage.

"Yeah, I guess, I mean, sure, it'll be great." I leaned closer to the vents which blew out deliciously cold air. The truth was I had no desire to learn about St. Augustine or to learn about Marine Science. But Nana insisted on a visit to St. Augustine this summer. She said it was time. Time for what, I had no idea and she wasn't willing to tell me which wasn't helping our newly strained relationship.

She and I had always been close; more a mother than a grandmother to me. But a few months ago she became distant and distracted. It started the night after my sixteenth birthday. We sat together on my swing set, like we did when I was little, looked at the stars and ate a second helping of cake. We picked out the Big Dipper and Orion and I talked about how my growing pains seemed to be getting worse. She turned and looked at me and her eyes went wide, almost scared, but then as quickly as the expression appeared it disappeared and was replaced by a weak smile. I asked what was wrong, but she just said it was getting late and we should go inside. Later that night I heard her talking to Dad about St. Augustine.

"Matthew," Nana whispered, "it's time to go back."

"Mom, she's not ready."

"Matthew, it's time. We aren't the ones that need to prepare her. We both knew this day would come. Time is now running short and she'll need every moment of it. It is down to only three possible outcomes, either I'm able to find it, she is able to succeed, or they win."

"It's not safe."

"It'll be safe with Z and the others to protect her. I will also be sure to keep them focused, as my family has done for generations, until she can protect herself."

"Right. Z did such a grand job last time," Dad shot back.

"We're still here aren't we? There was no choice back then, if someone had found out, it would have been disaster for us and for them."

"It WAS a disaster last time!" Dad's voice rose.

"Hush. You'll wake Storm," Nana reprimanded in a strained whisper.

"It was a disaster last time," Dad hissed. "We barely got out alive and for what? To simply send Storm back to them on a silver platter? "P..."" Dad's voice stuttered, "Storm's mother sacrificed herself for us because Z couldn't even control her own sister. This time the stakes are just as high if not higher. Who's going to have Storm's back this time?"

"I will. You know as well as I that Storm must go back."

The soft chink of ice being swirled in Dad's glass filled the silence. *He must be thinking. He always swirls his glass when he thinks.*

That was the last time Dad and Nana spoke about the summer plans. Dad thumped around the house for the next few weeks in a perpetual grumpy mood. Nana shopped and packed and ignored my dad. To top it all off, Nana enrolled me in a Marine Science course for the summer! So not only did I have to spend the summer in a town I'd rather forget existed, but I also had to go to summer school to learn about the ocean. Why Nana thought taking a course about the ocean in the town where my mother died of drowning would be something I'd consider a fun way to spend my summer was beyond me. Her answer to why I had to come, "Because it's time." And Dad's answer every time I asked if I could stay home was,

"No."

"But..."

"No!" He said firmly. The heat rose to my cheeks and my vision blurred as my eyes filled with water. Dad was never very good at handling tears and I saw his face change from determination to concentration. He and I both knew that one wrong move and he'd have a full blown sobbing mess to clean up. He motioned me to come over and sit next to him on the couch. Despite my best efforts to stay willful and make it as hard as possible for him, my adrenalin ebbed. I leaned against him and inhaled. Automatically, my body relaxed as it inhaled the familiar and comforting aromas of Old Spice and Jameson's Irish Whiskey. Those two scents enveloped me in a protective shield called, Dad.

"I don't want to go," I whispered on an exhale.

"I know, honey, I know." Dad stroked my hair slowly. The ice in his glass shifted position. We sat in silence for a few minutes and listened to the rain.

"You don't want me to go, either, I know you don't," I finally said.

"You're right, I don't. But what I want and what you need are different things this time."

"Why can't you come with us?"

"I have to get this manuscript finished. The deadline is...well, I have a lot of work still left and it's just..." His voice trailed off into a jumble of mumbled words.

He was lying about the work thing. He wanted to avoid St. Augustine as much as I did. The difference was that he could say no because he was an adult. I had to do as I was told because I wasn't. I turned my head to see his face and then followed his gaze to the painting on the wall. A beautiful oil painting of three mermaids in rough, nighttime seas. It was one of the few objects that we managed to take with us when we fled the storm in St. Augustine sixteen years ago. It was painted by my mom.

One mermaid sat in the foreground on an exposed rock, her torso was tall and proud as she caressed her deep red hair. Her skin was opalescent in the moon light and her tail hung into the dark water. A second mermaid swam in front of the rock with swirls of black and brown hair. The third mermaid was the least detailed. She sat on a rock in the background, her most defining characteristic being her blonde hair and a touch of white highlights. The overall feel of the painting was slightly ominous like a storm was likely to hit. But the expression of the red haired mermaid was so confident that she seemed to be nearly daring the impending confrontation. She always made me feel confident. Like if only I could be as strong as she was, everything would be okay.

When I was little, I pretended one of the mermaids was my mom. I changed which one was her every time. I figured that if she were a mermaid then she wouldn't have drowned. I suppose it was my way to keep her alive...I suppose saving the painting was Dad's. The painting was a piece of my mom. Her hands had touched the canvas and her brush strokes had created the picture. As long as the painting survived, so did a part of my mom.

******

"Stormy, you awake?" Nana's voice dissolved my memory like salt in water.

"Hmm mmm." I opened my heavy eyelids and peeled my cheek from the window. The world outside moved much slower than my last conscious vision of us speeding down I-95.

"Where are we?" I asked with a yawn, a stretch, and a bunch of pops in my joints.

"Saint Augustine!" Nana exclaimed. "Look to your left, there's the Fort. And up ahead is the Bridge of Lions."

Following Nana's excited directives, I rubbed the sleep from my eyes and looked around. Two story homes, restaurants and inns, all with railed porches made colorful with masses of bougainvillea in full bloom, lined the waterfront street on one side of the road. On the other, a stern, stone fort was seated atop a rolling knoll of manicured grass. Sail boat masts bobbed beyond the low seawall, people walked in small packs, children ate ice-cream and a row of horse drawn carriages awaited tours. Cars, horses, Harleys, bicycles, and walkers all shared the same space.

"Is that a pirate?" I pointed to a man strolling in full swashbuckling attire.

"Yes."

I stared at Nana for a moment, unsure if she was joking me. Apparently not. I rolled down the window and took a deep breath. A unique mixture of horses, roasted garlic, jasmine and seaweed assaulted me.

I jumped suddenly as the roar of cannon fire echoed in the air. "*Jezzus!* Are we under attack?"

Nana laughed. "No. The fort does reenactments and shoots off cannons throughout the day."

"Didn't anyone bother to tell them what century we're in now?" I asked.

"St. Augustine tends to keep its own sense of time."

We drove over the Bridge of Lions and the famed Lighthouse tower came into clearer view. It was striped black and white, topped with a light tower painted red. The feel of the medieval, fairytale town was replaced by that of a tropical resort. A bright, wooden marquee welcomed us to St. Augustine Beach.

Surfers in baggies crossed the two-lane road with boards tucked under their arms and skateboarders rolled down the sidewalks dodging unsuspecting walkers. I tried to spot the ocean, but mounding dunes followed by a hotels blocked my view. Palm trees lined a park that welcomed us to the Pier where an open-air pavilion stood and children splashed in tiny fountains of water. Volleyball players jumped and slid along a row of sand courts and kites decorated the sky like confetti. We eventually turned left onto a short street that ended in sand dunes and Nana parked in the driveway of a yellow, two-story house. My mouth closed with a sharp click of my teeth.

We're here. Great.

An odd mixture of excitement, fear, and nausea jockeyed for position in my stomach.

"I've missed this place more than I realized," Nana beamed with excitement.

The yellow house at which we'd arrived had been Nana's childhood home. She'd grown up, raised her son, welcomed a granddaughter into the world, and then fled from here sixteen years ago. It had been rented ever since. Now it was hers again. Not sharing Nana's excitement or her fond memories, I grabbed my backpack and climbed the stairs to the back deck with the excitement level of a prisoner climbing to the gallows. I was about to ask something but that something flew right out of my head because my mind couldn't make sense of the images my eyes were giving it.

I had, of course, read about the Atlantic Ocean. We had studied it, and the other oceans, in science, geography, and history. But no words or photographs could have prepared me for the intensity of the experience of actually seeing it firsthand.

The deck I stood on was at the height of the dunes. Beyond the sandy, oat-covered hills was a blindingly bright white expanse of sand. I squinted against the reflective glare. Waves of heat morphed into waves of water. Large swells rose. Waves of turquoise capped in white froth broke one after the other onto the smooth, darkened sand. The sound of the crashing water reverberated within me. It was a sound old as the earth, a sound of time passing, of eternity, of beating hearts...BOOM, swoosh...BOOM, swoosh...BOOM, swoosh...the waves chanted their endless rhythm and consumed me until I was nothing more than an extension of their bodiless heart and soul.

Brilliant diamonds sparkled on the water's surface beyond the breakers and the colors of the water changed endlessly; deep blue surrounded circles of light green that blended with tan and cream. And with all of its immensity and strength, it appeared to stop at one, continuous line that divided the light blue sky from the deep blue water. How brave the explorer must have been to sail to that edge, to take on such an unknown, to leave the land behind. "Whoa!" I finally managed to utter in a complete understatement.

"Beautiful isn't it?" Nana put her arm around my waist as she stood next to me.

"I was so angry at you for making me come here," I confessed in a whisper.

"I know you were."

"I'm sorry."

"Why?"

"Because I've been acting so mean to you."

"Thank you for apologizing.

I looked over to Nana. She looked back at me. "I had no idea," I said.

"Of what?"

"That it could be so beautiful."

"Sometimes we don't always see things for how they really are," she replied.

"What do you mean?"

"Well, sometimes we need to see things for ourselves rather than take on the truth of others."

"Oh." I thought of how I considered the ocean. Adjectives included cruel and dangerous and deadly. But those were words given to me by my father. They were words put upon me rather than words I created for myself. Now as I looked out to the ocean I had an entirely different set of words floating around. They included awe-inspiring and beautiful and powerful.

Nana gave my waist a gentle squeeze and whispered, "Welcome home." I wasn't sure if she was talking to me or to herself.

Chapter Two

As soon as I was able to tear my eyes away from the ocean, I went inside and found my bedroom; upstairs, first door on right. My room was on the beach side of the house, directly over the deck. After taking in the view of the sparkling water from my window, a strange desire came to mind...I wanted to touch the water. I needed to feel it. I wasn't sure why, but it had to happen. I dropped my bags on the floor and skipped down the stairs two at a time.

"Sunscreen!" Nana called after me from the kitchen.

"Yeah, got some," I called back, *in my bag*, I finished in my head. I needed to work on my tan anyway.

"I'm certainly glad to see your attitude so much improved!" Nana smiled as she peered around the corner of the wall dividing the kitchen from the main hall.

I smiled. "This all feels like some strange dream."

"Dream is better than nightmare," Nana said with a smile. "Hey, I don't want you going in the water alone, okay? The ocean is beautiful, but you also need to beware of its dangers, especially to someone who's never been in anything deeper than her own bathtub."

"Of course not, I'm not that brave," I laughed nervously at the thought of actually swimming in the ocean. "I'm not even wearing my bathing suit. I just want to check it out."

She held my gaze in hers and smiled. "You're okay?"

"Yeah, I am...but I'm not sure why."

Nana just nodded and smiled. "Because you're Storm, that's why."

"Naaanaaa," I rolled my eyes.

"Okay, okay, but you don't give yourself enough credit for what you've already accomplished. You got on that plane and you came to the place that has long been a very valid reason for a nightmare. You are strong and one day you're going to realize it and when you do, everybody else better watch out."

"Right, thanks for the vote of confidence. But I'm not sure how much choice I actually had in it all."

"Well, behind every great woman is a great Nana," she smiled. I laughed. "Okay, if you're sure you'll be fine, I'm going to run to the market to pick up some food. Is there anything special you want me to get?"

"Whatever...well, maybe some cookies."

"Okay." Nana said.

"Ooh, and vanilla ice-cream," I added.

"Okay."

"Oh, and that caramel sauce and maybe some..."

"Sprinkles. Yes, I already had them down," Nana said with a laugh. "You and your sweet tooth. You get that from your father."

Out on the deck, a black and white cat lounged in a small spot of shade. The cat yawned and lazily rolled over as I knelt beside her. "Nana!" I called, "Look who's here!" I scratched her soft belly fur.

Nana came out wiping her hands on a kitchen towel. "Oh, hello little cat. She's probably one of the beach cats that have roamed these dunes since I was a little girl." Nana knelt next to me and gave the kitty a tickle behind the ear. The cat rolled back and forth contentedly on its back. "According to local folk lore, if a beach cat shows up at your door on your first visit you will be blessed with love and opportunities for new adventures!" Nana said with a wink. "Perfect don't you think?"

She stood back up with a soft grunt. "Are you sure you put on enough sunscreen?"

"Yeah," I said with a barely perceptible amount of hesitation. "I won't be long anyway." I gave her a quick hug and headed out. I crossed the little wooden walkover right next to our deck with my towel tucked under my glowing white arms. The screech of birds made me look up to one of the tall palm trees. Two small, black headed, green bodied parrots peered out at me from a hole in the trunk.

"Hi there," I offered their inquisitive faces.

They turned their heads sideways in a very parrot-like way but I suppose they didn't find me all that interesting because they disappeared back inside and picked up their squawky conversation.

"So, we have forts, pirates, and parrots here. Sounds like a Jimmy Buffett song," I mumbled to myself with a shrug. Leaving my parrot friends to their own discussions, I reached the powdery white sand on the other side of the walkover. The heat from both the air and the sand hit me like a wall of fire and literally took my breath away. Drawing in painful gasps of scorching air into my lungs, I began the journey toward the promised oasis. Barefoot and inexperienced, what started as a walk soon became a jog because of a very uncomfortable burning sensation under my feet. Uncomfortable became painful and then unbearable.

The fire was finally extinguished following an all out mad dash toward the water and an awkward plunge into an oncoming wave. I was still catching my breath when the next wave rolled up and the water lapped at my calves.

The third wave, more eager than the previous ones splashed my knees and my heart beat nervously behind my ribs. My temples pounded slightly and my breath came too quickly. Little spots of lights that looked like fireflies danced in front of my eyes. *Oh God, Storm, don't faint*, I thought. "You're okay. Just keep it together," I said with pinched lips during forced, slow exhales.

I felt a conflict of urges, one wanted to race forward into the blue-green frothy water and the other wanted to turn tail and dash back up to the safety of the dunes. Determined not to make a fool of myself by running back across the fire pit, or drowning in the ocean, I compromised and backed slowly (and calmly) away from the water's edge and settled in the damp, packed sand. The sand gave way so easily under the slightest pressure of my toes but as soon as the pressure was released, it filled back in as if it had never been disturbed. My impression was forgotten nearly as soon as it was made. So fleeting, so unremarkable...so me...the pale, nondescript girl from Indiana. "Well, at least you didn't faint," I said to myself as I spread out my towel.

******

The smell of suntan lotion and a freshening of the salt air stirred me from my sun-induced trance. With a little stretch, I looked around to reorient myself. Propped to my elbows, I noticed the water had reached within inches of my toes. *What time is it?* I wondered as two swimmers wearing silver swim caps, black goggles, matching silver pendants and black suits walked past me into the oncoming surf. They jumped gracefully over the breaking waves. The urge to dive into the water surged within me again.

My wandering eyes then settled on a group of three surfers, two girls and one boy. I couldn't hear their words but the timber of their voices carried to me with the onshore wind; two sopranos and one tenor. They appeared completely at ease; like they ruled the seas. The shock of water on my feet startled me.

Seriously, what time is it? I wondered again and sat up. My shoulders and arms felt tight and prickly.

I gathered my now half-soaked towel with a quick glance back to the surfers. The blonde girl surfer faced me while the boy and brunette laughed together. "Yeah, hi," I whispered self deprecatingly, "I'm Storm, the dork who gets burned on her first day in Saint Augustine."

******

"NANA, I'M HOME!" I yelled in the open space of the front hallway.

"Hey sweetie," Nana called from the kitchen, "Be sure to rinse your feet with the hose out on the deck to get all the sand off."

Damp footprints outlined in sand traced the path I had taken from the front door to the stairs. "OKAY!" I called back and continued up the stairs. *I'll take care of the sand later*, I thought, *I need a shower first.*

Submerged beneath the deliciously cool waterfall, my skin instantly felt better. *For all my fear of the ocean, who knew the sun would do me in*, I thought as cold water cascaded over my shoulders.

"Storm!"

"AHH! Ah-Ack," I screamed, jolted suddenly out of my reverie, and then coughed out the water I swallowed. "You scared me."

"Are you ever going to come up for air? I've been trying to get your attention for five minutes now." Nana's silhouette moved around the bathroom.

"Sorry, just rinsing off," I said peeking around the edge of the curtain.

"Mmm mmm. And the sand downstairs?"

"Oh, yeah, I was going to get that when I got out."

"Don't even try to use that smile on me. What am I going to do with you child?" Nana chided. "Well, come on then, get dried off and put some clothes on. I thought we'd celebrate the start of our summer by eating out tonight." Nana's gaze shifted to the arm holding the curtain back and she made a 'tsking' sound with her tongue. "You also may want to put some extra lotion on that pink skin of yours. Next time try actually rubbing the sunscreen *onto* your skin rather than just waving the bottle near you."

I looked down at my arms and saw just how *more* pink, not less, they were. "It doesn't feel too bad," I lied. With the water off, the slightest bend of a joint stung so much tears welled in the corners of my eyes.

"I left a bottle of special aftersun lotion on your dresser."

"I'll give the lotion a try if you insist. But it's really not that bad." *Ouch*, I thought.

After Nana left, I reached for the soft, fluffy, pink towel. My skin yelled at every soft, fluffy, pink touch. The girl in the mirror looked back at me with wide eyes and a shocked expression. Her bright red skin had the perfect outline of shorts and a tank top. Her eyes, the color of new leaves, shone brightly within her very ruddy face. I touched my leg gingerly with the tip of one finger and saw the impression on mirror girl's leg go from pink to white back to pink. "Youch!" I whispered. "Great going, Storm," I scolded myself. "Really great."

During my rant, I noticed a small, green, glass bottle on the dresser. I unscrewed the cap cautiously, like it was some kind of witch's brew and wafted my hand over the opening like my chemistry teacher taught me. The first whiff proved surprising, a strong smell, but very pleasant...a touch spicy. I poured some into my hands and rubbed it on my barbecued body as gently as possible. The thick, slippery liquid felt like cool, moist air blown onto my seared skin. *Thanks Nana*, I thought.

After dousing my body in the lifesaving mystery lotion, I rummaged through my disheveled suitcase tossing clothes out until I came across the thinnest, lightest, softest sundress I owned. Vowing to take care of my unpacking first thing in the morning, I slipped the dress carefully over my shoulders and let it hang loosely around my body. I felt fine as long as no part of the fabric actually touched the burned parts of my skin.

Nana sat at the kitchen table flipping through a magazine, she had changed into Capri pants and a thin button down linen shirt. She looked so at home in this beach house I could almost picture her as a young girl running around barefoot in the sand with her silver-haired ponytail a deep brown instead.

"Okay Nana, I'm ready!"

"Oh! Don't sneak up on me like that. You're gonna give me a heart attack one of these days." But her words were full of love as she smiled at me. "How did the lotion work?"

"It was, umm, really good. Thanks. I guess I got a bit more sun than I thought. Did you buy it at the store?"

"No, an old friend of mine makes it." Nana stood up slowly from her chair, the only time she ever seemed her age was when she stood or sat down. "Well, let's get goin' Stormy, the evening isn't getting any younger and neither am I!" Nana picked up her hand bag from the table. As we turned for the front door, I noticed my trail of sand was gone.

"Sorry about the sand. I was totally going to clean it up."

"It's okay, but next time *you're* sweeping!" Nana winked and gave me two, quick firm pats on my shoulder. I winced in pain.

"Sorry, Dear. I forgot about the burn," she said. I wasn't quite sure I believed her.

******

The Beachcomber, a beachfront restaurant just a couple of blocks from our house, guided wayward beach wanders, like a lighthouse in foul weather, with a beacon of blazing tiki torches and signs promising icy drinks. We chose a table in the far corner closest to the mountainous dunes. The wind carried an intoxicating scent of blooming jasmine mixed with the brine from the sea.

"Are you okay?" Nana asked.

"Yeah...just feeling for the fried fish they have on special tonight," I smiled weakly.

I looked up from the menu as a young waitress approached our table. She wore short khaki shorts and a blue tank top that had *Beachcomber* sprawled in large letters across the front.

"Hiya! Welcome to Beachcombers!" She said in an alluring European accent. British? Scottish? Australian? I couldn't place it for sure but it made me want to hear more. Her strawberry blonde hair fell in gorgeous waves down her back, her smooth bronze skin shimmered in the fading light of the sky and her light green eyes reflected the gold of the torchlight and ohmygod where's the bag to place over my head so as not to be compared to her in any way.

"Hi Pearl, it has been a long time," Nana said. *Huh?* My mind broke from its self-conscious worries. *Nana knows her?*

"Rean!" Pearl exclaimed in her smooth, resonating voice. "You've changed!" *She knows Nana?*

"A few more wrinkles on the surface, but I'm still young at heart, dear. You, of course, look as divine as ever," Nana said.

"You look good, too."

"Good for an old lady, you mean."

"No, just good," Pearl smiled and then leaned in for a hug. "How's Matthew?"

"He's fine. Or at least as fine as to be expected."

"Has it been a long time for you?"

"Sixteen years," Nana replied. Still confused, I just sat quietly.

"Sixteen years. That's a lot for you." Pearl's eyes widened. "Then..." Pearl's eyes locked onto mine and a chill ran through my body. An eruption of goose bumps covered my skin and with those came the unpleasant sensation of now chilled, burned skin.

"Yes, Pearl, this is Storm."

"H'allo," Pearl said mechanically. And as if she struggled to break out of a trance, a disconnected voice whispered, "Nice to see you again, Storm."

"Again?" I smiled weakly.

"Storm is here for the summer, Pearl," Nana spoke the words quietly.

Pearl nodded her head and looked back to Nana. "Time is nearly up then. It's nearly over, except, well, Storm," Pearl looked back to me with a gigantic grin, "you're back!"

A sudden swirl of wind blew our menus from the table. Sharply scented smoke drifted toward us from the now extinguished torches.

Chapter Three

"But Nana, how did that waitress know you?" My skin was about to burst into flames and my patience with her strange behavior was short.

"Stormy, I told you, I knew Pearl's mother from before we left Saint Augustine. She and I were close friends."

"But that doesn't explain why *she* knew *you*. She looked just a little older than me and you haven't been here in *forever!*"

"Perhaps her mother shared stories about me," Nana offered.

Why is Nana being so difficult?! "Well, can you at least tell me what you guys were talking about?"

Nana looked toward the ocean. Smooth waves rolled in under the twilight sky and a line of a dozen pelicans played follow-the-leader as each skimmed the surface in turn; an astounding display of grace in flight despite the species' ungainly appearance on land. By the time I turned back to Nana, she had already started walking again.

Or not. "I guess that's the end of *that* conversation," I whispered and kicked at the sand with my toes.

******

"Nana? Aren't you going to bed?" I asked after we returned to the house. She was straightening some pillows on the living room sofas. I really wanted to ask her more about that waitress.

"In a bit, dear. I'm going to enjoy a little time outside on the deck."

"Do you want some company?" I offered.

"Not tonight, Stormy, you need your rest and I need my thoughts."

"But..." The urge to argue about being treated like a kid reared within me but when Nana's eyes met mine, I recognized that look of distraction about her. I had no idea what was bothering Nana these days but I decided that I wouldn't add to her worries tonight by fluffing my teenage feathers. "...I love you," I offered.

Her eyes softened with unspoken thanks. "I love you, too."

"We'll talk tomorrow?" I asked.

"Tomorrow, yes. Goodnight and sweet dreams."

******

Hearing the sound of the waves outside my window was a new experience for me. I was shocked at how their rhythmic pounding relaxed me. With closed eyes, I imagined rising and falling with them. Floating, drifting, sinking below the frothy surface until water caressed all parts of my body. At first it felt good, like a silky blanket but as I sank deeper, the silk turned to ice and the tickles turned to clamps.

Oh, I thought apathetically, *this place again.*

The sound of waves may have been new, but being trapped below the ocean's surface was very familiar. As usual, once I realized that I was in my recurring nightmare, I struggled and flailed my useless limbs in every direction. They were sluggish and ineffective. Heavy like a limb that's fallen asleep; you know it's still attached, but moving it is like shifting dead weight.

With equal ineffectiveness, I opened my eyes. Frustratingly blurry images filtered back to me and I had to blink continuously. I hated this nightmare. I was trapped, helpless and totally without control.

But then I felt it, something cool and smooth took hold of my hand. I looked to the left but my eyes refused to stay open long enough to make out the form. I felt the rush of water over my skin...whatever it was, was guiding me forward. I was like an inexperienced dancer guided by a skilled partner and even without eyes to see, my limbs learned how to move. They swayed effortlessly and the water turned once again to silky fingers.

Smoother and faster I soared. I rose, swooped and spun...it felt like flying, effortless, weightless, powerful...until, the hand disappeared. I sunk rapidly and my stomach lurched in fear. My limbs lost coordination and I fought the icy tentacles that gripped at my skin. *Mom*, I called. *Come back, Help*. My mind screamed.

"HELP!" I cried with a great gasp as I opened my eyes. My arms were stretched over my head and when I rotated them back forward shooting pains of pins and needles startled me into full consciousness. I rubbed my arms to encourage blood flow.

"OUCH!" I totally had forgotten about my sunburn. "Okay, seriously?" I asked the universe of unfairness. I sat up gingerly but still felt trapped. A quick glance at my legs solved that mystery as my sheet had spiraled around and cocooned my legs.

I really hate that dream, I thought.

The clock next to my bed proudly displayed 3:23 in laser red numbers. "Great," I groaned and stumbled toward the dresser in search of the lotion Nana left for me.

I sighed as the pungent lotion worked its soothing magic. Even the parts that weren't burned got a dousing, which in all honesty were few. With the last of the flames extinguished and the remnants of my dream suppressed, I was ready to find sleep again except that my ears picked up faint murmurs intermingled with the monotonous surf.

Peering out my window, I saw two figures sitting on opposing chairs engaged in deep conversation on our deck.

They sat in profile to my window and the one on the left, with her legs extended onto the other chair, was unmistakably Nana.

The figure on the right, also with legs extended, was in the middle of laughing at something Nana said. The mystery woman's long hair, dark brown or possibly dark red, was untied and blew lightly about her like the wisps of newly made cotton candy. There was an air of confidence, bordering on intimidation. In her presence, Nana appeared delicate, fragile, and old.

"...very risky," Nana spoke quietly to the woman.

"Perhaps, but this is our last chance," the woman answered in a voice that resonated like a large brass wind chime. Her sleeveless, long, white dress danced around her and her bare arms appeared bleached, bright, nearly iridescent under the crescent moon's dim glow.

"I wish it didn't have to..."

Only snippets rode on the wind up to my window. I wished I had opened it before I went to bed. Not wanting to give away my presence by lifting the squeaky frame, I pressed my ear more firmly to the clammy glass pane.

"...she will be protected from this moment on...Others do not yet suspect....Storm will not know....the future of...depends on her success..."

They're talking about me?

"...but can you be *sure*..." Nana sounded worried.

Be sure of what?

The woman laughed softly. "Sure is not something I can be in this case. But I am counting on you, dear friend, to help them all to stay focused on this important task. As always, our weakness is why we must turn to you, our trusted Harn. Help them as they become distracted. This is one time we can't afford to drift off."

The fragmented conversation tidbits were killing me! For all my years of listening in on Nana and Dad's discussions, I never had this much trouble. The combination of sea breeze and waves seemed to push the words off course before they could make it to my ears.

"When will...start?" Nana asked.

"It will happen naturally, she'll...training will begin immediately..." The woman deep smooth voice lulled me and I remembered that I was really tired. Forgetting for a moment that I was eavesdropping, my head clunked lightly against the pane.

The voices stopped. I opened my eyes and peered out again at the two figures. The woman's eyes, glowing like coals left smoldering after a bonfire, locked on mine.

Unable to move, to duck or even to blink, I just stared back. The moonlight caught a sparkle of teeth as the corner of her lips turned upward ever so slightly. She blinked and I dropped to my knees below the windowsill. My heart thumped loudly in my chest and my breath came in short bursts. When the woman spoke again, her words were easy to hear. "The walls have ears and loose lips, sink ships."

"But my dear Z, we still have so much to figure out!" Nana protested.

"There is still some time my old friend," Z responded.

"Who are *you* callin' old? At least *I'm* only double digits!" Nana said. Both women laughed.

"You were right to bring her here," Z said. "It's begun and we must use our remaining time wisely."

"I honestly wished that it wouldn't happen, that she would be more her father's child than her mother's," Nana said.

"I understand your fears," Z replied. "If all goes as I hope, she will pass the test and take her place this summer solstice and at least one of our worries can be eased."

"And as for the other worry?" Nana asked.

"We need your help more than ever dear friend. You are the last and our time is up. Perhaps your friend could assist you as before."

"No, not after what happened. It was a mistake to include him; a mistake I will never forgive myself for. This is my burden. I could never ask him for more than he's already given."

"Oh yes, he lost something. What was it again?"

"It wasn't a what, it was a who."

"Oh yes, I remember, now. Sharon was it?"

"Sophie."

"Yes, dear Sophie. Well, as you desire. Till the morrow," Z said, "get some rest and remember to give Storm the items I told you to make the transition easier. The calmer she stays, the easier it will be."

"Can I tell her anything?"

"No. She must discover the truth on her own and we need her to stay safe until the time comes."

"It won't be easy to keep the secret from her. Have you had to deal with teenage determination lately?"

"Thankfully, no. Not for a few centuries anyway. But if she is anything like her mother, you had better be prepared for the worst. Perhaps I can help by providing a bit of a distraction."

"Just as long as it is a safe distraction."

"Oh, he should be safe enough."

"I'm not sure I like I sound of that."

Muffled laughter rang lightly in the air. "Goodnight, Dear Friend. And welcome home."

The front door squeaked opened and closed.

"Yikes!" I squeaked.

I leaped clear across the space between my window and bed and dove under the covers. My heart thudded heavily in my chest.

The creaking stairs betrayed Nana's location.

I buried my head in my pillow and tried to slow my breathing. My door opened slowly. A subtle fruity scent of white wine drifted in on the air. A cool hand lay on my back.

"Z says you have grown into a beautiful young lady with a level of curiosity quite similar to that of your mother. Sleep now, darling. The excitement is over for tonight and the morning comes quickly around here." Two quick pats on my back and she left.

After the door closed behind her, I rolled over onto my back. Sleep was far from an option as my brain spun with too many questions.

******

I created a theory on where the phrase, 'bright and early' originated...St. Augustine. Nana wasn't joking when she said 'morning comes quickly'. It came fast and furious in the form of a colossal, burning, intense yellow orb hovering in the sky. And lucky me, that orb rose directly in front of *my* window and succeeded in heating my room to a balmy 90 degrees.

I tried keeping my eyes closed against it, but the backs of my eyelids burned bright orange and my limbs dripped with sweat.

"Good morning Stormy!" Nana announced as she trotted into my room. The aroma of hot coffee surrounded her. "Rise and shine sleepy head!"

"Hmm mmm." I managed to mumble into my pillow. "Just a few more minutes...please, Nana."

"Whew, it's a bit musty in here, Storm, let me open your window for a fresh breeze," Nana chirped. I heard the reluctant wooden frame creak and felt the rush of warm, moist air blow over my damp skin. "We're meeting Mr. Manistar at the Lighthouse at nine."

"kay," I muttered but didn't lift my head.

"Breakfast in fifteen minutes," Nana added cheerfully and breezed out of the room as quickly as she had entered. The scent of her coffee lingered in her wake.

"At least my sunburn isn't yelling at me," I announced to the empty room after a roll of my shoulders. Pushing my mane out of my face and blinking into the brightness, I reached my arms overhead to stretch but stopped in mid-movement.

"What is that smell?" A memory of the way our science lab smelled when Mr. Turner brought back samples of kelp from his trip to California popped in my head. "Yuck." I sniffed tentatively at the pungent air. Following my nose around the room, the source eluded me until I reached up to close the window figuring, by way of elimination, that the smell must be from something horrible lying dead on the beach. "Ugh!" I exclaimed and turned my nose to my armpit. *Oh my God. It's me!* I quickly rubbed my deodorant on but the odor wasn't fazed. It also wasn't just my armpits! My skin smelled like something that would have been found drying or *dying* by the high tide line. *Yuck!* While searching desperately for something to fix the smell, a rainbow dancing on the wall caught my eye. It was from the morning sun reflecting off the lotion bottle Nana left for me.

There was no time for a shower so I quickly poured a generous amount of the clear liquid into my hands and rubbed it on my skin. The scent of cloves, ginger and cinnamon relaxed my offended nostrils and my spinning mind. *Well, that's one problem solved...hopefully.*

I stood in front of the mirror with a critical eye. "Huh, sorry to say, not much to look at dear girl." I turned side to side. *Not a curve to be found,* I thought. I still held a sliver of hope that all of the pain in my joints and limbs would somehow transform into curves. So far...nothing. Even more distressing was the mass of dirty blonde waves, curls and bits in between that sat on my head. The name Medusa came to mind. The scent of bacon wafted into the room just as I finished forcing my unwilling hair into a ponytail.

It will only be seconds before..."Storm, you'd better be out of bed!"...*she calls up here.*

"Yup, be right down," I said with one final look and a quick sniff. Both of which proved satisfactory.

******

"Here you are, sleepy head." She handed me a plate with two sunny side up eggs and a piece of bacon. She had arranged them to look like a happy face just like she did when I was little. No sooner had I smiled than a yawn forced its way through.

"Sorry, I'm pretty tired. I had my nightmare again last night."

"Oh, I'm sorry."

"And then when I was trying to get back to sleep..." I broke off mid sentence, unsure if I should tell her about what I overheard. Did she really know I was listening in? Maybe she was just playing a hunch. Maybe I really had fooled her into thinking I was asleep.

Nana looked at me inquisitively as she took a seat and folded the newspaper neatly beside her plate.

"My sunburn hurt a lot," I said quickly and diverted all attention to my eggs.

"Huh," she sipped her coffee and picked up the paper, "well, sorry you had such a rough time last night. I was worried that perhaps Z and I kept you up with our talking downstairs. Listening in on other people's conversations can be quite draining." I nearly coughed up my bite of eggs. She winked as she looked up from the front page.

How does she always know?

"Oh, that, well, um, I guess I might have heard something downstairs. Not too sure, but who is Z anyway?" No point keeping up the charade as I was totally busted.

Nana gave a little chuckle, she loved busting me. "Z is my old friend I mentioned yesterday on the walk back from dinner. She's Pearl's mother. She and I go way back and we had a lot to catch up on. Don't you like the eggs?"

I hadn't noticed that I was pushing them around my plate rather than eating them.

"Is there any salt?"

"Yes, I'll get it." She brought a green container back from the counter. "Z recommended this brand."

"Coarse Sea Salt," I read the label aloud. With a shrug of indifference, I poured the large, white grains onto the eggs.

"Z suggested that with the summer heat, you need to make sure you replenish the salt you'll lose from sweating."

"Umm, okay." *Whatever, I just thought the eggs were a bit bland.*

"So, almost ready to go?" Nana asked when I was nearly finished. "Mr. Manistar is expecting us in fifteen minutes."

"Yeah, just gotta brush my teeth," I said as I shoved the last bit of bacon into my mouth. I slid my finger across my plate and enjoyed sucking off the last few salt granules. *Funny*, I thought, *I've always been more of a sweet tooth.*

******

Just a few minutes drive from our house, we pulled off A1A beyond the Anastasia Island State Park entrance. Under a canopy of enormous oak trees and dangling Spanish moss was the dirt parking lot for the Lighthouse. Unseen cicadas hummed loudly and mosquitoes zoomed past my ears sounding like the high pitched whine of a dentist's drill in a surround sound movie.

"Well this is new," Nana spoke under her breath.

"Got one!" I exclaimed with a triumphant swat on my arm. "What?"

"That building," Nana motioned with her chin to the building on the left. "The Keeper's House is the one on the right, but that one on the left is new."

She clutched her bag tightly and by the briskness of her steps, I sensed tension. Nana was very protective over the Lighthouse and its history and she rarely supported change, especially if it involved kitschy souvenirs and my guess was that anything labeled Visitor's Center was likely to have merchandise. By the time I looked up from killing another mosquito on my leg, she was nearly to the front door and I once again had to catch up.

Inside the "new" old-fashioned looking, two-story house, an extravaganza of lighthouse and mariner paraphernalia greeted us along with a blast of ice-cold air.

"Ahh," I sighed happily and fanned my shirt.

There were lighthouse pictures in gilded frames, stained glass lighthouses, lighthouse key chains, lighthouse tee shirts, lighthouse books, and lighthouse magnets. There were model ships of the pirate variety, some in bottles, also bottle openers shaped liked sailboats, ships wheels and wind chimes with tiny, dangling, crystal lighthouses and ships. If it could have a lighthouse or boat on it, it did. And if it didn't have a lighthouse or a boat, then it had a light or oars.

"I had no idea this was such a big merchandise market!" I said to Nana whose crease between her eyes betrayed her dislike.

"Ms. Harn! It is such a pleasure to finally meet you!" A portly man approached with his arm outstretched and a smile on his face that extended to his flushed round cheeks.

"Hello Greg," Nana said to the man and shook his hand. "Please call me Rean."

"Well, of course, Rean. We are so glad to have you visit," Greg replied. "Things must look quite a bit different from when your ancestors lived here, eh?" He looked so proud. He didn't seem to notice Nana was less than thrilled with the changes. "This is of course our new visitor center, built a few years back. Such a demand of visitors required more space you see."

"And I suppose the $9 charge is just part of the recovery fee for this fancy new place?" *Uh oh*, I thought. But the man just smiled, unfazed.

"We are dedicated to the preservation and the safeguarding of this great monument and all of her treasures. Through educational programs, scientific research and public awareness, we're able to generate revenue to protect all that your relatives held so dear. Your family did such a great service to St. Augustine and I hope that in some small way I can be a part of the preservation of those memories. We just needed more space and, honestly, we needed to generate a bit more money. Sort of a win-win."

Wow, he's good, I thought. *At least Nana relaxed the crease a fraction of an inch.*

"Hi! I'm Storm." I thrust my hand out. Best not to tempt Nana with too much quiet.

"Oh, yes, forgive me, Storm, this is Mr. Manistar, curator of the Lighthouse." A smile returned to her face and I exhaled.

"Storm, nice to meet you. You know, I have a son about your age, how old are you, sixteen? Seventeen?"

"Sixteen, sir," I answered.

"Ahh, my son as well. Perhaps you two could get together some evening and he could show you around the town. If that's okay with your grandma," Greg said.

I winced inwardly at his use of 'grandma'. *Please*, I thought, *just play nice, Nana.*

"Sure. That'd be, umm, nice," I said and did my best impression of a smile. *Great, a blind date with the lighthouse curator's son.*

"So, Rean," Greg's attention back on Nana, "you mentioned wanting to chat about some documents on the phone. Whatever you need, I hope I can help."

"Lewis Tressman."

Mr. Manistar's face lost its rosy glow and his smile faltered. "Oh, well, I'm not sure that I can...when you mentioned research, I didn't know you meant..." He sputtered.

"Stormy, why don't you wait here," Nana turned to me, "we'll be back in a few minutes. I think Greg and I need to talk about a few things in private." Turning back to the still pale Greg, she kept the pressure on, "Is your office still upstairs in the Keeper's house?"

Greg nodded, his jaw clamped closed and the muscles on the side of his neck looked tense.

"Wonderful, let's go sit down and have a chat," Nana said with a smile as she hooked her arm through his.

Good luck, Greg, I thought. *I'm not sure what Nana wants to know about this Tressman guy but when she sets her mind on something, she usually gets it.*

Left alone in the lighthouse palooza, I wandered around among all of the trinkets. After a full circuit of the shop, I planted myself in front of the book display. Titles included, Southeastern Lighthouses, Ghosts and Gravestones of St. Augustine, Ghosts of St. Augustine, Haunted Lighthouses and How to Find them, Legends Behind the Legends of St. Augustine, Oldest Ghosts, Florida's Shipwrecks, Incredible Tales of the Sea,

The Standard Guide to St. Augustine, Myth Truth and Folklore of Merfolk and America's Oldest City.

"Wow," I whispered, "between the apparent abundance of ghosts, tragic sea tales and myths, St. Augustine is pretty creepy." I chose the book Legends Behind the Legends of St. Augustine, by M. Humpphrey to pass the time.

Black and white photographs, reproductions of yellowed newspaper publications and transcribed journal entries were interspersed with the typed pages of the paperback. A grainy photograph of a group of young girls caught my eye. The article that followed, dated July 11, 1873, said,

'a tragic incident occurred yesterday at the construction site of the town's new lighthouse. Three young girls, Mary (15) and Eliza (13), both daughters of Hezekiah Pittee, the superintendent of construction of the tower, and a young black girl fell into the ocean after riding on the supply rail car. Mr. Pittee's children were known to ride the supply cart from the lighthouse to the ocean for fun, but something happened yesterday and five children ended up in the ocean. Workers were able to save a boy and a girl.

Mr. Pittee and his family are newcomers to St. Augustine. They lived in a house on-site and were known around town as a very happy family. Our condolences go out to the family.'

"Sad, huh?" A boy's voice whispered over my left shoulder.

"Whoa!" I gasped. My heart thumped loudly in my chest. I spun to my left and scolded the voice, "You scared me."

The voice belonged to a decidedly non-scary boy around my age with messy blonde hair and light brown eyes. He wore wrinkled khaki shorts and his red-collared shirt was embroidered with the word "STAFF" on the right side.

"Sorry," he said. "I saw you standing over here and thought you might need some help or something. Are you here on vacation?"

"Sort of, well, not really. I'm here for the summer," I said, feeling inwardly stupid for being startled. My heart returned to its normal pace and I collected my thoughts to sound at least somewhat coherent. "My name's Storm."

"I'm Jonathan, nice to meet you." I accepted his outstretched hand and gave it a quick shake.

"So, Jonathan,"

"Oh, you can call me Jon, everybody does," Jon said.

"Oh, okay. So, Jon, do you work here or do you just go around trying to scare customers while they're reading?" I asked him.

"Yeah, sort of. I mean, no." He laughed. "How about I start over."

I smiled. "Sure."

"I sort of work here, not sort of scare people. But, I guess based on your reaction, I do a bit of both." He gave a snort of laughter. "My dad is the head curator so in the summer I help out with tours and cleaning up around the exhibits and stuff like that. Kind of boring, but at least I get paid."

"Oh, your dad's Greg...Mr. Manistar?" I asked.

"Yeah," Jon said.

"My Nana's meeting with him now. I'm just waitin' for them to get back."

"Oh," he replied. And then as if a light switch turned on in his brain, "OH! *You're* the girl dad mentioned. You're Ms. Harn's granddaughter? Wow. She's pretty famous 'round here."

"Really?" I asked. "Weird. She's just Nana to me."

"Well, she must be somethin' pretty cool because my dad's been excited for weeks to meet her and he only gets that excited when it's somebody linked with the lighthouse in some important way." He rolled his eyes in parental embarrassment. I smiled in understanding. "So, what do ya think of the book?" Jon took the book from my hand and opened it back to the page on the drowning.

"Well, I only just read the one story about the girls. Is it true?" I asked.

He smiled a half smile and said, "There are plenty of stories I could tell you about this place," he winked. "And yeah, that one's true."

"Stormy," Nana's familiar voice broke through our conversation. "ready to walk around the grounds?" She stopped and looked at Jon, "Oh, who's your friend?"

Before I could answer, Greg who stood next to Nana, said, "Jon, so glad you met Storm. How are you kids getting on?"

Jon rolled his eyes again and I giggled under my breath. "Great Dad, thanks."

"Perhaps you would like to show these lovely ladies around?" Greg said to Jon. "Of course, Ms. Harn might be able to teach *you* a thing or two about this place."

"Yeah, 'kay Dad," Jon replied.

I went to put the book back on the shelf before starting the tour.

"Why don't you keep it?" Jon asked. "On me, it's really a good book. Lots of stuff about how the myths around here may have gotten started. The author is a local character. He has crazy things to say about this place. Worth a read since you're new in town."

"Oh, no, I couldn't..."

"No really, it's fine," he said and put the book firmly into my hands and then led the way out of the back door.

The three of us strolled the garden path toward the colossal Lighthouse tower.

"How'd the meeting go?" I asked.

"Not great. I didn't get the help I was hoping for," Nana replied. She seemed pretty upset. "Not that I expected Greg to be forthcoming with information on a rather dark period in the general shining past of the lighthouse."

"Oh, sorry. Who was this Tressman guy anyway?"

"Lewis Tressman?" Jon asked. Nana nodded. "He was an assistant to one of the old Head Keepers, William Russell, back in the late 1800s. I read one old story that said he build secret rooms, almost like puzzles. They were so hard to get into that even the folks he built them for sometimes forgot how to get in!"

I laughed. "That's pretty funny. So, why is Mr. Tressman important?" I asked Nana, looking up from a sign post that identified the plant we stood in front of as a Shrimp Plant.

"Well, like Jon said, he liked to build secret rooms. And one of his rooms may have held something of great importance to someone I know," Nana replied. "I thought perhaps Greg could help me with some information regarding its location, but he said the records from that period were sparse. I personally think he didn't really want to delve into the controversial side of that time. Anyway, it's no concern of yours, Storm."

"Oh." *Whatever, I was just asking.*

"So, children, how about a more interesting challenge. She pasted on a smile and turned her gaze skyward toward the black and white striped tower.

Chapter Four

The challenge, as Nana described it, was just that. Two-hundred and nineteen spiraling steps up, a panoramic view of the Inlet from dizzying heights, two-hundred and nineteen spiraling steps down, a walk through the keeper's house and a trip back through the gift shop...my legs were officially jelly.

"I guess I'll see you around," Jon said as we stood together back in the gift shop.

"Yeah," I said and fidgeted with the book in my hands.

"I'm starting a summer course next week, but maybe we can get together sometime," Jon said, his hands buried deeply in the pockets of his shorts.

"I'm doing a course, too. It's the marine science one."

His face lit up. "No way! That's the one I'm taking."

"Well, cool," I said, "I guess I'll see you Monday." *And at least I'll know somebody there*, I thought with a private sense of relief.

Extracting his hands from his pockets, he wrote his number inside the front cover of Humpphrey's book. "Give me a call if you want to get together or something."

"Thanks," I said and then we hit the moment when we both realized we didn't really have anything else to say. After an awkward pause and a final look around the gift shop, I finally just smiled and walked to the door.

******

By the time we got home, the noonday sun broiled the sky and land with unbridled strength. Want-to-be rain clouds holding the promise of relief simply disintegrated into thin wisps of condensed air as they drifted seaward. I sought refuge under the umbrella on our deck. It was hot and I was damp with sweat but the breeze carrying the scent of the seawater smelled so good that I was willing to suffer the heat to keep inhaling it. But that wasn't the entire truth as to why I chose the deck over air conditioning. After Nana and I had returned from the lighthouse, I spotted the three surfers from yesterday. The two girls and the guy. They were really beautiful and he was perfect. He was well worth the discomfort of the heat, and more! Quite happily I settled back into the chaise lounge.

"Yikes!" I squealed. Something had rubbed against me. And without further warning, the black and white cat from yesterday jumped on my lap.

The cat looked up at me and kneaded my stomach. "Do you have a name?" I stroked her tenderly. "I could call you Jello," I said softly as I tickled her along her soft side. The cat dug her claws in deeper. "Ouch. Okay, maybe not Jello. I wasn't saying you were fat or anything, jeez." She returned to her gentle kneading.

"Nana said beach cats are a sign of new adventures and love." I giggled at the love part. I wasn't sure a boy's phone number counted as love, but it was a start in the right direction! "Hmm, you need a name that reflects this new life. How about Zelda? That game was all about adventure!" I waited for the pain of another set of claws, but instead, she curled into a ball and purred. The combination of her breathing and purring made a sound like a cricket.

My trio had headed pretty far out and it was hard to keep track of them. The heat combined with squinting into the harsh, afternoon light made a nap nearly mandatory. I put the book aside and Zelda and I drifted in and out of a very peaceful rest. My mind wandered back to the morning...I'd never had a boy pay attention to me like that before. *Maybe I'll give him a call later*, I thought dreamily. *But what would I say?* "Hi, this is Storm, the girl you met at the Lighthouse." *Or*, "Hi Jon, this is Storm.

What'r you up to?" *Umm,* "Jon, it's Storm. I love the book you gave me." *Right, maybe I'd just wait to see him in class.*

When I opened my eyes again, my shadow stretched in front of me and Zelda had disappeared. Along the line of breaking waves, a handful of eager surfers speckled the water's surface. Off to the right, on their own, was my trio. The wind brought laughter and bits of conversation to me. Two of the three surfers paddled backward quickly and before the third reacted, a wave rose and knocked the lone surfer off the board. More laughter, like soprano chimes drifted to shore. I focused on the spot where the boy disappeared beneath froth and bubbles. His board floated peacefully but there was no sign of its rider.

Where'd he go? I wondered.

I watched. *Surely he should be up by now.*

Just as I sat up in my chair to get a better view, both girls *and* their boards flew into the air. The boards went one way and the girls went the other. Everything landed with a splash.

"What the..." I said aloud. The girls popped back to the surface and a splashing fight ensued between them and the now-surfaced boy. Laughter rang on the wind.

Done for the day apparently, the trio bodysurfed into shore. I stared without fear, safely anonymous on my deck. Both girls had long hair that hung more than halfway down their backs. One was blonde and the other brunette. The boy had hair to his shoulders, also brunette. I pulled my towel around me suddenly struck self-conscious compared to how beautiful they all were. It reminded me of when I met Pearl the other night. She was so gorgeous and I was so not. *Look away,* I scolded myself. But I didn't want to...or perhaps couldn't. They were just so beautiful. The boy's skin glistened in the sun...the muscles of his back begging to be stroked and caressed...he was better than any cover of any romance novel I'd ever seen.

"How was your snooze, sleepyhead?" Nana asked, startling me out of my Atlantic fantasy.

"Good. I feel much better," I tried to sound normal. "Just relaxin' and enjoying the view out here."

"Yeah," she chuckled, "and the ocean is sort of good-lookin', too."

My gaze broke from the trio. I blushed. *How does she always know?*

"Ahh, to be young again. Alright, well, dinner will be in about an hour," she said.

"Thanks," I said. I really just wanted to keep watching my surfers and hoped Nana didn't want to sit and chat. Fortunately, she left after she did a quick wipe of the table.

But the moment was gone and so were the surfers. I scanned up and down the beach. They were gone.

"Nana, I'm gonna go for a short walk on the beach, okay?"

"Sure Stormy, enjoy," Nana's muted voice rang through the screened window.

Once to the sand, I looked around. An orange butterfly drew my gaze as it made its erratic flight past the fanning sea oats. With no other more significant leads, I decided to follow my little fluttering friend. "Okay, South it is."

Retracing the path Nana and I walked last night to the Beachcomber, I scanned for the trio. They weren't in the water and they weren't on the beach. *They have to be somewhere*, I reasoned.

I meandered to the A-Street ramp next to Beachcomber and watched cars drive onto the beach. One Camry got stuck briefly in the soft sand but after a little push from a passer-by made it through.

Quaint beach cottages lined sandy A Street. Shutters hued in blues and greens, signs on doors read "Relax, you're at the beach", pink, tacky, plastic flamingos stood as comical sentries, yellow dune daisies sprinkled tiny lawns and fragrant pink and white flowers of tall oleander bushes perfumed the air. Near the corner of A and A1A, I passed a house with a sign above the stairs that read Stir It Up. People lined up in front of a window while others munched on yummy looking food. My stomach growled but I kept walking. Sharing the house with the restaurant, I discovered as I turned the corner, was a surf shop called The Pit.

Three surf boards leaned against the railing in front of the shop. *The same surf boards from my three surfers!*

Without hesitation, I climbed the steps to the shop's entrance. It wasn't until I opened the door and a bell jingled to announce my entrance that I wondered what I going to do if I saw them. I walked in quietly and let the door close gently behind me. The bell jingled again.

A boy who looked nineteen or twenty came out from a side room. My heart lodged in my throat. It was *him*!

So I completely underestimated the beauty of this guy. I mean, he looked perfect from a distance, but up close, well, OH MY GOD! My jaw dropped open with an audible clunk.

I couldn't move, speak or breathe as he approached me with a big smile. His electric blue eyes glowed from the surroundings of his deeply bronzed skin. His wet hair, the color of roasted chestnuts, hung down to the tops of his shoulders. The bottom edge of his light blue tank top was wet. I futilely tried to look away from the perfect muscles of his bare arms but my gaze just budged to the outline of his washboard stomach below the tee. I tried again to move my eyes, but they traveled up past the silver starfish pendant hanging on his neck and got stuck on his square jaw line and prominent cheekbones. Giving up, I settled back at his jewel-tone eyes.

"H'allo, gorgeous!" He said in the same accent that the waitress had. He stopped just in front of where I stood. My head came to his chin. "Can I help you find something?"

Nope, I thought, *Already found it, thank you.*

Storm? A voice spoke to me from somewhere deep inside.

Not now, I thought, *I am staring at the most beautiful boy in the world.*

Storm. The voice chimed again.

Busy, I thought.

STORM! The voice screamed. *BREATHE!*

I inhaled deeply. The room spun as oxygen returned to my body.

"Are you okay?" He asked. His eyes glimmered. His mouth was in a half smile, looking quite smug and amused.

"I was just browsing," I managed to squeak. Then I quickly turned to a rack of clothes. *Did I just say browsing?* I shook my head, completely embarrassed.

"Well, take your time, love. The women's is over here." He pointed to a rack across the store. A proper glance at the clothes on the rack in front of me confirmed my second embarrassment for the day...they were all men's clothes. *Ugh.*

"If you need anything, the name's Rowan."

"S-S-Storm," I forced out willing my cheeks to extinguish their blaze. He raised one perfect eyebrow at my response. "I mean," I cleared my throat, "my name's Storm. Nice to meet you."

"Your name is Storm?"

"Yeah," I struggled to keep meeting his intense gaze.

"Huh. Interesting," he smiled and my limbs turned to rubber. He seemed to be enjoying some private joke as he turned back to the counter.

"I think I may actually enjoy a job from Z for once."

Chapter Five

"What was that?" I asked Rowan.

"Hmm?" His innocent eyes faced me again.

"Just now, I thought you said a name I knew," I repeated, fighting the lure of his liquid blue eyes.

"Oh, who?"

His right eyebrow arched like a rainbow.

"Umm, I thought..." The scent of seaweed mixed with the wet neoprene smell of the shop.

"Yes?"

A small, unimportant part of my brain reminded me I was trying to ask him something; something important about a letter or a person or his eyes. Yeah, it was about Rowan's eyes. I've never actually seen that shade of blue before. They were almost transparent in color, like crystal clear water, with a deep, dark center that goes to infinity. His beautiful eyes narrowed slightly and my mind went quiet.

He smirked and walked behind the counter. As he bent to unload a stack of things that looked like bars of soap, my thoughts returned but they were all muddled like after waking up from a confusing dream.

"Sex wax!" He chuckled. "The name always cracks me up!" With a shake of his head, he stacked the bars in the glass display case.

Desperate to keep his attention, I struggled to find something to say. "So, how were the waves today?" Not necessarily the best topic being that I know less than nothing about surfing, but beggars can't be choosers.

"Oh, they were alright. The sets were okay but the breaks were a bit sloppy.

"Yeah, I hate that, too."

He looked up from the cabinet, now half full of the wax bars, "so you surf?"

"Oh yeah, totally!" *Oh totally not. What the heck am I saying?*

"Excellent to hear Storm. We should totally head out together sometime. Do you have a board?"

Phew, a way out of this mess. "Right a board. No, I wasn't able to bring it with me. Huge bummer."

"No problem, we have boards you can borrow. Like, take this one over here!" He came out from behind the counter and grabbed a large, blue surfboard that had an evil looking point on one end and what looked like a cutout fin on the back. It looked like some strange smooshed shark. He lifted it easily and handed it over to me. I grabbed hold awkwardly and the board immediately crashed to the ground.

"Oh, sorry," I said, my face burning with embarrassment. "It's a little bit heavier than the one I, umm, have at home."

"Where's home again?"

"Indiana." *Oh, shoot.*

"Ahh, yeah, I've heard some good things about the surf in Indiana. What ocean is that on again?" Rowan grinned.

"Oh, umm, I meant..."

"Rowan, have you seen the new shipment of boards?" A girl's voice chimed. Her accent matched Rowan's except rather than pure masculine hers was pure feminine. Listening to her speak was like listening to a beautiful soprano melody compared to his ultra sexy tenor.

I recognized her as the dark haired surfer from the trio. Her hair was also still wet. She wore a thin, short, white sundress over a green bikini. Her bronze arms glistened with moisture. "Oh, sorry," she shot Rowan a questioning glance, "didn't know you had a customer. I just figured you were lazing around laughing at the Sex Wax again."

He chuckled. "Come on, it's funny. But no, Sara," he winked at me. I blushed. "I'm working here as you can see."

"Yeah right, that would be a first," she said.

Their bantering reminded me of brothers and sisters or perhaps...*ugh*, my heart sank, I didn't even want to entertain the possibility that they were...were...together.

"Hi," I squeaked. "He was working, I promise."

"Well then this *is* a first!" She said and held out her hand. "I'm Sara."

"Sara," Rowan spoke, "this is *Storm,*" he emphasized my name.

Sara's arm froze in mid-shake and her nose twitched with a quick inhale of air. "Really! So you ARE working."

"Told you," Rowan replied with a smile. "Best job I've been given by Z for ages."

"Well, pleasure to meet you, Storm." She let go of my hand and glanced at Rowan. His head tilted with an unspoken question and then she turned back to me with a smile. "Your eyes are so beautiful. The green is bright, like sea glass and the little flecks of gold look like tiny islands."

"Thanks." I was caught a bit off guard by the compliment since I never thought of any part of me as beautiful before.

"So, is Rowan taking good care of you? We want only the best for our newest arrival."

"Oh. Well, yeah, I guess. I mean, how did you know I just got here?"

"Small town, and the bright cherry color kind of gives it away," she laughed.

"Ugh," I moaned and felt embarrassed for the second time in just about as many minutes.

"Oh don't fret little one. It happens to all newcomers."

"Well, I guess I should go and let you guys get back to work." I turned for the door.

"Oh, don't rush off on my account. As long as Rowan's with you, he's totally doing his job," she winked at him and he gave her a shove with his arm.

"Hey, I have a thought," Sara said.

"Don't strain yourself, that makes two in two years," Rowan interrupted.

"Nice," Sara scowled. I smiled, they were funny in a strange way.

"Anyway," her attention back on me, "do you want to hang out with us later? We're going to head over to Jacks across the street for some music after work. If you aren't doing anything...."

"Oh, well," I really wanted to go but they seemed quite a bit out of my league...Rowan interrupted my internal debate, "Yeah, come on! We're fetching Sara's sister when she gets off work and heading over. Join us!" He smiled at me. *Debate over.*

"Okay!" I hoped my voice didn't betray the excitement I felt.

"Great," Sara chimed. "Meet here around six-ish; the back door will be unlocked."

"Sure," I replied.

She smiled and left out of the same door she had entered from. The tiny suspended bell tinkled.

"Your girlfriend seems nice," I said as I examined my feet.

"What? Oh you're talking about Sara? She's not my girlfriend." He smiled at me. I smiled back, perhaps a touch too quickly and a touch too broadly.

"Oh...okay. So, see you later," I said.

"Looking forward to it. And Storm,"

I stopped, one hand holding the door open, "Yeah?"

"Welcome back to Saint Augustine."

"How did you...?" I started to ask how he knew I had lived here before as a baby but before I could finish, the phone rang. Rowan smiled and reached under the counter for the handset. "The Pit, Rowan here." I mouthed the word *bye* and floated on the tide of anticipation toward home.

******

"NANA!" I called as I burst through the front door.

"NAAANAAA!" I called again and darted into the kitchen.

"NAAAN..." I was cut short as I nearly collided into Nana.

"Stormy, what is all the yelling about? Are you okay?"

"Oh, yeah, I'm more than okay! I just met some kids at the surf shop and they invited me out to Jacks later! They seem really nice and they invited me and..." I paced as I spoke, not sure whether to run upstairs to find something to wear, or to grab some water or to sit down. Unable to decide on an activity, I just circled.

"Whoa, Stormy, slow down. Catch your breath. I can barely understand your words." She placed her small hands on my shoulders and guided me to the kitchen table. "Have a seat and tell me about your new friends. That's a girl," she said, "slow deep breaths. Here's some water."

I sipped the cold water thankfully. It really was very hot outside. That storm that threatened earlier never materialized and even the late afternoon sun was intense. "Right," I tried to speak slowly in between my sips of water, "so I met some kids at the surf shop down the street and they invited me out tonight. Can I go?"

"Do they have names?"

"Rowan and Sara. I guess Sara also has a sister; she was going to meet us as well. *So* is it okay? I won't stay out late."

"I'm not sure. Your classes start tomorrow, remember?"

"C'mon Nana. The class doesn't start until nine and I won't be tired. Please, please, please?"

"Their names are Rowan and Sara?"

"Yeah." *Do their names affect her decision?* I wondered.

"Alright." She seemed reluctant but resigned.

"Thank you, thank you! You're the best!" I jumped up and gave her a bear hug.

"Hang on there Stormy." She struggled to speak until I released my hug. I didn't realize how strong I was. "Listen, be home by ten, not a moment past. Got it?" Her face was stern.

"Yes Ma'am!" I gave a mock army salute. Now with my evening organized I turned my attentions to my stomach. "Nana, do we have any pretzels?"

"Since when do you like pretzels?"

"I don't know, just sounded good I guess." I took another large gulp of water but my thirst raged on.

"Dinner will be ready soon, can you hang in there?"

"I guess so. What'r we havin'?"

"Spaghetti and meatballs."

"Any Parmesan?"

"Since when do you like Parmesan?"

"Since now I guess. This salt air must be affecting my taste buds."

"Yeah, I suppose so." Nana turned to the stove where I noticed steam rising from a silver pot. "I hope Z knows what she's doing," Nana mumbled.

"What's that?" I asked

"What? Oh, nothing," Nana replied.

"Okay, well, I'm gonna go find something to wear while dinner's cooking."

"Yeah, sure." I had the impression that she wasn't even listening to me anymore.

"Although, I may just go naked, okay?" I said.

"Yeah, that would look great on you," she said.

Definitely distracted.

******

UGH! I have NOTHING to wear! Mirror girl looked at me with open disgust. After trying on clothes for twenty minutes, the best I could come up with was a knee length, blue skirt and a yellow tee with "HUG ME" across the front. *Seriously? These are my clothes?*

I settled, or perhaps just gave up, and wore the blue skirt but traded the tee for a white tank top. I put on some more of the lotion. I loved seeing the shimmer on my skin from whatever stuff was in it. I slipped my feet into a new pair of flips and made one last grimace at my reflection before hurrying downstairs.

Dinner was already on the plates.

"Well, you look cute!" Nana remarked when I entered the kitchen. "I mean, you look beautiful!" She corrected her obvious blunder in the use of the "c" word and I forced a smile.

"Dinner smells great!" I sat and took a large bite.

"Thanks, Dear."

"Nana," I spoke when my mouth was empty again, "can you pass the salt?"

******

What is going on with Nana? I wondered as I strolled along A1A toward The Pit. *She barely said a word to me at dinner. Was she mad that I added salt? I didn't mean it as an insult. Maybe she's not feeling okay. Maybe I should give Dad a call. I don't know, I don't want him to worry. Ugh. No, I'll talk to her in the morning and make sure she's alright. And she calls* me *moody. Jeez.*

Only a couple of cars remained in the parking lot in front of the shop and the wooden surfboard racks were empty. I walked around to the back of the shop, hopped up the stairs two at a time, and gave the weathered wooden door a tentative push. It creaked open slowly and the bell at the top cheerfully announced my arrival.

"Hello," I offered to the quiet shop.

"Oh hey, Storm!" Rowan called from a side room. "We're just back here. Come on in, we're nearly finished."

"*We're* nearly finished? Exactly what part did you do to be included in 'we'?" Sara's melodic voice chimed in.

"I brought the drinks!"

I crossed the store and peeked into the little side room. Rowan and Sara were sitting on the floor with a stack of boogie boards between them. They each had open amber bottles next to them and a black Sharpie in their hands. Rowan had changed into khaki shorts and a tee shirt. His hair still glistened like he had just gotten back in from surfing again. Sara wore a short, blue cotton dress. Both of them were barefoot and somehow made me feel overdressed and under-dressed at the same time.

"Hi Storm. Want one?" Sara motioned to her drink. I didn't recognize the label; it was light green and had gold cursive writing on it. I figured it was a beer of some sort.

"Oh, no thanks." Conflict rose internally about whether I should feel responsible or lame by refusing her offer. I settled for knowing that I would never be allowed to see the light of day if Nana found out I drank alcohol while out and therefore, I made a good choice. I prepared to have to defend my answer and practiced a few lines in my head, 'I'm training for a marathon...', 'I'm on a new diet...', but before I had a chance or need to use either excuse she just nodded and continued labeling the boogie boards. Like it really didn't matter to her either way.

"Sorry we're running late. Rowan was supposed to price these this morning, but *apparently* he was too busy," Sara's voice dripped with sarcasm.

"Hey, I told you I'd get to them," he said.

"Uh, yeah, as in I'd end up doing them," she replied with an eye roll.

Rowan gave Sara a boyishly charming grin and they both laughed.

"Do you need any help?" I asked.

"Nah, nearly finished. Have a seat." Rowan motioned to a black leather couch along the wall. Half of it was taken up with already priced boards.

"So, Storm, Rowan told me you just arrived in Saint Augustine." Her eyes were so big and inviting. They reminded me of large, swirling pots of melted dark chocolate. It was hard to concentrate and look at her at the same time. Her hair was damp like Rowan's and she wore the same silver starfish pendant as Rowan, also.

"Uh huh," I stammered and forced myself to look away from her. "Just got in yesterday. I'm staying in the yellow house up the street."

"Is Rean with you?" She asked.

"Yeah. How do you know her?"

"Oh, my mum mentioned she was coming with her granddaughter. That's you, right?"

"Yeah. That's me."

"Sixteen years sure fly by," Rowan said with a wink in my direction.

A marker made a dull 'thunk' on the right side of his head.

"Hey!" He turned to Sara and threw it back. She gave him a serious look that I didn't understand.

"Whatever," he replied. "I was just saying that..."

"Right, well, how about less saying and more labeling," Sara responded curtly.

Rowan stuck out his tongue when Sara looked over her shoulder for another board.

They were really funny together and I couldn't contain a giggle.

"Hey Sara," Rowan said with a quick wink in my direction, "I know a word of letters three. Add two, and fewer there will be. What's the word?"

"Hmm, a word of letters three..." Sara repeated quietly.

"Do you know Storm?" Rowan asked.

"Know what?" I asked.

"The answer to the riddle of course," he said with a smile.

"Oh, I get it, a riddle. Umm, no. I've never been very good at riddles."

"Well, it's about time you got good then, you never know when you'll need to know an answer!" Sara said.

Rowan leaned over toward me and in a mock whisper said, "Sara's not very good at them either."

"Hey, give me a sec," Sara said, she was still writing a price on the last board. "Finally done!" Sara said with excitement. "The answer is *few*. Now, let's go."

"Nice," Rowan said. "Do ya get it?" He asked looking at me.

"Not really," I said.

"A word of letters three...but when you add two more you get fewer...*few* plus *er*. The answer was in the riddle, you just have to know where to look!" He said with a smug expression.

"Oh, I get it!" I said.

"It's a good skill to have...picking out the things hiding in plain sight," Sara said. "Now, let's go grab Pearl."

"Pearl?" I asked.

"Yeah, Pearl. She's my sister; works over at the Beachcomber. Do ya know her?" She looked at me with those hypnotic eyes again. My thoughts jumbled together in my head.

I fought against the strange sensation and forced myself to answer. "I met a girl named Pearl last night when my Nana and I had dinner at Beachcomber. She knew Nana, too." My voice sounded mumbled in my ears.

"Stop it Sara," Rowan spoke quietly. "She's not a new play toy. Z told us to take care of her."

Sara looked at Rowan with something between a smile and a sneer, "Actually, Z told YOU to take care of her. Z never asks me to do anything like that, not anymore. Anyway, I was just playing. Z didn't say anything about not playing."

"Whatever, Sara. Let's go. Hey, Storm, want some?" Rowan asked, holding a small bottle in my direction

"What?" I asked, my brain trying to get itself back together in coherent thoughts. *I must be more tired than I thought.* A familiar spiced scent of cinnamon, ginger, clove, something peppery like licorice filled the room.

"Some lotion for the road!" Rowan rubbed some lotion between his hands.

"You may need some more there surfer boy, nobody likes a stinky water baby," Sara teased.

"Who you callin' stinky?" Rowan shot back.

"If the stench fits..."

Rowan and Sara were both rubbing lotion down their arms. Remembering the gross smell from my room this morning I figured it may not hurt to put on some more.

"Uh, yeah, sure," I replied and took the bottle from Sara when she was done. *Maybe it has to do with the heat or something, I mean if Rowan and Sara use the stuff, I guess I'm not the only one.* Sara took the bottle back from me and put it in the bottom drawer of a filing cabinet. *The smaller the town, the bigger its secrets...* I thought. *Where did I read that?* I wondered.

We left through the back door and took a side alley to the Beachcomber. I recognized Pearl immediately by her hair; golden ringlets, half pulled up into a lose bun while the rest danced in the light breeze. She appeared to float effortlessly around the Beachcomber's deck as she lit the surrounding tiki torches. Her hips swayed to the music playing from the restaurant's outdoor speakers.

"Hey Pearl, you gonna light those things or just dance?" a voice yelled from inside. Pearl stopped dancing, but her hair still flirted around her head, and she very ungracefully stuck her tongue out. Rowan chuckled. "That a girl, Pearl," he said.

"I'm only doing this to help you out, Terry, you know," Pearl called to the voice in the restaurant. "I'm not even on tonight! Try to enjoy happy hour without me! Ooh, Rowan and Sara are here! See ya." She tossed the lighter that was in her hand to the building where I suppose Terry stood and skipped toward us.

"Guys! Just in time, I..." she stopped in mid-sentence and in mid-stride.

"Um, Pearl," Sara said through the silence, "Storm here stopped by the shop earlier to talk to Rowan about surfing lessons so we invited her along to Jacks."

"I hope that's okay," I offered weakly. "I mean, no big deal if it's not, I can head...." But before I could finish my verbal backtracking her face morphed from shock to pleasure. Her smile was as bright as the rising sun.

"Why Storm, it is perfectly okay!" Her eyes sparkled and a pleasant sea breeze blew her hair into a random dance about her shoulders. She closed the gap between us, "It's so wonderful to see you again." And then she hugged me. Strangely, I didn't feel weird about being hugged by her. In fact, I hugged her back and we stood at the edge of the deck and embraced like dear friends that hadn't seen each other for years.

Finally, she stood back from me, still holding my hands and looked me up and down.

"Stormy, you are gorgeous. I always knew you would be," she whispered.

Self-consciousness returned as did the heat to my cheeks as I thought about my totally lame outfit and obvious sunburned body.

"Uh, thanks?" Not quite sure how to take my second unexpected compliment of the day, I laughed nervously, "I don't think I'm so much to look at, especially standing next to you three."

"Well, you may need to look more closely at yourself next time!" Pearl offered. "Come on, let's go."

"I see your sunburn's much better," Pearl spoke as we walked up A Street toward the sound of Reggae. "Did Nana give you our mum's lotion?"

"Yeah, it's been really helpful," I blushed and hoped that the faint scent of ocean wasn't coming from me.

Sara giggled under her breath. Pearl gave her a shove.

"Old family recipe," Pearl added softly with a smile. "We all wear it, although it smells like Rowan could use a little more."

"Told you," Sara said with a tiny wrinkle of her nose. Rowan gave her a shove.

"Anyway Pearl," Sara said, "I'm excited Storm's here this summer. This place was getting rather tedious but now, well, exciting things are bound to happen! Don't you think Sis?"

"Sara, let's not..."

"Hey, Pearl," Rowan interrupted Pearl, "I know a word of letters three..."

"Few," Pearl responded.

His smile changed to a grimace. "Someday I'll stump you."

"Maybe, but that day's not today!" Pearl chimed with a large grin.

"Well, maybe not mentally, but physically! Race ya!" Rowan called and took off at a mock run toward Jacks. He glanced back and shouted, "Last one there's a hagfish!"

Something inside of me begged to play along. I made a quick glance toward Sara and then Pearl. We held our walking pace for a moment but then our legs couldn't resist. We ran and laughed at each other as we cut down Rowan's lead. I passed Sara and then Pearl passed me and then I passed her and Rowan kept dancing just in front of us, taunting us to go faster.

"Is that all you got ladies?" Laughter surrounded us all the way to Jack's as Rowan triumphantly crossed the imaginary finish line of the bar's open deck a half a second ahead of me.

"You are a quick little thing aren't you, young one!" He picked me up and spun me around as if I weighed no more than a feather. He put me back on my feet and smiled.

Pearl and Sara pushed past, "Not so fast!" Sara called as she passed us.

"You didn't make it to the pool!" Pearl continued Sara's sentence as she passed us. "So easily distracted," Sara finished.

"Hey!" Rowan exclaimed to their backs but before he could take a step a giant splash was followed by giggles.

"Good effort!" Sara shouted from the pool.

"Yeah, so close. Maybe next time hold off the celebration dance until you've actually won!" Pearl teased.

"Every time," Rowan said while shaking his head. "No fair because Storm distracted me!" He shouted toward the pool. He smiled down at me, "We'll get 'em next time, eh?" He reached to my hand, entwined it with his and walked us both to the pool. To say I felt on top of the world is a bit of an understatement. I floated alongside Rowan and hoped with all of my might that I didn't wake up if this was some crazy dream of mine.

"Alright ladies, a deal's a deal, what can I get you?" Rowan spoke in a bit of a monotone voice as he led me to the pool's edge where Sara and Pearl awaited us.

Pearl answered my unasked question. "The last one to the pool has to buy the first round."

"Oh, I see," I looked to Rowan apologetically and then burst into laughter again. "Are you pouting?" I asked between giggles.

Both girls hung onto the edge, elbows on the cement, bodies floating weightlessly behind them. Their clothes were tossed to the side of the deck.

Mental note, always wear a bathing suit.

"Margarita for me, with salt!" Sara exclaimed with enthusiasm.

"Make that two!" Pearl chimed.

"And you my dear?" Rowan looked at me with his turquoise eyes shining brilliantly in the late day sun.

"Oh, I don't know. I don't need anything." I felt like an idiot as I sat down at the edge of the pool.

"Of course you do!" Sara responded, "Get her a margarita too! Extra salt for the changeling."

"Oh, no, I really don't..." *What's a changeling?*

Pearl rescued me, "A virgin one, please, just like the rest of us. We don't want Nana thinking we aren't responsible not to mention, Z..."

Sara stopped her joking. "Right. Irresponsible would be the last thing we would want to be labeled." She said softly but with a defiant edge and a slight pout of her perfect rose hued lips. She pushed away from the edge, sank effortlessly underwater and glided to the other side of the pool. She rose up at the opposite wall. She seemed to have taken an interest in the drummer of the band.

My feet dipped into the warm water while Rowan walked over to the bar window to order our drinks.

"Is Sara mad?" I asked.

"Oh no," Pearl smiled up at me her eyes shining like little green flames, "she just gets carried away sometimes; sort of forgets limits which has lead to some bad consequences in the past."

I looked over to Sara and saw the drummer she was watching drop one of his sticks. Her giggles carried over to us on the air of the music.

"See?" Pearl nodded over toward Sara, "she's already gotten over whatever bothered her and is having quite a good time torturing that young man. We rarely stay unhappy, or angry, or, well, any emotion for long."

Pearl's smile was so warm and sweet. It sounded pretty awesome to feel accepted and to be around people that were so happy and carefree!

The clear water rippled gently and I relaxed into the music. I looked back to the inviting crystal water and I realized my skin ached to get wet. My mouth felt all cottony. Even my scalp tingled at the thought of it. I extended my hand into the water and swirled my fingers around a bit. I had never felt such a strong desire for anything, well, perhaps for Rowan, but this was different, it was like an impulse, an awakening of something. I wanted, no, I *needed* to be in that water! I took one more look down at my feet as they swayed effortlessly underwater. Just a tiny bit deeper. The water licked up my legs, it felt cool and so very delicious.

"Careful, beautiful!" Rowan called, breaking into my water-obsessed thoughts.

I sat back up. The hem of my skirt was wet from hanging over the edge so far. *Did I seriously almost fall into the pool? Did Rowan seriously just call me beautiful?*

Rowan gave a chuckle, turned back to the barman and continued his conversation while he waited on the drinks.

"Here we are ladies!" Rowan announced and handed each of us a full plastic cup rimmed in chunky salt crystals.

"So nice of you!" Sara said as she popped up next to Pearl and laughed.

"Really, you shouldn't have!" Pearl added.

"Alright already. Next time, just you both wait! What are you laughing about Storm?"

The girls' giggles were infectious and I forgot about my embarrassment and joined in the lighthearted moment. I got the impression that these three lived in perpetual lighthearted moments. I bet they made a fun time out of most every situation.

"Cheers!" Rowan announced above our laughter and held his cup high. "To fair weather, fairer seas and the fairest maidens," he touched his cup to each of ours' in turn.

His eyes totally lingered on me when he said that last part. No, they didn't, I'm being stupid. Or, maybe they did. I hope they did. I think they did. They did, right?

Pearl and Rowan exchanged a glance I couldn't interpret but I didn't really care. I let the heavy beat of reggae music fill my ears and body.

How quickly my life seems to be changing, I thought as I sipped my sweet and salty drink.

"What are you thinking?" Rowan looked at me with questioning eyes. I felt the heat rise from my neck and creep toward my cheeks.

"Oh, nothing, really. I was just thinking about how different my life was just a few days ago."

"You ain't seen nothing yet!" And with that he grabbed my hands and pulled me to my feet. Despite my protests, I found myself intertwined with him dancing to the music. Pearl and Sara joined us.

The four of us swayed in rhythm. The song drove us and we drove the song! Pearl spun Sara and Sara spun me and I spun Rowan. The rhythm filled every pore and happiness flowed freely. Rowan smiled at me and took one of my hands and spun me to him and then I did a little dip into his arms, like in the movies. Despite his glowing appearance, he was cool to the touch and goose bumps appeared on my arms. I spun back away and couldn't help but laugh loudly.

I'd always loved music and I'd always loved dancing but most of my friends at home were too shy to ever dance. This was the first time I felt normal dancing. And dancing with them slowly pushed my many questions about that lotion, about their necklaces, about Nana, and about Z out of my mind. Those things could wait. Right now, all I wanted to do in the entire world was dance and laugh with them.

Pearl and Sara's skin was still wet from the pool and it shimmered in the setting sun. They looked like they were lit from the inside the way they glowed and their long hair hung down their backs in thick ribbons. Rowan glowed also in the light but his glow was deeper, like hot coal. He smiled his breathtaking smile and I forgot to breathe momentarily. It wasn't until he broke his gaze from mine that I felt the rush of fresh oxygen into my lungs.

The deck where we danced next to the pool slowly filled with other people. We kept moving away from them, edging closer to the pool, but the people filled in the space quicker than we could make more. Despite the gathering crowd, we still managed to play to the music.

My skin was damp from the heat of the air and the surrounding people kept pushing closer. I was right next to the pool, on the edge and men and women kept dancing next to me; closer to me...too close to me.

I need space. Too close. There's no room. I closed my eyes and did what felt natural to do, as if I had known the solution all along.

When I opened my eyes again, a liquid sky stared back.

One minute I was dancing, the next I was getting choked by people and now I was alone and quite content. But what had changed?

Bubbles drifted past my eyes.

Oh, I thought, *OH! I'm underwater!*

The sky was blurry because I was looking up at it through water...from the bottom of the pool to be exact. The hard cement pressed against my back and I looked down at my legs and saw my skirt billowing slowly around me. The heavy, steady beat of reggae still reverberated through me.

I should be freaking out, right? I thought. But this was exactly where I wanted to be all evening. My skin was cool and my throat was no longer parched. Like a person lost in the desert that finally found a source of water, I felt that I had been dehydrated my entire life and had finally replenished my lost water. I could just lay here forever!

Is this some new version of my underwater dream? I wondered.

I noticed with some detached amusement the movement of cartoon-looking heads above the surface of the water. Faces appeared and then disappeared. Then the surface of the water exploded in a mass of bubbles. Rowan was at my side instantly with a look of playful curiosity in his eyes. Not quite sure what I should do, I smiled. He smiled back and held out a hand to me. I looked at it, but didn't move.

I don't want to wake up yet, I thought.

Come on my wee fish, his voice spoke in my head. *Z would have my head if I lost you the very first day.*

He tilted his head and then glanced to the surface.

But I don't want to go back to all those pushy people, I thought.

You can't stay here, not now, not yet. He replied.

With a sigh, I reluctantly reached to him. He knitted our fingers together and we floated up. But as we got closer, he started to pull away.

No, stay with me! I shouted in my head.

His teeth glistened as he smiled.

My fingers slipped from his grasp and I thrashed to reach for him. My head broke the surface.

"WAIT!" I gasped.

Chapter Six

I didn't dare move. My eyes adjusted to the darkness and the outline of my bedroom revealed itself.

What a strange dream, I thought and tried to recall the last memory of it. "Ahh!" I gasped. Something moved in the corner of my room.

"Shh." A soft voice whispered from the rocking chair.

"Pearl?" I asked. The skin of her left arm shimmered as a sliver of moon light slid over it.

"Sorry to frighten you. I stayed to make sure you were okay," she whispered.

"How did I...? How are you...? Where is...?" My brain had too many questions loaded and ready to fire that my mouth didn't have time to get each one out before the next arrived.

Pearl sat on the edge of the bed. She brushed some hair out of my face with a soft touch. "Shh. You're okay. You, eh, fainted while we were dancing," she whispered. "I should have made sure you drank more. The heat makes it easy for us to get dehydrated. Especially now, for you, so much is happening. Gosh, you're burning up." She put the back of her hand on my forehead and then on my cheeks. "Such big changes during this time. Sara said she offered you some salt ale at the shop but you didn't drink any."

My brain was still entirely too groggy to make sense of this conversation. *Is hallucinating a symptom of dehydration because it looks like Pearl's eyes are glowing.*

"I remember feeling crowded by all the people," I whispered after closing my eyes and using the pressure of my fingertips on my temples to push the strange sights from behind my lids. My head pounded with my pulse.

"The crowded thing happens sometimes with us. People love to be near a good vibe!" I risked another peak, her eyes still seemed lit from within but her smile was soothing. She smoothed my hair again like a mother would to a sick child. "I looked over just as you fell," she hesitated for a moment waiting for my memory to catch up. "...into the pool."

I grimaced with embarrassment.

"Rowan got to you immediately and pulled you out. He carried you all the way here."

"Oh, well, that's great. And here I thought falling into the pool was embarrassing, good thing Rowan carried me here."

Pearl giggled with delight. "Oh Stormy, it's really okay." It was at that moment that I heard the distinct sound of water dripping into the bathtub.

"My clothes?"

Pearl smiled with delight. "I hung them up for you!"

"What did Nana say?" I asked worried about the questions that were sure to come from this.

"Actually, she doesn't quite know." Now it was Pearl's turn to look sheepish.

"Seriously?" I forgot we were supposed to whisper. This was the first good news I had heard since I woke up.

"Shh."

"Oops." We sat in silence for a minute to make sure Nana hadn't woken up. Only the metronome of drips from my sopping clothes onto the tub floor punctuated our quiet breaths.

"Sorry," I whispered in my super quiet voice when it felt safe to speak again.

"Well, when we got here, she wasn't here. I think she was meeting with mum tonight. She checked in on you when she got home and I hid in the bathroom." A wicked smile breezed onto her face. I got the impression she had fun sneaking around. "I figured this was something we could keep as our secret so that you're allowed to play with us again! And I promise to keep a better eye on you next time! So does Rowan."

My mind went back to my dream in the pool and Rowan's face...his words...his touch...my cheeks radiated heat again.

"I've never fainted before," I said.

"Don't worry yourself over it too much. It's pretty common during transition."

"What do you mean 'transition'?"

"Oh," Pearl hesitated, "just, eh, during times of change, you know?" She looked toward the open window as she spoke. I couldn't help but think that wasn't all she meant but my brain was confused enough at the moment.

"But I made sure to drink lots of water," I said.

"It isn't just water you need." Pearl looked directly at me and her green eyes really did appear to glow in the moonlight. I thought about Nana mentioning the heat...and the taste of my finger after sliding over my plate and Sara's drink order...

"Salt?" I asked.

"Yes, salt." She smiled and stroked my hair again.

"But I don't under...."

"Soon. Right now I want to know that you feel okay," she said.

"Yeah, I guess," I said. *Except I think I'm still hallucinating because her eyes are totally glowing*, I thought.

"Good, because tomorrow, well, actually today," Pearl glanced at my clock, "is a big day for you. Starting your class remember?"

"Oh, yeah." I was suddenly not that excited about it. I would much rather find out what was going on with me and how it all fit with Pearl, Rowan and Sara.

"*Oh yeah* is right! You better get excited because Nana will have our bums if she thinks we're a bad distraction to you!" Pearl winked and gave me a playful shove.

I smiled.

"You get some rest. We have a long summer ahead of us." She got up to leave and I was moved suddenly to ask a very strange request of her.

"Pearl, would you mind staying a few more minutes? Just until I fall asleep?" I felt silly for asking but her presence was so soothing and I dreaded the thought of what kind of dream my subconscious mind would create from all of this.

"No problem, Stormy. Close those eyes and dream. Perhaps of someone who's name starts with 'R'."

My eyes went wide with shock and embarrassment. She giggled, amused at my obvious discomfort.

"Don't worry, your secret's safe with me," she whispered. "But, if it makes you feel better, I think you have equally distracted his subconscious thoughts."

At that I smiled. *If only it were true.* My eyes grew heavy with Pearl's soft tickles on my forehead.

******

I awoke to a bright, empty room. The smell of bacon aroused my belly before the rest of me intended to let go of sleep completely. I heard and felt a soft rumbling from within.

"Alright, alright," I mumbled, "I'm getting up."

Reluctantly, I rolled to the edge of the bed and flopped my feet over the edge. It wasn't an entirely uncomfortable position so I stayed. My stomach rumbled louder. "Fine, I'm going." Apparently, my internal snooze button had worn out its welcome. But in case there was any doubt, my stomach had a back up plan in the form of...

"Stormy, are you awake?" Nana spoke soothingly as she padded softly into the room, "breakfast will be ready shortly." She walked around my bed and opened the window. "Are you feeling okay?"

"Hmm mm," I mumbled and opened one eye to look at her. My

stomach grumbled triumphantly.

"I worried when I got home last night and saw you already in bed. Did everything go okay with your new friends?"

"Yeah, it was fun," I was nervous to say too much because I wasn't sure what she knew or didn't know. "We went to Jacks and hung out for a bit. I got tired so they walked me home. I suppose the travel and sun caught up to me is all." I stretched. Popping noises resounded as each of my joints adjusted themselves. Nana held my gaze for a moment longer than necessary.

"Well, it was a busy weekend! Are you ready for your first day of classes?" She finally asked.

"Yeah, I guess," I said.

"Any butterflies?"

I remembered the one that led me to the PIT and to Rowan. "Some." I smiled.

She kissed my forehead and then sniffed. "Better take a shower before class, dear."

"'kay." I yawned and stretched more. This time, a distinct soreness accompanied the few final pops.

"Oh!" Nana inhaled abruptly.

"What?" I sat up quickly and looked frantically around expecting to see some kind of spider or roach or another scary, tropical creepy crawly near my body.

"In your hair..."

I shook my head freaking out that the bug was in my hair.

"No, no...stop shaking around. There's a, a...Storm hold still. Thank you. Now let me see this."

"See *what*?"

"These beads. Now hold on a second."

"*Bugs*?!"

"Beads."

"What beads?"

She picked up a segment of my hair and held it straight in front of me as she examined it. "*These beads.* Now hold still a sec."

Where did that come from? I wondered.

As she looked with keen eyes, I also looked with intrigue at this new attachment to the left side of my head. Nana put my hair down gently and gazed past me. Her mind was far away. But she conjured a smile and looked back to me, "They're pretty."

"Are you okay, Nana?"

"Yes, dear. I'm fine. It's beautiful." She leaned in to give me another kiss on my forehead and I felt a dampness left behind by the brushing of her cheek. "See you downstairs."

"Thanks, um, yeah, I'll be right down." As soon as Nana left, I bolted straight to the mirror to examine the beads more closely.

They were silver and attached low down on a loosely braided portion of my hair. The beads were simple, made of shiny metal, which reflected the sunlight when I turned the little braid side to side. I rolled the beads back and forth between my index finger and thumb; so smooth, so pretty. I loved seeing the light dance on the walls from their reflection. I could have just stood watching the dancing light all day.

"Storm! I don't hear the shower. Come on, don't wanna be late!" Nana's call brought me out of my trance. I glanced at the clock, unsure how long I had been lost in the shimmery reflection of the beads. "Yikes!" I whispered and dropped the braid. A quick glance in my bathroom confirmed that the events of last night weren't a dream. My still damp clothes hung over the shower rail. I pushed them aside and jumped into the lukewarm water. I made sure to use extra soap and then a healthy dose of deodorant and lots of the spicy lotion. "Hmmm, that should do it!" I exclaimed triumphantly.

I rummaged through my pile of un-put-away clothes and found khaki shorts and my favorite green tee-shirt that my dad brought back from a conference he went to in Hawaii. I pulled my mane back into a loose pony. As I did, the silver beads on the braid jingled. The tune reminded me of my new friends. 'People love to be near a good vibe.' Pearl's words resounded in my head. I couldn't put my finger on what the vibe exactly was, but there indeed was a vibe. *Am I really a part of it?*

In the kitchen, breakfast waited for me on the table. Nana, already seated, had the newspaper opened in front of her and a cup of coffee in her hands. "Thanks," I said as I picked at my bacon and eggs. My mind was still on my braid and the beads and a perma-grin decorated my face.

"Glad you made it down...eventually. Are you gonna eat those or just decorate your plate?" She looked at me and raised her eyebrow.

I shoved an entire piece of bacon into my mouth and then smiled.

"Well, I'm glad you're in such a good mood, quite a rare sight these days before 11. I knew you'd be excited for the course."

"Yeah, the course. Super excited." *Not.*

"So, we should leave in about a half hour to get you to the lighthouse in time. I'll pick you up at four. What do you want to bring for lunch?"

"I don't care, a banana or something. Whatever is fine." Nana brought my mind back to the day's schedule and the butterflies caught up to me.

Nana rolled her eyes, "I'll make you a sandwich." She got up from the table and started assembling food for me to take.

"Hey Nana," she reminded me of a question I had been thinking of since last night, "did anyone other than you ever used to call me Stormy? Like when I was a baby?"

She kept assembling my lunch at the counter, "Your mom used to. I suppose that's where I picked it up." She looked over to me and smiled a brief smile. I smiled back but my mind, like hers also seemed, was far away. I ate the last pieces of bacon, the saltiness satisfied my limited hunger, and got up to go finish getting ready.

"Hey, what about the eggs?"

"I'm not super hungry this morning." Honestly, they were very bland but I didn't want to go through the whole salt thing again. Nana already seemed sort of freaked out by the braid.

"Alright, but really, you've nothing to worry about," she said.

"I know," I said. My mind was already off of the course and back on my new friends and my awesome braid. "Thanks." I skipped upstairs two at a time to check out my hair one more time.

******

Nana parked the car in the same parking lot we were in the other day when we visited the Lighthouse. My schedule said that we were using Room C.

Take a breath, I told myself, *nothing to be nervous about*. We went into the gift shop and Nana asked the woman behind the counter where Room C was. I heard her tell Nana it was upstairs in the house next door, the original Keeper's house.

"Do you want me to come with you?" Nana asked.

Yes! I thought. "No," I said. "I'll be fine." I attempted a confident smile. I'm not sure how it came out.

"Well, then, I'll see you at four. Enjoy!" Nana gave me a hug.

I walked alone out the back door of the shop and turned towards the Keeper's house. Outside, the wind had picked up and the fronds on the surrounding palms fluttered with waving fingers and the Spanish moss dangling from the enormous oaks bounced and swayed. It must have been low tide because I could smell a faint whiff of brine. The beads hanging from the end of my braid sung in the breeze. The cheerful tuneless chiming made me smile even with my stomach doing flip-flops.

"Oh! Sorry!" I exclaimed to an overly close, freckled face.

"That was a close one!" The girl, who I almost collided into, said. She was shorter than me with red curly hair and freckles dotting her round face. "Are you here for the Marine Science camp, too?" She smiled a metallic smile, her mouth full of braces.

"Yeah, I'm Storm." I smiled, feeling more confident with the presence of another student.

"I'm Samantha. Nice to meet you. I am so excited for this camp. I signed up for this *months ago* and I want to be a marine scientist and the professors teaching this are like totally top in their field. One is a geologist and one studies marine mammals. I totally want to do dolphin research. I already have started my own photo catalog of the dolphins that swim around my house. I live on the intracoastal and dolphins are always swimming past and after reading the professor's book, I started taking my own pictures of the dolphins dorsal fins. That's how you identify them, you know, by their dorsal fins. Each one is like a finger print. My dad takes me out in our boat and we follow dolphins until we're close enough to take their picture. I brought my pictures along to show him. I hear Dr. Ross is really great and I can't wait to meet him. I have read all of his books, even though they are for college students and I'm only fifteen. Have you read them?"

I stared at Samantha. 'Whoa' was all I could come up with and didn't think that was an appropriate response. Either she was way over prepared or I was way under prepared.

"Umm, no, I haven't," I finally pushed out of my mouth.

"Oh, well, I'm sure that's okay. I mean it wasn't like we were supposed to read them or anything." By her expression, I think she thought we should have read them.

We made it to the top of the stairs and I held the door open for her.

"After you!" I said.

"Thanks!"

"Well, I'm going to go get a seat. Ya comin?" Samantha turned back to me. I was still at the door.

"Yeah, right behind you." I took a deep breath and entered the large open room. Six tables were arranged in two rows and each table had two seats. There was one table at the front of the room facing back on the rest. I followed Miss Brown-nose into the classroom.

There were other kids already in the room. A couple of girls were talking to each other like old friends, a boy had on earphones while another was reading a book. My eyes paused on a third boy and a genuine smile filled my face. It was Jon. When he saw me notice him, he put on a big smile. I walked over to where he was seated, near the wall lined with windows that faced the water.

"Hi!" I said.

"Long time no see!" His grin made me laugh and relief washed over me with his familiar face.

"Yeah! Been banned from the gift shop for scaring the customers?" I asked.

"HA!" He laughed. "Nah, I only scare the pretty ones."

"Oh, please," I said rolling my eyes. "Can I sit here?" I pointed to the empty chair next to him.

"I was hoping you would."

"So, hi! My name is Samantha." Jon and I both looked up to see Samantha standing in front of our table. She sat down in an empty chair at the adjoining table and reached right in front of me to extend her hand to Jon. I leaned back in my chair to give her some more room. Jon took her hand politely and made a quick glance at me. I shrugged my shoulders.

"You guys know each other?" She asked.

"Yeah, well, sort of. We met the other day," Jon smiled at me as he answered. "Nice to meet you, Samantha," he added.

"The syllabus said that we're going on a boat tomorrow to learn about the coast. I love going on boats. My dad has a 32 foot Boston Whaler that he lets me drive. I hope we find some dolphins. Did you read the newest publication that Professor Ross was co-author on? It just came out last week."

Jon and I exchanged more glances. "Um, no," he said. I just shook my head and worried that we were about to get a line-by-line recitation of the publication and its findings, but luck was on our side because at that moment two men entered the room.

They each held mugs of steaming coffee, stacks of papers and were laughing about a conversation already in progress. They made their way causally to the front of the room and set down their loads. I presumed they were our professors. One was thin but muscular, in pretty good shape for a guy his age. His hair was longer, but slightly thinning. He wore old khaki shorts and an un-tucked Hawaiian shirt. The other was shorter and rounder. His hair was neatly trimmed, his shorts were pressed and his golf tee was tucked in. The din in the room of our mini conversations died away until only the two professor's conversation remained.

"No, you should have seen him climbing out of the water. Priceless." The one with the Hawaiian shirt said. The other laughed heartily and took a sip of his coffee. And then, as if they only now realized there were other people in room, they looked out to where we stared at them in nervous silence. I glanced to Samantha and her face was filled with undisguised awe, nearly worship-like reverence. The tucked shirt professor walked to the front of the desk where their papers were stacked, still holding his coffee, and sat partly on the edge of the desk and dangled one foot.

"Good morning!"

We mimicked his greeting in mechanical unison.

"I'm Dr. Jim Ross and this is Dr. Andy Briggs."

Samantha's hand shot up.

"Yes?" Dr. Ross pointed to the overly enthusiastic Samantha.

"I just wanted to tell you, Dr. Ross, what a pleasure it is to have you as my professor," Samantha said.

"Well, thank you, Miss,"

"Samantha Watson, Professor. Perhaps you know my dad, Phil Watson? He is a large contributor to the Oceanaria fund," she said.

"Ahh yes, I do know of him. Well, Miss Watson, good to have you in class. As I was saying, Dr. Briggs and I will be co-teaching this course. I will handle the difficult topics like ecosystems, ecology and fascinating marine life and Dr. Briggs will tell you about rocks." He said rocks with a roll of his eyes.

"Ahem." Dr. Briggs fake cleared his throat and Dr. Ross snickered.

"I'm standing right here, Jim," Dr. Briggs said with false indignation.

We all laughed.

"I believe what my esteemed colleague was trying to say," Dr. Briggs spoke now from his partly reclined, seated position behind the desk, "is that I will be handing the delicate, ever evolving infrastructure of the coast while Dr. Ross here will tell you about the warm and fuzzies."

We laughed more at their child-like bickering.

I like these guys, I thought. *They aren't at all like my stuffy teachers at home.*

"Yes, well, let's start with getting to know each other a bit." Dr. Ross held a piece of paper in front of him, "Arch, Abigail?"

A girl with bouncy curls and a big smile shot her hand up.

"Arch, Josh? Are you two related?" Dr. Ross looked between Josh and Abigail.

The boy rolled his eyes and with a hint of sarcasm replied, "Unfortunately, she's my sister." Abigail then stuck her tongue out at Josh. Dr. Ross went back to his list.

"Beller, Owen?"

"Here." The boy that was listening to his headphones when I walked in raised his hand.

"Bolen, Shannon?" A girl with long blonde hair that was sitting up front raised her hand.

"Harn, Storm?"

I raised my hand and I felt my cheeks flush...I always got embarrassed when my name was called.

"Mani..."

Before Dr. Ross could continue, Dr. Briggs interrupted him, "Miss, Harn," I looked up at him, "are you related to the Lighthouse Keeper Harn?"

"Yes," I said.

Okay, how red are my cheeks now, I wondered.

He raised his eyebrows a bit and nodded. Samantha fidgeted in her seat.

"Manistar, Jon." Jim continued roll call.

"Here." Jon raised his hand.

"Mr. Manistar, so nice that you could join us for the summer. How is your dad?" Dr. Ross asked.

"He's fine, thanks," Jon said.

Samantha shifted uncomfortably in her seat again. Her malcontent was nearly palpable. *Is it wrong that I want to smile?*

"Quinly, Kendall?"

The girl with curly blonde hair sitting next to Shannon raised her hand.

"Watson, Samantha?"

Samantha's hand shot up like an arrow. Dr. Ross nodded and gave a smile. Samantha smiled back and sat a bit taller.

"Wilkenson, Hayden?"

The boy that was reading a book looked up and nodded.

"Alright, let's get started," Dr. Ross said. "This course is designed to give you all some depth of understanding about the land and waters just outside these windows. This area is steeped in exciting maritime history as well as Oceanographic history not to mention its fair share of mysteries."

The kids around me mumbled excitedly to each other.

"And of all the miles of coastline of Florida, of the nearly *1200* miles of coastline, the few miles that make up your backyard here in beautiful St. Augustine are some of the most fascinating and some of the most temperamental." He paused a moment to let his words sink in.

"Dr. Briggs and I both teach at a University on the Gulf Coast and our plan is to keep this course at a college-level, if that is okay with you all." The room nodded, our egos sufficiently tempted. "You all will be learning what Juniors and Seniors in college learn. Sound good?"

I glanced around and saw bright eyes, excited nods and some nervous exchanges.

Dr. Ross continued, "We will divide our time between classroom lessons and hands on exploration that involves playing in the muck, one of Dr. Briggs' favorite pastimes." Dr. Briggs nodded in agreement and some folks giggled. "And also taking some boat trips out into the intracostal and near shore environments to hopefully catch some glimpses of the more interesting critters, like..."

"Warm and fuzzies," Dr. Briggs interjected.

"Did I mention intelligent?" Dr. Ross shot back.

"Biomatter," Dr. Briggs replied.

"So," Dr. Ross cleared his throat, "if everybody could come up and pick up a workbook from the table, we can get started."

The rest of the morning went quickly. Dr. Ross went over the syllabus and explained how the sections of the course were divided into basic marine science lessons on geology, oceanography, ecology and mammalogy. We ended the morning session looking at some slides of research trips they had taken off this coast. When photos of dolphins appeared, I thought Samantha was going to bounce out of her seat. She kept whispering that one of the pictures looked just like a dolphin she knew that swam by her house. She had followed the one out in her dad's boat and taken pictures of it. She had named it fluffy tail, or fifi fin or something. I nearly laughed aloud when Dr. Ross explained how it was illegal to approach a wild dolphin unless you had a special permit issued by the government. Samantha stayed pretty quiet after that.

Before I knew it, it was time to break for lunch!

"Stay close," Dr. Ross said, "we're going to get started again in about 30 minutes!"

"Do you want to eat outside?" Jon asked me over the din of the classroom chatter.

"Yeah, that sounds nice," I said.

Jon led me to a majestic oak tree near the picket fence. It was gnarled and covered with Spanish moss and resurrection ferns. Finger like branches twisted away from its trunk and reached to the ground. I had never seen anything like it.

"Wow! How old is this tree?"

"Depends on what story you believe," Jon replied. "But it's at least over 200 years old. This is where the girls that died use to play. Some say their spirits still do!"

The hair on the back of my neck stood up. I couldn't tell if he was teasing me or being serious so I buried my face in my water bottle.

"Really thirsty," I said sort of embarrassed. "Having a hard time adjusting to the heat, I guess."

"Yeah, I'd say so." He laughed and handed me his water. "Need some more?"

"Really?" Creepy stories aside, my body begged for more water.

"Sure, I can get more inside, no worries," He said.

I took the cold water eagerly and drank. The bottle was empty too quickly. My thirst had not diminished. *This is ridiculous.* I saw Jon staring at me and then he shook his head and chuckled.

"What?" I asked and bumped into his side with elbow.

"Nothing, really." He was laughing now. "I just never knew anyone who drank so much water."

"Nice one, Jon, feel free to laugh at my thirst. It's not my fault your town is like 200 degrees in the shade." But I couldn't help but laugh with him.

"So what do you think so far?" Jon asked through the side of his mouth as he chewed his sandwich. Nana made me a turkey sandwich and had put some of the left over bacon from breakfast on it. I wasn't all that hungry so I just picked off the bacon slices and ate them.

"So far so good. The teachers seem fun. I wish high school teachers were as cool as college professors."

Jon nodded in agreement. He reached down to a bag of pretzels and handed them to me, "Want some? I don't really like pretzels much, too salty."

"Oh, sure." I took a few and started crunching. He placed the bag between us. The pretzels totally hit the spot. I resisted taking any more even though I really wanted them. Jon must have picked up on my desire because he held the bag to me, "Really, take em all, I don't mind."

"Thanks!" I smiled and crunched away happily. My thoughts wandered back to my midnight conversation with Pearl...*it wasn't just water she said that I needed, but salt.* "Huh," I whispered as I munched contentedly.

A gentle breeze picked up around us and wicked some of the moisture off my skin. I lifted my heavy ponytail up to let the breeze tickle the back of my neck. My thirst finally subsided a bit and I felt much better but I was bombarded with the scent of brine again. *No way...please no...*I risked the quickest of sniffs toward my arm under the pretense of looking at a small bird hopping through the grass...*no...no...no...this isn't happening...*the smell I thought was low tide was really coming from my skin.

"Nice braid," Jon said as I quickly dropped my arms to my side praying he didn't notice the odor.

"Oh, yeah," I said, "a friend did it for me." *I think.*

"The beads are really..." He stared at it for a moment longer and the space between his eyes squinted together slightly like he was thinking hard about something or trying to remember something.

"Really what?" I asked.

But then the space smoothed back out. "Oh, nothing. They're cool. I feel like I've seen something like that before, in a book, or a picture some-where...I was trying to remember."

"Really?" I asked.

"Yeah, but I'm not sure where." He reached his hand to touch it. A shiver ran through me. "Huh, I'll try to figure it out." He stood up and held a hand to me. "Time to head in, round two is about to begin. Ding, ding," he made a sound like a boxing match bell. "Hmm, smell that?"

"No, what?" I stepped slightly away from him and tried to look confused.

"I don't know. But it smells sort of ..." He sniffed the air but a sudden gust of wind interrupted him. "Hmm, I don't know. It's gone now. Oh well, it was strange, sort of salty and musky but a bit spicy like chai tea."

I laughed nervously. "Weird," I replied with a little shrug of my shoulders.

"How's the book I gave you?" He asked as we neared the classroom.

"Actually, haven't started it yet." Embarrassed for the second time, *God, Storm, batting 1000 today.*

"It's okay, take your time. Let me know what you think. Of course, I hear the professor also has some interesting books if you prefer..."

"Stop," I fake scolded him but he dodged my shoulder punch and we both laughed as we made out way back to our seats.

Four o'clock arrived quickly. We had reading homework and instructions to come tomorrow wearing sunscreen and a bathing suit under our clothes for our first boating adventure. *Oh yeah.* I thought to myself, *don't forget the sunscreen! That's one lesson I learned well.*

Jon walked me out to the parking lot.

"Whoa, Storm, check out that bike!" He sounded very excited and directed my attention to a shiny blue motorcycle parked near the parking lot exit.

"Wow. It's really, uh, pretty?" I offered.

Jon looked at me with that look reserved for boys when they just don't understand a girl's reaction.

"Pretty? Are you crazy? That's the brand new Yamaha TMAX motor scooter!"

I smiled.

"Seriously? That means nothing to you. Four-valve-per-cylinder, 499cc parallel twin, liquid-cooled engine? CF die-cast aluminium frame, 43mm front forks, 4-piston mono-block caliper, dual front disc brakes? 47 mpg?!" He was now obviously flustered.

"Well, if meaning something requires me to think beyond *it's pretty*, then yup, means nothing," I said.

He just shook his head sadly. I gave him a push with my shoulder and laughed. But when I looked up again I did find something interesting with the bike. Or not so much the bike, but with the driver.

"Hiya, Stormy!" Sara called in her wind chime voice. She wore a thin white tank top and short black bike shorts.

"What'r you doin here?" I asked as we approached the bike.

Jon stood silently next to me. He was staring at Sara.

"To fetch you!" She chimed, a perfect smile adorning her glowing face. Her dark hair draped like a cloak around her shoulders. She held two shimmery blue helmets in her lap.

"Really?!" I started to move toward her and then I remembered Jon. "Oh, sorry, Jon, this is my friend Sara, Sara this is Jon." I looked at Jon but he didn't move and his mouth was hanging slightly open. *Boys*, I thought.

"Jon." I nudged him. "Earth to Jon." I guessed that between the bike and Sara he was in sensory overload.

He took a deep breath and blinked. "Hi," he muttered.

I shook my head. "So Sara, where's Nana?"

"Well, actually, I bumped into her earlier and asked if you and I could hang out this afternoon. It's my day off and I thought we could go shopping. She mentioned you may be wanting to get some new dresses or skirts or something. You know, if that's alright. I promised to have you back before dawn...or was it dinner...well, they're kind of the same thing really." She winked at me.

"Alright?!" I was over the moon. "Of course!"

I turned to Jon and he was still staring...no, more like gawking.

"So Jon," I spoke a little louder than necessary, "see ya tomorrow?"

"Uh yeah Storm, see ya tomorrow." He gave me an awkward hug.

He turned back to Sara, "Umm, nice to meet you."

"And it was *very* nice to meet you," she replied in a voice that nearly purred. She reached out her hand and stroked Jon's face lightly. His jaw went slack and his eyes didn't seem to be seeing anything. I felt a sudden urge to protect him, not that he was in danger, well, other than the danger of looking completely stupid.

"So..." I started and Sara turned back to me.

"Right, I'm sure I'll be seeing you around," Sara said to Jon with a wink and then turned back to me, "ready?" I nodded.

She handed me one of the helmets and helped me climb onto the back of the bike. "Toss your books in there," she pointed to a small compartment at the back of the bike. "I'm sure they're all so thrilling!" The sarcasm couldn't be missed.

"Okay then," she said after I climbed on, "hang on!" I gave Jon a parting wave and smile. No sooner had I wrapped my arms around Sara's tiny waist, than she hit the accelerator and the bike took off. I closed my eyes and happily let the wind tickle my skin.

Chapter Seven

"Doin okay back there?" Sara's voice broke through the wind as she weaved in and out of cars along A1A.

"YEAH!" I yelled back. I must have spoken too loudly because Sara answered with a giggle.

"Well, hold tight, Storm, I want to beat these cars to the bridge."

The bike leaned beneath me, first to the left, then to the right, and then back to the left. Each time she accelerated, my body tried to slip off the back of the seat.

We turned left at the base of the bridge and after a quick right, bounced our way along a narrow brick street.

"Ta da!" She announced after pulling the bike smoothly into a narrow space at the curb. My knees shook slightly from squeezing the bike tightly. Sara's driving was adventurous, to say the least.

She took off her helmet and looked back toward me with a grin that would have put the Cheshire cat to shame. Her hair, finally released from its confines of the blue helmet sprang out happily and caught the breeze. Shining dark strands fluttered this way and that and looked like a perfectly styled "bed head".

Of course she doesn't get helmet head, I thought dismally, *I should have known.*

But before I continued down that road of jealously, I noticed her smiling eyes. Her eyes made me forget I didn't look as gorgeous as she did. Besides, she wanted *me* to go hang out with *her*! My jealously shriveled in the brightness of her glow and I found myself happy to be with this goddess.

She reached into the back compartment that held my books and pulled out a vibrant, multicolored piece of silky fabric. It took me a moment to realize that the fabric was a wrap skirt. Sara pulled it around her and tied the thin strings on her right hip.

"Okay. Ready to shop! And based on the look you're carrying now, we don't have a moment to lose. Ooh, one more thing. Here." She handed me a jar of lotion from the back compartment. "Put some on so you smell...fresh." She winked.

My face burned slightly with a flush of embarrassment and Sara's laughter filled the air which caused my face to deepen from simply pink to crimson. "Come on little Stormy, put your big girl panties on. It's perfectly normal. Well, your outfit selection does need serious help, but as for the rest, it will all sort itself out with time. The lotion, however, is a must for us all."

We walked down the uneven brick street at a pace somewhere between a skip and a jog. Her feet were tucked into a pair of jeweled ballet flats. Mine were shoved into a pair of old sneakers. As dissimilar as beauty and the beast, she led me through downtown St. Augustine.

The tiny streets had curious names like Cuna, Hypolita, Treasury, Artillery and Cordova. A few times we criss-crossed the main walking street, St. George, where the largest crowds of tourists mingled. Each time we happened upon the crowds I noticed people staring at us, or I suppose at Sara. I picked up a sense that Sara loved the attention. She acted as if she was queen of this town and the admiring strangers were her loyal subjects! She flashed a brilliant yet condescending smile as we strolled past them. We stopped in quite a few tiny stores off the narrow side streets. In each one, the person working addressed Sara by name and they'd begin gossiping about the latest bands and who was "in" and who was "so not". I felt a bit of a celebrity just by association.

We were encouraged to try things on or look at something the owner thought Sara would find irresistible. Sara seemed partial to vintage Victorian circa clothing. However, a certain amount of rocker chic flair made itself present in some of her cravings. The combination of old lace and tattooed inspired art created a very unique and fantastically eye catching style.

As for me, I didn't really have a style, not one I knew anyway. But I wasn't about to complain about being pampered by Sara and her store acquaintances. I never had a sister or even a close girl friend before and it was fun to try things on, laugh, and play.

We eventually entered a small boutique on Granada Street. The smell of spicy incense permeated the air. I recognized the music softly playing in the back ground. It was an old Eagles song my dad liked called Witchy Woman.

"Paige!" Sara exclaimed as we entered the store.

The woman, who sat on a tall stool behind a glass counter filled with gold bracelets, silver rings, crystal earrings and jeweled necklaces, looked up from her magazine. A smile lit up her heart-shaped face.

"Sara, old friend! It's been too long. Tell me a tale!" Her voice rang out. I was familiar at this point to the greeting. Although I didn't understand it, it seemed to be the standard introduction in each store we went to.

Paige floated around the counter and gave Sara a hung. Their long, wavy hair mingled during the quick embrace, brown with black, milk chocolate with dark chocolate. Paige wore a fitted, floor length purple dress with spaghetti straps that criss-crossed her unbelievably toned back and a slit up the left leg that went to her perfectly shaped upper thigh. She had on knee high, gypsy tapestry boots with polished silver heels.

Seriously am I the only plain person in this town?! I wondered.

"Oh," Paige's soprano voice rang, "who is this gorgeous young thing? Barely of age, no?"

"Paige, this is Storm, she's sixteen," Sara said. Paige's eyes narrowed. "She's just arrived here and is in desperate need of some new outfits, as you can see.

"Hi," I said.

Paige gazed at me with dark eyes surrounded by darker lashes. Her eyes scanned up and down my body and I suddenly felt as exposed as if I stood in the middle of the shop naked.

She sniffed the air lightly and nodded, "Storm. Wow, it's really a pleasure to meet you. We haven't had many young ones for awhile. Mum mentioned a new arrival."

"Ahem, Paige," Sara interrupted, her tone serious, "Storm is *new* to this town." Sara emphasized the word new.

"OH!" Paige sang, "Yes, you guys *just* met, of course. Well, Storm, welcome." Paige held out her hand.

She reached for my hand and I noticed how long and delicate her fingers were. Each one was adorned with a silver ring with different sized and shaped milk-white stones embedded in them.

"Well, look around, please. Perhaps the rack over there; it has some junior sizes that may fit you," she said.

Her words were innocent but her tone wasn't. It was like thinking the spoon contained whipped cream when it was really sour cream. The store got darker and the three of us looked out of the store front windows. The sky had turned dark with thick thunderclouds and wind blew dust through the narrow street. Large drops of rain splattered on the hot ground.

I looked back at Paige and noticed a sly smile on her lips.

She walked over to Sara and whispered, "Storm, indeed. Never underestimate the ones that have been kept in the dark. Obviously one of yours, but who will claim her at the gathering?"

Sara smirked. "Yeah, she's ours. Not sure really. You know one or two usually pop up every few decades or so. Z just told us to train her up. I don't know anything beyond that."

"Right. They do, of course, but the timing is rather interesting, no? There was that rumor those many years ago," Paige continued. "It's nearly spot on for the deadline, but...no, it couldn't be. Or could it?" Her voice broke off and she looked accusingly at me again. I was frozen by her glare.

My ears rang and my head pounded.

"Are those new silver bangles?" Sara's voice chimed distantly.

Paige turned away from me. I exhaled in a huff and felt as if a great pressure had been lifted of of me. "Oh, yeah!" Paige's voice was high in excitement. "Just got them in yesterday, all hand hammered. Aren't they fabulous?"

Sara caught my eye and winked. She motioned for me to look around. *Whatever*, I thought. I wasn't so sure I wanted to stay in here. Paige seemed kind of mean.

The two of them continued to talk about jewelry as I walked from rack to rack. I stole glances at them between flipping through silk and cotton items. Sara leaned her hip against the counter, one leg casually crossed in front of the other, like a sloppy fourth position in ballet. Her long, thin fingers made tiny motions across the glass counter top as she talked. Paige sat back down behind the counter on her tall wooden stool. She flipped her hair over her shoulder in one smooth move and played absent-mindedly with a small, silver fish-shaped pendant that hung from a dark cord around her neck as she talked.

Sara looked over to me and then said something to Paige that sounded like "needs my help." Paige sighed with an arrogant nod. "Just a little," she whispered sarcastically.

"Paige likes to joke around. Don't let her get to you," Sara spoke softly to me as she pulled me over to the display of dresses that was labeled "New Arrivals."

I smiled weakly, but really I wanted to cry. I didn't like Paige and I didn't like being talked about. Thunder rumbled and lightning waltzed in the sky. Large raindrops still splattered to the ground.

"Come on, relax. Shopping therapy is just what you need! Young, yes, but it's never too early to look the part, Storm. These will all fit you in no time at all," she said as she shoved a bunch of dresses into my hands.

"Look the part of what?"

"A local. Or at least a local like us," Sara said with a wink.

Paige laughed wickedly without looking up from her magazine.

Sara pushed me, my arms piled high with clothes, toward the paisley curtained dressing room.

"Sara, are we still doing the full moon party at the point?" Paige asked.

"Same place as always. Z didn't want to take any chances."

"I'll pass the word to Daniel," Paige said. "How's Pearl holding up?"

"Well, she's been better. This year should be pretty interesting!" Sara said.

"So, no news, huh?" Paige asked.

"No. Nothing yet. But her little issue added to this new arrival should make it one interesting party. Hang on, howzit goin' Storm?" Sara called to me.

"Going good," I said.

Oops, I thought. I hadn't even started changing because I was too busy listening to their conversation.

The dressing room was small with two large mirrors on opposite walls. I call them infinity mirrors because I always feel like I can see to infinity with the never-ending reflections. The wall without a mirror had some framed pictures. There was one of a surfer half way down an enormous wave, a black and white one of the Saint Augustine lighthouse, and a third of a mermaid. A tiny date was hand written in the corner of the mermaid print, *1873*. The mermaid's tail was green and pink with a long, flowing fin. Her auburn hair billowed out behind her giving the impression of being underwater. The title of the mermaid print was written in cursive at the bottom.

"Sea Maiden," I whispered under my breath. "Beautiful."

"What was that Storm?" I drew my hand away quickly from the print. I felt like a kid caught with her hand in the cookie jar. I hadn't even realized it, but I was touching the picture of the mermaid. "Did you say the dress was beautiful?"

"What? Oh! No, still getting it on. I was just admiring one of the pictures in here."

How the heck did she hear me? I wondered.

"Well come out when you have something on, I have another dress for you to try. And you are going to LOVE this!" Sara called to me.

Paige and Sara started chatting about the party again and I slipped on the first of the sun dresses. To my surprise, it looked pretty on me, or better yet, I felt pretty in it! I pushed the curtain aside and stepped out tentatively into the shop.

"Now that is more like it!" Sara exclaimed. She walked over and spun me around. "Yes, this is great and you won't have a problem growing into it."

Paige giggled.

"Well, she needs room to grow. Especially around the, you know, the chest area," Sara said as she made a sweeping motion with her arms.

I didn't realize my growth spurts were of such importance or even of common knowledge, I thought.

"Okay, back in. Try on the others!" Sara said. She sounded giddy. It was infectious. I smiled and hopped back behind the curtain. It was fun being the center of shopping attention; especially by somebody who had such an obviously wonderful fashion sense.

I marched out for assessment with each new outfit. Some got thumbs up while others were tossed aside. Sara kept changing out colors "to compliment my light skin tone" and switching long skirts with short dresses, cottons with silks and solids with prints.

Each time I went to try a new thing on, the girls talked about the party. From what I could hear, it sounded amazing. They mentioned bonfires that got so big they lit the sky for miles, intoxicating aromas of delicious food, drums, songs and dancing until the sun rose. Each time I came out, they stopped talking and focused on my outfit. I wasn't sure if they were purposely keeping me out of the party conversation or genuinely interested in my looks.

"We just got some new suits in," Paige told Sara.

"I think these two will be perfect!" Sara replied and before I could even turn, two flimsy sets of material were tossed over the curtain onto me.

The colorful tissue-sized pieces of cloth fluttered into a scarily tiny pile on the floor of the dressing room.

"Seriously? I'm supposed to wear these?" They were a far cry from my usual tankini.

I held up the white one first. Then the green one. The green seemed to have a bit more coverage. *Okay, green it is,* I decided.

I gingerly slid the shimmery bottoms into place. *So far so good,* I thought. *Everything seems covered.* Then I tried to attach the top but I quickly realized this wasn't one of those tops that looked like a bra with simple arm straps and a back closure. No, this was far more complicated and honestly, confusing. I understood where the large, large being relative when speaking of this suit, part of fabric went, but other than that, strings went everywhere and nowhere at the same time. I had no idea what tied to what.

"Come on, Storm," I scolded myself. "It can't be that hard. It's a bathing suit for goodness sake."

I laid the top out flat on the small chair in the corner of the dressing room, splaying all the strings to the sides and examined the shape. Standing over it in nothing but my green bottoms, I willed the top to make sense.

If that string goes this way and this one goes over there and then I suppose these two tie back here. This was more complicated than the origami swan I made in the sixth grade. I gingerly slid the top into place and tightened down all the strings ending with one final tie in the middle. *Ta-da!*

I gasped when I turned triumphantly toward the mirror. I was so intent on getting the stings organized I had put the top on backward. *No worries, a little shimmy and shift and now...Ta-da!*

"Wow," I whispered, turning side to side mesmerized by the tiny shimmers of the suit and the way my skin seemed to radiate as well, like it reflected the shimmer of the material. *Is that really me in the mirror?* This wasn't as embarrassing as I thought it would be, *although I'm still not sure I'm comfortable showing this much skin.* "This is a lot of skin." I put my arms across my belly, then by my sides, then one across my chest and the other across my belly. There wasn't a way to hide the skin. But it wasn't really all that bad. *I actually feel sorta pretty.* And for some reason, for a quick glimmer of a breath, I felt inexplicably confident in my skin!

"Is that the last one?" Sara said as I came shyly back into view. "Ooh! That suit is perfect. It's a keeper also."

My keeper pile was very impressive. I was trying to figure out which ones I would pick so that I could stay within my cash limit. Sadly, I could probably only actually afford to keep two. Nana hadn't given me a budget for a new wardrobe.

"Okay, one more!" Sara said. She pulled a long, silk blue dress with thin straps out from behind her back. "Go on...try it on!"

"Oh, no," I said. "This is way too fancy. I mean, I won't have any reason to wear it, plus it'll look silly on me."

"It is perfect for you, Storm. And don't worry, it won't look silly by the time the party comes around," Sara said.

"The party?" I asked. My heart accelerated.

"Yeah, the party," Sara said.

"It's the best party the town never sees!" Paige exclaimed.

"Indeed. Haven't you heard us talking about it this whole time? You'll love it Stormy!"

I'm invited?

"You didn't think you weren't invited, did you?" Sara asked.

"Oh, well, I don't...I mean, I wasn't..." I stuttered.

"Please, Storm. You're the guest of honor!" Sara said. She pushed me gently back toward the curtain. "Go on."

I'm invited. I'M INVITED! I screamed in my head. I jumped up and down as quietly as possible in the dressing room. *Me! Plain Jane me, in-*

vited to the coolest party ever. But wait, what did she mean guest of honor? She's probably just joking again. Whatever! I'm going to a party! And not just any party, from the sound of it, the coolest party in town!

I hurriedly put the dress on and nearly forgot to feel foolish. But when I turned to face my infinite reflections, it was my turn to freeze and stare.

The dress was perfect. It hugged me and flowed with me all at the same time. It was like wearing water. And it may have been a trick of lighting, or the angle of the mirror but I swear curves had appeared on my stick-like frame. *Is this really my reflection?*

I didn't want to take it off. And to make it worse, I knew it wouldn't be anywhere near my budget.

"Well, come on and show us!" Sara exclaimed.

I walked out tentatively. Sara let out a whistle and made a circle motion with her hand.

I turned in a full revolution.

"Well now, looks like Storm here is coming into her own!" Paige said.

"And I happen to know," Sara said, "that blue is Rowan's favorite color!"

My face caught on fire.

"Relax," Sara said with a laugh. "Your secret's safe with us."

"Yeah," Paige said, "safe. You're not the first one to try to land that fish. Just be careful, he's as slippery as an eel," she giggled.

"Okay, well, Storm, go change and bring all the outfits we're getting to the counter."

"Oh, well," I said, "I'm not going to be able to get all of them." It was embarrassing.

"Why not?" Sara didn't seem to understand.

"I-I-I can't afford it," I mumbled.

Sara laughed loudly. *Is she laughing at me?* I wondered. *That's just mean.*

Thunder grumbled again outside.

Paige looked out the window and then to Sara. She raised one eyebrow and chuckled. "Such a quick little temper," she said under her breath and continued flipping through her magazine.

"No, Storm," Sara said, "I'm not laughing at you not being able to afford these. I'm laughing because you thought you had to! I didn't take you in here to tease you with clothes you couldn't get. These are on Z."

"What? Really? Does Nana know about this?" I asked.

"Yeah, silly. Z knew you'd need some clothes so she asked Rean if it would be okay if you and I went shopping today," Sara said.

"Oh. Well, wow!" I said. I was stunned by the generosity of this woman who'd I'd never even met. First, she gave me life saving lotion and now she just completely revamped my wardrobe. *Why is she doing all of this for me?*

"I'll go get the clothes!" Sara said with a smile as she walked past me. I was still standing completely stunned in the middle of the store. "Wow! This is amazing!"

"One more thing," Paige whispered as Sara ducked into the dressing room, "this is from me."

She reached across the counter and handed me a silver ring with a milky stone. I noticed her right middle finger was now missing a ring.

"It's a moonstone," Paige said, "for our newest little sister. Wear it to help guide you through the next few months."

The ring fit perfectly on my middle finger. As I turned it in the light, every color of the rainbow shimmered from it.

"Um, thanks," I finally managed. As Paige leaned back toward her stool, a beautifully intricate braid slipped out from under her hair. To call it a braid was an understatement, it was an elaborately woven masterpiece that instead of having three strands of hair woven together like mine, it had a hundred. It was about the width of my pointer finger with thin strands of green and gold thread woven through its considerable length. The colors reminded me of a monarch butterfly's chrysalis. Along with the thread, were tiny, silver, round beads interspersed top to bottom and a cluster of the beads, hung lower than her hair by a few centimeters, made a little flower shape. They were the same kind of beads as I had on my braid, but hers was a work of art, a masterpiece of design and intricate complex design!

"Wow," I exclaimed, "that's beautiful!" I motioned to her braid.

"Oh, yeah." Paige quickly tucked the braid out of sight. "Thanks." Her eyes darted quickly to Sara who had returned to the counter. I glanced as well and saw Sara's expression darken for an instant.

"Here you go!" Paige said as she handed me three large bags. "I'm sure we will be seeing each other very soon." Sara led me to the door.

"Try to stay out of trouble my friend," she spoke to Paige as we wove through the racks of clothes.

"Now what would be the fun of that?" Paige said and winked at me.

"See ya at the party Stormy. And good luck, hope they train you up fast enough to pass the test!" Paige snickered as the door closed behind us.

"Test?" I asked Sara as the door closed behind us.

"Oh, just Paige teasing again," she replied.

The weather had cleared outside but the brief rain left behind very thick and steamy air. I took a deep breath and wondered if it was more liquid than gas. Tree frogs croaked their tuneless songs as we splashed through the puddles.

"I don't know what to say about all of this," I said to Sara. "It was way too kind of Z to buy me all of these." Both of my arms arms held a large bag full of my new outfits.

"Oh, no, she wanted to do it," Sara said. Her attitude seemed more subdued.

"Well, I need to thank her somehow," I said.

"No worries, Storm. She wants you to feel welcomed here," Sara said.

"And this ring." I held up my hand to admire it more in the sun. "It's so beautiful!"

"Where did you...oh, Paige of course. Listen, you really need to cleanse it in the ocean as soon as you get home, okay?" She didn't seem as excited about the ring as I was.

"Why?"

"Just do it."

Did I do something wrong?

She led us back to the bike, unclipped our helmets and handed me mine. She untied her skirt and stowed it in the back compartment.

I hope I didn't make her mad.

The wind picked up and my hair blew about my face. The chimes on the end of my braid sang delicately. Then a second set of chimes sang in harmony to mine. I looked around and saw them. Silver bells attached to the end of a braid just like mine.

"Sara," I said, "I never noticed your braid before." It was only as she tied her hair up that I even noticed the glimmer of silver.

She quickly tucked the braid under the rest of her hair.

"Did you put this in my hair?" I said picking up my braid from under my hair.

"No," she said curtly. "And you should keep that under your hair. Best not to draw attention with it." Her eyes darted nervously around.

I felt scolded. How had the afternoon taken such a sudden turn? It was like some kind of switch flipped in Sara; she went from making me feel elated to making me feel like a spare part. A hot droplet left my right eye and made a torturous journey down my cheek and onto the corner of my lip. I looked away so Sara wouldn't see that I was crying. I felt like such a baby, but she kind of hurt my feelings.

"Storm," Sara said in a softer voice. "I'm sorry. I didn't mean to make you feel bad. Right now I need to get you home and you need to do your homework, okay?"

"Yeah, that's fine," I said, trying to stop the tears.

Some large rain droplets hit the cement around us.

"Storm, relax," Sara said. "I don't feel like getting drenched on the way home."

The look in Sara's eyes made it impossible for me to argue with her. I took a deep breath.

"It's just not my place to talk to you about this," Sara said.

"Well, who's place is it? I was just asking about your braid because mine just appeared on my head this morning and I'd like to know how it got there," I said as my emotions shifted from sadness to anger. "And then I see that you have one and Paige has, well, she has some crazy masterpiece attached to her head..." The words spilled out of my mouth. "What's going on?!"

"Stop, okay. I'm sorry to make you upset."

"Stop what?" I mumbled, still angry at everybody ignoring my questions.

Sara's eyes darted to the darkening sky. A yellow bolt zapped across the sky. Thunder rumbled and the buildings lit up with bright flashes. "Look, I'll tell you this, your arrival here is something of a big deal."

"Why? Is it 'cause Nana's related to the old Lighthouse Keepers? Jon said something like that about his dad being all excited to meet her."

"No, it isn't because of Rean. Well, not totally anyway. It has more to do with something we've been waiting and hoping for. And with your arrival, that thing actually has a chance of happening."

"What would that have to do with me?"

"Maybe nothing, but maybe everything. We're just excited and nervous and maybe acting a bit weird."

"Yeah, I'll say. I just don't get what it has to do with me?"

"Have you ever had to keep a secret?"

"Yeah, I guess."

"Like a real secret, one that you couldn't tell no matter what?"

"Umm, yeah."

"Okay, well, this is like that. I want to tell you, but I can't. Not right now anyway. But it isn't because I don't want to, it's because I'm not allowed to. You get it?"

"I guess, but..."

"I promise if you can be just a little bit patient, you'll get all the answers you want."

"Hmmm..."

"Really, I promise. And it's good stuff, for you, I mean. Like, today, look at all of the new clothes you got. They're pretty cool, right?"

"Yeah, they are." I smiled and felt the weight of the bags on my arms. Bags full of new clothes, all for me!

"I think we should go home," Sara said.

"Ok." I agreed. Not really satisfied, but temporarily content. I did get a bunch of awesome new clothes for really no reason. As I put the bags into the storage under the seat I felt my braid slip out from under my hair. The bells chimed melodically.

"Shh." Sara roughly tucked the braid back under my hair.

Her eyes darted back and forth again and then stayed glaring ahead of us. I looked and saw what was distracting her. There were three men standing near us. They were staring and whispering to each other.

"Where did they come from?" I asked. The hairs on the back of my neck tingled uncomfortably.

"Damn, I told you to keep it hidden," she said, not taking her eyes off the men who now started to inch closer. They were amazingly handsome, like Rowan, but unlike Rowan, they didn't look friendly. One had thick, wavy, brown hair, grown down to his shoulders. His face was very angular and his eyes reminded me of a cat's eyes. They were golden brown. I found myself staring; not wanting to look away. Sara's voice broke me from my trance.

"Get on the bike, Storm," Sara whispered. "Slowly."

The hairs on the back of my neck were now at full attention. I moved mechanically; my mind still drawn to the one man's eyes, like a moth to a flame.

Sara sat in front of me and started the engine.

"Come on Sara, why won't you let me meet your new friend?" The one with the crazy eyes asked.

"Go home, Daniel," Sara hissed.

She revved the engine until it whined. "Hold on!" She spoke in a low voice to me.

She released the clutch and we shot forward, right toward the one she called Daniel. As we passed, I noticed a silver fish pendant hanging down from a dark chord around his neck. *I've seen that before*, I thought, but before I could get a second look, we shot past him and his friends. I dared a quick glance behind and saw them staring after us. I ducked my head into Sara's back and held on tightly for the entire ride home.

******

Sara parked the bike next to the lattice. We were greeted by Nana's loving smile when we climbed up to the deck.

"Good evening ladies!" Nana said. She held a glistening glass of white wine in one hand.

I still felt shaky from the incident downtown but Sara seemed fully recovered as she glided over to one of the empty chairs and relaxed back like a lounging feline.

"Well, based on the look of things, shopping was a success," Nana said.

"I told you and Z that I could handle it," Sara replied. "Paige was fine. I don't think she suspects anything. Although, I'm sure she'll pass the word along to Laverna, but as far as she knows, Storm is just another random addition. Oh, there was one eensy weensy issue at the end with some stupid boys, but it's all good. You had fun, right Storm?"

"Um, yeah! It was really great!" I was still standing with my load of bags.

"So, what was this, how did you put it Sara, eensy weensy issue?"

"Oh, well, these guys," I started but Sara interrupted me.

"Why don't you go try on that blue dress for Rean?"

"Okay," I looked at Sara. Her mouth was smiling, but her eyes were serious. "Yeah, sure. Be right back! Hey Zelda!" The cat was lying in the middle of the deck. I reached and gave her a quick pet.

I heard Sara mention men, braids, and naïve as I went in the door.

Pulling the dress out, I slipped it carefully over my head. My reflection was just as beautiful now as it was in the store. My skin, whose embarrassing burn had turned into an awesome tan, tingled as the silky fabric slid down my body and I enjoyed getting lost in my world of satin and curves. Out of my window I heard Sara and Nana talking and then a third voice joined them. I recognized it from the other night. It must be the woman Z that everybody keeps talking about. I looked in time to see a tall woman with a long, thick braid of dark, red hair walk over to Sara. She seemed a bit angry and Sara was talking with a lot of animation. Then a bright flash of lightning and crack of thunder made me jump.

A second flash and sharp crack followed. The soft evening light was replaced by an ominous green glow. I raced downstairs in a whirl of blue silk as the third crack of thunder shook the house's foundation.

"Nana!" I called "Sara!" I went out to the deck. Nobody was there. The sky flashed bright white and I was momentarily blinded. I ran to the side of the house and looked over the railing. Sara's bike was still there, but where was Sara?

"Nana!" I called again but thunder drowned out my voice.

I ran back inside. "NAN..." I ran into Nana, "...a," finishing her name after the fact.

"What's going on? Where's Sara?"

"She had to go," Nana said. The space between her eyebrows was creased.

"Oh. In this?" I waved toward the outside and the impending storm. "How come you didn't call me?"

"She'll be fine. What happened with those men downtown?" Nana asked.

"Um, well, nothing really. We were leaving and these men sort of tried to block us."

"Did they say anything?" She asked.

"One talked to Sara. It seemed like they knew each other," I said.

"Okay," Nana said. "You're okay?"

"Yeah, I'm fine," I said. "Why wouldn't I be?"

"No reason, I suppose. You were in very good hands with Sara."

"So why did she leave? And was that Z? She gave me that awesome lotion and bought me an entire new wardrobe and everybody keeps saying how concerned she is over me, but I've never even met her. Did I do something wrong? Did I spend too much money on the clothes?"

"Not at all. She and Sara just had to go check on something in town. I'm sure you will meet her very soon." Nana glanced out the large window facing the ocean.

"Oh," I replied, unsure if Nana was telling the truth about it not being my fault Sara looked upset talking to Z.

"Stormy, do you," Nana looked back to me and stopped. Her eyes traveled slowly up and down, taking in my new dress. "Wow! Stormy, you look beautiful!"

"Oh, thanks." With the confusion, I forgot all about my new dress. Another crack of thunder made me jump. "Jeezus! Are we going to be okay? This storm seems really bad." I glanced uneasily out the window.

"We'll be fine. Summer storms come up suddenly sometimes. I'll search up some candles just in case we lose power," she said and gave me a quick kiss on the forehead.

"Okay." With nothing much left for me to do besides change and read over the chapters for tomorrow, I trudged slowly back up to my room. I took off my dress and hung it carefully in the closet. To take my mind off of the storm, I pulled the rest of the clothes from the bags and hung them up. By the time I had finished, the storm's intensity seemed to have worn off, or perhaps it just moved elsewhere. "Now what? I mumbled. My pile of science papers stared back at me from my bed. "Right." I climbed next to them and settled in.

Huh, I thought, *Special Publication NO. 35 Florida's Geological History And Geological Resource.* I tossed it aside.

"The Rising Tides of Northeast Florida," my voice filled the empty room. *Ooh, thrilling.* "Florida's Changing Coastline."

My eyes shifted back to my closet and I smiled. Then I looked to the little table next to my bed. The book Jon gave me from the lighthouse stared back. "Well, now that looks more fun." I reached for it. Opening to the introduction by the author M. Humpphrey, the first line answered my question from yesterday about the source of the quote that popped in my head. It said,

"I dedicate this book to St. Augustine Florida; the smaller the town, the bigger its secrets."

Decision made. My homework can wait.

Chapter Eight

A high-pitched and really annoying beeping dragged me from the depths of sleep. My right hand shot out and hit the clock to make it shut up but that didn't work. It just kept beeping. My eyes cracked open a half inch. *Come on stupid clock*, I thought. *I only just closed my eyes.* I stared longer but nothing dramatic happened to the bright numbers or the noise. They glowed 6:03. *Oh wait...6:04.* I fumbled with the clock desperate to find the alarm button. Then I realized the clock wasn't actually making any noise. The horrible sound came from outside the house. *Seriously?* It turned out to be a garbage truck reversing down our street. I rubbed my eyes and looked around. A jumble of scientific papers were spread over my sheets and stretched open on my left was *Legends Behind the Legends of St. Augustine.* I turned the book over as I yawned and stretched my legs. Each joint seemed to ache rather than pop and my skin felt tighter than usual. *Maybe I shouldn't have stayed up so late last night reading that book*, I thought, *but it was too good to put down. Well not good as in awesome, but good as in entrancing.* Reading it was like watching an infomercial on TV where for some reason you just couldn't bring yourself to turn the channel.

The book was open to the last story I finished. It was called, *The Legend of the St. George Street Angels or Devils, You Decide. This one was really weird*, I thought as I looked over the story again. Apparently in the late 1700's into the early 1800's, the busy port town of Saint Augustine was a rough place to live. Merchants, sailors, and pirates all came together here with less-than-peaceful results. But all of that miraculously changed in the early 1800's, after the arrival of a Spanish cargo ship that limped into port following a tremendous storm.

The storm receded and the thankful crew came ashore. As the weeks passed and the storm was forgotten, drinking, gambling, and fights returned as usual during the shore breaks of seamen. Many town merchants (and parents with daughters) dreaded these shore breaks for although the sailors spent their money in town, fueled by strong liquor, short tempers and unleashed desires, they also quickly got out of control. The locals' brief reprieve during the unusual storm and the thankfulness of that particular crew was by far too short lived.

The specific event this myth centers on involves four Spanish sailors on leave from their duties onboard. A few months had passed since the great storm but the tales were still on the tips of many tongues. A statue, believed to be the Virgin Mary, was said to have been the savior of the ship. The crew promised to deliver her to a place of honor if they made to to shore alive. They had landed, against odds, in St. Augustine, and had been most gracious to the town. The ship that carried these 4 sailors, however, did not share the same grace. For although they knew of the story of their fellow countrymen, they had made an effortless journey across the Atlantic and now they felt it their right to have fun. They had all been enjoying themselves and had taken their merriment too far as they had cornered a beautiful young girl down a dark alley. She, however, was new to the town, arriving around the same time as the storm, and seemed unaware of the dangers after dark. Most girls were kept at home when the sailors arrived, but this young girl walked bravely alone down the dark streets. It didn't take long for the sailors to find her. While pressed against the rough co-quina wall of a narrow brick-paved alley, she didn't cry out, rather she stared at the men and said calmly in perfect Spanish, "Respect this town or you shall be punished. Do you not remember the storm and the promises you made?"

They just laughed. "That was not us," one spoke in heavily Spanish accented English. "We hold no duty to this town."

"You're choice," she said with an unusually calm voice, considering her predicament. "Have you not heard of the Saint George Street Angels? They were carried here on the wings of the storm to protect Saint Barbara and those who carried her. They have also vowed to protect this town and won't have the likes of you attacking the poor girls anymore!"

"Well, miss," one sailor said in a drunken, Spanish slur, "they must be busy since you appear quite alone."

"Who's Saint Barbara?" Another asked.

"Who cares." A third jeered. The others laughed and closed in like a pack of wolves. She cried out with an ear piercing call. That's when the explosion happened. The men turned at once and saw three women, dressed in white with eyes that glowed. They held sticks of dynamite in one hand and lighted torches in the other. The hunters became the hunted.

"Respect." The angles chanted as they stalked closer to the terrified sailors. "Respect our town." When the sailors turned back to the girl, they were met with a wicked grin and a pair of eyes that glowed an unearthly phosphorescent green. "Respect," she whispered.

"Dear God save us. These aren't angels, they are devils!" One sailor screamed and then crossed himself as if in prayer.

"I suggest you run away now," the girl said in a quiet voice.

They did as they were told and ran back to their ship. The chilling sound of the girl's laughter chased them down the dark alley. The sound was described as eery chimes and raised goosebumps on the flesh of all that heard it, even on the sweltering summer night.

Myth or truth? It is true that in the 17 and 1800's St. Augustine was plagued by rowdy sailors. And it is true that the behavior of the sailors while they visited our town changed drastically following an eventful evening in the early 1800's. A statue did arrive on a ship, her name became the Hurricane Lady. Is she the Virgin Mary or the mysterious Saint Barbara? Were dynamite wielding Angels/Devils with glowing eyes behind the change? Decide for yourself. Venture downtown on a warm summer night and listen for the faint sound of wind chimes down the dark alleys. If goosepumps rise on your skin, you may be hearing the laughter of the Angles who some still believe protect the town's young girls and provide a safe haven for our revered, mysterious Hurricane Lady.

Be this the truth or be me a liar. And I tell you I ain't no liar.

"Angels with glowing eyes?" I asked my empty room with another yawn. "'Be this the truth.' Ha! What a loon. Right?" But my words didn't completely support my thoughts. There was something that struck me as familiar. It was the glowing eye part. *The other night, after Jacks. Pearl's eyes totally seemed to be...*

"Nah," I snorted.

My gaze then settled on the pile of unread papers. The clock now cheerfully displayed 6:33. *Hmm, plenty of time if I skim!* I grabbed the topmost paper and let my eyes fly over words and sentences, graphs, charts, and pictures.

Nana came in to wake me an hour later. My head spun with terms like 'high low water' and 'igneous, metamorphic, and sedimentary' and 'oolitic limestone'. I'm sure that these terms were supposed to have some context, but that connection was lost to me. *Oh well,* I thought, *better than nothing.*

"Well dear you sure are having an early start. You must be enjoying the class work so far, hmm?"

"Um, yeah, just couldn't put it down!" I smiled.

I hope my cram session will get me through today's lecture, I thought. Then I remembered, we were going on the boat! The professors surely wouldn't be asking us questions while we were on a boat! *Yay, I'm saved!* *The boat, we're going out on the...*and nearly in the same breath of excitement, dread washed over me like a rogue wave. *The boat...the water...the deep, unforgiving water.* My thumb fidgeted with the heavy moonstone ring still on my middle finger. I remembered Sara's instructions of cleansing it in salt water. *Well, I guess I can at least accomplish that today. Like when our boat capsizes and I sink to the bottom of the sea.* I gave a dark chuckle, not because it was funny, just realistic. *Ugh, I think I would have preferred to be called out as not having done the reading than to go out on a boat into the ocean*, I thought.

"Perfect." I groaned, "Just perfect." I climbed reluctantly out of bed. I walked to the bathroom and washed my face and then found the green bottle of lotion. I rubbed it all over my tight skin and immediately felt relief and remembering my embarrassment from yesterday, brought it with me to tuck into my bag.

I dove my hand into one of the bags of new clothes and found the purple sarong, In the other bag I found the white ribbed tank with the shimmery purple hibiscus flower print. *Perfect. Too bad today is the day I drown*, I thought morbidly and trudged downstairs like a person walking to their own funeral.

"Morning."

"Why the long face?" Nana asked after looking up from the paper. Her mug of coffee sent swirls of steam into the air.

"Oh nothing. Just tired, I guess." *And I'm going to die today out on a dumb boat because you made me take this course.*

"Okay. I thought maybe you were nervous about the boat trip. Well, I'm glad you're not. I was all ready to give you a pep talk. Okay then. Cereal for breakfast or would you like eggs?"

I honestly wasn't that hungry and neither sounded very good but I didn't have the energy to protest the necessity of breakfast. That was one argument I would never win against Nana. "Umm, I think just some toast and butter." *Wouldn't want to add getting seasick to my dread list today.* I felt her eyes on my back but she didn't say anything.

I ate my toast silently as Nana continued reading the paper. After a time she said, "well, you may not make it out today anyway. The paper mentions some storms are likely this afternoon."

The was the first good news of the day. I smiled, suddenly hopeful that we would be stormed in, but then it turned to a grimace as I remembered I needed the outing to hide the fact I hadn't really kept up with our reading assignments. *Talk about a rock and a hard place. I really hate today,* I thought.

"When are we leaving?" I asked.

"Now that is something I need to discuss with you. I thought I was going to use it to cheer you up for being nervous of the boat outing, but seeing that you are fine with it," Nana winked.

"Okay, fine. I'm a little," *A LOT,* "nervous."

"Needless to say, you will be fine," she smiled. "And to help cheer you, here is the good news. Sara left her bike here last night on purpose. She thought you may like to have a bit of independence." She watched my reaction. I couldn't help but smile.

"So you mean that I can drive myself on Sara's scooter?"

"Yes, but slow down a minute. I have a few rules. First, you have to stay on the island and you have to ride in the right lane only. Second, you ALWAYS have to wear your helmet. And third, if you get hurt your father will kill us both, so be safe!" She smiled at the last comment and slid the thick key across the table to me.

"This is awesome!"

"The rules?"

"Oh yeah, okay, okay, of course and you bet!" I picked up the key and rolled it back and forth in my fingers. "Well, I'd better get going, don't want to be late." My heart beat with excitement.

******

"Hey, Jon!" I called as I parked the scooter in the shade of one of the oaks.

He looked up from across the lawn but couldn't see me through the layers of dangling Spanish moss.

"OVER HERE...HEY!" I called again and this time his eyes located me. He smiled and walked toward me.

"Look at you!"

I wasn't quite sure if Jon was addressing me or the bike. In either case, since the bike couldn't respond, I did.

"Yup, here we are! Remember my friend Sara? She left me the bike to use."

"That's some friend!"

"Well, old family friend, I suppose. You were right with all the valve-thingies and twin cooled stuff and the spoons, it rides great."

"You mean front forks?" Jon asked smiling.

"Oh, yeah, the forks, whatever those things are, the bike is really nice!"

"I should think so." Stroking the side of the bike very affectionately, he shook his head slightly as if feeling sad that such a beautiful machine should be wasted on the ignorant. *Boys are so weird.*

"So, Jon." I was hesitant to interrupt his moment but knew I had limited time, "I started reading that book you gave me."

"Huh? What?"

"The *book.*" I responded impatiently because he was far too enamored by the dang bike. "Remember? The other day at the Lighthouse, the one by Humpphrey?"

"Oh yeah," He finally tore his gaze away from the shiny blue chrome, "Isn't that guy a nut?" Jon pushed his hair back from his eyes and laughed. "He's an old local and as loony as they come. And believe me, that is saying a lot when talking about good ole' Saint Augustine locals! I figured you would enjoy it."

"I am. He seems to have some pretty strange stuff to say about the history of the place, ya know?"

"Yeah, cracks me up every time, *'Be this the truth'.*" He did a great pirate/old person impersonation with his voice and then laughed again, cracking himself up by his own cleverness. "He lives only a few miles down the road. A real hermit, keeps to himself."

"So he is a loon, right?" I asked as I started walking toward the classroom. Jon seemed reluctant to leave the bike alone.

"Oh yeah! Why?" He gave one last glance and caught my stride.

"Oh, I don't know, I read that pirate story about the glowing eyes...I just wondered..."

"Oh yeah. I love that one. The Angels that protect the streets downtown? He's nuts!" Jon said as he drew a circle in the air with his index finger by his ear.

"Yeah, nuts." I repeated...*right*? I thought, *I mean Angles don't roam the streets and I doubt their laughter sounds like creepy windchimes. Like Sara sounded yesterday when we arrived downtown. And glowing eyes, Pearl's eyes...nah I was just tired.*

"Good morning guys!" Samantha called as bounced along the cement path to catch up to us. "Did you get through all the papers? Truly fascinating, I mean I had already read some of them before, so it wasn't really new to me, but still. Wow...I just never thought blah blah blah blah...." Her face beamed as she spoke. I tilted my head a bit to the side, like a curious dog. I watched her lips move but stopped listening to the words that came out. *Did she ever pause to breathe*, I wondered. I looked at Jon's face. His eyes were glazed over.

"...so did you all agree with his findings?" She asked.

Nobody spoke for an awkward moment. We had reached the steps up to our classroom. Samantha looked expectantly at me. I looked with wide eyes at Jon.

"Yes," he said definitively.

"Hmm mmm," I added with a smile. Our eyes back on Samantha.

"Oh, me, too!" Samantha added enthusiastically.

We walked up the stairs as quickly as possible and took our seats. My head hurt already.

Professors Ross and Briggs came in shortly after us with steaming coffee mugs in their hands.

"Good morning folks!" Professor Ross said as he passed.

"Good morning," we replied in unison.

"Exciting reading last night, eh?"

"Oh yes!" Samantha's voice rang out. Little circles of red bloomed on her cheeks when she realized how loud she had spoken.

"Yes, well, it should have kept you busy and will be helpful background for this morning's lecture by *Dr.* Briggs." Dr. Ross motioned to his colleague to take over. Dr. Ross sat in the chair behind the desk and sipped his coffee.

"Thank you *Dr.* Ross." I giggled at how they called each other 'Dr.', it seemed more as a joke than actual reverence to the title.

"This morning we will focus on the changing coastline of Saint Augustine. I trust you all enjoyed the literature?" There were rustles around the room as students retrieved notebooks and pens and pulled out the thick packet of handouts. I was pleased to note that I saw other shifty eyes when the mention of the reading homework was made. "Then if the weather holds we will head out on the boat for the afternoon." This led to more obvious excited chatter around the room.

"All right folks." The din quieted. Dr. Briggs walked to the front of the desk as Dr. Briggs took over the spot in the chair. "Now, who can tell me what the primary substrates of Saint Augustine are?"

The silence in the room was nearly deafening. Usually if you just waited long enough teachers answered their own question. But apparently not these two. Dr. Briggs and Dr. Ross looked quite comfortable in the silence.

Samantha's hand finally lifted into the air.

"Yes, Ms. Watson, right?"

"Yes." She blushed. "There are Cretaceous-Tertiary-and-Quaternary-limestone-and-Holocene-sediments-including-lithified-to-unlithified-shell-quartz-sands-with-minor-amounts-of-organic-matter-and-clay."

She looked quite satisfied with herself and was slightly out of breath. I had no idea what she just said. I wasn't even sure it was English.

"Very good, Ms. Watson. It appears that at least one of you completed your reading assignments." He gave Samantha a little nod. She beamed with delight, her freckles blending with the radiating color on her cheeks! *Whatever*, I thought.

"Let's start with our foundation." Dr. Briggs turned on the slide projector. He talked and clicked through slides for the next hour and a half. I was still trying to figure out how to spell 'cretaceous' from Samantha's answer when he stopped.

"Now, who can tell me the name of a subset of limestone that is used quite prevalently in this town's architecture?" Dr. Briggs asked.

I was surprised to see Jon's hand join Samantha's.

"Yes, Mr. Manistar."

"Coquina rock?"

"Exactly!" He smiled at Jon. Samantha looked a bit deflated. I was completely lost.

New slides appeared on the screen. This time the pictures were of some light brown rock that looked like a bunch of broken shells glued together. "Why is coquina so special in this town?" He asked and looked out toward us.

This time the girl name Shannon answered, "It was used to build the *Castillo de San Marcos*." She said and spoke the name of the fort with an exaggerated Spanish flourish.

"Exactly!" Dr. Briggs smiled at her. "The coquina is a fascinating conglomerate stone..."

The slideshow, discussion, and question-answer session continued until lunchtime. And to my surprise, I was fairly interested in the geology of St. Augustine by the end of it. Dr. Briggs showed us a short cartoon movie made by the Lighthouse Association of the St. Augustine coastline through time; the movie showed the morphing coastline from 1741 through to the present. I had no idea so much land could shift and change so quickly. It was almost like deals being made and broken between the land and the ocean.

"Should we eat outside again?" Jon's voice broke my trance.

"Oh!" I was surprised to see everybody moving about. "Yeah, sounds good. Hang on a sec." There was a question that I needed to ask.

"Dr. Briggs?" He looked over to me as he continued to gather his papers.

"Yes Ms. Harn? You've been very quiet this morning." Heat rose to my cheeks. "Yes well, this was all so fascinating. So much to write down." *And try to learn since I didn't read last night*, I thought. "I was just wondering, with the changing coast and all, how much did storms influence it?"

"Very good question. Saint Augustine seems to have a protective shield around it! The two major storms to hit this region were the Great Storm of 1880 and Hurricane Dora in 1964 and then one unseasonable gale that was unnamed about..."

"Sixteen years ago?" I ventured a guess.

His eyes brightened, "Why yes, it was!"

So the storm that killed my mom just after I was born and was the reason Dad, Nana, and I fled was one of the rare events in St. Augustine's history.

"And there was also an earthquake a year or so after the 1880 storm," Dr. Briggs continued. "So to answer your question, the extreme shifting of this region's coast is not due to large storms which are very infrequent here, but some other, yet to be understood, phenomenon. Other than the dredging of the inlet in 1940, the shifting is one of the reasons this area holds such interest to myself and Dr. Ross. Well, see you after lunch! Going to go check on the boat."

I smiled weakly and met up with Jon at the door.

"What was all that about?"

"Nothing really, I was just curious about something. Oh and that reminds me. I meant to ask you before, did you ever meet Mr. Humpphrey?"

"Me? No. Why?"

"I was sort of hoping to meet him. There's just something..." I lost my nerve.

"Why would you want to meet the looniest man in St. Augustine?" Jon laughed at me.

"Takes one to know one," I jibed back.

"Nice Storm, how old are you, 5 or 16?" I laughed.

"No really, I think he may be able to help me out with..." I thought quickly, "...with finding out about my mom's death and the no name storm that happened here when I was a baby. You said he's lived here forever, right?"

"Oh, yeah, I guess he may." Jon's expression was slightly embarrassed. I felt bad for making him feel bad since I used the "dead mother" card and it wasn't exactly the whole truth. I really wanted to confirm that the glowing eyes and that thing about the wind chime laughter was totally stupid. But it seemed so stupid, I didn't want Jon to think I was a loon for even considering it to be real.

"I'll ask my dad if we could go see him. No promises though, the guy's a hermit."

"Thanks."

"Hey, do ya want to see the basement? I realized I never took you there the other day when you were here."

"Sure, but I didn't think you had basements in Florida."

Jon laughed. "They are rare, but we are about thirteen feet above sea level here. Welcome to Mount Anastasia! The highest point on the island!" He opened his arms wide like a game show announcer.

I followed Jon into the Keeper's house. It was just like a home, warm and cozy and the walls were covered in vintage wall paper and oversized prints of historic photographs. Jon led me into a parlor-like room with a large fireplace. There was a glass case containing a china doll and a very out of place green metal spiral staircase that led down.

First impressions after winding our way down? Compared to the warm and cozy atmosphere in the house, the basement felt like a dungeon.

"It's sort of creepy down here," I said. Despite the sweltering temperatures outside, it was dark and cool in the basement. The musty air reminded me of the visit Dad and I made to the Marengo Cave back home. The mixture of brick, oddly shaped coquina blocks and relics provided the creepy factor.

A large multifaceted beacon light greeted us at the base of the stairs. The sign next to it said it was a Fresnel lens. On the other side of the small room were small oak barrels acting as stools in front of a rope tying game. Signs above each sample rope read the types of knots you could practice, Figure 8, Bowline, Reef Knot, and Carrick Bend.

"That looks like fun," I said and sat down on the barrel in front of the Bowline diagram. Jon sat next to me, in front of the Reef Knot. We tied knots, laughed, switched barrels and kept playing until we had mastered them all.

"Have you heard about the man in blue?" Jon asked as he finished his Figure 8.

"No, who's that?"

"Oh, just this story of a guy who hung himself."

"Seriously?" My body shivered.

"Yeah," Jon replied in a quiet voice. "The story goes in the 1930's a passing mariner came to work at the lighthouse. He supposedly committed suicide by hanging himself down here. There's no proof and the lighthouse society denies it ever happened but when we've come down here with the K-2's they go crazy! Lots of people have reported seeing an apparition of a man in a blue uniform wandering around down here!"

"What's a K-2?"

"It's a meter that measures electro-magnetic energy. They use them to find ghosts on those ghost hunting shows."

"Stop, you're creeping me out," I said as I followed Jon through a narrow passage that connected the South room to the North one.

"Is that where they tortured prisoners?" I asked peering through a tiny opening that showed an empty room constructed with thick walls of coquina.

He laughed. "Nah, it's a cistern." He peered in over my shoulder through the tiny hole. "Although, I'm guessing nobody would hear you in there if you screamed."

"Jon..." I pushed him with my hip. We entered the North room. It was about the same size as the South room. An ancient, seven-foot cannon sat on display with a rope guarding it and a little sign asking parents not to let their kids sit on it.

I laughed. "Since when do cannons have to be treated gently?"

"I know! The thing is like already 200 years old, looks pretty good to me." Jon defiantly reached over the ropes and gave it a solid pat.

I laughed and walked over to touch the solid, rough, coquina wall. It was cold and perspiring. It was strange to have just been learning about the origins of coquina and now to be touching it as it held up this entire building.

"This is the north wall," Jon said, still looking at the cannon, "remember those stars we saw outside on the second floor?"

I nodded. Jon had pointed out four large, seemingly decorative stars on the exterior of the building's North and South walls. Not decorative, he told me, but for structural purposes. I thought they looked pretty, nonetheless.

"We're right below them."

"Hmm." I nodded. The place felt strange, beyond the cold and the sort-of-creepy. A chill ran up the length of my spine and for the second time, a full body shiver.

"You're cold?" Jon asked. "We can go, we should probably get going anyway so we have a few minutes to eat before the boat." He started walking back toward the spiral stairs. I followed his lead but my foot got caught up in one of the cracks in the floor and I fell hard onto my knees.

"Ouch," I whimpered and looked back to find the offending bump. It was nothing more than a slight mismatch of the concrete. The area was stained a different color, like from some kind of old water damage.

"Whoa, you okay?" Jon knelt beside me. I rubbed my knees.

"Yeah, uneven floors and clumsy people don't often mix well." I tried to smile but I felt really embarrassed. Jon helped me up. The rest of our exit was, thankfully, uneventful.

We sat under the large Oak tree to eat.

"Thanks for the tour," I said.

"No problem," Jon said. "The basement is really the only part of this place I truly dig. It just seems so secretive and..."

"Creepy?" I offered.

"Yeah, sort of." He smiled.

"So where exactly was the old lighthouse?" I asked looking around.

"About a half mile that way." He pointed East and a little South of where we were sitting. We should walk out on the pier at low tide. You can see the remnants of the old tower to the left of it."

"Oh, like in the water?"

"Well, not always, but nowadays, yeah."

We had just finished eating when Dr. Ross summoned us all to the ramp.

How quickly emotions can change, I thought. *Happiness to dread in one short heartbeat.* My hair swirled around my face in the freshening breeze.

Well, here goes nothing, I thought.

I walked with Jon toward the white power boat that was docked at the wooden pier next to the boat ramp.

I really hate today.

Chapter Nine

"Sorry to cut your lunch short, but there's a chance some storms are due to pop up later this afternoon," Dr. Ross said as we gathered by the pier, "and a short boat trip is better than no boat trip."

"Ha! Storms. Get it Storm?" Samantha nudged my arm.

"Yeah. Funny," I said.

"Never heard that one before, eh Storm?" Jon whispered.

"No. Never."

Jon nudged my arm and despite my dread, I giggled at him.

Dr. Briggs was already aboard sitting on the captain's bench. I got the impression that he wished he had something other than a can of Coke in his hand.

"We should have a nice couple of hours with blue skies and then we can get back in before the storms hit." Samantha giggled again at the use of my name in a sentence. "Sound good?" Dr. Ross smiled, his round cheeks already flushed from the heat. We all nodded, climbed awkwardly on the boat, and found seats.

"All limbs must remain inside the boat at all times," Dr. Ross said. Owen and Josh looked up like deer in headlights and quickly pulled their arms back in from where they had been dangling over the edge of the boat into the water.

"Thank you gentlemen," Dr. Ross said with a smile.

"Any questions?" Dr. Briggs asked the group.

"Are there lifejackets?" Shannon asked. I was too embarrassed to ask that but I'm so glad somebody did.

"Yes, great question," Dr. Briggs responded. "The lifejackets are all stowed under the seats you're sitting on. Anything else?"

"Where are we going?" Abigail asked.

Dr. Ross answered, "We plan to head out of Salt Run and perhaps head out the Inlet into the Atlantic if the conditions are favorable. We are going to be looking for dolphins this afternoon. Does anybody know how we identify individual dolphins?"

Samantha's hand, of course, went up the fastest.

"Yes, Ms. Watson."

"By their dorsal fins!" She exclaimed.

"That's correct," Dr. Ross answered. He discussed the differences in dolphin fins as Dr. Briggs deftly pulled away from the dock and began our slow journey out of the Salt Run Channel. I sat very still fearful that any slight move may tip the boat over.

"We hope to start a catalog of dolphins for this region. There is already an active photo-identification study a bit farther south and to the north. Saint Augustine may be able to fill in some of the gaps and perhaps help us understand where some of the dolphins from the North and South disappear to for some lengths of time. Today is a bit of a scouting mission you may say. Does anybody *else* know another large marine mammal that calls Saint Augustine home for part of the year?"

Samantha took the hint and didn't raise her hand.

"Yes, Mr. Manistar."

"Right Whales," Jon answered.

"Indeed. The females of the North Atlantic Right Whales come down to the warm waters of Saint Augustine during winter months to have their calves."

"Ms. Harn, are Right Whales Odontocetes or Mysticetes?"

Huh? I looked up to Dr. Ross's smiling face.

No fair, I thought, *I didn't raise my hand.*

"Umm," a voice in my head said Mysticeti. *Well it's a 50:50 shot,* I thought. "Mysticetes?" I answered meekly.

"Very good! Yes, they are a member of the sub-order Mysticeti, the baleen whales. In contrast, bottlenose dolphins are part of the sub-order..."

"ODONTOCETI!" Samantha squealed. We all laughed at her enthusiasm.

"Yes, correct, the toothed whales," Dr. Ross finished. "So let's keep a look out. Scan your eyes back and forth to see if you can spot any."

We all did as we were told and Dr. Briggs drove slowly along the channel toward the mouth of the inlet.

"Remember the slide show you all watched this morning?" Dr. Briggs said. "The inlet up ahead has only been in its present location since the mid-1940s when the Army Core of Engineers dredge it. The original inlet shifted all along here," he pointed toward the east at a land mass, "up to 400 yards south of the current one. This extension of Anastasia Island, Conch Island, grew as a result of the forced inlet and this water, Salt Run, became a tidal lagoon. The Lighthouse used to be oceanfront property!"

It was very hard to imagine how different everything was from what I saw now. I tried to mentally remove the large mass of sand and dunes to the east and have the water flowing freely from the ocean to our boat. I imagined the lighthouse shining its beacon out to sea welcoming wayward vessels and trade ships alike. St. Augustine, a safe port where storms veered away and land and sea coexisted peacefully...most of the time.

"Like the inlet, the lighthouse you see now is not the original," Dr. Ross said. "The previous one should be somewhere about here." He pointed below us.

"What do you mean? Like underwater?" Shannon asked.

"Well, yes, actually. The previous lighthouse was destroyed by a large storm back in the 1880, known as the Great Storm. One of the very few hurricane-strength storms to make a direct hit here. The lighthouse tower, already in peril because of increasingly unstable foundations, received its final blow during that storm and sank into the sea during the fury. You can still see some of its remains during low tide," Dr. Ross said.

I looked over to Jon and he smiled, proud that he had already told me all of this.

"I read there was hidden treasure in the old lighthouse," Samantha said.

"Well, there are many stories about that old structure," Dr. Briggs said. "One of the architects hired before the tower collapsed to, of all things, reinforce the tower, was renowned for his building skills."

"Doesn't sound like he did a very good job," Josh said.

Dr. Ross spoke over the laughter Josh's comment created, "Well, after some failed attempts to reinforce, it was decided to build a new tower farther back. The same mason assisted with the construction of the new tower. But he was better known for his brilliance with the construction of other types of buildings...secret buildings. I think that's where the rumors got started."

"What do you mean secret buildings?" I asked.

"Well, one of the stories is that the builder, what was his name?" Dr. Briggs asked Dr. Ross.

"Lewis Tressman," Dr. Ross answered.

"That's it, Tressman," Dr. Briggs said. "He supposedly built some sort of holding room of sorts; a room that only he knew how to get into."

I looked at Jon with wide eyes.

"What did Mr. Tressman build his secret room with?" I asked.

"Most likely local materials," Dr. Ross said, "like..." He looked around waiting for us to finish his sentence.

"Coquina?" Samantha asked.

"Yes, very good," Dr. Briggs nodded.

"Who did he build it for?" Jon asked.

"That's part of the mystery. Nobody knows. Of course nobody ever found anything either, so the secret, if there was one, may have died with Tressman," Dr. Briggs answered.

"Or maybe not," I whispered thinking of Nana.

"You know, later next month, even that mound will be underwater," Dr. Briggs said as we passed a large rock structure that stuck nearly four feet out the water.

"Really, why?" Samantha chirped.

"Saint Augustine is due for an exceptionally rare tidal event called an Extreme Proxigean Spring Tide."

"But it isn't Spring!" Shannon said.

Kendall giggled, "Yeah."

"As you all will find out in tonight's reading, Spring Tides have nothing to do with the season of Spring but rather the proximity of the moon to the Earth. Proxigean Tides are a rare event and Extreme Proxigean Tides are even rarer," Dr. Briggs stated.

"The last one to occur here was in the mid nineties. Most of you were probably just born," Dr. Ross said. "I was also just a spring chicken, but my colleague Dr. Briggs has a clear memory of it, I'm sure, being so much older than I am!" Dr. Ross winked, we all laughed.

"Yeah, so much older," Dr. Briggs said. "Nearly two months!"

We laughed more.

"You said coquina was porous, right Dr. Briggs?" Jon asked after we all settled back down and got to looking for more dolphins.

"Yes. Coquina is a fascinating form of Limestone as it is relatively soft when first quarried but hardens after years of surface exposure It retains its porous nature due to a lack of a hardened matrix between the shells so is also very light weight and amazingly durable as witnessed by the age of your fort. When the fort was attacked with cannon fire, the coquina walls absorbed the projectiles rather than deflecting them."

"Bend like a willow rather than break like an oak," I whispered a saying Nana used to tell me.

"But," Jon asked, "if Tressman built a secret room with coquina and that room is now underwater, wouldn't everything be all wet?"

"Perhaps he wanted it to fill with water," Dr. Ross added.

"You mean that there may be some hidden underwater room?" Owen asked.

"That's awesome!" Hayden exclaimed and looked into the water apparently trying to find the room.

"That's what treasure hunters want to believe," Dr. Briggs said. "Unfortunately, no one has been able to search the area because of the city's very strict regulations. Since it's historic, getting permits for such undertakings is extremely difficult. This mystery may be one that remains unsolved forever."

"DOLPHINS!" A shrill call broke into the discussion. Abigail and Josh held out their arms with index fingers pointed toward the flat waters to our north. My body lurched a bit as Dr. Briggs put the boat in neutral. And then I saw them. Three larger fins and one smaller fin rose out and back under the water's surface. Chatter on the boat began immediately as we watched the group move around the channel.

"Good spotting you two," Dr. Ross announced. "Now who can tell me which direction they are heading?"

"North," answered Samantha.

"South," countered Owen.

"Any other guesses?" Asked Dr. Ross with a smile.

"It doesn't look like they are traveling anywhere, just swimming about," I said mostly to myself. My mind was still spinning with all the talk about the Keeper's room. *Underwater room. Why would Nana want to find an underwater room?* I wondered.

"What is that Ms. Harn?"

"Umm, it doesn't really look like they're going anywhere, just sort of hanging out?"

"Very good. They are indeed *just hanging out*, the behavior is called milling. That's the term we use when a pod is moving in no specific direction. Ms. Harn, venture a guess as to how many dolphins we are looking at here?"

"Well, three big ones and one small one here. But I think I just saw another two big ones over there." I pointed to the left.

"Also, well done. Five adults and one calf. I agree," he said.

I smiled. *I guess I'm kind of good at this stuff.*

"Are these two groups together?" Dr. Ross asked.

"Probably," Jon said.

"Okay, then who can tell me how these guys are staying in contact so far apart? The water's pretty murky; would eyesight be their favored sense?"

We all shook our heads.

"How about sound?" Dr. Ross asked.

"Echolocation!" Samantha shouted.

"Very good. They use sound to stay in touch."

As Samantha recited all she knew about echolocation, I zoned out and watched the graceful fins surface around us.

The one big one with the small one, I guess a mom and baby, started to swim toward our boat. Dr. Briggs turned the engine off. Silence filled the air, well, except for Samantha's very thorough description of marine mammal communication that was still going strong. I watched them approach and the large one stayed between the baby and our boat as they swam a full circle around us. Samantha finally got the hint, closed her mouth enjoyed the show with the rest of us.

It seemed as if the pair was observing us rather than the other way around. Light breezes picked up. My hair danced around my face and tickled my back. The beads on my braid jingled. I remembered the scare from Sara and my shopping trip and quickly grabbed the end of the braid to silence the beads.

But even as I tucked it away, the dolphin mom's eye looked at me from just under the surface as she passed next to where I was seated. She made a loud *squeeeeeak* all of a sudden and I jumped. Then she slapped her tale. She hovered a moment longer with her eye just above the surface of the water, her baby at her side. The rest of the dolphins gathered and they all disappeared out of the inlet.

"Extraordinary!" Dr. Ross exclaimed.

"Dr. Briggs, shall we follow?"

"Sure thing!" The engine roared to life and he throttled up until we moved smoothly toward the inlet. I held on tightly to the rail of the boat and closed my eyes. The boat rose and fell and made a repetitive "tha thunk tha thunk tha thunk" sound.

When I opened my eyes again we had exited the channel and were now out in the open ocean. I closed my eyes again.

"Storm, it's easier to spot dolphins with your eyes open," Jon said into my ear.

"That's okay, I'm good." My fingers were numb from the strain of holding on. *Soon this will be over and I will be back on land.... Soon this will be over and I will be back on land.... Soon this will be over and I will be back on land...*

When I felt the boat moving fairly smoothly, although rapidly, along the ocean's surface, I dared to take a peek. I gazed out to the open ocean and much to my hand's delight, relaxed my grip on the handrail. My fingers tingled as the blood returned to the tips. I scanned the surface of the water without really meaning to.

I sat up a bit taller, my fear temporarily forgotten and watched the water intently.

Just a trick of the light?

A splash and movement just twenty yards away. Everybody else's attention was on the water ahead of us. I looked back to the east and again, a body just barely breaking the surface and disappearing below the deep green swells. *Whatever it is, it's keeping up with us easily,* I thought.

I looked to Dr. Ross, about to ask about it, but saw him make a motion like a circle with his finger to Dr. Briggs. Dr. Briggs nodded in agreement and the boat turned in a wide arc. The lean of the boat made me nervous but soon enough we were even keeled on a beeline course for the inlet. I forgot about the thing I saw and enjoyed the thought of getting back to land. We entered the channel but instead of relief, I felt panic because the entire channel rocked and rolled and frothed with white caps.

"Hang on everybody; this is going to be a bit bouncy!" Dr. Briggs announced.

I felt like we were in a giant wave pool. Our tiny boat bounced, rocked and rolled. Dr. Briggs did his best to keep the boat steady, but we were no match for this turbulence. The boat struggled against the strong outbound current and every crash landing sent a jolt up my spine as I was launched inches above my seat only to land heavily down repeatedly. I thought I heard Jon holler, "Woo Hoo!"

I looked toward the St. Augustine side of the jetty. *I wish I could magically pop myself onto those rocks*, I thought, *right next to* that *lucky guy*.

I eyed the figure on the jetty of rocks. His long, dark hair glistened in the refracted light and his skin shined. It wasn't just some guy...it was Rowan!

I heard his deep, resonating laugh.

This is funny to him? I asked myself. *Seriously? I may die out here in this channel and he's laughing?* Rage built inside me. My brows furrowed. A large wave crashed into the jetty and water washed up and over him.

"Oh my God!" I said with a gasp but nobody heard over the roar of the struggling engine.

The water cleared and he still sat on the rocks. His laugh rang louder.

Then suddenly the water in the channel calmed. The white caps subsided and the current lost its hold on the boat. We turned the corner and headed back into the quiet waters of Salt Run.

******

I was the first one off the boat when it docked. My legs shook and I didn't trust myself to walk very far so I just sat on the grass and waited for everybody else to get off.

I was joined by the others shortly and then finally by Dr. Briggs and Dr. Ross.

"Let's call it a day with that," Dr. Ross spoke. "We'll plan to head out again on Friday. And we'll bring along a camera and data sheets for you all to practice photo-identification procedures."

"One last thing before you go," Dr. Briggs spoke now, "your first assignment is due next Monday." There were groans. "A ten-page paper, typed, double spaced, titled Saint Augustine's Changing Coastline; Causes and Effects. At least five citations and websites don't count." More groans. "Thank you all. Have a great afternoon and see you tomorrow!"

We all got up slowly and made our way back to the room to collect our books. There was a mixture of excited chatter about our boat ride and mumblings and grumblings about the paper as we meandered into the classroom.

"Ten pages double spaced shouldn't be that bad," Jon offered as we walked.

"Huh? Oh, yeah, not too bad." Honestly I wasn't even thinking about the paper. Jon kept on talking but my mind was still on Rowan.

"Earth to Storm!" Jon nudged my shoulder.

"Hmm?"

"I said it was pretty weird about the Tressman stuff."

"Yeah," I said. My mind struggled to contain all of its thoughts between Tressman mysteries, Humpphrey legends, and Rowan.

"And I'll find out what I can with my dad's collections," Jon said. "So, umm, are you doing anything this afternoon?"

"Not really, but I should get caught up on this class stuff," I said. Of the many things on my mind, the thing about Rowan was winning and I really wanted to get home and try to find him.

"Yeah, me, too. Well, I guess I'll see ya later."

"Thanks Jon. See ya tomorrow." I wiped some Spanish Moss off of the scooter seat, swatted two mosquitoes off my leg, and strapped on my helmet.

******

Two surfboards leaned against the railing of the stairs to the deck.

"Welcome home!" Rowan's velvet voice spoke. He walked down the steps and met me at the bike. His hair was wet and hung heavily over his bare bronze shoulders. He wasn't wearing a shirt.

Snap out of it Storm, my inner voice shouted, *you have questions to ask. Just one more minute of staring,* I begged.

My peripheral vision got wavy and distorted and I suddenly took a deep inhale. I had apparently forgotten to breathe...again.

"Hey, you okay?" Rowan asked. He was at my side now and looked concerned.

"Oh, yeah, I'm fine." I shook my head and took another breath. "Just got a little lightheaded." *Because I was staring at your gorgeous body and forgot to breathe because I'm an idiot.*

"Here let me grab those for you." He reached and took the load of papers from me before I could think to protest. His hand brushed mine in the process and I felt something akin to an electric current run up my arm and into my stomach. He smiled.

"Let's see what you have here. ' The geologic history of the east coast of Florida', 'Significance in the Sediments', 'Then and Now: St. Augustine's changing coastline', 'Photo-identification techniques of *Tursiops truncatus*', 'Marine Mammals of Florida'...wow, quite a stack here." The sun in his face turned his eyes to liquid turquoise. "Some light reading for the night?"

"I wish." My composure finally regained. "This class is really hard. I've never had this much work to do for school...like ever! And now on top of it all I am supposed to write a paper by next Monday about the coastline here." I let out a loud sigh and we walked up the stairs together. Rowan laid the papers down on the glass table.

"Well, in my opinion, you've been working too hard. I think you need a little break." He winked at me and led me over to the lounge chairs that faced the ocean. He gave me a gentle push on the tops of my shoulders to sit me down on one and he reclined on the other. "Go on, lie back." I did and let out a big sigh. There was something I wanted to ask him, but my head swam in the soothing tones of his voice and the tingling memory of his touch on my shoulders.

"There you go. Much better, m'dear. You are way too tense. I mean I'm surprised you can even move your hands after how hard you were gripping that boat today," he said.

I sat up quickly; memory jogged. He looked at me with a half grin and a mischievous twinkle in his eyes.

"So you *were* there. I knew I saw something, but how..." I couldn't think of the right way to finish. It didn't make sense in my head let alone saying it out loud.

"How what?"

"How were you out there?"

"Out where?"

"Oh come on. I *know* I saw something and it wasn't a dolphin and it was swimming and it had...it had *hair*!"

Rowan's pearly teeth shone brightly against his tanned face as his smile broadened. "Wow," he spoke calmly, "that is strange indeed. I wonder what it was."

"Rowan! It was you! But, how?" I asked.

I took another look at his iridescent skin, not a trick of the light, but a trick of his skin! I looked into his mesmerizing eyes, felt my breath and my will to protest disappear. I struggled with every ounce of my own will to stay focused.

"You made the water do that, didn't you?" I asked.

"Is that what you think?" He asked.

"Yes, I do. And stop answering all of my questions with a question. I don't know how, but it was you on the jetty and it was you I saw when we were full throttle along the coast. You almost killed us!" Finding an inner confidence I didn't even know existed, I refused to drop my gaze even as I tossed absolute crazy accusations at the most handsome boy I'd ever known.

His laughter threw me off guard. "Oh please. You were never in danger. I was just playing. You enjoyed being out there; feeling the salt spray in your face, the energy beneath you. And you enjoyed tossing that wave back in my face." He was still reclining on the lounger with his arms behind his head.

"What do you mean? I didn't..." I shook my head.

"Of course you did. But you only played back when I got you mad. It's kind of fun to find your buttons.

He sat up, turned sideways on the chair and faced me as he swung his legs around. He planted his feet on the deck. "Look, I'm no good at this. Z asked me to keep an eye on you and to not freak you out. Am I freaking you out? Because if I am I'll go."

"NO!" I spoke too emphatically. Rowan smirked. "I mean, no, you're not freaking me out. I just want to understand what the heck is going on," I said.

"Well, unfortunately, I can't tell you that."

"Well there's a lot of that going around. It seems that no one can tell me anything. Everyone apparently just wants to look after me and keep me happy and nobody will tell me one damn thing, not you, or Sara, or Nana! It's getting really old."

"Hmm, I may not be able to answer those questions, but, I *can* do other things." His impish grin returned and he reached over to my hand that fidgeting with the frayed fabric on the side of the chair. His cool fingers wrapped around mine. My stomach jumped in a most pleasant way; kind of like when you go down that first big drop on a roller-coaster.

"Look Storm, I'd like to hang out with you," he said.

"Oh?" I watched his eyes. They flitted between my eyes and my hands. On the one hand I really wanted some answers, but on the other hand, well, the other hand was being held by the most gorgeous guy in the entire planet.

I smiled. "I'd like to hang out with you, too." *Perhaps my questions could wait for a little longer.*

He slid closer to me and put my hand, still wrapped in his, onto his leg.

"So, what do you want to do?" I asked.

"Hmmm," his face was now mere inches from mine. I felt his warm breath on my lips. I longed to kiss those perfect lips. I wanted to wrap my hands in his hair and pull him close to me.

"What's that?" I whispered with a slight pout and leaned in as close as possible. He put his free hand up to my cheek. His fingers tickled my cheek, then my jawbone and stroked back toward my ear and along my braid which had made its way loose from my pony and then he continued along my neck. So soft, so smooth...

"I'd like to go surfing together!"

"What?" I sat upright in shock.

"Yeah, you said the other day how much you missed surfing since you moved here from Indiana." He smiled a wicked smile.

"Okay, fine, you win." I crossed my arms like an angry toddler. "I don't actually know how to surf."

He laughed. "Really? You lied to me? Storm, I'm shocked at you."

I smiled back. "Just a tiny white lie."

"Well, my little lying nymph who-doesn't-know-how-to-surf-but-goes-around-telling-people-she-does..."

"Stop." I gave him a shove on his arm.

"Ouch." He fake pouted and rubbed his arm. "A liar and a hitter!"

I wound up for another punch. "Okay, just kidding," he said quickly. "So, since surfing may take a bit more time for you to figure out, how would you fancy a walk on the beach?"

YES! YES! YES! I thought.

"Sure, sounds fun," I said as casually as possible.

He led me down the stairs hand in hand, over the walkover and onto the silky soft, sun-warmed sand.

I really LOVE today! I thought.

Chapter Ten

I floated on a bubble of excitement as I walked hand in hand with Rowan. Too nervous to look up, I feigned fascination with each glittering grain below me.

Just relax, I reminded myself, *and wipe the overly large grin off your face.*

I dared a quick glance to Rowan. He was already looking at me. I returned to my examination of the sand. He stopped me just above the tide line. He crouched and cleared some shells and seaweed.

"Sit for awhile?" He asked, blue eyes sparkling as he looked up to me.

"Sure." I smiled and sat down on the damp, packed sand. Our shoulders weren't touching, but I could feel the energy radiating out from his skin. I felt giddy inside, like I was on a sugar rush. My heart beat just a touch too fast. Low waves crashed one after the other onto the shore a few feet ahead of us and the foamy water raced toward our feet but retreated before it touched our toes. We stayed in a comfortable silence for many breaths and even more waves. Thousands of coquinas, exposed with the retreating waters, turned their tiny, rainbow colored shells upright and dug themselves back down into the protection of the cool, wet sand. It was a water ballet of mollusks, choreographed to perfection. Like spying the hidden coquinas, I felt the more you looked, the more this town revealed...surprises hiding just out of sight, or perhaps hiding in plain sight.

"I feel sorta guilty," I said after an orange coquina's struggle to rebury itself was cut short by the swift reflexes of a passing sandpiper.

"Guilty? Why? I was just joking you about the lying thing," he replied.

His eyes reflected the late afternoon light. He squinted a tiny bit making beautiful creases beside each of his eyes; like smiling eyes.

"I knew you were joking. It's not that. It's just that I am having such a good time here."

"Oh, right. I see your problem. I often feel guilty when I'm having a good time, too." His voice was laced with sarcasm. I broke through the inches that separated us and bumped his shoulder with mine.

"No, that's not what I meant. I mean that I feel like I should be more angry at this town for what it did to my family."

"What did it do?"

"It destroyed us, that's what." I looked at him waiting for some kind of sympathetic response.

"How did the town destroy your family?"

Unprepared for his decidedly unsympathetic follow-up question, I stared at him in confusion. "What do you mean how? A huge storm nearly killed my dad, Nana, and me when I was a baby, like a newborn baby. We barely got out in time. My mom wasn't so lucky."

He thought for a moment. "Well, that wasn't really the town's fault was it? It wasn't even really the storm's fault, I mean storm's don't have their own will. Storms are simply following the whims of the most powerful will at the time."

"The most powerful will at the time?"

"Well, yeah. Like if you and I were arguing and you wanted one thing and I wanted another, you may argue and try to force your will on me. I would be doing the same to you. Whichever one of us had the strongest conviction would steer the argument to their favor.

"I never thought of storms like that. But storms aren't like arguments."

"Well, they're tools, just like words."

"You make it sound like people are out there moving storms around when they get angry with each other."

Rowan didn't respond.

"Awe, come on. Stop messing with me."

"I'm not messing with you, I'm trying to help you discover some of the answers to your questions. I said I couldn't tell you the answers, but I didn't say I couldn't help you figure them out."

I thought back to the boat ride and to Rowan on the rocks and to the feeling of energy that surged through me just as the wave rose and crashed over him. My will, my strength, *my doing?*

"Your doing," Rowan echoed my last thought.

"What?" I drew my foot back from the rogue wave that had surround and submerged our feet before it retreated.

He smiled, "I just think you're on the right track. I could, eh, see it in your face."

"Oh." *How'd he know what I was thinking?*

"You know what else I think you're thinking about?" He asked as he shifted his body to an angle that required our legs to rest on each other. Happy goosebumps shivered up my body at the contact.

"What?" *If he gets this one right, I may just become the happiest girl on the planet.*

As if on cue in some perfect dream, he closed the small space still separating us. Seconds, minutes, hours, days, eternity, I don't know how long we remained intertwined, our two bodies blending together as one. His breath was warm and he tasted of salt. His lips were strong; resisting and giving all at the same time as he drew me in, ever closer, ever tighter. My fingers wrapped tightly into his long, silky hair as his long fingers cradled my head. A humming sensation developed deep in my belly, grew stronger, and expanded in all directions until my entire body vibrated with energy.

He was the one to break away. I moaned involuntarily, like a spoiled child being denied a treat.

"My siren," he whispered and kissed me lightly on my cheeks, my chin, my forehead, my ears, my neck and then finally back around to my trembling lips.

My fingers slid from his hair down the contours of his back muscles and up around to his chest. Both of my flat palms couldn't cover the expanse of his chest. I felt tiny. As my hand slid up, I lifted his silver seastar pendant and rubbed the smooth, warm metal between my fingers. It hung on a braided cord of brown hemp-like string. But unlike hemp, the cord was soft, nearly silky.

"Soon, ma'love, you will have one of your very own," he murmured into my ear as he nibbled the soft skin where it met my neck.

"I will?" I whispered, in total heaven with his caresses.

"Yes, you will."

"What does it mean?"

"It means you've come home," he said. Before I could ask anymore, he shifted focus from my ear to my bottom lip. He gave me tiny kisses and little tender nibbles and I forgot any follow-up questions I had. I felt all soft and gooey, like the inside of a marshmallow that had been held over a flame. I happily let him nibble his way around my mouth and when his tongue questioned me, I welcomed him with pure desire.

A rush of water up my legs and under my bum brought me back to solid form. Rowan and I jumped apart and simultaneously lifted up our bellies toward the sky. The wave retreated and we collapsed onto the saturated sand.

"Hmm, I can take the hint. High tide isn't for another hour." He smiled and offered me his hands after he stood up.

"Huh?" I asked slow to catch my breath and return from the stratosphere of desire.

"What I meant was, I'm sure Z would want you home safe and sound for the evening!"

Thoroughly confused, I accepted his offer of a hand up.

"What?"

"Well, the tide, you know, it comes and goes every day..."

"Not the *tide*." I pushed him jokingly and he laughed. "What does Z have to do with anything?"

He leaned in and kissed me again just as a new wave rushed up and around our legs.

"Oh, come on! I'm just doing what you asked," he turned suddenly and spoke in the direction of the ocean.

"Who are you talking to?" I asked. As far as I could tell, the beach was quite deserted.

"A certain overly protective sea witch," he said with a chuckle.

My mind had returned to the present and without the thoroughly enjoyable distraction of Rowan's kisses, the questions I had earlier returned with a force. "Tell me what's going on."

"Storm, we've already been over that. I can't tell you, but you can figure it out if you try. In fact, you need to start figuring it out."

"You're making no sense." I felt my anger of earlier rise to the surface again. A strong westerly breeze picked up around us. "I'm getting pretty tired of how everybody is acting around me. 'I can't tell, you.', 'Not yet.' 'Give it time.' My voice rising in volume and octave. The dry sand from further up the beach, made airborne by the gusts of wind, stung my skin. "And what the heck are your smiling about?!"

"That was a really good impression of Sara's voice," Rowan chuckled.

"OH MY GOD! You are hopeless." I stood straight and tried to look angry but his laughter made my lips turn up into an unintended smile.

"Have you ever noticed if you get a strong desire for someone to do something, they often will?"

"Well, I don't know."

"Or when you get upset, the weather seems to mimic your bad mood? It's you, Storm. You just never realized it."

"I still don't get it," I said.

"I know, but you will," he said. "You're more powerful than you realize and you will soon put all of the pieces together. I just hope to be on your good side when that happens."

"My good side? I'm not sure who you think I am, but I'm just Storm, no one special."

"Wrong. You, ma' dear, are more special to more people than you may ever know. And we are all determined to make sure you stay safe until you're ready to figure it out."

I squinted into the low slung, deep red orb of the setting sun as it dipped below the tree line behind my house.

"Why me?" I asked.

"Because you're Storm."

"I wish people would stop saying that."

******

Back at the house, we stood on the deck together. The wind had calmed and the twilight lingered. It was light enough to see, but all color had been washed out as nighttime marched closer.

"So, will I get to see you later?" I asked.

"I'm sure that could be arranged," he replied with a smirk and turned to go.

"Rowan?"

"Yes, ma'dear?" He stopped and turned to look at me from halfway down the stairs.

"When will I figure everything out?"

"I think you're already partway there. Relax and let things unfold naturally."

"I'd rather you just told me."

"Ha! Wouldn't we all prefer that, except then we'd only know the bits and pieces others believed to be true. Wouldn't you rather figure out the truth for yourself?"

"No."

He cocked his head and gave me a daring stare.

"Okay, fine," I conceded, "but I wish I understood more than I do now."

He smiled and winked. "Soon. I can say with absolute certainty that things will begin changing very quickly and once this particular ball starts rolling, there will be nothing to stop it, whatever it brings. So, perhaps for now just try to enjoy being you. Thanks for a lovely beach stroll."

"I had fun, too." I blushed as I remembered his kisses.

"Have a good night beautiful Storm." He turned and left. I watched him as he walked back to the beach.

"Storm? That you?" Nana called as I opened the door.

"Yup. I was out at the beach."

"Wonderful. I hope you're hungry because I made too much food as usual. Should be ready in about fifteen minutes or so."

"Okay." I wasn't hungry at all. Being okay with 'just being me' wasn't really my personality. I'd much rather figure out how to either get people to start answering my questions or find someone else that would.

Once in my room, I flopped onto my bed. Rowan's words raced through my mind. *You enjoyed feeling the salt spray in your face, the energy beneath you and you enjoyed tossing that wave back in my face...the only time you ever play back is when I get you mad.*

I closed my eyes and let his melodic accent resonate fully, *play...you're Storm...just be...*

The cold, dark water pressed down on me. My lungs burned for oxygen. Rowan's voice was gone. I was back in my nightmare and trapped as usual.

My arms swung slowly forward and backward in the liquid environment, slow and sluggish. My legs...umm, my legs....*where the heck are my legs?* I wondered.

I opened my eyes to the dark green murk of the water. *This isn't how the dream goes,* I thought.

I looked down toward the space that should have contained my floating, useless legs. Rather than seeing legs, I saw a tail. A fish tail to be exact. It shimmered even in the murk. I felt like an actress who lost her script or a writer who lost his notes. This was undiscovered territory, *this* dream had never happened before. *What do I do now?* I wondered.

Play. Chimed a familiar voice.

Rowan? I thought in my head. *Are you here?*

Play. He repeated.

Frustrated, I twisted and turned violently in the murk. *Where are you?* I yelled in my head.

Silence.

Angry now, I pushed with all my might against the pressure surrounding me. My arms were useless but my legs, umm, well, my *tail* responded to my anger. It pushed forcefully down through the water and I moved forward. I pushed it again and I moved farther. Again and again and the water rushed by me. It was cool, but no longer cold. There was laughter in my head. It took me a moment to realize that the laughter was from me. I was laughing. I was...*playing.* I swam up higher and higher and the water got lighter and brighter. I could see the sky now, distorted by the ripples on the surface. Just one more big push and then...

"huuuhhhh..." I inhaled so deeply that I sat straight up in my bed. Then I breathed again. And again just for good measure. I breathed too quickly. Dizzy now. Breathing slower. *Phew, okay, feeling better. Feeling...*

"GAH!" I gasped at the sudden realization I wasn't alone.

"It's okay," Rowan whispered.

My heart beat faster and not from fright this time.

"You said you wanted to see me later. This is later." Rowan smiled. I was still caught somewhere between my dreaming and waking. "Would you rather I go?"

"No, no," I said quickly and grabbed his arm. It was cool to the touch. "I was just surprised. I had the strangest dream, well, not really strange because I have the dream all the time, but this time it was different and well, strange."

Rowan looked at me bemused. His wet hair hung heavily over his shoulders. A drip of water fell onto my arm.

"Am I babbling?" I asked sheepishly as I rubbed my eyes to clear my vision. Just like the other night with Pearl, my sleep blurry eyes tricked me into thinking Rowan's eyes, like Pearl's, were glowing.

"A little, but I like it. Keep going," he replied.

"Well, you were in it." I looked away from his eyes, feeling shy. "At least your voice was in it. Anyway, we, or at least I, was underwater. That isn't the strange part. The strange part was that..."

I stopped and quickly moved the thin blanket covering my legs.

"Legs," I said to myself.

"And beautiful ones at that," Rowan whispered.

"No," I said, half laughing, "my dream...the strange part was I had a tail."

"Like a monkey?" He asked smiling.

"No," I gave him a playful shove, "like a fish...or a mermaid."

"Ahh." he nodded. "And?"

"And? What do you mean *and*? I had a tail in my dream. The dream that I have had forever and have forever been afraid of, tonight, I had a tail in it and I could swim and I could get out! I did get out....I..."

"Played," he answered, finishing my sentence.

His word stopped me short. "Yeah, that's what you said in my dream."

He just smiled.

Another drop of water landed on my leg this time. "Have you been swimming?" I asked. I touched his hair and it wasn't just a trick of the light, it was wet.

"You look tired, Storm. Come on, lay down and get some rest."

I searched his face for an explanation but received only his adoring, overly bright eyes and handsome smile. Maybe it was just a trick of moonlight, but his eyes still looked..."But..." I started to speak.

"Shhh...lay down. You need your strength, love. Changing...like the tides," He whispered as he lay back on the pillow next to me; one arm was bent behind his head and he closed his eyes. His chest looked so inviting.

"Rowan, can I ask you something?" I resisted the urge to lay my head down on him.

"Sure." His free hand stroked my hair lightly. The light touches felt like tickles that I never wanted to end.

"I noticed the girls, Paige and Sara, have braids also, but Sara's is like mine and Paige's isn't. Does Pearl have one, too?"

He hesitated for a moment. "She used to have one. It was like Paige's but it, eh, was lost." Rowan's cool hand reached behind my neck and guided my head onto his chest. I closed my eyes and breathed in his salty, masculine scent. I felt a bit feverish from all the nighttime excitement and his cool skin reminded of the damp washcloth my dad used to lay on my forehead when I got sick as a child. I wanted to ask a question but the words wouldn't stay in order in my mind. My body relaxed and although I was sure my question was important, sleep was winning the battle over curiosity. But at least I got one question answered, even if the answer didn't really help me figure anything out. Not yet...

The next time my eyes opened, I was alone and sunlight streamed into the room.

Was it all a dream? I wondered. I rolled over. Something crumpled beneath my hand.

Storm, will see you this afternoon. Be good. Love, Rowan

I smiled, the note in hand and sat up. Then I lay back down. *Ouch. I don't feel so good.*

I stretched my arms and legs. *Double ouch.* I thought again. *Everything hurts; my muscles, my bones, my joints, my hair!*

I felt my forehead, it didn't feel hot, but my chest felt like it was on fire and I was pretty sure a porcupine had taken up residence in my throat. *Great, now I have the flu? Come on!*

"Good morning, Sunshine," Nana chimed as she came into the room, "You sure fell asleep early last night. Didn't even eat any dinner!"

"Huh, huh," I croaked.

"Oh, you're not feeling good, Dear?" Nana asked as she paused next to my bed.

"No," I murmured weakly. My stomach lurched as the smell of her coffee fell heavily on me with its overly sweetened thick odor.

"What hurts, Dear?"

"Everything." I lay flat on my bed and tried not to inhale any more than necessary. "I think I have the flu or something."

"Well, I'll make you some salt water to gargle with and see if that helps at all. Z mentioned you may start feeling a bit off."

A bit off? Z? Why is Nana not getting it? I feel really sick.

"I'll put the salt water on your sink counter, Dear." Nana gave me a gentle hug.

"Can you stop calling me 'dear'? It doesn't make it sound like you're taking me seriously." I said angrily. But I immediately regretted my temper because now my whole body ached with the effort of emotion.

"Sure." Nana stopped moving around the room and looked at me. "I'll put the salt water on your sink counter, Storm." She spoke very purposely; a slight smile fighting to stay hidden. "Better?"

"No," I mumbled.

After Nana left, I forced myself out of bed. I cringed with each step to the bathroom. My bones were on fire. Each hair follicle ached from the weight of my hair. I picked up the warm cup on the counter and sniffed. It smelled like the ocean. I held a big sip of the warm salt water in my mouth enjoying the tingling sensation on my cheeks. Without thinking, I swallowed it. My throat rejoiced. *Huh? That should have been gross, not good.*

I stared into the cup. It was still half-full of the warm salt water. I looked at my face in the mirror. My hair was a wild mane and my cheeks were flushed, but my throat felt infinitely better. I took another gulp, gargled and then swallowed again. Now both my throat and my chest felt better, cooler. My cheeks were less flushed. I tentatively stretched my arms.

The aching seemed to have relaxed a bit. My head still rang slightly but it was bearable. Even my stomach stopped feeling like it was riding a roller coaster.

"Welcome to another strange day in Paradise," I said and swallowed the rest of the water and went to get dressed.

All of my old clothes were either too tight in my hips or too loose in my waist. Thankful the shopping trip had happened when it did, I went into the closet full of my new wardrobe. A flower print, silk dress caught my eye and my body relaxed as the delicate fabric slid down around me and soothed my fever sensitive skin. I was surprised that my hair didn't put up more of a fight against my brush. It actually was quite willing to tame itself beneath the bristles and the more I brushed, the shinier it looked. I think I could have stood there all day running the brush through it had it not been for Nana's call reminding me I had to get going.

I arrived just as class started so it wasn't until lunch that I got to talk with Jon.

"So Storm, I finally found out more stuff about that guy Tressman." I felt a bit better, less feverish but still not totally myself. Nana had packed me a bottle of water sprinkled with sea salt and I sipped it slowly. Every swallow was a welcomed relieve to the heat that threatened to creep back up inside of me. I was only half listening as Jon talked.

"Really?" I said in between swallows. *What is he talking about?*

"Yeah, and let me tell you that whoever this Tressman guy was," *oh right, Tressman,* "my dad doesn't like to talk about it. So, I did a bit of my own research in Dad's office yesterday afternoon after he left for a meeting. Tressman is mentioned a bunch during the construction years. He was here when the guy's daughters were killed in that weird accident and he was last seen before the Great Storm. Remember the one that destroyed the old tower?"

I nodded and shrugged off some chills, unsure if they were from my fever or from the memory of the story. "Maybe that's why Nana doesn't want us helping her. She thinks it's too creepy or sad. Maybe he was a bad guy."

"I think you're totally right. I found an entire folder in the back of our archives on Kate Harn, your relative!" Jon looked at me with wide eyes and waggling brows. I pushed him on the shoulder to make him continue. "There were lots of photocopies of letters and some pages that looked like a journal or something. In one letter that she wrote to her sister she said that 'Tressman had been fawning over the lighthouse nannies', she referred to them as 'pretty young lasses, one with hair as richly hued as melted dark and milk chocolate and the other shiny and bright as the silk of summer corn. The girls had such a knack with the children on the grounds that the mothers often joked the two were modern day pied pipers and it was wise never to cross the fair ladies or they may lead the children away, as in the fairy tale, never to be heard from again.'" Jon said, reading from a notebook. He looked up embarrassed, "I wrote some stuff down so I wouldn't forget." He went back to the notebook and skimmed down through his messy scribbles. "Kate was upset with Tressman's behavior toward the nannies, blah, blah, blah, worried that they would leave because of it and was supposedly going to speak to her husband. Ooh, here! Well then the kids had that accident and I think that did a fair bit to fuel the superstition of the girls' magic over the children. Some of the women thought it was retaliation for Tressman's behavior. But before anything could be done to either Tressman or the nannies, I guess Tressman went crazy or something because she wrote of his attacking one of the nannies."

I watched Jon tell me the story. He loved to gesticulate with his hands when he got excited. I had to give him space or else a random back hand might bop me alongside my head.

"Then this part I found in what looked like a journal entry. 'The one *with hair of spun gold*' Kate wrote, overly poetic in my opinion, 'came running with her clothes torn and weeping as I'd never seen. Her hair was disheveled and she cried "he took it, help me!" and then collapsed.' Apparently after the attack, Tressman continued his employment, but nobody dealt much with him. There was only one gentleman who he met with regularly and always at night. Kate described him as tall, handsome, and mysterious. The nannies also continued working for Kate but stayed away from the other local children as many of the mothers were too superstitious to let them near their children following the incident. I take it tensions were high for awhile around the lighthouse."

"Wow."

"And that's not all!" Jon used a salesman's voice that made me laugh. "One last journal entry, or at least it was the last page in the folder, said this, 'our efforts have found nothing but I will continue the search as will my daughter as long as we are spared from the tempest.' The crazy part was the date. She wrote the letter the same night the Great Storm took place; the one that toppled the old lighthouse and flooded the area. The keeper and Kate survived, but Tressman didn't and the nannies weren't heard from again. In a newspaper article dated a few days after the storm, Kate is quoted saying she thought the nannies had been killed."

"Wow," I repeated. I felt slightly nauseous. "Why would Nana keep all of this from me?"

"I know, right? Especially since she's a direct descendant, right? She'd be continuing the search for whatever Kate had been looking for!" Jon looked quite smug with his secret information gathering. His hands finally came to a rest on his legs. "The other strange thing is that Kate seemed really fond of the girls."

"Huh? Why is that strange?" My mind struggled to keep up.

"I mean, she wrote with so much expression and like a dozen too many words to describe stuff, but in the letter she tells her sister that the girls must have died in the storm also, she just says 'they died.'" He looked at me, waiting for my slow brain to catch up. He gave up and spelled it out more clearly, "It was like she didn't believe they died, but for some reason wanted others to believe they had. I mean, all she said was the girls died, no mourning, no sadness over the loss of the beautiful young girls, no tear stained ink in a letter detailing the tragedy. Just a simple, they must have died, period. I kind of think she lied...on purpose."

"Oh. I get it. Yeah..." My mind spun slowly which really didn't help settle my stomach.

"Hey, you feel okay?" He asked, his eyes looked concerned.

Do I look as bad as I feel? I wondered.

"I'm okay, just caught some bug or something. So, what did he take?" I asked, sipping more saltwater.

"Who?"

"Tressman. You said that Kate heard the blonde nanny cry *he took it*. What is *it*?"

"I don't know. But, I'm thinking something." He looked serious. "I think the thing he took is the thing your nana wants to find. What if *that* is the secret treasure? And what if he hid that something in the mysterious room he built? And what if Kate was trying to help find it but keeping it a secret by lying about the nannies' deaths?"

"You really do like mysteries, huh. That sounds more like a crazy movie plot than something that happens in a small oceanfront town. I just can't see Nana having anything to do with treasure hunting let alone an almost 200 year old treasure hunting myth." My head couldn't make sense of the information, the puzzle pieces just spun randomly around in my mind.

"Oh, I almost spaced this!" In his excitement, he almost knocked me off the bench with his arms. He pulled a small, old looking book from his back pack. "I found the braid picture that I was thinking of, but I was wrong, it isn't your braid. But, here, check it out!" He opened to a page that he had dog eared. Pictured was an ink drawing of an intricate rope pattern.

I studied the picture. The short section of rope was made from at least a hundred individual smaller ropes woven in an exquisite pattern. Jon was right, it wasn't my braid, but it was just like a braid I knew...Paige's! The caption below the photograph said, "Fig.19. This drawing depicts a fragment of rope discovered near the foundation of the original St. Augustine Lighthouse. Its intricate weave was referred to as the 'mermaid's knot' by sailors of this region from the 1700's. Pen and Ink. Provided by M. Humpphrey.

"Are you thinking what I'm thinking?" I asked Jon.

"You want to see the crazy old Humpphrey, huh?" Jon asked.

I smiled my best smile.

"I figured. That's why after I found this and read about Kate's account of Tressman, I asked Dad if he could set up a meeting with Humpphrey."

"You rock!" I shouted and gave Jon a big hug. I nearly forgot how crappy I felt.

"I know, I know," Jon said, still in our embrace. Then he sat back quickly. Giant drops of rain plopped on us. I looked around, stunned. *The sky was clear a moment ago*, I thought.

"Hurry! Before we get soaked!" Jon called as he grabbed his stuff. He had already made his way halfway to the building, but I lingered and looked.

Is someone there? Leaning against the oaks? I wondered.

Rain fell harder but I slowed to a standstill. I kept staring at the trees and then I saw him clearly. His brown hair hung to his shoulders, his eyes were trained on me and glowed like blue infernos in the darkness brought on by the sudden storm.

"It was just a hug." I spoke as if he stood right next to me. I knew he would hear me, even though I wasn't sure how.

I held fast in his gaze for another moment and then turned away. I casually strolled the rest of the way inside and let the rain cool my feverish skin.

Chapter Eleven

On a good note, Dr. Ross canceled our boat trip for the afternoon due to the unpredictable weather. The downside of that, however, was that we had to break into discussion groups and talk about the papers we'd read and the progress we'd made on our writing assignment.

My participation in our group's discussion consisted of very few words, lots of "uh huhs" and some enthusiastic head nods. Fortunately, I don't think my vague contributions were noticed since Samantha was in my group. She had enough words for all of us combined!

While Samantha explained the intricacies of tidal flux, my mind struggled with my own tidal wave of questions. I knew Rowan made that storm. But I still didn't understand how he did it. Also, the hidden treasure thing, Kate's letters and the bit of *rope* in that book spun in my head. *Mermaid's Knot,* I thought. *What does that have to do with a treasure hidden for hundreds of years? And why does Paige have one hanging on her head?*

"So, do you want to hang around for a bit?" Jon asked after class. The air was extra thick this afternoon and steam rose from the paved road. Entire squadrons of mosquitoes circled me as I walked to the bike. I managed to kill six, but based on the angry welts on my arms and legs, many more successfully had their afternoon meal a la Storm.

"Umm, nah, I'd better get home." I swatted one more on my arm. Jon's face fell slightly and I felt bad so I added quickly, "I'm so behind with these papers. I just really need to get stuck in, ya know? And I don't want to push myself if I'm getting sick." *And,* I added in my head, *I think Rowan owes me another answer.*

"Yeah, true. I guess I should hit the books, too. Okay to give you a call tonight if I find out something from my dad about meeting up with Humpphrey?" He asked.

"Yeah, sure! I'll be home...all night...reading and working on this stupid paper." I made a fake pout.

"Awe, it won't be that bad, just throw in some stuff like metamorphic and tides and high-low water."

We both laughed.

"At least the weather cleared up," Jon added as he peered through the still dripping oaks.

"Yeah, thankfully," I replied.

Huh, I wonder.

"Well, bye. Talk to you later." Jon started to turn back to the lighthouse.

"Yeah, thanks again for finding out all that stuff." *Perhaps a little scientific experiment to stay in the theme of my studies*, I thought. I reached out, gave Jon another hug, and waited. Sure enough, thunder rumbled overhead. Hypothesis confirmed. Rowan was totally messing with the weather somehow. *What was it he said about weather?* 'It was simply a tool that could be controlled by the strongest will.' *He wants will? I'll give him will.*

I knew I'd probably regret it, but what the hell, a girl has to make a point sometimes. I landed a big kiss on Jon's right cheek.

Lightning peeled across the sky with a simultaneous explosion of thunder.

Both Jon and I jumped. "Whoa!" he exclaimed.

I turned quickly away and hopped onto the bike. "See you tomorrow Jon," I said. His cheeks were red and he had a goofy look on his face. Part of me felt bad for using Jon like that. I mean I really didn't have any romantic feelings for him but I refused to let Rowan think his will was stronger than mine...whatever the heck that meant.

Thunder claps accompanied me for the entire ride home but the sky never opened up. "Is that the best you got surfer boy?" I spoke to the air as I pulled next to the house. I turned off the bike's engine and nearly jumped to the second floor window when I turned to stand up.

"Jeez, don't do that!" I griped, face to chest with Rowan.

A smirk appeared on his lips, "First of all, Stormy, no, that isn't the best I got," he answered in an imitation of my voice. "But I would get in a heap of trouble if you got killed in a scooter crash because you drove that thing in a downpour. Secondly, stop hugging that Manistar kid."

"Skipping the obvious questions regarding your apparent ability to control weather and to hear me from great distances away, what's it to you if I hug Jon?"

"I just don't like it is all."

"Oh, I see. You don't like it. Hmm. Sounds similar to how I don't like everybody keeping secrets from me and telling me to be a good girl and to just enjoy being me." I pushed passed him and walked up the stairs to the deck. Nana was sitting in a chair under the big table umbrella.

"How was class?" She asked, looking up from her book with a smile that I didn't return. "Oh, what's wrong?"

"A lot is what," I replied. "Everybody seems to know stuff about me but me. And every time I ask about it, I just get blown off. Then, Jon tells me today that you're working on some kind of a treasure hunt that has been going on for like 200 years. Something to do with that guy Tressman, Kate Harn, and some nannies. And then there's this stupid braid, weird guys that Sara knows who try to attack me, Rowan and his knack for controlling weather, and let's not forget Z! Oh no. The mysterious Z who apparently cares so much about me but hasn't even met me. Z who bought me tons of clothes and who everybody is afraid will be upset if I get upset! Well guess what? I'M UPSET!"

"Storm, relax. I can't..."

"Let me guess, Nana. You can't tell me about it. GOD! I'm sick of this.

Nobody will tell me anything!" My voice rang above the rustle of the sea oats and the discontented squawks of the little green parrots in the palm tree. "Someone needs to start talking to me or I'm going to totally lose it!"

"Storm, relax," Rowan said as he walked up next to me.

"No. I'm not going to relax," I said as I brushed his hand off my shoulder. "Tell me what's going on!"

"They can't do that, Storm." A deep, richly feminine voice resonated through my chest. Nana's gaze shifted to behind my left shoulder and Rowan also turned to look. Based on the angle of their gazes, the powerful voice belonged to someone that was quite a bit taller than I was.

"Turn around, Child," the voice said. The words rang through me like I was a bell that had just been struck.

I turned slowly. I saw a woman who took the breath from my body and the thoughts from my head.

"You're," I attempted to speak. The woman just stood silently, giving me a moment to process and collect the jumbled pieces that had once been coherent thoughts. "You're," I stopped again. My eyes were absolutely overwhelmed by the sight of the woman. I closed them for a moment and assembled the words I needed to say. I opened my eyes back up.

"You're Z," I whispered.

"Yes. Sorry our meeting had been thus delayed. It is a pleasure to meet you, Storm."

I stood still and silent. She was tall, nearly six feet. The afternoon sun shimmered off her deep auburn hair that hung in soft ringlets past her slim waist and gave the impression her head and torso were ringed by fire. Her sleeveless dress was a loose drape of silky fabric in varied hues of green, ranging from a shade so lightly tinted to be almost white to a beautiful rich emerald. It gathered in to her middle by a wide braided belt. Her feet were bare except for green beads that were strung around the second toe on each foot, like toe rings, and then attached to single strands of milky stones over the top of each foot, which then attached to multicolored beaded anklets.

It was like a necklace for your feet.

"I'm afraid your frustrations are my fault," she said as she walked over to where Nana sat. "Thank you Rean and Rowan for doing your best. I had asked the others to tell you as little as possible because I need you to be as strong as possible. The more you figure out on your own, the stronger you will be. And as for Rean's secrecy about Tressman, she is helping me with a special task. A task I want you to stay clear of since it is not entirely safe. And, I know you are frustrated, but your safety is of the utmost importance to me right now. You are not making it easy for us. However, I didn't expect you to. I never had doubts you would be one of the most strong-willed young ones we'd ever experienced. And Rowan tells me that even as untrained as you are, you are already stronger than any he's encountered."

"Any what?" I asked.

"Any of our kind," she replied simply and sat in the empty seat beside Nana.

Right, that clears it up, I thought sarcastically. Her face was unbearably perfect. She didn't look much older than Rowan but the way she acted and spoke made her seem years older than even Nana. *It...this...she just doesn't make sense.*

"So the questions remain," Z continued, "how much should you know and when should you know it? On the one hand we need you to begin training, but on the other we need you protected. The less others know of you and your abilities the better, but the more you discover about your abilities the more chance we have of succeeding."

I waited silently, even more confused. Nana and Rowan stayed still. Z got up and walked toward the railing that overlooked the beach. "I fear that you are not one to be delayed for much longer, regardless of the benefits to you and to us." She turned and looked at me, her eyes smoldering like red hot coals. Without removing her gaze from me, she said, "Rowan."

"Yes?" He replied.

"Take her now to the ocean. I think it's time she learned to swim."

"Is it safe?" Rowan asked, "After what Sara told me happened downtown and then I saw him today talking with Paige. They may suspect more than we think."

With a sigh and a prolonged blink, she finally released me from her stare and turned to Rowan. "Yes, there is a risk. There has been ever since her return and there will be until the solstice. But, I trust you to bring her back safely."

I stole a quick glance to Rowan and in contrast to his usual self assured, nearly cocky expression, he looked nervous and concerned.

"Umm, it's okay. I don't need to...." I stammered, unsure what they were all talking about but sensing that if it had to do with my personal safety I'd rather choose the safe route.

"No, Storm. It's time," Z responded.

"Time for what?" I asked for about the millionth time.

"Time to know," Nana replied. "Trust Z. Rowan will help you. All will be okay." She smiled, but her eyes betrayed internal conflict.

"But..."

"No 'buts' Stormy," Nana stopped my protests, "you've been at me since we left home to explain everything to you. I wasn't able to but now you can find out. You need to find out and dear..." her eyes became serious, "remember to wipe up the sand when you get back."

Remembering the first day I went to the beach when Nana cleaned up my sandy, wet footprints I made on our floor, I had to smile a little. Even though I had no idea what was about to happen, and I wasn't sure I wanted to know, I knew that by her making that joke, everything would be okay.

"Come on, Storm," he rubbed my back, "go grab your suit. It's a beautiful afternoon to go for a swim."

After a quick change upstairs, I came back down. My head was jammed with questions and my stomach was full of butterflies at the thought of going into the water. I was excited to find out what all the mystery was about but I was also scared to death of getting in the water. I wasn't sure that being led to the gaping jaws of the mighty Atlantic was a very good place to have my first lesson. As Rowan and I walked hand in hand across the sand, I felt Nana's and Z's eyes on our backs.

Excitement stayed ahead of dread all the way down the beach and even through the first few steps into the frothy water. It wasn't until the first wave hit my knees with enough force to push me back 2 steps that I lost my nerve.

"You know, I'm good," I said as I pulled against Rowan's grip. "I get it. There's some big thing that I shouldn't know and I've been a pain asking stuff. So, how about I just stay quiet and you all can just go about your business."

"Nice try, Rainbow Fish. You asked for answers. Z is giving you a chance to find some out." Rowan's grip tightened and he led me further into the water. The waves broke one after the other. I felt the strong pull and push against my legs. My feet sunk into the sand each time a wave retreated, threatening to trap me in place. I rose on tip toes and then made full jumps to get past the continuous assaults.

My heart raced in my chest as the water rose higher up my body. My breath lost all rhythm. I pulled more desperately against Rowan.

"Breathe, Storm," his voice purred. He sounded just like he had in my dream. *Play, Stormy. You can do it.*

"Did. You. Say. Something?" I asked as I tried to breath and jump and not pass out from fright.

He smiled his radiant smile and I heard his voice again in my head, *No, but I thought something.* He winked.

I'm scared. I thought.

"There's no need to be scared," he answered.

"You heard my thought?"

He nodded.

I glanced back to shore, the house was small in the distance but I was sure Z and Nana were still watching. I looked back to Rowan. "We're nearly there. The water is calming down, see?" Rowan motioned to the water just a few feet ahead of us. He was right. The waves had become more rolling hills rather than craggy, snow capped mountains. It really looked surprisingly beautiful and inviting. My breath even calmed. "Rowan, I..." But he dove away from me into an oncoming swell before I could finish my sentence. I waited for him to return.

Nothing.

I waited until 3 more swells rolled past me.

Five breaths, six, seven. I scanned the water frantically.

"If this is some kind of joke, it isn't at all funny! I'm going to kill you when I find you!" I spoke out loud to the rolling waves trying to create braveness through words. I walked a few feet deeper. The swells now crested at my chest but didn't break. The water seemed to cradle me and despite my fear and rising anger, the water was delicious on my heated skin. I felt energetic, invigorated, alive and really, really irritated at Rowan. *Where the heck are you?*

His voice returned to my head, *That's it, Storm. Come on. Play. Dive in and I'll catch you.* I looked around and hoped to catch some glimpse of his suit or a flash of his skin but he was totally nowhere, well, he was in my head, but nowhere to be seen.

Stop resisting! His voice said.

Scared, I thought.

Calm down, as soon as you stop resisting what is, what is will be really fun!

I don't understand.

Accept rather than resist. Resisting what is happening at the moment is such a horribly human trait. I had such higher hopes for you.

Now you are making even less sense than the fact that we are apparently having this conversion in my head.

Two souls of the sea, connected by the sea, he responded. *Think about it and you'll have the answer.*

I looked down to my legs submerged in the water. We were both *in the water. Connected by the sea...*but that was only half of what he said.

Go on, he prompted.

It wasn't just any *two people in the water,* he said two *souls of the sea. What do you mean of the sea? I'm from Indiana.*

You can take a fish out of water, Storm.

The water now lapped at my chin. *A fish? Me? That's a good one, I can't even swim.*

Then how do you explain what you're doing right now? He asked.

And that's when it hit me. I'd been so focused on Rowan's voice in my head that I didn't even realize my toes were no longer touching the velvety sand. I floated, effortlessly, on the ocean's surface. When the wave rose, I rose; when it fell, I fell. Unlike my dream where I flailed and felt helpless, my legs moved in unison, crossed at the ankles. They gently swayed beneath me. They knew what to do somehow. My arms under the water looked shimmery in the sun's rays that penetrated the uppermost layers. They, too, moved with an unconscious grace. My hair fanned out lightly around me.

How am I doing this? I wondered.

Don't think, just feel! Rowan responded.

My mouth was level with the water's surface and the salt tingled the skin on my lips. I licked my lips and a surge of energy filled my limbs. With one, spontaneous, powerful kick, I rose three-quarters out of the water. But what goes up, must come down and down I came with a splash and submerged completely for the first time.

Laughter resounded in my head.

The coolness that surrounded me was like a waterfall of bliss. I remembered that strange dream of lying in the bottom of Jack's pool after dancing with Rowan, Sara, and Pearl. *It was a dream, right? I mean, I wasn't actually lying on the bottom of Jack's pool and Rowan didn't actually swim down to me and smile at me, right?* I remembered the feeling of peace and of calm. I didn't want to come up then and I didn't want to go back up now. And the best part was that I didn't have to. I had no desire to take a breath of air, I just floated, weightless and content, except, *wait. I had to breathe. Nobody could just stay underwater without breathing. If I didn't get back to the surface, I'd die. Got to get up, NOW!* Panic resurfaced and so did I. I popped my head back above the surface because I just thought I should. The harshness of the air shocked my lungs and I coughed violently. More than just the shock of the air, the loud sounds of the people talking and laughing and screaming and crying on the beach made my ears pound and the sun made my scalp feel like it was on fire. A hand on my back made me spin.

A smiling Rowan leaned in and whispered into my ear, "you can take a fish out of water, but when she returns she'll still remember how to swim." He brushed his lips to my cheek, "welcome home, Storm."

I looked into his eyes and realized that all I thought to be true of my world and myself was rearranging. My beliefs of possible and not possible, my understandings of real and imaginary, fact and myth were no more solid than a lacework veil.

By home, he didn't mean the yellow house. He meant right here, in this water, in this ocean. Two souls of the sea...he called me his siren. It could only mean one thing. One. Very. Strange. Thing. Something that, until now, I believed only existed in books on mythology. My eyes grew wide and he knew the light bulb finally blinked on. *He means that they are, well, they AND I are mer...*before I could finish my revelation, my legs were yanked down and my head flew below the surface.

My arms dragged beyond my head and my hair flowed straight behind me. Each follicle tugged on my scalp with the force of the water that flew by. Something painful gripped my ankles. I opened my eyes and saw the filtered light from the sun grow dimmer. The colors changed from light green to olive. I fought the rush of water and bent my neck forward for a glance toward my feet. Through the now deep green, nearly black water, I made out a pale form with some sort of billowing cloak even darker than the water. I struggled, but to no avail. The clamp on my legs was an unbreakable vice. My chest burned and my head felt squeezed with the pressure of the increasing depth. My neck muscles gave out and my head flew back. I was at the mercy of whatever had a hold of me.

I'm going to implode, I thought. *This sucks. My first time swimming, a huge revelation and now this octopus or other stupid sea animal is going to kill me? No way.*

I struggled with renewed strength. The pressure on my ankles intensified.

Let her go! Rowan's voice rang loudly in my pounding head.

What? Rowan's here? Help me!

Calm down lover boy, her fate is inevitable, why prolong it? Pearl will never find it and without an heir, your clan is doomed. Why protect this one when it no longer matters? Or does it?

Leave her! Rowan shouted. *She's not strong enough for this yet.*

All this trouble for this little half-ling freak. Her mom already abandoned her once, obviously. Who's to say she'll even claim her at the Solstice?

Hey! I thought. *My mom? Did this thing know something about my mom?* I pulled my legs against the iron grip again.

Oh half-ling, the voice scolded me, *stop your struggles, it isn't like you're going to drown...apparently.* High pitched laughter filled my head.

So, Rowan, Paige told me about your babysitting job. How's it going so far? The voice continued. *I suppose Z may be a tad upset if you bring this one back in less than perfect condition. Although, it isn't like you all haven't lost a few before. Sara helped break the way in that department, huh.*

Get away from her now. Rowan growled.

Awe, you didn't tell the little one? Tsk tsk Rowan. Messing with a woman's heart is just not a very gentlemanly thing to do. Child, you didn't actually think Rowan cared for you did you? He was just following orders, as always. Z says, he does. Laughter, cruel laughter rang in my head until I thought it would burst apart.

*What do you...*I started the thought but then stopped. Since arriving in St. Augustine, I had been treated like a kid, called a bunch of names all referring to my youngness, told what to do and what not to do, been ignored when I asked to have things explained to me, and now this voice, after dragging me under the water, is telling me that the one boy who has ever shown the slightest interest in me was just following orders. All this time with Rowan, his smiles, winks, touches...kisses...*a job? Orders? Young one? Child?! Screw you and Rowan and everyone else who insists that I'm not old enough or strong enough or smart enough to handle whatever is going on!* The water's pressure no longer bothered me, my body, swelled by my anger and determination, pushed against it. The iron grip, that just moments before felt unbreakable, seemed no more hassle than my blankets wrapped around me after my nightmare. In one sudden motion, I flung my legs apart and then spun forward so I was vertical, rather than horizontal in the dark, cold water.

Get here and face me you jerk! I shouted in my head to the darkness that surrounded me. I spun in circles, flaring my limbs in hopes of making contact with either the thing that brought me down here or Rowan. Hitting either would be just fine with me. *You think you're all tough. Well both of you get back here and face me now!* For a moment I thought I was absolutely alone.

Stronger than I thought, the voice rang out. *Mother will be very interested to hear about this.*

I wouldn't keep pushing her. Rowan's voice rang through the darkness. *She'd tear you limb from limb if she knew how to find you right now.*

More laughter filled my head. *You may be right. Interesting arrival indeed.*

Who the hell are you? I shouted.

Every dawn begins with me, At dusk I'll be the first you see, And day-

break couldn't come without, What midday centers all about, daises grow from me, I'm told, And when I come, I end all cold, But in the sun I won't be found, Yet still, each day I'll be around.

What? My mind spun. *A riddle? Seriously?* Something pulled my hair. I spun and swung my right arm but it was in slow motion; its forward motion fighting against the thickness of the water.

There's a reason not to mix our kinds, the resulting freak is never able to keep up.

I don't know, she nearly hit you with that right hook. Rowan responded.

Coward. I thought angrily.

Something brushed against my right shoulder. This time I purposely waited a moment before reacting; like luring a mosquito in for the bite before squashing it. Learning from my previous fail, I moved my left arm slowly across my body. The pressure on my right shoulder increased slightly. Fingers curled around my collarbone. My hand, now only inches from the pressure, didn't have to move far through the heavy water. Instead, I darted it suddenly forward to close the small gap that remained, and just like a well timed pounce, I succeeded in grabbing the hand that held me. Not having planned what to do if I actually succeeded grabbing hold, I did the first thing that came to mind and after that, I held on as tightly as I could.

Let GO! The voice shouted, multiple octaves higher than it had been. *She's biting me!* The hand pulled violently but instead of shaking me off, I went with it. I bit even harder, grinding my jaws side to side. I was dragged suddenly forward through the darkness. Rowan's laughter rang in my head. *Atta girl!* He cheered.

But my triumphant moment was short lived. My body started to shiver and I lost feeling in my limbs. The surge of anger and adrenalin that had kept me going this long was not going to keep me going any longer. The hand kept pulling and my jaw released; unable to hang on any longer. I had been underwater for I don't know how long. Maybe I was already dead and this was some sort of weird afterlife experience. I didn't think being dead would feel so cold, or be so dark, but whatever.

And to think for a moment I believed her to possibly be a reason to worry, the voice growled.

I floundered alone in the cold abyss but even though I had run out of physical strength, I wasn't ready to let that bratty voice make fun of me again. *And by the way you stupid voice who is too cowardly to face me,* I thought with the last of my strength, *the stupid answer to the stupid riddle is the stupid riddle itself! Dawn begins with me...dusk...daybreak...the center of midday. The answer is the letter D. Now go away.* I felt a swish of water next to me and then nothing. I was alone and I was going to die. I wrapped my arms around my legs, turning myself into a tight ball. I let myself just hover. If I was sinking or floating I really had no idea and I was beyond caring.

Come on, Storm. Rowan spoke softly in my head.

What? Rowan? You're still here?

Come on my brave one. You've done quite a lot for your first day. Fingers interlaced with mine. Then a strong body wrapped itself around me, trying to subdue my uncontrollable shakes. I felt rather than saw the rush of water as the body undulated in a smooth, porpoise-like rhythm. The water turned from black to deep green then to blue green as we rose. Ribbons of sunlight made the water look like we were in the middle of a striped mint candy. My body stopped shivering as we entered the sunlit waters and my legs extended out of my fetal position. My ankles crossed and my legs moved as one. They kicked to Rowan's rhythm, the muscles of his legs pressed hard against mine. Our upward speed increased. As the water got warmer and brighter I felt stronger and kicked harder. The water was now the color of sparkling emeralds. Rowan and I continued to shoot upward. I craned my neck back and arched slightly, desperate to close the final gap between me and the blurry mirage of sky and clouds. We pushed and I reached until we finally soared from the water like some trained dolphin act at a seaquarium. Still held tightly in Rowan's arms, we leaped as one, half rolled in the air, and then fell back to the water with a giant splash.

"Huuuuuuuuuu!" I gasped the biggest breath I'd ever taken as I surfaced for the second time and then coughed and gagged as the air came in too quickly. My chest ached and my head pounded.

"What just happened? Where are we? Why aren't I dead? How did we do that? What did we do? Who was that down there? Why did it try to kill me? Am I dead? How did I hear you in my head?" There were so many questions to ask they just all came out at once, stepping on the previous one and getting stepped on my the next one and then all of them getting confused by my coughing fits. "How did you hear me in your head? Where..."

Rowan's lips suddenly pressed against mine. That put a stop to my outpouring of questions. He cradled me in his arms, one arm under my knees, the other reaching around my back with his hand spread wide behind my head. *Shh.* I heard softly in my head.

Rowan released me from his kiss. His mouth and eyes sparkled with a smile. "You were great down there!" He exclaimed. "I mean really amazing. Like seriously impressive!" He pulled me back in for another kiss. His mouth was strong, almost rough, against mine, like he couldn't control himself. This was not a side of the ever calm, controlled, and self assured boy I had experienced before. And the kisses we shared had surely never been this full of passion. *Wait a second.*

"Wowan." I tried to speak but his lips made me mumble. I pulled away and tried again. "Rowan. Wait. Hang on." His eyes still sparkled; tiny droplets of water hung on his dark lashes. Our bodies spun in slow circles. "I need answers." My voice sounded scratchy and it made my throat sore to speak aloud.

"42." Rowan said with a smile.

"What?"

"You asked for an answer. 42 is an answer." He winked and hugged me.

"What?" My head continued to pound. "No. Stop it. I'm being serious." I shifted in his arms so I could face him. It's hard to be taken seriously while being cradled.

"Okay. Sorry, couldn't resist. I will do my best to answer your questions, but I'm afraid that I may not be able to tell you all that you want to know. Some things need to remain unknown for a bit longer. Also, we will need to head back shortly as I hadn't planned on ending up where we are. So, how about this? You pick your top three questions and I'll do my best to answer them, then we can get back home.

My eyes wandered. Nothing but water surrounded us. Bright sun warmed my shoulders and the water below us continued into a blue infinity.

"Where are we?"

"About 20 miles east of Saint Augustine. One down, two to go."

"What do you mean 20 MILES east of Saint Augustine? We're in the middle of the friggin' ocean? How are we supposed to get back? How did we get here? Why..."

"Wait." He put his fingers to my lips. "That's more than two questions. You're getting wrapped up in resistance again. We'll be fine, trust me."

"What was that down there?"

"It wasn't a what, it was a who. And that who was doing what he does best which is to make trouble for us. He gives all of our kind a bad name."

"Our kind?"

"And now you've hit on the question I've been waiting for. Yes, Storm. Our kind."

"What kind would that be?"

"Are you sure you want to use your last question on that? I bet you know the answer already."

"Well, I..." I did have an idea, but it was absolutely crazy. It was Disney crazy, it was teenage movie crazy, it was mythology crazy, it was....

On the right track. Rowan's voice chimed in my head.

"Hey!"

"Sorry."

"It's not possible, though," I whispered.

"Why not?"

"They don't exist, that's why!"

Rowan's eyes squinted in thought and then widened in resolution. Then before I could even ask what he was thinking, he pulled us both underwater.

*What the...Rowan, why...*I struggled in his arms. I fought to get back up to the surface; to the air. *I need air, I need to..."*

Breathe. Rowan's voice interrupted my frantic thoughts.

LET ME GO! LET ME GO! I NEED TO GET UP! I twisted and pulled and fought against his hold.

Storm, look at me.

I did and saw his bright blue eyes shining through the water. *Breathe.* He repeated.

I'm trying to! That's why I need to get up. Let me up!

No. Not breathe up there. Breathe down here.

I can't.

Can.

How?

Because of what you are. What we are. Say it Storm. Say what we are.

There really was no other explanation. But even so, it just seemed so ridiculous.

Say it.

We're mermaids?

I immediately felt really stupid.

Well, yes and no. Yes, you are. No, I'm not, that would be daft. I'm a merman. Together we're merfolk or merpeople and to be absolutely honest, you're a half-ling, half human, half mer.

I nodded slowly. *Huh. So, I'm not human and merpeople really do exist?*

Well of course they do! Humans are so limited.

Hey!

Well, my dear, your only half human, so you're only partially limited. He laughed.

Pearl and Sara?

Mermaids.

That thing that tried to kill me?

Merman. Part of a different clan, the lionfish.

Z?

Mermaid. Actually, she's Pearl and Sara's mother and our clan's leader. We belong to the seastar clan. And you do, too!

I'm pretty sure my dad is human, so, do you know who my mom was?

Yes.

Yes?

Yes.

Who was she?

You mean who is she.

What? She's alive? SERIOUSLY?! WHERE IS SHE?

Sorry, but you already got answers to way more than three questions. That's all I can do right now.

Are you kidding me?

Nope.

Nope?

Nope.

That's it?

There are very few rules in mer society but one of them is the protection of truths. It's what Z meant when she said you needed to figure things out on your own to become strong. The more you are told by others, the more others define your truths, and in turn, the weaker you are.* He smiled. The filtered light made his teeth glow with a strange green tint.

I shook my head a bit to try to stop the spinning. It didn't really help. *So, that's why you never just came out and told me what I was? What we are?* I shuddered a tiny bit on the use of *we*.

Right. That would have been me defining your truth. You have to determine your truth. Get it?

I think so, it kind of sounds like not believing everything you hear. Like the time Mindy Marrow told me that Joan Pultz, a new girl that came to our school in sixth grade, was mean and two-faced and I should never talk to her. I believed Mindy and stayed away from Joan for the entire year. It wasn't until that next summer that Joan and I were in an art camp together that I finally spoke to her and it turned out that she was really nice. Apparently, Joan had been voted to be the classroom representative and Mindy was jealous so she told everyone lies. I felt really bad for just believing them after realizing that Joan was a really cool person.

Exactly! Everyone views the world through their own filters and makes judgments based on those filters. Mindy had a filter of jealousy and by you taking on her truth, you also took on her filter and lost the ability to figure out your own truth."

I nodded slowly. *This is so crazy. I mean so totally crazy.* I didn't know if I wanted to shout for joy or cry in fear.

Now what? I looked up and saw the bright sky beyond the thin membrane of water still above my head. We had been underwater for minutes. *This is seriously unbelievable.*

Now breathe.

I CAN'T! I thought back.

Mermaid. Rowan replied and rolled his luminescent eyes.

I inhaled slowly through my nose and felt the warm ocean water slide in. I could taste the salt in my mouth. It didn't hurt and I didn't cough like when I surfaced and breathed air. It was thick and pleasant. *Ahhhh.* I stared wide-eyed at Rowan. I felt great!

Well done my little nymph. He smiled.

What is that feeling? I thought back. Energy surged in my limbs. They felt full of some combination of pins and needles and tickles. It took nearly all of my concentration not to shake everything out.

You are doing splendid!

More tingles hit me and the energy this time was unable to be ignored. I couldn't help myself. I gave one huge push with my intertwined legs and surged upward, right out of the water. I flew! The hot sun kissed my wet skin, my hair tickled my back in the wind and then as suddenly as I took off, I landed with a splash. Some of the energy tickles were gone, but my limbs still wanted more. They wanted to move and twist and push through the water. I had never felt this alive, this energetic, this *graceful* before! Another leap, and another and...just about to take off for a fourth time, I felt pressure on my arm. I spun underwater, my hair momentarily blocked my vision. It drifted slowly behind me revealing a very close up Rowan. His eyes smiled at me.

Hold on there, flying fish. Rowan thought, his eyes now full of laughter. *What do ya say we make our way back to shore. I'll answer your questions, as long as they're about mers and not about personal stuff, okay?*

Okay. I began to surface.

What are you doing?

Well you said we were heading back, I just figured...

Mermaid.

Oh right. Swim underwater. I get it.

How do your legs feel?"

It wasn't until he asked that I noticed my legs had been moving slowly through the water beneath me, once again coordinated in a slow swishing motion. *Pretty good, I suppose.* They were crossed at the ankles again and my muscles felt locked in place. I'm not sure I could have separated them even if I wanted to. *Hey, how come we don't have tails?*

Oh ma'dear, you don't honestly believe everything you see in the movies do you? Rowan's lips were in a half smile and he winked.

So no tail, huh? That's a bummer because your would have looked really pretty with a shimmery pink one. I was then tossed out of the water. I landed with a splash and came up sputtering and laughing. Rowan surfaced next to me also laughing. I repaid him by dunking him under and he got me back by spraying me with a fountain of water in my face.

"Okay, okay, Storm, let's continue shall we?" Rowan's eyebrow rose in challenge.

"Okay, teach me oh great one of the sea." My voice oozed with sarcasm.

"Hmmph. Now Storm, I realize you're still a baby..."

"Don't start that again!" I protested.

"Sorry, I didn't mean that in a bad way, just that you're still very young in mer terms. Pearl is so much better at explaining all this than I am. Young ones tire quickly. And half-ling young ones, well, I'm not sure what they do. I honestly didn't think they even existed, but then I met you!"

"You didnt think *I* existed? This day just keeps getting weirder."

"Just let me know if you need to take a rest once we get started, okay?"

"Why, what happens when I get tired?"

"Well, you'll sink."

"Oh, yeah, that sounds bad."

"Your muscles need two things to rest and recover, salt and sun. The younger you are, the more sun you need, that's why we've been hanging at the surface so long. Do you feel how your legs are moving right now?"

"Yeah, they're just sort of doing that on their own."

"Exactly, you don't have to over-think the mechanics. Your body knows what to do. It's in its element! That's it, just relax. What would your body like to do now?"

That answer was simple. My lungs burned from breathing the too-thin air ever since we resurfaced. My nose and throat felt dry and scratchy like I was coming down with a cold. "Go back underwater," I answered.

"That's my girl!"

Chapter Twelve

Which way? I looked around in all directions. The water, although surprisingly clear to me being that I wasn't wearing goggles looked pretty much identical in all directions. I felt a soft hand touch my cheek and guide it around.

This way. He pointed my face to our left.

How he knew that, I had no idea. Apparently, realizing I was a mermaid didn't help my sense of direction in any way.

Okay, a few things to keep in mind, his thoughts took on a serious tone, *we're fine near the surface as light still penetrates. But stay alert below the Photic Zone because your body will start to tire.*

Below the what? I questioned.

Oh Stormy, you really are behind on your reading. He made a tsk tsking sound and shook his head side to side. *The Photic Zone is the depth at which visible light penetrates through water. Different waters, depending on clarity have different depths of light penetration. Our bodies absorb the energy from the light wavelengths to stay strong. Longer wavelengths, more energy for us. Shorter wavelengths, less energy for us.*

Oh, right, I thought back, *wavelengths, of course.* To myself I added how glad I was that Samantha wasn't here to share an hour lecture on the properties of each wavelength of light. I chuckled at the thought.

Well, at least she's read the papers, Rowan chided.

Hey, I wasn't thinking that to you.

Sorry, Babe, can't help what I hear. Don't worry, eventually you'll be able to control the thoughts you send out, but until then, watch out because somebody is bound to be listening. Sunlight sparkled on his green-tinged toothy grin.

'Kay, fine. You said there were a couple of things. Got the sunlight thing, what's the other?

Not to worry now, let's just work on the breathing and swimming. He gave me a kiss on the lips, which felt really weird...and nice.

I took a deep breath. The energy pulsed and I kicked powerfully while simultaneously laying my body horizontally in the water. I kicked again and again. It felt so good; like flying underwater!

Swimming, as it turned out, was effortless. The real challenge lay in keeping a constant speed...and direction. Breathing was more complicated since it required effort to draw in the water and then even more effort to restrain myself from the burst of energy that followed. I had some trouble doing everything at the same time and kept stopping to breathe and then swimming fast and then remembering that I was going too fast and then slowing down and then remembering that I was supposed to be going the direction Rowan led us. Kind of reminded me of the time my dad tried to teach me to drive a stick shift; lots of short, swerving bursts followed by stalls and reminders to pick only one lane. I'm really not sure where I would have ended up if Rowan hadn't been there to guide me and correct my path every couple of minutes.

My coordination did finally improve after an hour or so. We soared silently and smoothly through the water. My mind also quieted and my eyes opened wide at the sights I beheld. There was just so much to take in as we swam slowly a few feet below the water's surface bathed in the rippling sunlight.

I realized I had never seen so clearly before. I was horribly nearsighted on land. When I was little, I had thick, total nerd glasses. After begging and pleading for months after I turned fourteen, my dad reluctantly took me to get contacts, thank goodness, but I still hoped someday to get laser eye surgery. As I looked around me now, everything was crisp! I saw for what seemed like miles through the blue-green water. I saw sharks hundreds of meters away, small silvery fish darted by and I could make out their individual tiny gills, mountains of rock intermittently rose from the depths adorned with colorful sponges and long branching tree-like corals and the colors, far from muted, were brilliant like an underwater rainbow. The tiniest of shrimp floating along the currents inches from my eyes were as clear as ones floating yards away. They were orange and white with teeny tiny legs and even teenier claws...were those krill? *No way.*

Your eyes are designed to see in water, not air, that's why you've probably always had trouble on land. Rowan's voice echoed in my head, interrupting my half-thought, half-daydream in my underwater paradise. *Our eyes are more like marine mammal eyes. You did at least read the papers on vision in marine mammals, didn't you?*

Umm, well...I mean, I was going to...

Rowan laughed, little waves of water rose above our heads. We swam together in silence.

You said before there are very few rules, what is another one? I thought as we swam side by side. The surface was still just a few feet above our heads, close enough that the heat of the sun penetrated and made my back pleasantly warm.

Free will. Taking away a mer's free will is like death to us. This time he was the one to shudder.

Huh. So, self-discovery of truth and free-will. But I'm only a half...what was it called?

Half-ling, yes.

So, what does that mean for me? I thought I was just a dork as a human, now am I gonna be a dork as a half-mermaid?

He laughed. *Oh Storm, far from it! So far you're more skilled than most mers I've ever met! You're like, well, unbelievable.*

HA! You're a merman and you tell me I'm the one who's unbelievable.

You don't even know what you're capable of. To be honest, none of us do.

Pearl, Sara and I felt your strength the moment you arrived. You're the one we've been waiting for. Z made sure we kept an eye on you to protect you until you had time to make the transition when you can take your rightful place in our clan.

What do you mean until the transition?

Mers age differently than humans. We develop similarly to about the human age of puberty and then we take on our adult form and strength within a few months or so after we turn sixteen. The transition is completed at the summer solstice after your sixteenth birthday. Then pretty much never change much again, or we do, but the change is so slow that it appears we're frozen in time.

You mean you never get old? You're immortal?

No, we get old, but our time scale is on millennia rather than decades. We age, but nearly imperceptibly to humans. Think of it like dog years and human years. Humans age in what seems like dog years to us, but on an even faster scale, like a thousandfold faster scale.

So, you aren't a teenager?

No.

Early twenties?

Umm, no.

How old are you?

I'm ten K'atun.

You're ten what?

Ten K'atun. I suppose that's just shy of 200 solar years. I never was very good at your math.

K'atun, wait a minute, that's part of the Mayan counting system.

Yes. Its scale is more appropriate for our lifespan. You okay?

Truth was I was feeling quite dizzy and my legs no longer acted as one. I started twisting and kicking without making much headway.

Hey Storm, come on, up we go! Rowan reached an arm around my waist and we both glided up to the surface. My body shivered uncontrollably. The air felt thin and unwelcoming in my body, but the sun was delicious on my head and shoulders. I leaned into Rowan's chest. He supported me effortlessly.

"So," Rowan said, "I suppose that was your strength limit. Good to know."

The shivering continued even as the sun's warmth radiated through me. "Yeah, I-I-I g-g-guess s-s-s-so," I chattered.

"Let's float for a bit," he said as he stroked my hair back. I laid like a baby otter on his chest as he floated on his back. Every bit of exposed skin hungrily absorbed the heated rays of the sun.

"Of course direct light gives the most energy and your body is still adjusting to absorbing the energy through the water. You did great, though, for your first time!" He kissed my head.

"Hmm, hmm." I still clenched my jaws together to stop the chattering of my teeth.

"I remember the first time my mum took me swimming in the open ocean. I was no more than six or seven but very headstrong, mind you."

"Rrreealy," I chattered, "you...hhheadsstrong?" I smiled. Rowan cocked an eye toward me.

"Anyway..." Rowan continued, "we had recently moved to Cape Horn and I wasn't used to the power of the seas. My mum said, 'now Ro, you mind where I go and follow exact what I do. No wandering off, this isna the tide pools.'"

Rowan chuckled at the memory. His accent increased when he mimicked his mother's voice.

"I was ready to prove I wasn't her babe anymore, you see, I was the youngest; three older sisters and me. I was coddled and babied and treated like a doll in every which way imaginable. I was ready to be treated like a man!" I couldn't contain a chuckle when I pictured a young Rowan being coddled by three adoring sisters.

"I was already skilled at manipulating of water, so..."

"You were what?" I asked.

"Oh, good at moving water. It's one of the skills we'll be practicing when Pearl gets back."

"Oh, right." I grimaced when I remembered the turbulent waters of the inlet after our first class trip.

"Anyway, I had no fear of going to the sea 'cause I figured that whatever happened, I could just make the water do what I wanted it to do. Well, as I quickly found out, manipulating small tide pools of water is much different that manipulating endless oceans."

"What happened?" I asked. I closed my eyes and allowed Rowan's voice to lull me while the sun warmed my skin. We still floated toward home but I could have cared less if we ever made it back to land.

"Well, I, of course, didn't mind mum. The lesson started just fine. We swam together and I practiced sensory navigation. Eyes do you little good, so you have to use your other senses to figure out where to go." He answered my unasked question. "At some point, she turned into a small cove to give me relief from the endless current and swells but I was too busy chasing schools of sardines to notice. Well, after I lost interest in the fishes, I called to mum. But she didn't answer. I called again and still got nothing. It was then that I realized I was alone. The current was strong and I was tiring quickly. I tried to change it like I did in the small pools, but it wouldn't budge. Disoriented and scared, my desire to be a man completely vanished. All I wanted was to hear my mum's chime and smell her near me."

"Her what?"

"Her chime and scent. Sorry, I forget you're new to this. Every mer gives off a vibration underwater, also a distinct smell; more like a taste really. Anyway, my mum tasted of lavender and mint and her chime was solid and comforting like the a middle C note. But as I struggled to swim in the gloomy water I couldn't find any hint of her. My heart raced and I felt myself panicking. I thought of going to the surface, but then I thought my sisters would make fun of me if they found out, so I kept swimming, trying to pick up on mum's scent and sound."

"What happened?"

"Well, I sunk lower to see if the patterns in the sand could help me navigate, but as I did my legs bumped into something big and solid. I jumped a bit and tried to swim harder. I bumped the thing again and then my legs got sorta stuck. I turned and looked and came face to face with the head of a giant hammerhead shark. Its teeth were bared and its eyes were like black glassy beads. I nearly shat myself! I screamed and struggled more but it seemed to follow me as I moved. Suddenly I heard laughter ringing in my head."

"What? Sharks laugh?" I asked.

Rowan chuckled. "No, but sisters do. Figuring that I was a dead mer, I stopped struggling and waited for the jaws to clamp down on me. But when nothing happened, I looked again and saw that the wide shark head was held by three sets of slender hands. I hadn't noticed in the gloom, but the shark head was just that, a head. My sisters had come along on the swim and decided to scare me a bit after noticing I had wandered off from mum. So after watching over me to make sure I didn't get too lost they decided to have some fun with the shark head."

"Ooh, that's mean," I said, but couldn't help laughing.

"Yeah, did teach me to listen, though."

"Did you ever find your mum...I mean mom?"

"Yes, she found us and wasn't all that chuffed. My sisters got in trouble for scaring me and I got in trouble for wandering off. The four of us couldn't sit down for a week." Despite the painful memory Rowan laughed. "Mum was not quick to punish, but when she did, you were sure to learn the lesson and not soon to forget it. Mers tend to have short attentions and after that, my mum made sure I learned to focus because although the sea is our domain, it doesn't often forgive absentmindedness."

"Your mom sounds really great." I couldn't hide the sadness in my voice.

"Awe, Storm, your mum is great, too."

"Good to know. Too bad it doesn't matter since I don't even know who she is."

"But you will, when..."

"Don't say, 'when it's time', that phrase is really pissing me off."

"As a matter of fact, I wasn't going to say that," he replied with an air of indignation. "I was going to say when you finish transition."

"Really? When's that again?" This was even better news than finding out I was a mermaid. Okay, well maybe not better, but...

"The Solstice Party."

"But what's..."

"Nope, can't go down that line of questioning."

"Ugh," I grunted with frustration. Every time I felt like I was finally making progress and getting information, a question of mine would be unanswerable.

"Well, can you at least tell me if my mom knows I'm here?"

"Yes she does and she's very proud of you."

"Will the secrets of this place never end?"

"Well, I hate to break it to you, but the secrets actually increased by one just a few weeks ago."

"Huh?"

"You're the newest secret."

"Oh."

"Any regrets?"

"No."

"Good! Ready to swim a bit more?"

"Yeah." I smiled. I liked thinking of Rowan as having some trouble learning this stuff, too. I knew he must've told me that story to make me feel less awkward, like all mers go through a learning period. *And at least I won't get my bum spanked if I don't behave.*

"Don't count on it there, missy," Rowan said after he heard my thoughts. He turned quickly onto his side and dumped me with a splash into the water.

"Hey!" I said as I spat water.

"Come on, let's not be late for dinner." I followed him underwater, still laughing.

After another half hour of swimming, sand angled up from the depths and light played on its rippled contours. A small silver shark coasted past, a full one, not just the head. I noticed feet dangling in the water above me, suspended on either side of an oval shadow. We were near shore. The water pushed me slightly forward and then back. The feet and the shadow disappeared. We were swimming under the back line with the surfers.

Ready my little mermaid?

For what?

For this! Rowan pushed forward and shot out of the water into a froth of white. He body surfed into shore.

I looked up, felt the surge of water that indicated an approaching wave and then with one welcomed, powerful kick, I shot through the water and emerged in the surface foam. I laughed and rode the wave and for a brief, splendid instant, let all of my concerns of secrets and unknowns wash away. I flew in the water. I was free to play! I heard one of the surfers shout, "Good one!" as I soared past on my belly and giggled as the foam tickled my nose.

Chapter Thirteen

Between classes and swimming lessons with Rowan, the days flew by! Nana and I weren't on speaking terms yet since we got in a huge fight about me being a mer and her keeping the secret form me, but whatever, I had other things to focus on. She was wrong and I was right. It was just going to take her time to figure that out and until then, I'd just stay busy with Rowan.

I felt stronger each time we swam and by the following week I barely had to take breaks. But ego aside, I still feigned exhaustion because when it came to the choice of swimming or snuggling on Rowan's chest, a girl's gotta have a bit of reward for all of her hard work. Our time spent floating around the Atlantic also gave me great insight to the mer who had taken my heart. Rowan was a wonderful story teller and based on the stories of his youth, he was not one for rules.

He came to St. Augustine to find Z after a dream his mom had.

"So you had never met Z before you took off from half way around the world to find her?

"Only once, at my coming of age solstice and that was more ceremony than talking. We only all gather at Solstice Parties and there are so many mers there that you don't really get to meet personally with the Clan leaders, unless of course you are with an heir or are coming of age. Also, mermen travel around a lot once they come of age. We can even switch clans during certain festival years. So heading here was a pretty normal thing to do."

"Did your mom know Z?"

"They had met at Solstice Parties but nothing more. When she had the dream about me, she knew enough to listen. Dreams are very important to mers and are used as guides for large decisions. She spoke to Z and Z agreed I should join them here. Okay, enough yacking, more swimming my lovely procrastinator."

I was thinking about that conversation as we walked hand in hand through the narrow streets downtown. I no longer worried about what that mean mer, the one who tried to kill me on my first swim, said about Rowan just doing his job by being with me. From the little I could find out about the neighboring lionfish clan, they weren't very nice at all. He was just saying mean stuff to try to hurt me. Rowan really liked me. And I really liked Rowan.

We walked between 18th century Coquina buildings and 21st century storefronts. St. Augustine was a town of extremes. We had finished swimming for the day but I was anxious to hear the end of his story he had started during training. The late afternoon sun was still hot but the angle allowed us to hug the shaded side of the street to get some relief. My scent made me nervous but Rowan assured me I smelled just fine. 'Delicious' was the word he used. I liked that word.

"So, now can you tell me your mom's dream?" I asked.

"Yes." He smiled. "She saw me across the sea with Z. Z held a mounded pile of salt in her hands. A great wind then blew and the salt covered me in shimmering crystals."

"From that she knew you had to come to Saint Augustine?"

He gave a short laugh. "She said it meant that Z needed my help and that I would meet with a great storm that would make me complete."

"So, did you? Get stuck in a storm, I mean."

He smiled and then squeezed my hand. "Eventually, yes." He looked intently into my eyes.

The great storm...Storm..."What? You think *I'm* the great storm?" I exclaimed, eyes wide with disbelief. I couldn't swallow. My pulse throbbed uncomfortably in my temples. "But I'm just an orphan Halfling, I'm sure your mom would have wanted more than *this* for her only son." I motioned to me with an offhanded wave.

Rowan stopped walking. His look, his eyes on me at this moment felt like a hug to my soul. "You are everything I have ever wanted. You are lovely and witty."

I smiled.

"You are hot tempered and stubborn..."

"Hey!"

"You are warm and smell like..."

He side stepped my punch to his shoulder.

"...spice and salt...and..." Rowan winked, "...you have a really cute butt!"

I lunged and hit him square in the chest. I had a much more advantageous landing, since he broke my fall. Rowan appeared a touch winded but his eyes still sparkled as he looked up at me through a curtain of my hair.

"My Storm," he whispered.

"My Rowan," I whispered back. He kissed me and then we stood back up, brushed off and followed our noses to Claude's Chocolates for a late afternoon treat of sea salt truffles.

******

"Hmmmm." I sighed and reluctantly left my memory of Rowan and the truffles. The present was much less comfortable as I stretched every inch of my body and, of course, felt sore all over.

So much had changed so very quickly. Each day I changed, grew, and became something so much more than I thought I was. I think I even got an A on my class paper that Rowan helped me with, although I had to edit out the parts about mer clans affecting weather patterns. Rowan was upset, but I didn't think it would have gone over well with the professors.

And yesterday, when Z, Sara, and Pearl returned, we all sat on our porch and I listened to stories of a world I had no idea even existed a few weeks ago.

"STORM! BREAKFAST!" Nana called.

"YEAH, COMIN' NANA!"

"DO YOU WANT JUICE OR MILK?"

Ugh! I climbed out of bed and pushed my hair out of my face. "JUICE...AND BACON!"

"PLEASE?" She called back.

"Please," I answered curtly.

"Hiya!" Pearl exclaimed as she bounded into the room and onto my bed. "Ooh, sorry, did I frighten you?"

Holding the edge of the dresser with white knuckles, I waited for my heart to return to its regular rhythm, "oh no, I'm fine."

Pearl giggled at me. "Are you ready for your lessons today?"

"Yeah, I guess. What are we gonna do?" I took my green bathing suit with me into the bathroom figuring that whatever we did would involve some sort of water.

"Hmm," Pearl chimed, "maybe some simple wave manipulation, wind induction and human attraction and repulsion."

"Oh," I replied though the closed door, "is that all?" Beads of nervous sweat dripped from my armpits. *Glad we're taking it slow,* I thought. I gulped a glass of salt water to quench my burning throat and relax my nerves a bit. It helped one out of two.

I met Pearl's shining eyes and glowing smile after I emerged from the protection of the bathroom. She looked like a kid about to go to Disney World. So happy and carefree. I wasn't happy and carefree. I worried about a lot of things. I figured that must be due to my human half. I knew now why men would follow her anywhere, even to their watery deaths because even though I am like her, I would follow that smile anywhere. *Will I have that power, too? Or maybe because I'm only half-mermaid I could only lure men to like swim a few laps in the pool.*

"What's so funny?" Pearl asked.

"Oh, nothin'. I just wondered, well, how do you do it?"

"Do what?" She asked. She played with one of the shiny sequins on my comforter cover.

"Always look so confident and happy?"

She stopped fiddling with the sequin and looked in my eyes. I couldn't have looked away if I wanted to, which I didn't. "Storm, you are the most beautiful creature I've ever met. And I'm not talking about your new appearance, which is absolutely stunning, my siren. You are pure and kind and one day, you will feel your strength, your confidence. Beauty is more than this," she motioned to her body, "the real magic comes from the light that shines from within. I've watched humans over the years find ways to create beautiful exteriors but without inner beauty, it still looks, well, ugly."

"Oh," I said and thought about her words. "So, this," now I looked in the mirror at my newly developed body, "this is..."

"Helpful," she said with a smile and walked over to where I stood. We looked in the mirror together. "But *this*," she put her hand first over my heart and then onto my forehead, "is where the true power and beauty resides."

I smiled. "Thanks."

"You're welcome." She kissed me lightly on both cheeks. "Now, let's get going sleeping beauty, Nana's got food all set out and then Rowan and Sara are meeting us at Lorelie's Point."

"Where?" I asked, as I pulled another one of my new tee shirts over my head, I took an extra glance at my reflection in the mirror. Sara was amazing at being able to pick out these clothes for me back before I was, well, before I looked like this! It was so hard to believe that the reflection I saw was me! I mean, the curves were unbelievable, but I still struggled to shine, like Pearl put it. I was getting the body, but the confidence lagged behind.

"You'll see. Come on my little water fairy!" Pearl hopped off the bed and grabbed hold of my wrist. Her strength was surprising even in her playful mood.

"Hang on a sec, let me grab my YOUCH!" I exclaimed as I dropped the moonstone ring to the ground and stuffed my right fingertips into my mouth.

"You okay?" Pearl asked.

"No, well, yeah, it's just that ring. Ouch." I sucked on my two fingers to stop the pain. "I picked it up and it was hot like fire. It totally burned my fingers!" I looked at them and sure enough, the tips of my thumb and pointer finger were red and pulsing and tiny blisters were forming.

"Who gave you that ring?"

"Paige, back when Sara and I went shopping," I answered as I nursed my sore fingers.

"Of course...Paige. Very clever cousin," Pearl whispered. She was lost in her thoughts but then looked back to me, "You need to cleanse it in salt water, Storm. Didn't Sara tell you that?"

"Well yeah, that's what I was going to do today during training. But what does that mean?"

"It means Paige is clever and you need to be more clever. Promise me after practice today you'll salt the ring."

"Okay. But why not now?"

"It'll burn you now. Wait until later, after I've gone."

"Okay."

She smiled. "Great, let's go!" She pulled me out of my room before I had a chance to contain my mane.

Nana was very quiet at breakfast. Dark circles highlighted her sleep-deprived eyes. She was in deep concentration on a conversation with Pearl. Pearl did enough talking for all three of us and her voice was so soothing to listen to, I really didn't want her to stop talking and didn't have much interest in talking to Nana. Their conversation was a continuation from last night. It was about finding Pearl's braid. Well, really about how it was taken in the first place. I just munched on my bacon and sipped on the salt ale Pearl brought over. The amber bottle wasn't beer after all, Pearl called it salt ale and it tasted sort of like a strong and slightly spicy ginger ale.

Conversations and stories from yesterday afternoon repeated themselves in my head as I sucked the salt from a piece of bacon...

"She was brilliant again today!" Rowan said. "A natural." He winked and my cheeks became uncomfortably warm.

"Well, of course she is!" A new voice chimed in. Pearl, beaming as she spoke, walked up the steps and Sara trailed closely behind. "Is this a private party or can any mermaid join?" Sara asked with a laugh. They gracefully crossed the deck and gave Z hugs. They sat in the empty chairs and tucked their legs under them just as Z did. Pearl gave me a wink. I glowed inside.

Snacks of olives and sliced Parmesan cheese were on the table and the conversation din grew and ebbed with intermittent refreshing sips and deliciously salty nibbles.

Z, with a warm smile, drew the meeting to order after we all had a chance to get our own exciting tales out of the way. "We must begin our preparations for this year's Solstice Gathering, a very important one for our newest child." Z tipped her glass toward me.

"Can't we postpone this year?" Pearl asked.

"My love, we have pushed it as far as we can. In addition to the transition ceremony, I must make arrangements as it appears we have failed to recover it," Z answered.

"What arrangements?" I asked.

At this question, Pearl looked up. Her eyes were tinged red.

"During the summer of 1873," Pearl said, "Sara and I worked as nannies. It was such a busy time with the new lighthouse being built. We were in charge of the children and trying to keep an eye on one of the builders."

A memory came to my mind. A story, a picture in a book...

"Oh my God! Did you kill those children?" The words blurted from my mouth before I could stop them.

"No! Well, yes, well, not really," Pearl stammered.

"I did it," Sara replied softly. "It was an accident."

"I was on my way to talk to Kate about the accident when the builder we were keeping an eye on, Lewis Tressman, stopped me."

"Lewis Tressman?" I shot a glance at Nana.

"His eyes were fierce with rage and his breath smelled strongly of some white liquor he used to make in house. He grabbed at my dress and pushed me to the ground. I fought him with ease and to my own fault, let my guard down when he told me he had been praying to the Hurricane Lady after the deaths of the children and *she* told him what I was. He rushed at me. It wasn't until the pain tore through my body that I realized what he'd done." Pearl's hand reached to her head, her missing braid like a phantom limb, only the memory of the pain remained.

My hand unconsciously touched my braid. The bells tinkled softly from the end. But then my eye caught sight of Z's braid, it was intricate like Paige's, like the drawing Jon showed me, the Mermaid's Knot. Suddenly her words from earlier rang with new meaning, 'ruling family', Z was a ruler, she had the intricate braid, the symbol of the ruler. Paige had one also, she must be the heir to her clan, some kind of fish. Sara had a simple braid like mine, Pearl had no braid, but once upon a time...

I gasped with the sudden realization. "Pearl, you're the heir to this territory?"

She smiled subtly. "Yes, or at least I was until my braid was taken. Now without it, there is no longer a rightful heir. If we don't find it in time, or have another female descendant to take the place, then this territory, the rest of the Atlantic, and Sea Star clan, will belong to Z's twin sister, Laverna.

"Laverna rules the North Atlantic, their Clan symbol is the Lionfish." Rowan answered my look of confusion.

"But this *is* the North Atlantic," I replied, even more confused.

"Yes, it is and that is why Laverna desperately wants to regain control of this town and its waters," Z replied.

"How long can a clan be without an heir?" I asked; letting go of the geography issues for the moment.

"An heir must be designated within two and half Calendar Rounds," Pearl said.

"Just shy of 150 years," Rowan whispered to me. "The time is up at the new moon following this summer's solstice."

"What about Sara?" I asked. "She's your daughter, too, couldn't she..."

"You cannot choose another from the same generation. Z chose Pearl as the first born female." Sara answered; her voice seemed a bit cold. *Perhaps a touch of sibling rivalry there*, I thought. *Oh! That's probably why she got so cranky after I complimented Paige's braid, Sara will never be heir while Paige will be.*

"The royal braid is only given from ruling mother to one daughter at the Solstice Party during the daughter's coming of age," Z explained. "It replaces the Braid of Mar that denotes all female offspring. The daughter, in turn, can designate one to her daughter when she comes of age and so on. You cannot have more than one ruling daughter within a generation, which is why Sara cannot simply replace Pearl as chosen heir. Many a territory has shifted hands due to either a lack of female descendants, untimely deaths, or mishaps of a chosen heir."

"Don't you and your sister get along?" I asked.

Z sighed. "We are a bit of a special circumstance. We are twins, as Pearl mentioned, and therefore have divided the Atlantic equally as per my mother's designation. What was once one territory is now two. However, being twins doesn't mean we share many common beliefs. My sister holds little regard for human life and very high regard for power. An event long ago, resulting in our mother's death and solidifying Saint Augustine as a permanent residence for our clan, tore us apart. We've yet to recover our bond. We, Laverna and I, do meet peacefully each year as per my mother's final request. We are true to our mother, but it is simply from duty rather than emotional desire. I still vow to protect and my sister still vows to take or destroy." Z spoke those last words with a twitch of her lip that looked like the start of a smile, like the difference between her and her sister were some sort of drawn out game of chess, a battle of wills and wits. "But on the one night of the year we meet, we try to put aside our differences and allow the clans to relax. We celebrate coming of age ceremonies, rejoice in any clan marriages and mourn losses. We meet where we do, at the crossing of the Ley lines; where energy is neutral and magic is pure of heart, so that neither can take advantage of the other. We are all on equal footing as it were."

"But if the missing braid is found?" I asked.

"Then Pearl can take her place as heir and Laverna will have no more hold over our territory than she does now," Z answered. "But despite all of the generations of chosen female descendants of Kate Harn who put in valiant and oftentimes dangerous efforts to find Pearl's long lost braid during the past century, we are now nearly out of time. Rean, I can't thank you enough for all you have done. We owe you and your ancestors a world of thanks. You have kept us focused over the centuries as well as kept our secret."

I turned my attention to Nana. She was so quiet and small looking but a fire burned in her eyes. "I'm not through yet my dear friend," Nana said.

"I can help," I said. "Jon said we could..."

"No," Nana replied in what I call her "mom voice". "You are not to help with this task."

"But..." I protested.

"I agree, Storm. We need you safe and sound for the Solstice. Transition is a hard time for any mer and I think my sister will challenge you even harder than most."

"No buts," Nana said with a slight scowl which I returned right back to her.

Z smiled then, perhaps to break the tension. "Time, Rean, as I mentioned before, is not on our side. You've done all you can. You and Miles both."

Who's Miles? I wondered.

"How do you even know it's still around, Nana?" I asked just to stay included in the conversation.

"Braids are energetically connected to the mermaid," Z answered. "Even when removed, by choice or otherwise, the connection remains. If the braid was destroyed, Pearl would also have perished. And likewise, if Pearl is killed, the braid would turn to salt. Pearl and the Braid can live separately as they have been but not for much longer." Pearl's face paled at Z's statement. *So it wasn't just the clan's future at stake, but also Pearl's*, I thought.

Being part of a royal line must be so stressful. And here I thought my training was hard; poor Pearl had the entire future of her territory resting on her sunkissed shoulders. *Not just a beautiful face*, I thought.

"Mermaids are so complicated," Rowan said.

"You don't know the half of it," Sara replied. And we broke into fits of laughter as only great tensions can bring on. Like a release of sorts, it felt good to laugh.

"So, Laverna seems pretty keen on getting her hands on this territory," Rowan said after our laughter subsided, "and not so keen about human or mer life, why doesn't she just flatten the place and get it over with? Destroy Saint Augustine, the braid, Pearl, you..."

"Well, for one thing, as long as this is my territory her powers are weak within the boundaries. There have been a couple of attempts to mess with our town, but none were overly successful." Z looked over to Rean whose gaze shifted to the distant water as she took a long, slow sip of her wine. "Secondly, if Laverna were to destroy me, our mother's designation of our territorial division would be no more and then our Auntie in the Pacific would have claims to both of our territories. Neither of us may die by the hand of the other, directly or indirectly. No, Laverna doesn't want to kill me. Being in possession of Pearl's braid, and as a result, in possession of Pearl, heir to the territory, is her intent. It would giver her the ability to go around our mother's final ruling put in place just before her death." Z smiled a sad smile and her eyes became distant. When she returned from wherever her mind had taken her, her voice was no more than a whisper in the wind, "And that, my children, is enough for today."

"So, Storm," Pearl spoke with an extra lightness, "now you know why you need to get some rest and continue your training. We need you ready to kick serious tail for the party!"

"What do I have to do at the party?" I asked, all worries of territories and power disputes flung from my mind at the thought of my own impending challenge and most likely embarrassment.

"That's when you'll be welcomed as an official member of our clan, silly girl!" Sara chimed.

"Oh," I said. "Will it hurt?"

"Not much," Rowan said.

Everybody laughed again.

He's just kidding me, I thought, *right?*

******

"Stormy, you ready to head to the Point for your lessons?" Pearl asked cheerfully.

I looked up and the memories faded. Nana and Pearl were done with their discussions. I forced the last bit of bacon past the newly formed lump in my throat.

Chapter Fourteen

Two ancient looking beach bikes leaned against our porch rail. *Held together by rust and a prayer*, I thought with a laugh. But apparently the laugh was on me when Pearl stopped next to them. I looked from the bikes to Pearl and then back to the bikes.

"No, no, no." I said with a shake of my head.

"Yes, yes, yes!" She smiled.

I frowned. "You're kidding, right?"

"What do ya mean?" She climbed onto the one that at some time in the far distant past may have been red.

"I mean it's like already a zillion degrees and we're gonna have to ride not just bikes somewhere, but *these* bikes somewhere?"

"Well, yeah, they'll get us where we need to go. What did you think we were going to do, swim?"

"Ha ha, okay, really, what are we doing?"

"Really, hop on! We've got to get going if we want to reach the point before noon. These classics haven't any gears so it'll be good exercise for your legs." She must have noticed I didn't move any closer to the nineteen seventies circa bikes. "Stormy, you need to build your endurance! You never know when you'll be trapped too deep. You need to be strong to survive that. You're nearly physically mature for a mermaid so you don't have much time left to build your strength. Not to mention, I *love* when the wind tickles my skin!" Her face as sweet as a grinning toddler, she giggled and a gentle breeze picked up around her.

"Seriously? We're mermaids and we're riding bikes."

"Yeah, seriously. Come on!" She took off up and over the beach walkway and through the deliriously soft sand to reach the water's edge. Her delighted giggles drifted back and sounded like the mocking calls of the sea gulls. I fell over three times before I finally gave up on riding. I ended up pushing my fossil bike to the water.

Sweat dripped from every pore of my body by the time I reached her and I smelled like the debris line baking in the morning sun. She waited patiently as I struggled to the packed sand. Her face was turned into the north wind and she giggled as her hair brushed her neck and back.

And they call me *a child*, I thought.

"All set?" She smiled at me when I finally reached her.

"Just a sec," I panted and pressed one hand on my side. "Cramp."

She giggled.

"I'm not having fun yet, just so you know."

"I know." She smiled and turned back to the North wind. "Let me know when you're ready."

"Hmph." I took deep breaths and eventually the grip on my side released and I felt okay. "What did you mean I'm nearly mature?"

"Leading up to the solstice following your sixteenth birthday, a mer transitions from human aging to mer aging. It's a period of rapid change, growth, and physical development. It's a hard time, tiring and sometimes painful."

I nodded, Rowan had mentioned that. I thought of all the growing pains and feeling feverish and sick. I seemed to be doing better now...despite my cardiovascular shortcomings.

"It all ends on the solstice when you will be physically mature." Pearl looked at me, "So, although your mind will continue to develop, your body will stay basically the same. We need to get you as physically strong as possible because after the solstice there's not much physically you can change."

"Oh." I looked down at my body. So this was nearly the finished product. There was just so much I never knew about mermaids, so much that wasn't in the fairy tales or the myths. Of course, who knew the myths were actually based on the fact that mers really existed. I suppose that was a pretty big detail to hit spot on.

"You've already figured out why we use the lotion?"

"Well..." I was embarrassed.

"Don't worry, Storm, every mer goes through this time. Your body is shifting so rapidly that the energy is released through sweat and in turn through scent. It isn't really a bad scent. I've been told by some that it is a bit addictive, like puppy breath. But it is rather distinctive which is why it's helpful to mask it with the lotion."

"Who told you that, about the addictive thing?"

"Oh," Pearl looked away, "a human I used to know."

"Oh."

"So, enough talk, let's get going."

"Fine." I tried to smile.

Lorelie's Point was literally the northernmost point of St. Augustine Beach. I recognized it as the place Rowan stood as he teased our marine science boat a few weeks ago. Recognizing it was easy, getting there was an entirely different matter. Apparently, merpeople are very fit. I'm not yet one of those people. The first mile wasn't so bad, but we just kept going and going.

When we reached the end of the land, Pearl dropped her bike and gracefully skipped up onto the rocks. She looked refreshed and full of vigor. I felt like a half-dead hippo and collapsed next to the rip rap as I fought to catch my breath, again.

"How far was that?"

"Hmm, about five miles, I suppose. Here, drink some." She handed me a perspiring amber bottle of salt ale from her backpack. I rubbed the cool bottle on my forehead and then drank.

My throat was once again moist and my limbs felt rejuvenated from the salt. Biking was much harder than swimming.

"This is one of the few places that we can just let our hair down, so to speak." Pearl took her hair out of the clip that held it back. She, of course, didn't have any chimes singing from the end of a braid. I stared a moment, too long perhaps.

"Go on, Stormy, let your hair down. It'll feel delicious."

"Okay," I said. I was nervous remembering the effect the braid's chimes had on humans, but then I realized what Pearl meant. There wasn't another soul around us. We were all alone. And she was right, it felt wonderful!

We, Pearl and I, sat together in silence for a few minutes. Our eyes closed, our faces toward the sun, our hair down which tickled our backs and the tiny bells from my braid sang their lighthearted tune.

"Did it hurt?" I asked tentatively without looking at her.

"Yes." Her voice was no more than a whisper carried on the wind.

"Are you scared of not finding it in time?"

"Yes."

"Why can't I help look for it?"

"Because we don't want to take any chance with you."

I didn't ask any more questions.

I like Pearl, I thought. I felt somehow connected to her even though we'd only known each other for a few weeks.

"Hiya!" A soprano chime rang.

"Sorry we're late, Sara's fault."

Rowan and Sara emerged from the water in front of us. They argued the entire way as they approached out little camp.

"Was not, Rowan," Sara said.

"Yeah, whatever," Rowan said.

"I'll *yeah whatever*, you," Sara said.

"Clever, did you think of that all by yourself or did a toddler write it down for you?" Rowan said.

"Children, children. Come on and let's get started," Pearl said.

Rowan and Sara quieted but as I turned to look, I saw Rowan give a playful shove to Sara. Sara stuck her tongue out in response.

Wait a minute. I thought.

"Hey!" I said as I stood up. "Pearl, you said we couldn't swim here."

"No, I said we *wouldn't* swim here. Sara and Rowan don't need the training for their muscles like you do," Pearl replied.

Sara laughed.

I scowled.

My body, still sore from yesterday's swim and the day before that and well, the entire week, was already feeling the new muscle strain from the ride. I thought being a mermaid was all sitting on rocks combing your hair. I had no idea it was actually more like boot camp.

"Alright, let's," Pearl began but interrupted herself, "Rowan, Sara, quit it!" She said with a stamp of her foot and a glare in the direction of the still-fighting mers. I laughed because that's exactly what I did when Nana or Dad made me mad.

"Let's begin Stormy." She emphasized each word as she glared Sara and Rowan into submission. Once they were seated on the rocks with us, she turned back to me, "now Storm, I believe you and Rowan have been practicing the basics of swimming. Still going well?"

"She rocks!" Rowan replied. He gave me a little nudge with his leg.

"Thanks," I said and nudged him back.

"Oh God, get a room, you two," Sara said.

"How many miles have you been taking her?" Pearl asked Rowan, ignoring Sara's comment.

"We've been working up to nearly 50. She still tires around 30," he answered.

"Okay, keep it up because we need her hitting 50 by the Solstice," Pearl replied. "How's the navigation going?"

"Better," Rowan said with a wink directed to me.

I winced remembering last week when he had me lead us back to shore and we ended up flying North in the gulfstream. *Oops.*

"Okay, well I'm not too worried about that because we'll get more into that during the night lessons," Pearl said. I noticed Sara wrinkle her nose like she had just smelled something offensive.

"Storm, what two things do you have to be aware of when you swim?" Pearl asked.

"Depth and water clarity," I answered.

"Good," Pearl said. "Why?"

"Because I need the energy of the sun and if I go too deep, the sun's rays don't penetrate. Also, if the water is very murky, the sun won't penetrate."

"Good, you're right on all accounts! Nicely taught, Rowan."

He smiled and winked at me.

God he's hot. I thought. *Especially all glistening and shirtless. So many perfect muscles, such a tight tanned belly...*

"AHEM, Stormy!" Pearl spoke. Sara giggled and rolled her eyes.

"Huh?" Wide-eyed like a child caught with her hand in the cookie jar, I looked at Pearl.

"Thanks for joining us again. I was saying that today we're going to practice manipulation of the elements. I asked if you knew how we exert our will over others and over the elements like waves and wind." Pearl's eyebrows were raised and there a slight smirk on her lips. It was as if she knew what I thinking about. I looked down at my foot. It was dangling in the water. I looked around the circle and everybody's feet were in the water.

DANG IT, I thought. *She...they did know what I was thinking about because they could read my stupid mind since our stupid feet were all in the stupid water.*

Totally embarrassed, I pulled my foot back onto the dry rock.

"Later, love. When we're not practicing to save our world," Rowan whispered and rolled his eyes toward Pearl.

I gave him a quick sideways glance then tried to focus on the lesson. "Umm, sorry, waves and wind? Umm..." I stammered.

"Energy," Pearl answered. "It's all energy. We exert our will, our energy onto others or onto elements. It requires focus and stamina. You can't be wishy-washy about your desire and you must set your intentions wisely."

"But how does it work?"

"It has to do with what mers are made of. We are mostly salt and salt is made of ions. Meaning when it dissolves in water, it has a charge; a positive and negative quality to it. Like magnets, our entire being is set up to either attract or repel depending on how we direct our energy and focus."

"Why can't humans do the same thing?"

"Too much water, not enough salt. Humans don't have enough ions in their system to create enough polar charge. Okay, let's begin," Pearl said.

"Finally," Sara said and then yawned.

Rowan and Sara shifted into a line with Pearl. Not sure what I was supposed to do, I scooted into a line with the rest of them.

"Okay Rowan, why don't you start us off with a two foot wave traveling west."

I watched Rowan's eyes focus on the water of the inlet and a subtle tension wrinkle appear in the corner of his right eye. Looking over to the water a bulge appeared and it grew into a sizeable wave.

"Steady now, not too big. Back it off a bit," Pearl advised.

The wave, seemingly acting of its own accord grew and then shrunk and then steadied itself. It began to move to our left, slowly at first, but then gathered speed.

"Steady...control..." The wave sped up and grew bigger.

"Rowan, back it off, come on, we're supposed to be teaching not showing off," Pearl scolded.

His eyes squinted more and he smiled a wicked grin. I could tell subtlety wasn't his strong suit. Keeping a small wave moving slowly was boring for him.

"Rowan..." Pearl's voice warned but the wave kept moving and growing until suddenly it reconsidered and reversed its direction of travel. It sped toward us and crashed over our heads.

"Hey!" Sara protested.

"Rowan, you have to practice the fine tunings, doing *less*," Pearl chided. She was still dry.

"Oh balls, it's just so damned boring," Rowan said and laughed at Sara who was now soaking wet. He shook his head side to side to dry off.

"Okay Storm. You try to make a wave," Pearl said, trying to keep a straight face after Rowan's example.

"How?"

"Just think of the water doing what you want it to do. Imagine molding it with your hands like soft clay. If you make it your truth, it will happen."

Sounded simple enough. I stared at the moving water sloshing by us with the incoming tide. I imagined pushing the water together like a pile of sand.

Nothing happened.

"You have to *want* it and believe it," Sara added. "Like *make* it do what you want!"

I thought about picking up piles of water with my hands.

Nothing.

I imagined myself splashing the water like a child.

Not even a ripple out of the ordinary.

My mind was full of wave images but unfortunately, they were limited to my mind only. The actual water did nothing in response to my thoughts.

Finally tired and frustrated after ten fruitless minutes, I let out a huff and slouched back.

"I can't do it," I said.

"Whether you think you can or you can't, you're right," Pearl replied. "Try again."

Sara reclined on the rocks and twirled her fingers in the water of the tide pool below us. Rowan sent waves across the inlet to splash unsuspecting beach-goers. I tried my hardest to muster a ripple and got the same exact, frustrating results.

My new lessons as a mermaid were not going so hot. After hours of maddening work, Pearl declared it lunch time. *Nobody ever told me this whole mermaid thing was going to involve hard work. I'd rather just stick with swimming and maybe add in some reclining on rocks like Sara.*

Reaching into her pack, Pearl pulled out four tinfoil wrapped packages.

"Please tell me you remembered to ask for extra hummus," Sara called over.

"Yes, sister dear. Here you go." Pearl hopped back onto the rocks and handed one of the packages over to Sara.

"And no tomatoes, right?" Rowan asked.

"Yes, Rowan." She handed another package over. "You two get worse by the century!" Pearl said as she rolled her eyes and laughed.

"Here you go, Storm." Pearl handed me a foil package. "I wasn't sure of your specific high maintenance needs," Pearl looked over to Rowan and Sara, "so I just got you the same as I like."

This was my first meal with other mers. I opened the tin foil slowly. *What if mermaids eat fish heads or eel skin or something?* I worried. *What if they eat raw lobster or sea lettuce or...*

I looked around. Everybody was munching happily. In my hands lay a delicious looking veggie wrap stuffed with tomatoes, cucumbers, sprouts, olives, creamy garlic dressing and hummus.

Rowan saw my surprised look. "What'd you think? That we ate fish heads or something?" He asked.

"No!" I said with a snort. "Of course not." I took a big bite.

"So who're you meeting tonight Sara?" Rowan asked in between bites.

"This cute human boy I met yesterday at the PIT. He's taking me for drinks."

"Please be more careful with this one, Sara," Pearl said.

"It's not my fault they always try to show off," Sara replied.

"Um, it sort of is."

Sara laughed. "Well, maybe a little, but whatever, a girl's gotta' have a wee bit of fun, right? I mean we've been stuck in this stupid town forever. It's hard to keep things lively."

"What happened last time?" I asked.

"Oh, just some poor bloke Sara was stringing along nearly drowned when they went out for a midnight swim," Rowan said.

"Oops," Sara said with a girlish giggle. "I told him he wouldn't be able to beat me to the channel marker, it's not my fault he didn't believe me."

"You have a bit of an unfair advantage, don't ya think sis?" Pearl said.

"Whatever. He didn't actually drown, remember?"

"Yeah, thanks to Pearl," Rowan said.

"Oh, I had it under control," Sara said. "He could have stayed under a few more minutes before any permanent damage was done. Besides, *Mr. Surf Instructor*, what about that little cutie last summer? Explain *that* one!"

"What?" Rowan asked, his face the image of innocence.

"Yeah, what?" I asked, not quite sure I wanted to hear about 'some cutie from last summer', but curious enough to find out if she lived. *What was it Paige had warned me about with Rowan? 'Many have tried to catch him, but he's as slippery as an eel.'*

"Look, waves happen," Rowan said offhandedly.

"Yes they do," Pearl said, "however, waves that strip bikinis off of women in the middle of their surf lesson *don't* happen all that often."

Sara and Pearl laughed. I blushed at the thought of some poor girl stuck naked in the ocean.

"Exactly! Freak thing!" Rowan said with a grin. "Thank goodness I was there to rescue her. Poor girlie, held on so tight. She was so grateful that..." Rowan looked up at me, "that, well, really, that's an old story. Isn't it time we get back to our practice?"

Rowan threw some of his sprouts at Sara. Sara, in turn, lobbed hummus back at him, but hit Pearl so Pearl tried to toss tomatoes at Sara, but they flew apart and some splattered against my arm.

"Hey!" I protested. Before I knew it, a full-fledged food fight had started. It was every mer for themselves.

Sprouts, cucumbers, hummus, tomatoes and olives covered us all by the time we finished.

Rowan bounded to my side, grabbed my hand and shouted, "Time to rinse!" My feet left the sand and my body was pulled beneath the water's surface before I even knew what hit me.

I shook my head underwater to clear it.

Oops, you must have fallen in the water, gorgeous, Rowan spoke in my head.

Really..., I thought back.

Yeah, crazy stuff, huh? He laughed. He wiped away some stubborn hummus from my left arm. Small blue and yellow striped fish swam over to eat the floating bits.

You are the most beautiful little mermaid in the world, my darling. He said. Then he kissed me tenderly on the forehead. *Even covered in hummus!*

Thanks! I thought. *You're not so bad yourself.*

Feeling protected by our veil of water, I let him kiss me on the lips without embarrassment. His salty lips tasted divine. *Now this part of being a mermaid is pretty cool.* Our hair danced together under the water and our weightless bodies wrapped together. We drifted, underwater, out of the inlet, letting the tide have its way with us. I could have very happily stayed kissing Rowan forever.

Tick tock tick tock. Sara's voice broke into my head.

I looked behind Rowan and saw Sara and Pearl. They also drifted happily, wiping bits of food off of them and laughing at the fish coming to feast after our folly.

Hey Sara! Rowan called, *I'm full of holes and yet still full of water. What am I?*

Your head! Sara said with a giggle.

Ha Ha. Rowan said. *But no. Pearl?*

A sponge. Pearl said.

How does she always figure the riddles out so quickly? I wondered.

Lots of practice, Pearl said. *And speaking of practice, let's get back at it. The Solstice will be here before we know it.*

Climbing back onto the rocks, we split into two groups. Rowan and Sara practiced making waves jump over other waves. I practiced staring at a motionless tide pool, which Sara so nicely described as the baby pool, while Pearl tried to give encouraging advice.

Great, I thought, *being a teenager as a human was embarrassing enough, now I have to start over again as a mer.* It was all so easy for the other three. I mean Rowan's big issue was making waves and storms TOO big. Sara and Pearl didn't even have to try, waves just wanted to do their bidding.

I was nearly in tears with frustration. *Maybe my mom, whoever she is, isn't a very talented mermaid, either.*

"Pearl? Do you know who my mom is?" At my question, Sara and Rowan's waves collided and created such a large standing wave that both our side and the Vilano Beach side of the inlet got swamped.

"Yes, I do," Pearl answered simply.

"What's she like? I mean, is she good at this stuff?" I motioned around me to the water and the air.

"Storm, your mother is one of the best."

"Oh. Why did she leave us... Dad, Nana, and me? Did she not want me because I was only a half-mer?" Memories of the words that mean mer said the day I first swam with Rowan kept haunting me at random times.

"Oh no, Storm. That wasn't it at all. She loved you with all of her heart. In fact, she loved you and your dad with all of her heart but the only way to save the both of you was to let you go until it was safe for you to return."

"What do you mean?"

"Well, you were in danger as an infant. Mer children are similar to human children. They aren't nearly as indestructible as mature mers. It wasn't safe for you to be here until you reached maturity. It broke your mom's heart when you left, but she knew it was the only way."

"When will I see her?"

"At the party. But, you have to complete transition and I'm afraid we don't have much time to get you fully trained. So, let's get back at it, kiddo. Let's give the water a rest and play with the air!"

Prepared for another frustrating lesson, I was pleasantly surprised to find that I was much better at wind manipulation. *Dad did always say I was full of hot air*, I thought sarcastically.

I successfully knocked shells and even small rocks off ledges with varying strengths of wind. Like the waves, Rowan had trouble *not* tumbling the jetty rocks into the ocean with his tornado-like bursts.

"But I knocked the bloody little rock off just the same, right?" He complained.

Pearl simply shook her head.

Toward the end of the afternoon when the sun's angle increased and our shadows were stretched like funhouse mirror reflections before us, Pearl called it quits.

"It's about time," Sara complained.

Pearl pulled out some more salt ale for us to drink.

"I'm sure you have plenty of time to get ready and look stunning, sis," Pearl said.

"I already have stunning down, I'm thinking of going for drop-dead fabulous!" Sara said with a flourish of her hair.

"Please, not drop-dead," Pearl begged.

"Oh, okay spoil sport. Just fabulous then...perhaps a touch of take your breath away?" Sara winked at me. I think she thoroughly enjoyed toying with humans.

"Sis, I was wondering something," Sara said as she took a few sips of her drink.

"No, you can't play an underwater breath hold game with the boy."

"No, not that, but, *really*? Not even a short one?" Sara asked.

"No," Pearl said.

"Oh well, doesn't matter anyway, that isn't what I wanted to know."

Rowan and I laughed quietly at the two of them. He held my hand and I leaned lightly against his sun-warmed side.

"I wonder what the Hurricane Lady would do to Storm? I mean, she's only *half*-mer, so maybe the statue wouldn't mess with her like it does us."

"What are you getting at?" Pearl asked.

"I was just thinking, you know, we've all tried it. Maybe a Halfling could get up close and..."

"Are you mad? Maybe the human half would be okay, but the mer half would die trying," Pearl said. She sounded angry.

"I'm just saying I was wondering about it, that's all. I mean, Stormy," Sara looked at me, "we've all tried it, wouldn't it be fun..."

"Wait, tried what? What's the Hurricane Lady? *The name sounded familiar, but I couldn't remember from where.*

"The Hurricane Lady is a story told to all young mers here. It's about this guarded statue kept in an old museum downtown," Rowan answered.

"Oh it's more than a story!" Sara exclaimed. "She's deadly to mers. If we go too close to her, we can die. The legend part is that what she takes, she also gives. So, although she may take a life, she gives one back in return! And although mers may die trying, a half-mer, well..."

Before I could respond, Pearl shot back, "Get off it Sara. Stop trying to get Stormy to do stupid things. It's the girls all over again. We're supposed to be protecting her, not trying to get her killed!

"It is nothing like the girls, Pearl. But thanks for bringing them up again." Sara's voice was low and ominous. The wind picked up around us. "Everyone's been thinking the same thing about Storm, but I'm the only one to voice it. She may be the one. And by the way, if it weren't for the search for your stupid braid, I'd have been out of this dull town decades ago!"

"Quit it! She's a baby for God's sake. You just thrive on the drama without a thought for repercussions. And if you want to leave, leave. By all means, dear sister, don't stay on my account."

Pearl and Sara continued their argument. Their voices, so lovely just moments ago became menacing sounding hisses. Their faces contorted into angry masks and the muscles on their arms and back became pronounced. They looked really scary. The water in the inlet grew steeply sided, choppy waves and the wind swirled. Again the words came to my brain, 'what Z says, they do.' and with those words my insecurities rose to the surface and grew larger. Nobody cared about me, they only cared about keeping me safe for some duty or position I was supposed to fulfill. A duty that nobody would even tell me about. Just 'be good', 'do as your told', 'don't ask questions', and my favorite 'when it's time'. God! And now this stupid Hurricane Lady thing. Pearl and Sara fighting over me. My family torn apart because of me. Just "STOP ALREADY!" I shouted.

My hands were balled in angry fists and my voice rang out like thunder. In the same moment the waves and the wind all stopped. The inlet reflected the sky like a mirror and the heat blanketed us as all the wind seemed to be sucked away like in a vortex. 'Every action has an equal and opposite reaction.' Newton's third Law of Motion echoed in my head. And the equal and opposite action to my stopping everything dead still was something near to a mini hurricane that soaked us instantly with a wall of water from both the inlet and the sky. Lightning sparked from the black clouds overhead to the ground around us, wind howled and blew sand at our bodies so hard it felt like being hit by a million tiny shards of glass.

"Storm," Pearl's voice cut through the wind and wall of rain easily.

I turned to look at her. I picked out 3 outlines of Pearl, Sara, and Rowan through the sheets of rain. My mind still somewhere between anger, resentment, and guilt. The air and downpouring water had a pink tinge.

"Reel in that feeling. Focus it!"

"WHAT?" I screamed angrily. "I DON'T WANT TO F..." But I stopped talking. The air was still tinged and I knew I had created this out-pouring of energy but for the first time it didn't feel uncontrollable, even as big and strong as it was.

More to spite them for treating me like a china doll than for any learn-ing aspect, I focused on a spot in the water and reaching out with the now orange-tinged shimmery air, pulled at the liquid and made it mound. Sur-rounding the shimmery mercury-like tendrils were little pockets of blue and green that moved to my desires. They were the wind, nothing more than a thin haze compared to the thick, bright shimmer of the water-mov-ing energy.

I am totally moving water, I thought! *I am controlling the wind. Take that Pearl, Sara, Rowan, Z, Nana, Mom, and you stupid coward who tried to kill me.*

My breath slowed and my anger ebbed. The colors faded, the seas calmed, and the wind died away. I clung to the last of the visible energy but then it was gone and I felt exhausted. I sat down heavily onto the soft sand.

"Well done!" Pearl and Rowan came over to give me hugs in turn. Sara stayed where she was.

"I thought that may work," Sara said indifferently as she shook her hair dry.

The three of us looked at her. Answering our confused looks with a shrug she said, "oh don't get your tails all tied up in knots. I just thought she needed a little encouragement to tap into her emotions is all. Guess I was right." She winked at me.

I wasn't sure if I wanted to thank Sara or hit her.

"Well, everybody, a successful day," Pearl said, I think more to break the tension than anything else. "Come on Storm, let's head back!" She smiled brightly at me. I smiled back, but a small ember of my anger and my insecurity over their real motives behind hanging out with me burned within.

******

The bike ride back home was quiet. We had the wind at our backs and the sun was nearly below the roof line on the western horizon. The tide was out so we rode smoothly over the packed sand. Every now and then, I thought I saw Rowan and Sara leap from the water beyond the breakers.

I bet I could take on the Hurricane Lady if I wanted to, whatever that meant, I thought. And I bet I could figure out the stupid Tressman mystery, too. I didn't notice Pearl had slowed her pace to mine.

"Storm, you okay?" Pearl asked as she rode on my left. Her eyebrows were wrinkled with a look of concern. "I mean, you did really great today for your first manipulation lesson and all." Her voice was no more than a whisper, but I could hear her perfectly. I understood mermaid ears now; the reason my hearing had always been so good. They're designed to interpret sounds underwater where sound travels so much faster so picking up sounds in air is no problem at all.

"Yeah, I s'pose."

"This time is hard on all mers. It's when you have to learn to make the unconscious become conscious. You're picking it all up really quickly, honest!" She smiled. "I remember when Sara came of age. She was hopeless, not for lack of skill, but all she wanted to do was manipulate." Pearl laughed at some private memory. "It was a pretty crazy time for all the teenage boys. I couldn't leave her side for months, scared she'd take it too far."

"But what about what she said with the Hurricane Lady."

"No. That was all talk. She was just trying to get a reaction from me knowing it would get a reaction from you. Manipulation is still Sara's strongest trait. The Hurricane Lady is not something you can take on. Many have tried to challenge her and none, as far as I know, have succeeded. Besides, the whole life for a life thing is just a myth. The Hurricane

Lady is just plain evil and deadly for mers."

"But what is it?"

"It's a statue that was made ages ago by some mer with some very dark magic. That mer manipulated humans to transport it from Spain to the Americas. The story is that it caused havoc all across the ocean. Mers fought each other the entire way trying to get a hold of it to bring someone back or trade someone in for another. It has caused nothing but trouble since its creation. The ship, as you may imagine had a horrendous journey and nearly sank many times. It did, however, eventually reach the shores of Saint Augustine."

"When was this?" I asked.

"Just after the last big gathering, late 1700's, or early 1800's I suppose. It was why we came here, actually. Z was asked to protect the statue and in turn protect all mers. That's what started the real troubles between the Lionfish Clan and our own. I mean, this used to be their territory until Z and Laverna's mother chose Z over Laverna to be the protector of the Hurricane Lady. And since then, we've been in Saint Augustine, the heirs of the Sea Star Clan, rulers of the South Atlantic, ruling part of the North Atlantic...and also having some fun protecting this little town." She smiled with a private memory.

That was it! Humpphrey's story about the Angels mentioned the Hurricane Lady.

"Have you ever gone near it?"

Pearl laughed. "Of course."

"And?"

"I made it just inside the door before I fainted."

I smiled. *So not even Pearl is perfect.*

"What if I'm not ready for the Solstice Party?"

"You'll be fine. I know it."

"But what if I don't want to? I mean, what if I just want to hang out and not take my place in the clan?"

"Well, it would mean disaster for us all. We need you, Storm. You have a very special place in our clan once you make it through transition. It's going to get more dangerous for you, not less, the closer we get to the solstice. The problem is, not every mer wants to see you succeed."

Pearl's eyes locked on mine. They were bright green and beautiful. We had just gotten back to the house and straddled our bikes at the edge of the high tide line. "Remember that, Stormy," Pearl whispered, "your success means..."

"HEY SLOWPOKES!" Rowan called to us.

Pearl and I turned toward the water. Sara and Rowan bounded toward us at a jog. I looked back to Pearl. *I was so close; she was going to tell me something.*

"A lot," Pearl said quietly.

"Seriously?" My heart thudded, my mind raced. *I had been so close. Damn. If only Rowan hadn't yelled out. If only...* Rowan interrupted my thought by pulling me from the bike and spinning me in a circle in his arms. He gave me a kiss.

"Hello darling. Imagine meeting you here," he said with a smile. His body dripped with seawater and now, the front of me dripped as well.

I laughed despite my disappointment. He was such a big kid. Mers may live to be thousands of years old, they may be strong in body and manipulative of mind, but the innocence of childhood seems to overrule everything else.

And along with the innocence, comes the attention span of a flea. With Rowan so close to me, the only thing I could concentrate on was his glistening skin and his delicious smell. My mind had already lost its focus on my worries about my mother, my stress over my control issues and my concern over whether Sara's behavior was kind or cruel.

So quickly distracted, I thought. *Like a cat with a shiny object. Rowan is my shiny object.*

I buried my head in Rowan's wet, salty hair. His strong arms wrapped tightly about me and I felt the warm sand under my feet disappear and the sensation of spinning take over. I dove into the feeling of flying as I let him swing me in luscious circles.

The sky was dressed in its tie-died evening attire, stripes of pink, purple and orange blazed across the heavens. Rowan and I had landed in a dizzy heap on the soft sand and watched the shifting color display. I lay half on top of Rowan and he was propped up slightly on his own arm, which rested behind his head.

Not a bad place to be, I thought, but then he started squirming beneath me. I started to move thinking I was too heavy but he held me easily in place with his left arm.

"Oh no you don't." He winked. He reached under his back with his right arm and pulled out a very disgruntled ghost crab. "There you go buddy," he said as he set it free on the sand, "sorry 'bout that." We both watched it scuttle away sideways toward a nearby hole in the sand.

"Much better," he said and leaned in for a kiss.

I looked up just in time to see Jon turn quickly to walk away. I pulled back from Rowan's lips and pushed up with my arms.

"JON!" I called.

He froze in mid-stride but didn't turn around immediately, like if he stood really still, he wouldn't be seen.

Rowan let out a loud sigh.

"JON!" I called again, ignoring Rowan's not-so-subtle outburst of displeasure.

This time Jon turned around slowly. I hopped off Rowan and landed on the sand by his right side. Jon looked terribly uncomfortable as he walked slowly back toward us.

"Sorry," he said, "I stopped by the house and Sara said I could find you guys down here. She thought you were still doing some surfing lessons." His cheeks flushed. "I can go." He turned to leave.

"No wait!" I replied. "You don't have to go. We were just, umm, well, the waves weren't that good."

Why would Sara send him down here? I wondered. *Except to create a very uncomfortable situation. I pictured her eyes and a satisfied smirk on her face. Manipulation...does she have no limits?*

"But if you need to be somewhere else," Rowan continued, not bothering to sit up, "don't let us keep you."

I glared down at him. He looked up at me innocently.

"No, Jon, he's joking, come on over. What's up?" I asked.

Looking briefly between Rowan and me, Jon seemed to battle some force within him. Finally, he walked over, somewhat reluctantly, and sat down stiffly. The onshore breeze intensified. I attributed it to Rowan's displeasure.

Why did he have to be such a baby? I wondered.

"I just wanted to tell you that my dad talked to Humpphrey."

The wind now picked up powdery sand and pelted it against my skin. It felt like I was getting a rough exfoliating treatment.

"Wow!" I exclaimed, ignoring Rowan's weather outburst as much as possible. "That's great! What'd he say?" I asked, deliberately cheerful.

Jon finally found his smile at my excited response. His animated demeanor came back and his face lit with excitement. "I guess he just told him about us. My dad and Humpphrey used to work together a lot, deciphering the old lighthouse logs and journals. But then, Humpphrey's wife died. After that, he kind of just stayed holed away."

"Huh, that's pretty sad about his wife," I said.

"Yeah. My dad visited him for awhile. Tried to get him to come back out and work at the lighthouse again but he said he couldn't."

"Why?"

"Said he was waiting."

"For what?"

"Dunno."

"Weird."

"I guess. But when Dad mentioned you had some questions about his book and that rope drawing, he agreed you and I could come over."

"What questions?" Rowan asked. His voice sounded tense.

"Storm had asked some stuff about the stories in his book and a sketch I found of a rope," Jon said.

"No," Rowan said.

"No, what?" I asked Rowan.

"No, you aren't bloody going to Humpphrey's house," he said, his voice low and dangerous sounding. "You know the rules."

"What do you mean? I want to ask him about the lighthouse. He might know something about..." I looked at Jon then back to Rowan. Rowan raised one eyebrow. "About the lighthouse," I finished lamely. I knew I wasn't allowed to tell Jon about Pearl's braid.

"No. Z and Rean are handling that. You know you aren't to get involved," Rowan continued. His voice still low and dark, like the distant rumble of thunder.

"I think he could be a big help. I can't believe nobody has gone to him before!" My voice, contrary to Rowan's, was rising in both octave and decibel. The onshore breeze was now more of an onshore gusting wind.

"Gone to him about what?" Jon asked.

"Storm, didn't you listen?" Rowan asked, ignoring Jon's question. "Things don't end well when we mix and you need to stay safely away from that search. One wrong place at the wrong time may be the end for you. Remember your first swimming lesson? If I hadn't been there..."

"If you hadn't been there? I was only there because you brought me there!" The sky rapidly filled with dark clouds.

"I had to, Z..."

"Umm, guys, I don't mean to break up this little discussion, but it looks like we're about to get walloped," Jon said as he looked nervously between Rowan, the sky and me. A lightning bolt streaked between two ominous clouds.

"A job from Z. That thing was probably right. You, me, it was all just a job for you. I'm not some object that needs looking after!" I shouted over the wail of the wind. "You've had, what, like over 100 years to figure it out? How's your method working so far? Huh?"

"Yes it is a job and one I'm taking seriously! Bloody 'ell, so what, a sixteen year old *little girl* is going to fix everything?" Rowan shot back, but then his eyes changed. They softened. He knew he went too far, but unfortunately, words can't be taken back once they're spoken. In fact, they often hang in the air, hovering, echoing and stabbing long after they're spoken.

Thunder clapped so loudly Jon jumped. Rowan and I stayed still as statues.

"You know what? I do have one regret." I glared at Rowan. "Ever.Trusting.You."

His breath let out in a rush like he'd been sucker punched.

"And you know what else, Rowan?" I said as I stood up. "I do think exactly that. I may be just what's needed to fix everything and maybe it's time the rules had a bit of a shake up. Perhaps you should stick to surfing and being the knight in shining armor to your helpless students. Go for it, I won't stand in your way. And as for your damn job. Consider yourself fired." The words spat from my lips, full of anger, dripping with venom.

Rowan sat silently; his face an emotionless mask.

Thunder clapped, the air was charged with electricity, wind howled and the waves crashed fiercely. The first large, hard drops of rain exploded onto the sand around us. I looked at Jon who was absolutely terrified and frozen in place.

"Come on, we'd better get out of here." I looked back down to Rowan. "You wanted a storm? Well, you just got yourself one," I said coldly.

He made no move to stand or leave.

Fuming and with the wind at my heels, Jon and I ran up the beach to the yellow house.

"Will he be okay out there?" Jon asked above the wind.

"Who cares," I replied. I was so angry with Rowan. I was so angry with everything.

Jon put his arm around me when we reached the steps to the deck. I accepted the gesture and leaned into him.

Rowan said he loved me; I thought I loved him, too. But it wasn't real. It was never real. I mean, duh, Storm. He's an amazing, hot, perfect merman and you actually believed he'd fall in love with a kid. It was all manipulations. He was no better than Sara. I didn't ask for any of this. Well, maybe I wanted the body, but definitely not the drama. I seriously just want out. I just want to be normal. No mysteries to solve, no clans to deal with, and definitely no challenge to undertake.

My legs stopped moving but my mind kept spinning. The adrenalin of the fight dissipated from my veins and my anger was replaced with an empty, horrible sinking feeling in my stomach. My limbs turned to jelly. Burning tears singed the corners of my eyes.

UGH, I thought. *What the hell have I done? The horrible things I said. I didn't really mean them, or maybe I did...I don't know anymore. I am so tired, so confused, so overwhelmingly...sad.*

Drenched from the downpour, I collapsed into a sobbing heap. Jon sat next to me. I heard him call for Nana. All I felt was a terrible emptiness; a loss; a broken heart.

How had everything gone so wrong so quickly? I wondered.

Chapter Fifteen

Jon weathered the storm at our house since Nana wouldn't even think of letting him ride his bike home.

Pearl and Nana spoke in whispers downstairs and I happily ignored them. Choosing distraction rather than confrontation, Jon and I sat on my bed and worked on the second paper assignment for our class. With a sickening feeling in my belly, I pushed away the memories of when Rowan helped me on the first paper. It wasn't Rowan sitting with me now, it was Jon. Jon who had a cowlick on the front, right side of his hair and a dotting of small freckles across his cheeks. His body was totally average, his voice was completely non-magical, and he smelled like Ivory soap. Jon...the sweet, normal, human boy.

I stared at him as he skimmed through one of the papers. His finger traced the words he read on the paper and his mouth moved as he read the words in his head. A small crease appeared between his eyes as he thought about the information. That was his look of concentration; I'd seen it before in class when we struggled to keep up our notes as the professors talked. His eyelashes were long, almost girlish and when he blinked they brushed his high cheekbones. I tried to muster attraction beyond that of a friend. I imagined me kissing him. I imagined him kissing me. I waited for the butterflies to flutter about in my stomach and the racing of my heart to make me feel lightheaded and giddy..."Nothing," I whispered.

"Huh?" Jon looked up.

"Oh!" I said, caught off guard. "There's umm, nothing in here about the weathering rate of coquina." I tossed the paper in front of me off to the side. Not such a surprise since the publication was titled Age Determination of the Florida Manatee.

"Oh, that's okay. Try this one," he said with a smile and handed me a different paper to look at.

"Thanks," I replied.

There were papers on photo-identification of dolphins in the Indian River, the effect of red tide on marine mammals, and of course about manatees who were thought to be the legendary mermaids by some very confused sailors. I barely suppressed my giggles at that one. I mean really...

"I think it's time for another Humpphrey story," Jon proclaimed with a toss of the paper he finished reading.

I smiled. "Yay!" I scooted closer to Jon as he flipped through Humpphrey's book. "Do you think he's as crazy as he seems?"

"Yeah, I think he is," Jon said with a chuckle.

Why would Rowan have such a problem with me meeting this crazy old guy? Gah, stop thinking of Rowan, Storm.

By the time we finished the papers and read most of Humpphrey's book, my brain overflowed with both factual and fanciful information.

I understood *and* could explain the porous nature of coquina rock, the cycle of tides in Northeast Florida, and diagram the changing coastline of the region. And I knew stories about strange diversions of storms, one big direct hit called Hurricane Dora, ghostly apparitions, and mysterious disappearances that haunted St. Augustine's past.

"Hey Jon, have you ever seen a proxigean tide?" I asked. I had just finished the last science paper in my pile and it mentioned the unique tidal event.

"No. There have only been like thirty or something in the past 400 years! Hey, wait a sec," Jon said with an arm flourish. He flipped wildly through Humpphrey's book. "I think he mentions one somewhere in here." The pages hummed like bat wings as he flipped forward, then backward, then forward more. "Huh. I guess not." He dropped the book and looked disappointed. "I swear I read about them somewhere recently."

"Was it in Kate's stuff?" I asked.

"Oh, yeah!" He said with bright eyes and a slap on my leg. "It was when I researched Tressman. Kate mentioned about the mason, Tressman, working down by the old lighthouse for weeks making a small, temporary structure to hold supplies. But then, one morning, in early summer the tide came up with a fury..." Jon's forehead creased as he concentrated on pulling up the images from the pages, "or a force, I can't quite remember the word she used, anyway, it was higher than she had ever seen it and the water covered his entire project."

"Bummer."

"Yeah," Jon said. "Not such a great master builder, huh, if he builds something where it would go underwater. I guess he didn't know about Proxigean tides."

"But what about the rest of the time, like during normal tides?" I asked.

"I don't know, I guess it would only go a little underwater? Still not so smart," Jon said.

"Yeah," I laughed. "I guess not."

"So, you ready to type these papers?" He asked.

"Sure."

He dictated and I typed on his laptop, my sensitive, burned finger tips pulsing with every right-handed letter. Then I dictated and he typed on mine.

Jon was so human. No magic, no out of control desire when I was near him, just him and me...laid-back and comfortable. Hanging with him was as relaxing as putting on a pair of old sweatpants. So maybe there wasn't that spark of desire but sparks could be overrated since they tended to burst into flame and explode in your face. *Maybe what I really want is to snuggle in a pair of old sweatpants.*

"Storm?"

"Yeah?" I looked up to Jon's face and saw his eyes, slightly gazed, staring at me.

Oh no, had I just taken his will? Shoot, shoot, shoot, I didn't mean it. I shook my head slightly to clear the thought of Jon as my old sweatpants.

"You okay?" I asked.

"Uh, yeah, umm, never mind." He replied with a little shake of his head.

That was too close for comfort.

"And done!" Jon announced while pressing the save button triumphantly. "Let's read just one more Humpphrey story!" A loud clap of thunder caused us both to turn toward the darkness outside my window. I felt a guilty pleasure that Rowan was still upset. Not that I was thinking about him.

"Hey," he said, "Tressman!"

"What?"

"Right here, on the page I just opened to."

Jon read aloud from the book, "...that Tressman himself was in the tower when the unexpected storm hit." He eagerly turned the pages back to the start of the chapter.

"The story's called, The Mysterious Mason." He waggled his eyebrows at me which made me laugh.

"Go on, read." I nudged him, excited to hear what Mr. Humpphrey had to say about our mystery mason. So he continued from the book.

"Back in the late 1800's there was a well known master builder named Lewis Tressman. He was hired to help save the coquina lighthouse. Due to the changing coastline and the years of erosion, the lighthouse was in danger of collapse. Although Tressman had a reputation for being a hard drinking, verbally abusive man, he was a master at his craft.

"His reputation for being difficult and rude was tolerated because of his expertise with coquina. One woman, the wife of a future keeper named Kate Harn, however, was not willing to turn a blind eye. She complained openly about Mr. Tressman's behavior toward the other women as well as what she considered a lack of work ethic. A hardworking woman herself, she was unimpressed when she would happen upon the master builder sitting under the large oak outside the keeper's house muttering to himself and scribbling in a small notebook. He also wasted many weeks excavating a portion of the land on the water's edge, near the old tower, building it up with coquina, and then watching the space fill with seawater upon the return of the tide. He continued to excavate and add coquina and mark the height the water reached during each high tide. His excuse was that he was experimenting with the permeability of composite material.

"The Head Keeper, William Russell, was concerned that her meddling was slowing down the lighthouse project since Mr. Tressman, who had started enthusiastically on the project, had suddenly refused to work. They reasoned that it could only be Kate's behavior that caused the change. She was ordered to keep away from Tressman and not to interfere with his method of work.

"Not one to be easily controlled, Kate outwardly followed her husband's instructions, but secretly continued to watch the builder's actions. Her accounts of his behavior showed an increasingly disturbed individual. She often observed him muttering to himself, disappearing into the woods for hours, and harassing with extreme brazenness the young nannies who recently came into the Harns' employ to watch over the children of the many craftsmen.

"Despite the efforts to save the old Lighthouse, it became clear to all that not much could be done and all efforts were then focused on the building of the new one at a safe distance from the water. Bad luck seemed to shroud the project from this point on. Three young children drowned, one of the nannies was attacked by an angry Tressman and the weather became unpredictable creating multiple delays. Tressman was still instrumental in the planning and construction, however, his already hot-tempered personality only got worse as the months progressed and he spent more and more time alone in the basement of the Keeper's house on the pretense of strengthening the foundation. Kate mentions only one who was allowed to visit the ornery Tressman. Never knowing his name, she describes him as tall and dark-haired. The nannies didn't like him.

"Her watching and worrying came to an abrupt end when a violent storm in 1880 claimed the old coquina lighthouse with Tressman, apparently caught unaware below the tower as the storm struck.

Following the storm and Tressman's disappearance, the basement was searched for clues as to what he was doing. No traces of construction were ever found and the tall, mysterious man was never seen on the lighthouse grounds again.

"Today, some hunters of treasures and collectors of secrets believe the master mason was building a secret room in the basement. For what, no one knows. For whom, no one knows. No such room has been found, despite extensive surveys of the basement. Believe what you will. But, during high tides, when the moon is at its fullest, sightings of a man pacing the lighthouse grounds outside the keeper's house have been reported. During low tides, the same apparition has been reported pacing the shoreline. Be this the truth or be me a liar," Jon finished reading in a deep, ominous voice, "and I tell you I ain't no liar."

"Whoa," I replied after a bit of silence.. I remembered Z's description of the storm, 'only one casualty, Tressman, two if you count the lighthouse.'

"What was it you said about Tressman making something at low tide?"

"Some kind of storage something," Jon said. "But, like Kate noticed, it would have gotten drowned with the tide. Why build a room that would be mostly underwater most of the time and entirely underwater during the crazy rare high tide?"

"A room?" I asked. "I thought you said he was just playing with coquina."

"I don't know, he built secret rooms, I just figured he wasn't telling the truth. I mean he didn't exactly seem like a nice guy, so why would he tell anybody what he was building? And remember the professors talking about hidden treasure? The myth of the treasure, the secret room thing in the basement, and what your Nana is looking for could all be the same thing. I mean, the common link with all of them is this guy Tressman, right?"

"Yeah, but that was just a legend, Jon. Nobody's ever found anything and you'd think by now an entire room would have found."

"Be this the truth," Jon said in a deep voice.

"Or be me a liar," I added in my deepest voice.

"And I tell you I ain't no liar," we chimed in unison; barely finishing the line before belly laughs took over.

"Okay, okay, maybe it is just a legend," Jon said, "but let's just say for fun that Tressman built something he didn't want anybody to get into." He sat silently for a moment, the depth of the crease between his eyes gave away how hard he was thinking. "Maybe it has to do with the basement!" His face brightened but then an instant later faded as he countered his own thought, "but that's like hundreds of yards away from the thing he was building in the water," Jon admitted with a sigh of disappointment.

"Wait a sec," I said, "what if his whole point was to make this room visible, rather than secret. Maybe it wasn't in the basement, but next to the water."

"You lost me."

"Well, if something just looks like it belongs there or like it's nothing special, then people wouldn't think anything of it. There must have been lots of piles of coquina and broken bits while they were working on the lighthouse back then. Maybe he built a secret place right in the middle of it all! Like hiding in plain sight!" I said. *Like the mers*, I thought, *like me.*

"Great, so Tressman built some kind of not-so-secret, secret room that doesn't look like a room at the edge of the water. What on earth would he have wanted to put in there?"

"Something that obviously didn't have to stay dry since anything he would have built would eventually be completely underwater, at least according to our professors and what they said about the Proxegean tide thing." I replied sarcastically and then stopped short. Pearl's voice rang in my head, 'the builder flew into a rage...he knew what I was...he tore my braid...'

"OH!" I exclaimed.

"What?!"

"What, what?" I replied, caught off guard. I obviously couldn't tell Jon, but I knew what was in that secret room.

"Umm, you said, 'OH!' really loudly. *Oh* what?"

"Oh, nothing I suppose. I had a thought, but I'm sure it's way off base." I looked out of the rain-streaked window. *How come nobody had put these pieces together yet?* I wondered.

"Oh."

"Yeah," I said as I stared out of the window trying to figure out how to find this room in order to retrieve Pearl's braid. *Do they know? I have to tell them, except I'll probably just get told to stay out of it.*

"This storm is crazy strong," Jon said, changing the subject.

"Yeah, I suppose." I frowned to myself remembering soberly why the storm pressed on.

"So, uh, Storm," Jon took the still open book from my hands, "I was wondering if you wanted to go out sometime." His cheeks burned crimson as he spoke.

"What?" my mind was slow to comprehend Jon's intentions and then like a snap of a rubber band, I caught up, "OH!"

"It's okay," he blurted quickly, "If you and Rowan are..."

"No, it isn't that, well, sort of, but," I wanted to explain that I didn't really feel that way for him when an especially large thunder clap interrupted me.

That's it! I thought. *Enough already.*

Changing tacks mid stride, I answered Jon, "Yeah, that would be great!"

Jon's smile stretched ear to ear, and so did his flush. He gathered up his computer and books in a hurry and bid me a quick goodnight. But before he rushed from the room he came back to me and gave me a quick, awkward peck on the cheek.

"See ya tomorrow," he stammered and turned to head out the door, bumped into the wall, re-aligned himself and then successfully left on his second attempt.

I didn't move a muscle. I heard his footsteps retreat downstairs. I listened to Nana asking if he was okay riding his bike. He responded he had never felt better. The door opened, then closed.

What have I done? I'm no better than Sara toying with her boys. I totally messed with Jon's feelings. I really am a witch...a sea witch.

Eventually I lay back on my pillow and closed my eyes thinking about secret rooms, stolen braids, unknown mothers and what a horrible creature I was.

******

"Stormy..." a velvety soft voice tickled my ears, a voice of dreams, of memories, of a time before I understood what time was.

"Storrrrmy..." It was so pretty, so relaxing, like an angel's lullaby. "Storrrrmy..."

I snuggled deeper under my covers and felt something solid next to my back. As my eyes opened a vision of Pearl's smiling eyes, shining like phosphorescence, greeted me.

"Hey sleepy head. Time to get up!"

With a stretch and a yawn, I contemplated her words. They were simple enough to understand but the other cues that usually accompanied those words were missing and my brain was very confused. For when I opened my eyes briefly to meet Pearl's, the room was dark. As much as I listened, no birds chirped and not even one car drove past on the main street a block away. By all accounts, it wasn't morning yet.

Just a dream, I thought and rolled over sleepily.

"Is she up yet?"

A different voice in my dream, I thought. Still soprano and beautiful but without the soothing quality.

"She's getting there."

Ahh...back to soothing.

"Well, we're not getting any younger here, sister," said the shrill soprano.

"Yes, but we're also not getting any older." My favorite voice laughed softly.

This is a very strange dream dialogue, I thought.

"Is she up yet?" Enter the rich tenor.

An orchestra in my head. Perhaps a symphony, perhaps...*yikes! Perhaps an earthquake! Why the hell am I bouncing?* My eyes popped open.

"What the..." I tried to figure out how my dream had morphed into this strange scene. Dream or reality I wanted it to stop.

"Okay, Rowan. I think she's awake. Not quite the master of subtlety but I suppose it was more effective than my approach," Pearl whispered. "As I was trying to tell you, Stormy, it's time to get up. We have more practicing to do."

Still bewildered, I took a moment to respond. "But it's night out," I finally managed to say with a sleep thickened tongue.

"Well, early morning, actually," Sara responded with a sigh as she finger brushed her hair in front of my mirror.

"We have to do some swimming practice," Pearl continued, "and for what we're working on, darkness is best."

"Yeah, so you're...I mean, *we* aren't seen," Sara added.

I sat up and pushed my hair back out of my eyes.

"So we'll meet you downstairs in five, Storm," Rowan added coolly and made for the door. I watched his beautifully masculine silhouette leave. My stomach dropped. His voice was cold, no *babe* or *love* or *little nymph* followed his directions. He never called me Storm. *Crap*, I thought, and put a pillow over my head. *It's too early to have to deal with all this again.*

Pearl leaned over, moved the pillow out of the way and gave me a kiss on my forehead.

"Don't be so hard on him. He's never experienced anything like you before."

With the look in Pearl's eyes, my anger and frustration softened. I attempted a weak smile. "He doesn't care about me. It was just a job to watch me."

"Actually, Z told him he could stop hanging with you weeks ago. She felt that the biggest danger had passed since you were now aware of what you were and had begun training."

"You mean he didn't HAVE to be with me this whole time?" My heart fluttered excitedly.

"Nope, not at all. He's been with you totally because he wanted to be with you. And honestly, I've never seen him get so upset about another mermaid before. You should have heard him last night. He was a mess." She smiled. I let her words settle on me like a warm, fuzzy blanket. I smiled back.

"Better," she said. "Now get changed and come on down."

"Wait, there was something I figured out that I need to tell you about."

"Tell me on the way, we have to go before we lose the darkness," Pearl said as she skipped out the room.

I stretched again and got out of bed. In front of the mirror I stared in wonder. My eyes glowed like the others'! They were like phosphorescent emeralds in the darkness, like Pearl's. Not quite as bright but still obviously glowing and my skin! It shimmered in the dim light of the moon and seemed as if a thin layer of talc was brushed across it.

I really love this part of being a mermaid. I thought. *Why couldn't we just call it a day at being beautiful? Maybe practice staring in the mirror for hours, or brushing my hair 100 times, or...*"Storm!" A voice hissed from my door. "Come on!" Sara said.

"Oh right." I turned to go. *Oh wait*, I scolded myself, *duh, I almost forgot the ring.* It was still where I dropped it the other day. I touched it hesitantly, unsure if it was going to burn me again but this time was like the first, it was cool to the touch. *Time to salt this thing like Pearl and Sara keep telling me to do.* I slipped it on my middle finger and hurried after the others.

Drenched in moonlight, we walked leisurely in the cool, soft sand toward the water. We were all spread out with Rowan nearly to the water's edge by the time I had only made it halfway. Pearl and Sara split the distance between is and talked in whispers and giggles. The waves called to me. Each rumbling crash of water was like a caress to my soul but also like an itch that couldn't be found. The only way to stop it, I knew, was to submerge below the deliciously warm, salty water.

"So Pearl," I called to her, "last night I was doing some reading and I think I figured something out." Pearl slowed down to let me catch up.

"About what?" She asked.

"About," I wanted to tell her about the Tressman story but couldn't speak due to the fact my hand felt suddenly as if it had spontaneously combusted! I clutched my hand to my chest. My mouth opened but was unable to make any sound.

"Storm, you okay?" Pearl's voice chimed through the darkness. I barely heard her through the pain. Still clutching my hand, I finally squeaked out a cry and collapsed to the sand.

"Help!" I whimpered. "My finger, it's on fire!" I struggled to take off the ring but I couldn't touch it and the pain and heat increased until it actually felt cold rather than hot.

"Rowan! Sara! Help!" Pearl's voice called. "I can't do anything, it's Paige's ring."

"What? I told her to salt it," Sara replied.

"Well obviously she didn't!" Pearl hissed, her tone as sharp as a knife.

"You know Paige can't be trusted but you insist on hanging out with her anyway. Are you determined to destroy our clan?"

While Pearl and Sara argued, I was lifted in the air and carried on swift, strong legs toward the ocean. Unable to see or think beyond the pain of my burning flesh, I just closed my eyes and cried. With a splash, I was underwater.

Open your eyes, Storm. Rowan's voice was in my head.

I did as he told me. *My tears of pain blended with the salt water that surround me.*

You're okay now. He held my scalded hands, examining it. The burning had stopped. He gently slid the moonstone from my scorched finger and concealed the ring in his palm.

We resurfaced just beyond the breakers. Both Pearl and Sara bobbed at the surface a few yards away.

She's okay? It was Pearl's thought to Rowan.

Yeah, she'll live but the finger looks pretty bad.

I hadn't yet looked at my hand and kept it protectively cradled in my other hand.

"Let me see," Pearl said when we were close.

"No."

I was too scared to open my fist.

"Storm, I have to see it."

"No, I don't want to. It hurts."

"Storm...."

Reluctantly, I opened my left hand and Pearl gently drew my right hand to her.

At the hissing sound of Sara's sudden inhale, I opened my eyes and saw the damage. Bad move. I struggled to keep from getting sick. At the base of my middle finger, where the ring had been, the skin was completely burned off and angry red, blisters rose above, below and on the adjoining fingers.

"WHAT THE!" I screeched.

"Hang on, Stormy, it isn't that bad." Pearl said, still holding my right hand in hers.

"NOT THAT BAD?! I SEE BONE!" My vision blurred as my equilibrium tilted with shock.

"Well, now, this *is* turning into quite an interesting summer!" Sara said.

"What are you all talking about?" I cried, hot tears streaking down my face.

"Calm down, Storm. I need to know what Paige said when she gave you the ring," Pearl said.

"She said, it was to help guide me." I took my ruined hand back and buried it once again in my other hand.

"I bet Laverna put her up to it," Rowan said.

"Yes, I'm sure of it. She's the only one who would dare use the Enfiar Spark. But I can't believe Paige followed through with it. Those damn Lionfish will stop at nothing."

"Storm, it's okay, well, it's okay now. The ring Paige gave you was not just a ring."

"Yeah, I figured out that much!" I snapped back. Anger reared within me, overriding my confusion. I was getting really tired of mer games that resulted in me getting hurt. I never asked for any of this. I didn't want this. Being a mer, fine, great. I can work with that. Getting chased, nearly killed, and now burned was not in my contract.

"The ring was energized with what we call the Enfiar Spark. It's old magic that uses the wearer's own energy against her depending on what the spark was designed to do."

"In English."

"Ooh, little Stormy is getting snippy," Sara said teasingly, floating on her back with her head resting on her interlaced fingers. "This is even more fun than I could have imagined."

"The Enfiar Spark is used for identifying a heart's desire," Rowan answered, ignoring Sara's comment.

"But..." I started to question.

"But," Pearl interrupted, "its method for telling is rather painfully old-school. The spark, however, is neutralized by salt water. So, by you wearing the ring without salting it, as I'm sure Laverna and Paige intended, once an answer to some desire of yours was met, the ring focused your energy and created heat as a way to communicate to you."

"But I don't even know what the desire was."

"I know," Pearl said, "but Laverna does." She gave a piercing glare to Sara.

"What?" Sara responded. "There wasn't anything I could have done. If I made a big deal out of it, Paige would have known something was up. I told her to..."

"Salt it, yes, I know. Thanks for your help, sister. I told her, too. But I didn't think she'd wear it tonight."

"It's not my fault."

"Your devotion to Storm's well-being is nearly overwhelming. Now Storm, the good news is your finger will heal since we got the ring off before it completely burned through."

"Oh, well that's a relief." I didn't even try to hide my sarcasm.

"No really, Storm, you're a mer. We heal remarkably well," Rowan said.

"In case you didn't get a good look, Rowan, I can see my bone!" I said for the second time and held my hand up for emphasis.

"See?" Sara said.

"What? Oh!" I exclaimed. The bone was no longer visible and the burned skin had already begun to grow back. My hand still throbbed but it already showed visible healing.

"Do you want the ring back?" Rowan asked with a smirk.

"Umm, not right now, thanks." I said and re-examined my finger.

"See? It's already better. Do you think you're ready to practice?" Pearl asked.

"I guess." I replied. "The night couldn't get much worse, I suppose." But I was still angry.

I dove into the darkness. My legs crossed at the ankles and pumped gently through the water but the feeling of energy wasn't like in the day. I gulped a big breath of water and waited for the surge, but only tiny tingles rippled through my limbs.

Nighttime, Stormy. Pearl thought. *Remember what you need to be at your strongest?*

Sun. I replied curtly as I swam alongside her undulating form. *Whatever, I'll keep up.*

You're not still mad at the ring thing? Sara's voice chimed.

No, I'm perfectly fine with nearly having my finger burned off. Just like being dragged out to sea was totally awesome!

Well, nobody ever said being a mermaid was easy. Sara replied.

Well, nobody really gave me a chance to realize it was apparently quite dangerous either, did they?

Sink or swim, Stormy.

Enough, Pearl thought. *Storm, we are terribly sorry about all that you are going through. It is hard and we are trying out best. Soon it will all be over and everything and everyone will be okay.*

Well, not everyone, Sister, Sara replied.

It will be okay for the clan, Pearl replied. *That's what matters most.*

I followed the forms of Sara and Rowan ahead of me. They weren't hard to see as they left a trail of glowing phosphorescence in their wake. I slowly relaxed as we swam. It was hard to stay upset when I was swimming. It just felt so good. I never had the luxury of feeling graceful on land. My attempt at ballet when I was five was disastrous and the teacher asked that I not return following a little incident with the bar. My jaunt into gymnastics when I was nine was just laughable; although I'm sure at some time or another almost everybody got stuck upside down in the jump harness with an embarrassing wedgie. And team sports just didn't work since apparently there is no "I" in "team" and the teams, after watching me trip over my own feet during tryouts, certainly didn't want one. I had given up on anything that required coordination, depth perception or tiny outfits. But now, here I was, as graceful as any creature built for a life under the water. I finally belonged somewhere. I was home! Although home was turning out to have quite a few surprises what with dueling clans and magical rings. But Sara was right, who was I to expect that being a mermaid was supposed to be easy.

Seriously, you got trapped upside down in a jump harness? Rowan's laughter and Sara's voice filled my head.

Um, yeah. Damn, I forgot about the mind thing.

You get used to the thought sharing thing. Pearl added. *Don't worry, eventually you'll be able to close off the thoughts you'd prefer not to share with the entire ocean.*

Thanks, maybe we could practice that sooner rather than later.

Awe, and ruin all our entertainment? Sara thought with a giggle.

Speaking of entertainment, how'd your date go Sara? Rowan asked.

Oops. Sara thought.

Oh no, thought Pearl, *what'd you do?*

Do? Nothing really, but I may have left him in the restaurant. Sara thought.

For how long? Rowan asked.

Umm, what time is it now? Sara asked.

Seriously? I thought.

Well, it wasn't my fault. I got up to talk to some people I knew at the bar and then I ran into a friend who works in the kitchen and then I saw someone outside wearing the most awesome boots so I went to ask her where she got them and then we got to talking and walking and well, I sort of forgot about the guy. Huh. Bummer, he was pretty cute, too.

Well, it was probably most fortunate for him in the long run. Pearl thought. *Okay guys, we're here. Sara, you work with Storm on navigation.* Sara's amber eyes came near and she held out her opalescent hand for mine.

And Sara, Pearl thought, *please don't lose her.*

Who me? Come on Storm, you're in good hands.

I took the hand she offered me and the two of us headed for the surface.

Taking the first breath of air was uncomfortable. I felt disoriented until the beacon of light flashed above my head. To our left, standing proud, tall and bright against the night sky was the St. Augustine Lighthouse. I had been so entranced by watching the phosphorescence trail behind Sara and Rowan I hadn't even noticed that we swam all the way around Lorelei's Point, and into the protected waters of Salt Run.

"Protected, yes," Sara added aloud to my unspoken thought. "But don't let its peaceful appearance deceive you."

I couldn't think how it could be dangerous here. Land was on both sides, the water was calm and most of it was quite shallow.

"Not by the things you see, Storm..." Sara paused and listened. She whispered after a moment of silence, "but the things you can't."

"Okay," I replied but I was still not quite sure what she meant.

"Pearl knows I hate this place." The water rippled about Sara's shoulders. "Well, come on. Let's get this over with."

She dropped below the surface and I followed.

Okay Storm. Sara's voice rang in my head. *Find me.*

I looked around but saw only the black-green water. *Is this like a crazy version of Marco-Polo?*

Sort of, she replied.

Her response rang in my head. But aside from her thoughts, I had no way to find her. Without the trail of phosphorescence to follow, the darkness seemed to close around me. The night ocean was seriously creepy. It reminded me of my dream.

Life underwater is not a life where eyes make much of a difference. You need to learn to trust your other senses. What do you feel? What do you hear? What do you taste?

I feel freaked out, I hear you in my head and I taste...what do you mean what do I taste?

Sara giggled.

Oh so glad I'm amusing you.

I swam in a random direction. The silt bottom rose up to greet my searching hands. My eyes strained to see in the darkness.

Don't focus on your eyes, Storm...tell me what you feel.

I feel the sand. I thought to Sara. The frustration in my head's voice was obvious.

Go on, tell me more. This time, close your eyes, they are no use to you here.

I followed her directions, closed my eyes and waited. I thought about Rowan's tale of his childhood, about how the water was so murky he had to use other senses. *What was it he mentioned?* Exhaling slowly I tried to concentrate.

I feel the water, I feel a current.

Good. Which way is the current moving?

Umm...it's moving over me from right to left.

Okay...anything else?

I remained motionless and tuned into the sensations on my skin. Sara was right, it was much easier to focus with my eyes closed. My other senses seemed to come alive with information. The steady flow of water brushed across me like a gentle breeze. It was constant, it was directional it was...wait a minute. The flow was interrupted on my left calf. The water there seemed to swirl, like it was disturbed.

Good...now, what do you hear?

I listened. Now that I thought about it, it was really quite loud down here. *There were clicks...*

Those are the shrimp, Sara answered.

...and pops...

Mullet, Sara answered again

...and a grinding like sandpaper...

Shark pups. Sara sounded like she was bored.

...and a different kind of sound...like a hum...

Go on, Sara said with a spark of interest in her tone.

It sounds like a musical instrument holding a prolonged note. Soft and sweet.

And finally, the prize goes to Storm! That's the sound of a mer.

And the other one? The lower, almost gong-like sound?

Also a mer, but a merman rather than a mermaid, Sara continued. *Each of us has our own tone that we emit in the water. So, how many different tones do you hear?*

Oh yeah! Rowan had talked about his mother's chime! Well, I thought, *I hear a high chime-like one to my left, an even higher, softer one to my right as well as the low gong. So, there are three different notes, one left and two to the right.*

Good.

So I guess Pearl and Rowan are to my right and you're to my left. But why can't I hear their thoughts?

They're blocking you. Mers can block thoughts, but we can't stop or hide our vibration. So, you realize that you can now feel me and hear me to your left. Anything else?

I took a gulp of water and realized that I could sense something else, a taste beyond the soothing salt. It was sort of sweet, but also tart...kind of like key lime pie.

Sara chuckled. *Thanks,* she added with a touch of indignation. *Yes, you can also sense how close another mer is based on the taste of the water. That is your last clue, if you can taste another, he or she is very close indeed.*

Reach out your left hand.

I did as I was told and I rubbed against soft skin. Sara was just inches from me.

The water's disturbance by my calf shifted up my thigh and over to my right side.

Follow me.

Instinctively I opened my eyes and lost all connection to the rest of my senses as my eyes strained to see.

Not with your eyes, silly girl.

Frustrated by Sara's tone, I closed my eyes tight and clenched my jaw until it hurt.

Her chuckle made me even angrier. *I'll follow you alright, right up your...*

A shrill shriek stopped my thought and made my head hurt. *What the...Sara? Are you okay?* I thought to her as I swam blindly forward.

Sara? Where'd you go? OUCH! I cried in pain. In my panic to find Sara and while trying to follow the new rule of keeping my eyes closed, I happened to swim into a very large rock. Breaking the rules, I opened my eyes and felt it with my hands. The surface of the rock was rough and sharp and sliced my fingers as I slid along it. I put my nose nearly to it and was able to identify the rough mixture. *Coquina,* I thought. The rock, if that's what it was since it was so huge it was more like a ruins or something, was way wider than my arm span. I swam along it trying to find its edge.

Sara! I called frantically in my mind.

Seriously? Is she blocking me? Is this just a test or something? Totally uncool if it is because I'm really getting freaked out. Come on Sara, little hint for the newbie, please.

I finally got to the end of the coquina wall thing, turned its corner and swam in my original direction again. *When I find you, I'm going to kill you.*

I tried to remember her instructions. *Think, Storm.* 'Close your eyes, take a breath.' *Oh, right. Breathe and taste.* I stopped moving and drew in a large mouthful of water. I didn't taste anything beyond salt. *Oh wait, she said the taste thing is only when they're close. Her chime...okay, listen.* This time I was rewarded with a faint note. I listened more intently and with my eyes closed swam slowly and allowed my movements to be guided by the sound of Sara. After a moment I tasted the water again. Still nothing, but her chime had gotten louder. I continued swimming, listening, and tasting. My progress was painstakingly slow but I eventually caught a hint of key lime pie.

Keep going, you got this, Storm. Swim, listen, taste, swim, listen, taste, swim, listen, OOMPH! I smacked right into Sara's back.

Ha! I exclaimed. *Found you!*

I opened my eyes in triumph and then shrunk back from her in fear. She floated absolutely still in the water and her face was frozen in an expression somewhere between fear and hatred. Her skin was milky in the dimly lit water and her hair flowed weightlessly around her. She looked really creepy, like a dead body that was pretty pissed off.

Sara? I questioned. But before she gave any response, I felt it. There were others in the water with us. But they weren't mers and they weren't sharks or fish or crabs. They were something entirely different. They were...humans? No, not human, but something like human. My eyes strained. My ears picked up faint whispers and my skin rose into bumps as a shiver traveled from my crown to my toes.

Faint as a butterfly's wings in flight, Sara whispered in my head, *they are the lost souls of Matanzas.* Before I could even comprehend she continued, *the souls of those that have drowned or been killed in these waters. Damn Pearl, she knows how I feel about them.*

So, they are...

Spirits, ghosts, the damned, whatever. Sara snarled and suddenly turned her face to mine. I backpedaled in the water as she looked truly frightening. *They're always here. I hate them. I can't help them, not one of them, espe-*

cially not the little...oh, forget it, she turned away and with a mighty kick left my side. *Come on, lesson over.*

Still unable to formulate a question from the tidal wave of thoughts in my brain, I followed silently in the wake behind Sara. The more I tuned into the faint, human like murmurings, the clearer they were. There were voices of men, women and even children. They chattered nonstop. It was like being at a party where the host forgot to turn on the lights. Sara stopped swimming again quite suddenly and I bumped into her backside for the second time.

Children's voices rang in my ears. They laughed and giggled. *Did one of them call for Sara?*

Yes. Sara responded.

Who are they? I asked.

The children, she responded.

Who?

Never mind, she answered and swam with powerful strokes. I struggled to keep up. I felt like the new running partner that hadn't trained yet.

Please slow down, I gasped.

In a moment, she replied.

What about Pearl and Rowan? I wheezed.

They'll find us.

Sara's kept up her pace until I felt the open ocean swell caress my body.

Thank goodness, I thought as she finally slowed down. I stretched my body in a luxurious arch. I rounded back and forward several times to stretch and twirled in some circles to relax. I definitely didn't ever want to be in a race with Sara. I swear she must have twin 250hp motors hidden somewhere.

What's with the rush there Rainbow fish?

It was Rowan's voice in my head.

Sara, she freaked out, some weird ghost things in the water?

Every time, he thought. *You okay?* His eyes glowed like two electric orbs in front of my face.

Yeah, I'm okay. It was awkward talking with him since I wasn't sure if we were still fighting.

Hey, he put a hand on my shoulder, *I was thinking about last night. Are you still mad?* He swam next to me, his eyes wide and curious, his body just barely brushing mine as our legs moved in unison.

I don't know. Are you?

I asked you first.

I shrugged and wondered if perhaps I was making a bigger deal than necessary. I remembered what Pearl said about how he could have stopped hanging out with me weeks ago but didn't. And he did save me with the ring thing.

Exactly! Rowan thought and interlaced his fingers with mine.

Hey! I protested. *That was* my *thought.*

Yeah, but I heard it, and I totally agree. He smirked.

Did you start hanging out with me because you had to?

Yes. It did start that way, but I found out very quickly that I wanted to hang out with you, even when I didn't have to. I still want to protect you, no, I need to protect you. I want you safe.

Yeah, I know, I know, for the clan and all whatever that means.

No, not for the clan. For me. I want you safe for me. I don't ever want to lose you, Storm.

Really?

Really. You're getting stronger every day. You don't really need my protection anymore, but I still want to give it to you because the thought of anything possibly happening to you would kill me. In fact, based on that razor sharp tongue of yours, it may be me that needs the protecting!

I laughed at that. *Sorry for the horrible things I said. I don't regret trusting you at all, in fact, I love you, you big, overly emotional mer...maid!*

I gave a powerful kick with my legs and tried to swim away but he grabbed my feet and pulled me back. I squirmed and laughed playfully.

Hey, who you callin' a mermaid...mermaid? He tickled me and I rolled around trying to get away from his solid grasp of my torso. Then he stopped and brought me in close. Our noses nearly touched and his eyes, shining brightly in the nighttime waters, gazed lovingly into mine.

You just said you loved me! Rowan thought.

Yeah, I did.

His smile made his entire face light up even brighter than his eyes. He put his hands around my waist and with one giant shove tossed me clear out of the water. I caught a glimpse of the starry night sky and felt the warm air on my wet skin. My hair felt heavy as it hung down my back. Then as quickly as the air appeared, it disappeared. With a splash, I landed back in the water upside down and into Rowan's awaiting arms. I lay there cradled like a baby looking into his face, which glowed with an indescribable iridescence.

So truce? He asked.

Truce.

He leaned closer and we kissed; slow, soft, and intimate. Not just a kiss of playful youth, but also of maturity, of trust in each other, of knowledge of the challenges that were sure to present themselves and most importantly, of the security of knowing neither of us would have to face those challenges alone.

No regrets, he whispered.

No regrets, I answered.

Pearl's voice suddenly entered my head, but she wasn't talking to me, she was letting me hear her talk with Sara. Pearl must have caught up to her when Rowan stopped with me.

Pearl was mad about what happened in Salt Run. Sara's thoughts sounded angry and short. I didn't understand Sara. One minute she seemed so nice and helpful and the next, well, the next I sure wouldn't want to depend on her to have my back. *What could have happened to make her act so selfish?*

I thought about the story Z told us about the conflict between her mother and aunt and her and her sister. Maybe Pearl and Sara were like that also. Maybe it's a thing with mer sisters.

Nah, Rowan added, *Sara's still caught up with the kid thing. You know, those little girls.*

Oh...OHHH, were they the voices I heard back there?

Happens every time we go there. I mean I get why Pearl insists on going there but it really twists Sara's knickers.

Pearl said something about having to keep looking. Is that what you two were doing? Looking for her braid?

Yeah. We haven't found it there yet and I don't know what's goin' to change. But she says she feels it there... somewhere in those waters, so we keep looking but the children always search us out.

Before I could ask more, the water became more turbulent and the surge of the shore break pushed and pulled at my body. With a quick smile to Rowan, I gave a powerful kick, timed with the ocean's momentum and burst through the slope of the breaking wave. I laughed into the clear night air; Pearl, Sara, the water souls and my struggles with training were put aside for this moment of pure joy and unabashed, effortless bliss.

I rolled onto my back and watched Rowan glide past me along the surf, silhouetted by the dawn's blood-red sky.

Chapter Sixteen

"Am I boring you Ms. Harn?" Professor Ross asked. My eyes popped open and my drooping head snapped to attention.

"No," I sputtered and scribbled words onto my page of notes. I threw in a weak smile while fighting the urge to yawn.

"Good. Then would you mind actually trying to keep your eyes open while I talk? It makes me feel so much better inside." He spoke sternly, but there was a glimmer of a smirk on the edge of his lips.

"Of course, Sir." My cheeks burned and sweat dripped from my armpits. *This is the longest week EVER and it's only Thursday!* My dual life as half girl and half mermaid-in-training was taking its toll on my attention span in class. On my paper were mere scribbles; faint, poor attempts at note-taking where I started with the best of intentions but drifted off mid-word. The temperature rocketed above 90 and my attempts at wind manipulation succeeded only in making the corner of my paper rustle in an apathetic quiver. I was just too exhausted to put my heart into it. I settled for nursing my bottle of saltwater.

"What's up, Storm? You look exhausted," Jon whispered as Dr. Ross explained the difference between k-selected and r-selected species.

"Nothin', just tired frooaa..." a yawn interrupted my reply, "from staying up studying, I guess."

I left out the part about how I spent the past four nights swimming around Salt Run, practicing sensory navigation and fleeing from underwater spirits. Despite Sara's protests and increasingly bad temper, Pearl made us go back night after night to practice.

Last night, I nearly didn't make it back thanks to a surprise run in with the little girls...

HA! That's two to nothing, little sister. Sara's voice chimed brightly in my head as I lost yet another game of seek-n-seek. Like hide and seek, except underwater and each player searches for the others while trying not be found first. I was losing...of course. Ready to start our third round and prepared to once again to be humiliated by Sara's skills, I was shocked when her hand suddenly grabbed my shoulder like a vice. I cried out in pain.

Shh. Sara said. *Come on, let's get out of here.*

What?

Come on! Sara pushed me forward and took off in a blur.

Hey, wait! I called, but she was already gone. Before I could start to follow, I heard them. The voices of the children. They seemed to come from all directions. Faint traces, like smoke, swirled in the water and an occasional face formed in the swirling fog. It would disappear only to reappear a few feet away. Disoriented, I spun in a circle seeking a way out of the cloudy water, only to realize I was surrounded.

What do you want? I asked timidly.

Children giggled and the smoke-faces appeared, disappeared and reappeared all around me. With no other option, I decided to swim through the cloudy water. As soon as I entered it, I realized it was a very bad idea.

Giggles that weren't my own reverberated within me. My head rang with sound and my limbs became weak and numb. As my legs fluttered weakly, I slowly sank to the soft, silt bottom of Salt Run.

Does the water lady want to play hide and seek with us? A child's voice asked.

I don't know, another child said. *Do you want to play?*

I'm bored, a third child's voice, *I don't want to wait anymore.*

We have to, the first child answered, *he said to guard it from the star people then he'd bring us a present.*

Oh, yeah! The third child said.

Their voices got excited and overlapped. It felt like being in a small space filled with excited canaries.

But the lady can play with us till he comes. She's so pretty! The first child said.

She reminds me of Sara, the second said.

Sara won't play with us anymore, the third said.

She's a star person, dummy, she's bad, remember? He told us it was her fault, the first said.

Oh yeah. I miss Sara.

Me too.

Lady, will you play with us?

Play? No, I can't play, I thought. *I just want to sleep.*

But I knew there was something important in the children's ramblings. *Sara...some man...star people...*I gathered what little will I had left to stay conscious and asked, *who is the man?*

He's a fish person! The third girl answered.

Yeah, he's so nice, he told us he'd always play with us, not like Sara, the second girl answered cheerfully.

And he tells us how pretty we are! The third girl exclaimed.

And he said he has a surprise for us if we keep away the ones with the stars. You don't have a star on your neck, so you're okay. Back to the first girl.

I wondered if they were talking about the clan symbol. *He's a fish person you said? Because he swims underwater?* I asked.

No, because of the shiny fish on his necklace, one girl answered.

It's not a fish, remember he told us it was a lion, another interrupted.

Don't be stupid, it's a catfish, the third laughed.

No, it's not.

Yes, it is.

No it's not.

It's a lionfish, the first one said.

Oh yeah! They all giggled. I was vaguely aware of water swirling around me but my body was numb, like I had been injected with Novocain. Breathing water was too hard, it was easier to be numb, to drift into the sparkling lights that twinkled behind my closed lids.

Hey, Lady wake up and play with us! The girls' giggles stopped.

There they are, come on, one girl said.

See ya lady, the second said.

Yeah, see ya. Maybe we can play next time, the third said.

And suddenly, I was alone.

A tiny part of my brain thought it heard Pearl's voice. *Where?* She asked. She wasn't talking to me which was good because I was too tired to answer. Tiny lights exploded behind my closed eyelids.

I don't know, over there somewhere. Sara's voice entered my head. She sounded cranky and defensive. *Look, I gave up being a nanny long ago.*

I told you not to leave her.

It's not my fault she couldn't bloody keep up. Ever since she returned it's all Storm this and Storm that, it was fun at first, but it's getting pretty old. She's nearly of age and she should be able to watch out for herself.

Damn it Sara! Pearl growled back. *It's my life! And the clan's future!*

Right, well, it's my life, too. First the braid and now Storm. How much do you need from me Pearl?

I need more than you gave those children!

I knew you blamed me.

Well, who else should be blamed? Hmm?

It wasn't me! I loved them, I took care of them, I...

Right, sister, just as well as you made sure Storm salted that bloody ring! You killed them and you doomed me. And now you may have doomed the clan as well.

Stop your bickering, you old hens. Over there, I hear her, Rowan said.

Chimes surrounded me and warmth radiated from the tips of my fingers and toes to my core.

Just relax, Rowan's voice hummed in my head. His arms wrapped under my back and legs and we floated to the surface.

"What happened?" I mumbled with a sleepy tongue. A pounding in my head emphasized the beating of my heart.

"A drain," Rowan whispered as he stroked my wet hair back from my face. The night air was calm and the lights behind my eyes were now transformed into stars sparkling across the clear sky.

"A what?" I still couldn't move my limbs and my fingers tingled with pins and needles. I lay motionless on top of Rowan's prone belly.

"A drain. It's when you enter water without any of the sun's energy. Instead of the water sending energy into you, all of your energy drains into the water around you," he said. "Or at least into what's in the water around you."

"Those little girls."

"Hmm hmm. When water souls gather, they absorb all of the latent energy in the water. They love collecting energy because it makes them stronger for a short time. So they often linger near us and try to talk and play so they can take some of our strength. Usually it's no big deal, but tonight the three of them gathered together and it was too much for you." I must have made a face revealing my inner anger at being the "weak one" because he quickly added, "Oh Storm, three water souls are too much for any of us. I'm just happy we found you before you were drained completely."

"Yeah, lucky me," I said and remembered wanting to drift away from consciousness, of losing touch with the sensations of my body. I had no idea that feeling was closer to dying than sleeping.

I reached my hand up and touched his silver star fish pendant. "The ones with the stars."

"What?" He asked.

"The children kept talking about a man who wanted them to keep the ones with stars away from Salt Run. The girls said he had a pendant; like yours but different," I said.

"Daniel," Pearl said. She and Sara surfaced next to us. "He's keeping us out of there for a reason...it has to be my braid. But how do you get in there to look with his little guard puppies always on the prowl?"

"Well, he obviously doesn't know either or he would have gotten it by now," Rowan said. "But he knows something to be using those kids to keep us away."

"Well, there's one thing he doesn't know and Storm, I need your help to solve this," Pearl said. "At night they come without being fetched. By day they are lost without being stolen. What are they?"

"Seriously?" I asked lifting my head off of Rowan's chest. The pounding in my head immediately increased and painful electric currents shot through my limbs. *Ugh*, I thought and lay my head back down.

"Relax, Stormy, you've been through a lot tonight," Pearl said. She gave Sara a frightful scowl but turned a soft smile toward me. "It's a very old riddle that has something to do with the location of my braid. The night before Tressman stole it, I saw him write the words on a piece of paper on his desk."

"Really?" I asked. "Do you know the answer?" The spinning sensation slowed but the spikes of pins and needles continued as feeling returned to my limbs.

Pearl laughed lightly; a really lovely sound. "Yes, but the answer hasn't helped. You're new to the game and therefore have a fresh perspective."

"Okay," I said dreamily. *I'll get right on that*, I thought as I snuggled closer into Rowan's chest.

******

"Storm?" Jon waved a hand in front of my face. "Earth to Storm."

"Huh?"

Kids in the class moved, stretched and talked.

"Tomorrow? Are you still up for it?" He asked.

"Oh, yeah, of course." *Our date.* "It'll be great!" I tried to sound excited and I suppose it worked as a smile replaced his look of anxiety and his eyes brightened in response.

"So what're your plans now?" Jon asked as I drank greedily from my bottle of saltwater. The fire in my throat diminished slightly.

"Nothin' I guess," I answered in between gulps. "Just head home...maybe take a nap." I smiled.

"Oh, okay. I thought I'd take a ride over to see Humpphrey. My dad said he was around today and that we could stop by. But if you're too tired..."

I stopped in mid-stride. His eyes twinkled with excitement.

"Ouch! You been working out?" Jon exclaimed in response to my punch that hit home in his shoulder. "So is that a 'yes' to joining me?"

"Yes, of course!" I exclaimed. A second wind surged through my veins, saltwater or excitement not sure which, but all traces of tiredness vanished and every ounce of teenage rebellion surfaced. *Finally, a meeting with Mr. Humpphrey. Now I just have to keep my thoughts to myself because I'm pretty sure that despite being required to protect me, Pearl, Sara, and Rowan will just as soon kill me if they find out I'm talking to the forbidden Mr. Humpphrey.*

"How are we getting there?" I whispered. My eyes darted from tree to tree making sure we weren't being watched,

"Some old bikes we keep around back!" Jon whispered back. "It's only a few miles. And Storm,"

"Yeah?"

"Why are we whispering?"

"What? Oh," I said in a normal, though still quiet, voice. "No reason. We should go." I walked quickly with Jon to the bikes. *Why is it always bikes*, I thought with a self-pityingly sigh.

We left the Lighthouse grounds and I couldn't help but look over my shoulder every few minutes. No one seemed to be following us and the sky remained clear. *So far so good. Hopefully the others are too busy to worry about my whereabouts for a few hours.* I followed Jon's turns until we ended up on a short, dead-end street completely shaded with giant Live Oaks.

At the second house on the left, Jon hopped off his bike and wheeled it onto the brick paved drive. There was an arbor in the front of the one-story, stucco cottage. To the right of the door was a tangled memory of what were once jasmine vines. A neatly planted vegetable garden in a raised bed looked out of place among the hodgepodge of plants that filled the small front yard. I parked my bike next to Jon's and wished desperately for something cold and salty to drink.

Bienvenidos was painted in large, bright colors of red, orange, green and yellow above a tall wooden gate which, in contrast, was weathered to a dull gray. A gray striped cat jumped on the fence to greet us and a moment later we heard the sound of reluctant metal being moved and shifted. The massive gate creaked open slowly and in its place, nearly as weathered, stood a man, barely taller than us, with a mass of shiny, silver hair and friendly, deep set wrinkles in his copper-colored skin. He was barefoot and wore a lose button down, cotton shirt and khaki shorts with frayed edges. His eyes, sparkling and ageless, absolutely twinkled with excitement and reminded me of a look I once saw from a small boy that stared wide eyed in anticipation at his towering vanilla ice-cream cone decorated with multi-colored sprinkles.

So this is Mr. Humpphrey, I thought. *He doesn't look crazy.*

His smile widened, "Ah, Mr. Manistar, you've grown into quite the handsome gentleman. Not even a trace of the barefooted toddler digging for worms below the oak trees."

I stole a quick glance at Jon and the pattern of a rose took shape on his cheek.

"And, his beautiful young friend." He turned to me.

"Storm," I said and held out my hand.

He accepted my hand in his but instead of a shake, he lifted it to his lips and gave it a kiss.

"Please, won't you both come in. I believe I've been waiting for you," he said.

"Wow!" I said. My breath was taken away by what lay in front of me. It could only be described as a beautiful and HUGE secret garden.

For the unassuming, nearly unkempt appearance of the front of his house, this utter surprise of beauty, space, lushness and life was breathtaking. My eyes tried to take in all the plants, fountains and assorted sculptures that filled this seemingly unending space. There were purple flowers toppling over blue flowers that were all surrounded by giant leafy ferns. There were brilliant pink stalks interspersed with wooden sculptures painted in the brightest hues. Statues of stone and wood peeked over lush bushes or stood sentient along meandering paths defined by mosaic pavers. There were working fountains, small bubbling pools, rocks and decks. I lost count of the number of winding paths and I followed at least five different kinds of butterflies flitting among a vine that crept unending along a side wall.

"Yes there's a lot of love and years of work in this garden," Mr. Humpphrey spoke softly, nearly reverently, as he answered my unasked questions. "Every part, living or otherwise has a story to tell! Sometimes it gets downright maddening in here with all of them trying to talk at once." He winked cheerfully. The three of us stood in silence as Jon and I looked around.

He led us over to a table that was set for tea and nestled under a shady oak. I chose the ornate green metal chair to sit in. Jon chose a solid wood piece with sturdy arm rests. Mr. Humpphrey settled into a stocky wooden chair with a low back and whitewashed appearance.

Nothing matched and yet they all fit so perfectly together. They also all shared the same yellow and blue floral cushions that looked like at some point they were quite bright and stunning. Now they were faded by time and sun and reflected only memories of the once vibrant colors.

"Lemon?" Mr. Humpphrey's voice finally broke into the song of the cicadas that filled my ears. He poured three large glasses of iced-tea and held up a juicy slice of lemon between tiny metal tongs. Part of me longed to drain the tall glass in one gulp but another part of me remembered that the liquid would do me no good. I needed salt to dampen the fire that raged in my mouth and throat.

Mr. Humpphrey turned to me and again as if he read my mind, he said, "I am afraid I have developed a rather peculiar habit over the years of dipping my lemon into salt before adding it to my tea. Would you like me to fix you one the same way?"

I nodded eagerly. "Yes please!"

He turned to Jon and waited for his reply. Jon shook his head, "No sir, if you don't mind I'll skip the lemon and salt and just have the tea." Jon shot me a look that seemed to say, 'See? this guys is totally nuts.' *Nuts?* I thought. *Or knowing?*

"Very well." He handed Jon the tall glass. Totally embarrassed, I realized too late that both Jon and Mr. Humpphrey had watched with amusement as I drained the glass and sucked the salt from the lemon. My lips puckered with the sour lemon juice, but my throat finally stopped screaming at me and I felt a touch of energy surge into my limbs.

"I guess I was a little thirstier than I thought!"

Mr. Humpphrey let out a hearty laugh, "Indeed you were child!" He re-filled my glass and popped in another salt covered lemon slice and settled back into his chair.

"Thank you." I used some restraint on the second glass and sipped rather than gulped.

"So, how is your father these days?" Mr. Humpphrey turned to Jon who fidgeted uncomfortably.

"Umm, he's fine sir. Working hard like always."

"Yes, I admire his work ethic. You don't see such dedication very often anymore."

"Uh yeah, I suppose."

"So to what do I owe the pleasure of this visit?"

"Well, Sir," Jon answered. "my friend," he looked to me, "she thought you may be able to help her answer some questions."

Until that point, I sat happily inconspicuous and sipped at my second glass of iced-tea. I was suddenly thrust into the spotlight.

"Umm..." I stammered, "well, yeah, I hoped, well, I mean I thought, well, I guess I...." *Oh my God I sound like such an idiot. Get it together Storm*, I chided. The breeze picked up around us and the sun disappeared behind a dark grey cloud.

Mr. Humpphrey looked calmly at me, then glanced to the sky and then back to me. He chuckled, took a silver flask from his pocket, and poured the contents into his tea.

"Purely medicinal," he said as his eyes twinkled.

"I know that everyone thinks I am a crazy old man that makes up stories and drinks too much. The truth is I do drink too much but even I am not creative enough to make-up the stories I tell! And as for the crazy part, well, perhaps there is some truth in that. I do talk to myself, so that may appear crazy, but to me, it is more of a habit developed from living alone all these years! I talk to my cats, my plants and I still talk to Victoria when she honors me with a visit. If that's considered crazy, so be it."

"Victoria?" I asked.

"She was the love of my life." His blue eyes glittered with moisture. "The reason I lived and the reason I can't yet die! She was the one person in this world that understood me. She put up with wild ways, my traveling for months at a time chasing my tail or someone else's. She defended me when people said I had lost my mind but she knew me better than I knew myself."

He reflected for a moment and then continued, "They say you are lucky if you find love once in a life time. Not puppy love, not infatuation, but real love. The kind of love that makes you want to dance in the rain, to run with each other to the end of Earth and back again and to spin in circles together until you both fall down dizzy and laughing, The kind of love that defies the odds, that challenges death and wins!" His eyes danced with excitement.

"What did you mean when you said she's the reason why you can't die yet?" I asked.

"Because I have more stories to tell and she won't let me go until I have told them all to those that need to hear them." He looked me straight in the eyes and maybe even straight into my mind. "I intend to do just that! Like I said, I've been waiting for you because the truth needs to be told, I am old and honestly my child, I'm tired."

I shivered visibly as chills ran across my arms. I took a slow drink from my glass.

"I need your stories if you'd tell me some."

"Yes. I believe I will tell you some." He stood up. "Let's get out of this sweltering heat and go inside shall we? I think I have something you'd like to see."

French doors stood open to a very small and very overcrowded living room. Every chair and table I could see overflowed with books and loose papers. He chuckled as he scooted a black and gray tabby cat off one pile and cleared a space on the settee.

"Please sit," he said and motioned to two chairs. He sat on a small sofa opposite the chairs and picked up a worn looking pair of reading glasses that were hidden between two stacks of loose papers. He shuffled through a pile of books stacked haphazardly on the table to his left. He exclaimed triumphantly as he pulled from the pile a dusty, very old looking, over sized blue leather book with torn bindings.

"Ah, here it is." He opened the book and a flutter of dust motes floated into the air. A grainy photograph looked back at us. "Mr. Lewis Tressman was hired to repair our proud Coquina Lighthouse. But eventually, repair was no longer feasible and he was kept on to help with the construction of a new lighthouse. Am I correct in that it is he you wish to ask me about?"

"Yes," I answered, unable to look away from the eyes of the man in photograph. His face was gaunt and smile-less. He was dressed in loose pants held up by suspenders over a worn, partly untucked shirt. *Where did you hide Pearl's braid Mr. Tressman? And who did you hide it for?*

"As I'm sure you both know, he was something of a local expert at coastal building projects. His specific expertise was working with coquina. Beyond his daily employment, he was also sought after by the wealthier townspeople for special projects. Do you know what they were?"

"Safe rooms," Jon replied.

"Very good. I see you have come here well prepared. His creativity was unparalleled in building these secret rooms for valuables. Each room was unique and no one but he and the owner, once payment was made, knew all of the tricks to get into the room. Funny enough, today people are still finding secret passages and hidden rooms in some of the houses downtown. No valuables have been found, but then again, they may not have even made it to the final holding room."

"But I thought he was a mean man," Jon said.

Mr. Humpphrey chucked. "Yes, well, being a good man and skilled man are two very different things. He provided a service, one that protected people's most prized possessions, so many were able to ignore his severe character flaws. One person, however, refused to turn a blind eye and it is *she* that deserves our attention now."

"Kate," I whispered.

"Yes," Mr. Humpphrey replied with a smile. He turned the pages in the book and stopped on another grainy photograph of a stern looking woman. But although her face was stern, her eyes showed a sparkle that made me want to smile. Her eyes...*Nana's eyes.*

"You, Storm, as you must now be aware, are her descendant. Her husband was made Lighthouse keeper in 1875 and she was known for her good nature, beautiful family of six lovely daughters, hospitality, and honesty. Mrs. Harn believed, among other things, that Mr. Tressman altered the books during his logging of supplies used during both the restoration of the old lighthouse and the construction of the new one. She openly disliked and distrusted Mr. Tressman which in those times was outspoken of a woman, even a woman of her status, and I'm sure it didn't win her any extra invitations to tea with the ladies. She wrote many entries in her personal journals about her speculations on the mismatched supply numbers, strange behaviors, and uneasy glances." Mr. Humpphrey paused.

"Are you okay?" I asked.

"Yes," His eyes still sparkled but he simultaneously looked drawn and tired, like telling this story drained him of his energy. "I was just remembering the last time I spoke of Kate and Lewis. It was a long time ago. Time is taking its toll on me, I suppose, but that is not something you will understand, is it?"

Struck dumb by his statement, I glanced sideways at Jon. "I," I started to speak but Mr. Humpphrey waved me off with a smirk.

"No teenager ever does," he said quietly and winked at me.

I exhaled.

"Tressman was, of course, the very person the Keeper at the time of restoration, Mr. William Russell, turned to for consultation of the Coquina Lighthouse stability. After much discussion, it was decided the only solution was to begin construction of a new lighthouse farther inland, beyond the greedy fingers of the inlet waters and the temperamental dealings of the tidal shoreline. Without haste, construction of the new, brick-over-coquina lighthouse began in 1871. The superintendent of construction of the tower was Hezekiah Pittee and the local consultant was none other than our Mr. Tressman."

"Mr. Pittee, originally of Maine, moved his wife and five young children down here for the construction. They lived in a small house on site and the children often amused themselves, watched by the hired nannies, with the trolley car that ran supplies from the ships to the construction grounds."

My heart sank. I already knew the tragic ending to this story.

Mr. Humpphrey again flipped pages of the old book and stopped on a picture of two beautiful young women, one with light hair, one with dark, surrounded by a group of smiling children.

"On July 10, 1873 a tragedy happened. The rail car's breaks failed and the car went into the water. Workers were able to save the youngest daughter and the son but Pittee's two older daughters Mary and Eliza and the young black girl drowned." Mr. Humpphrey finished his story in barely more than a whisper.

"I read about them," I replied. I left out the part that I also swam with them and their nannies, Pearl and Sara.

"Yes, but the importance lies not in the tragedy itself, but in what occurred after the tragedy," Humpphrey continued.

"Pe...the nanny," I whispered.

"Yes. The nanny. Following the tragedy of the young girls, Lewis Tressman, what is the phrase you kids use, went bonkers?" I smiled, despite the heaviness of the moment, at hearing Mr. Humpphrey say 'bonkers'. He smiled, too. "Tressman attacked one of the nannies. We know of this since Kate wrote of the incident in her journal as well as in..."

"A letter to her sister," Jon interjected.

"Very good, Son. Clever like your father."

Jon nodded shyly.

"Kate wrote that Mr. Tressman took something from the nanny. Do you know what it was?" I asked.

"Yes."

He rummaged through more piles on a different table until he pulled out a very old looking, yellowed paper. Drawn in pen was the image of a frayed piece of rope that looked exactly like the royal braid, labeled, of course, as The Mermaid's Knot. My scalp tingled where my own Braid of Mar was firmly attached. It was hidden from sight, safely tucked safely under my mass of hair. The Mermaid's Knot, the Royal Braid, Pearl's Royal Braid ripped mercilessly from her head in a rage by Tressman.

"The Mermaid's Knot?" Jon asked. "So it's real?"

"Oh very real indeed child. Originally named by a Spanish Captain who frequented St. Augustine's port. He made note in his log of a special rope he sought to find after coming across a piece in a small port on Spain's Atlantic Coast. He drew the rope in his log and dubbed it the Mermaid's Knot for its strength and beauty."

"Why would Tressman bother to hide a piece of rope?

"Perhaps because of its strength or perhaps because of its beauty. We may never know of his motives. Or perhaps you, Storm, will discover why in the near future."

I looked at him and he smiled. Jon looked between the two of us, confusion on his face.

"Right, so Tressman built a secret room that no one has found all because he wanted to hide some rope that he stole from the nanny? This is the dumbest treasure hunt ever," Jon grumped.

"Where did Kate talk about this? We didn't find anything in her letters," I replied, ignoring Jon's comment.

"No, not her letters because this wasn't something she told her sister. In fact, this was something she told only one other soul about, her eldest daughter. And since the 1880's, descendants of Kate have searched for the stolen Mermaid's Knot. The original fragment was passed down through the generations. I had the honor of touching it years ago. And believe me that it was softer than silk, brighter than polished gold and stronger than iron; a masterpiece of design, beauty and strength. The trouble was, and still is, where does the rest of it hide? Where did Tressman put it? That is still the mystery. A mystery that Rean is now in charge of."

He stood up and opened one of the French doors. His cheeks were flushed. "It's getting quite stuffy in here, no?"

"But how do you know all of this?" I asked, already leaning toward my own conclusions.

Mr. Humpphrey's face went from rosy to pale. "I've lived in Saint Augustine all of my life. Choices made long ago, before I had any mind for consequences, made this town's secrets my secrets. Now I must still bear them, along with their consequences. But bearing them and working to solve them are two different things. I gave up trying to solve them decades ago when I realized it wasn't just myself that was at risk by my actions. Unfortunately, my decision came too late," he replied in a monotone voice. I followed his distant gaze and for the first time I noticed a small, framed photograph hung on the wall behind me. It was in a weathered, wooden frame. Pictured under a canopy of Spanish Moss and vines was a much younger Mr. Humpphrey, a beautiful woman who I guessed was his wife, Victoria, and a toddler. The little girl wore a white, sleeveless dress and was laughing while being held in her mother's arms.

Chapter Seventeen

"Yeah, here we are," I said. It was the first either Jon or I had spoken since leaving Mr. Humpphrey's house. *Was that little girl his daughter? Was she part of the tragedy he spoke of? How had he found out about the mers and Nana's search?*

"I guess I'll see you tomorrow?" Jon asked me.

"Yeah," I mumbled. My mind was still on Mr. Humpphrey.

"Awe, do ya have to leave so soon?" Sara asked in an overly affectionate voice as she sauntered down the stairs from the porch to where we stood in the driveway.

Jon's eyes looked glazed.

"Hey," I said as I noticed what was going on. "Stop it, Sara!"

"What?" Sara asked as her long fingers slowly stroked Jon's hair.

"That!" I motioned to her and then to Jon.

"Oh, whatever, you're no fun. I bet he's hot, aren't you?" Sara's voice purred with her question to him.

Jon nodded slowly, like he was in a trance.

"I bet you want to come for a swim with me." One of Sara's dress straps slipped off her shoulder. A stupid grin was on Jon's face as he nodded again. She picked up his hands and guided him to the beach walkover.

"Stop!" I growled. A strange haze flitted in and out of my vision. I refused to let Sara treat Jon like one of her play things. As Rowan once told me, the stronger will prevails, regardless of whether you are guiding water, weather, or people. Right now, the stronger will was mine because Sara froze in mid stride. She dropped Jon's hands.

"Whatever," she said back to me. "I wasn't really trying anyway. Hope you're strong enough to win a real war of wills when the time comes. And as for you, little Johnny, perhaps some other time for that swim." She winked and kissed him on his cheek. Then she turned and strolled, alone, over the boardwalk to the beach. Jon still stood frozen and followed her longingly with his gaze.

"Jon," I said.

No response.

I walked over and gave him a shake. "Jon?"

"Huh?"

"You were going to go home, remember?"

"Oh, right. Home. Yeah." He looked at me with a confused expression.

"Go home, Jon."

"Okay." His eyes were still on the walkway.

"Jon." I shook him again by the shoulders.

"What?" He gave his head a little shake of his own. When he looked back to me his eyes were focused again.

"You sure you're okay with the two bikes?" I asked.

"Yeah, no problem." He smiled at me. He seemed back to normal but still stole a glance toward the beach like there was something he meant to do but forgot.

"Home, Jon."

"Yeah. Okay, right. Home. See ya, Storm," he said as he hopped on his bike, held the other bike out with his right hand on the handlebars to steady it and rode off. With a sigh, I headed up to the deck after I saw Jon ride out of sight.

"Hi, Nana."

Nana looked up from her book. She gave me a smile. "Did Sara find you?"

"Yeah, she sure did," I said still feeling angry about how she treated Jon. I rubbed the small bumpy scar left behind by Paige's ring and wondered just how many others Sara was going to hurt by her carelessness? I sat down on the chair next to Nana and curled my legs around to the side.

"Oh, well she said she was going to surf for a bit. I think that's her down there," she said and motioned with her glass of white wine to a slim figure near the water.

I looked to where Nana pointed and sure enough, Sara's beautiful silhouette stood near the water. Two guys were talking with her. Then all three of them headed into the waves.

Good luck boys, I thought. *I sure hope you're good swimmers.*

"Pearl and Rowan were over earlier also," Nana said.

"Oh?" I tried to keep my voice casual as I turned my attention back to Nana.

"I told them you were doing some extra work for school." She glanced sideways at me with a grin.

"Oh my God, thank you Nana," I exhaled. "They would have totally freaked if they knew I went to see..." I stopped talking because Nana had also forbade me from seeing Humpphrey.

"It's alright. I knew you'd go there eventually, Storm." Her eyes met mine. They looked sad.

"Oh," I replied.

Nana looked back to the ocean. "Anyway, they said they had to work on setting up for the party this weekend but Rowan plans on stopping by tomorrow to, now what did he say...oh yeah, to see if his little fish wanted to fly again."

I smiled at the memory of his strong arms tossing me from the water the other night after our practice session. And then those same strong arms wrapped around my waist and his lips and his...

"Ahem," Nana cleared her throat. "Am I right to think I may not want to know what he meant?"

Embarrassed, I stuttered a few words, but she thankfully waved me off, "there are some things best left unspoken. Pearl also mentioned something about a task she gave you to work on. She wanted to know how it was going."

"Oh, well, that's not going so great." *I'm horrible at riddles!*

"Well, she said you need to get it done before the party."

"Okay." *Seriously?*

We watched the ocean in silence for a few minutes.

"So how was the meeting with Mr. Humpphrey? Is he still as garrulous as ever?" Nana asked.

"Umm," I wasn't really sure what to tell her. *Every previous time I tried to talk to her about the Tressman mystery she told me to stop asking questions and just let her and Z work on it. Meeting with Humpphrey would obviously be a direct ignoring of her instructions. But then she seemed to know I'd ignore her. So, if I told her now about today, would she get mad or would the information help her? Of course it would help her, but right now I'm not so sure I want to help her.* We still hadn't made up for the fight when I made it back in from the Atlantic after my first swim and near death experience. I was still angry about being kept in the dark all those years, but I also felt bad about some of the words that were said. To make it worse, neither of us had apologized. And now the days had turned to weeks and like an untreated cut, our unresolved issues had festered and become infected to the point of not even knowing where to start...

"How could you have kept this from me?" I yelled at her, still dripping wet from my first swim in the Atlantic.

"I had to, don't you understand? If anyone knew of your existence, including you, chances are you wouldn't be around today!" Nana, who so rarely raised her voice, made her own strong stance.

"But all those years I felt different, strange, awkward and you just sat there, silently watching me struggle! And today, you and Z just stood there and watched Rowan take me to the water. And then that THING attacked me. I almost died! Do you even care about that? Did you and Z even think about that? If I had known all along, I could have prepared. When do I get control over my own life, or death as the case may be."

"Many people have risked their lives for you and you need to understand that. While I did watch you struggle, I knew the struggling would end."

"UGH! Great, that's very comforting. Did you also know I'd be attacked on the same day I found out I was a mermaid?" I stamped my foot.

"Actually, we always knew it to be a possibility which is why we tried to prolong it as long as possible. Believe it or not, the entire planet is not centered around you. You are one piece in a very complicated and convoluted puzzle that has been twisting and changing for centuries. And we are all doing the very best we can."

"Great, so now I'm just some puzzle piece. Nice. Way to make a girl feel special."

"Damn it!" Nana hit the table with her fist. "Stop the Goddamn attitude. There are more people than you may even know who depend on your survival. Beyond that, your father and I have given up nearly everything for you. We love you and would give our own lives for you. But you are so stuck on your pity train that you can't even see what others are doing for you.

"What others are doing for me? Like what? Keeping secrets from me and then telling me I'm all important but then telling me to stop asking questions?"

Look Stormy,"

"DON'T CALL ME STORMY! I'm not your Stormy. You gave up that right when you kept this from me because if you actually cared about me, YOU WOULD HAVE TOLD ME!" I screamed, tears of anger streamed down my face and my hands were clenched tightly in fists.

Nana's mouth opened as if to respond, but then she just closed it again. Her lips tightened into a straight line and she walked out to the porch and left me huffing and dripping on my own in the kitchen...

And now we sat together. Separated by an invisible barrier of tension and separateness created from the weeks that had passed since the argument. I had been so busy with my training and with the class that I hadn't seen much of Nana, anyway. I suppose she's been busy on the mystery of the braid. I should tell her what I thought about the secret room, but like the meeting with Humpphrey I wasn't sure I wanted to.

"I'm going to tell Jon," I said flatly.

"Oh Storm," Nana's voice took on a sad tone. She took a slow sip of her wine, "I was afraid of this. You have to understand something about us." She looked up and met my inquisitive eyes. "Us humans."

Oh! I was taken back...*she isn't including me in the 'us'*

"We are limited. Limited in strength, limited in our ability to survive, and limited most of all in years on this earth. You don't have those limitations. You must, however, respect ours."

"I didn't ask for this. I didn't ask to be what I am. I don't even think I want to be a mermaid anymore." Tears welled in my eyes. I felt so very alone. Whether I wanted to admit it or not, I missed talking to Nana.

"You don't have that choice."

"I never have the choice, apparently. Everyone else just gets to decide for me. Well just let me know where I can sit or stand or take a pee. I sure wouldn't want to screw up everybody's lives even more than I already am."

"Storm, stop."

"Stop what? Being angry? I don't want this! And now I feel like I'm just screwing up everything by being me."

"You're not screwing anything up. This is a very stressful time for all of us. But, like it or not, you have to rise up and take this on. We are depending on you, just like my mother depended on me when she passed the secret of the braid and the mystery of its location on to me."

"And if I don't?" I lashed back at her.

"Then you are one selfish little girl who a lot people risked their lives and the lives of others to protect until you were old enough and strong enough to return the favor."

"I'm not being selfish."

"Well, then stop acting like it. I am doing everything in my power to make good on my promise to the clan, your mom and dad sacrificed everything they had to protect you. Z, Pearl, Sara, and Rowan are working to get you up to speed by the Solstice and you still find reason to complain. It may not be easy, but like it or not, you have responsibilities beyond your own moods. Nobody promised life would be easy, for human or mer, so it's time to stop this woe-is-me pity party. Your visit with Humpphrey today with Jon, that was stupid but understandable. I didn't stop you even after Mr. Manistar called to let me know. You're going to do what you want, I understand that. You are now at the age where we can only protect you so much; while nearly mature for a mer, you are also creating your own vulnerability because of your impetuousness. Others can take advantage of you if you let them and believe me they will try."

"If it's so serious, why can't everyone just tell me why! Why is seeing Humpphrey or hanging with Jon such big deals?"

"Humans are fragile, Storm. We can't keep up with your kind for very long and when we try, often tragedy strikes. I know you're still angry, but don't let your anger at me cloud your listening to what I have to tell you now. You asked for an answer. I'm going to give you one."

"Fine. I'm listening."

"As you know, I was the one chosen by my mother to continue the search for the braid stolen those many years ago, which is also why I kept my maiden name, to keep the Harn name alive. Each generation of chosen daughter kept her maiden name so she could be traced back to Kate and to the Mermaid's Knot. I was only just a touch older than you when my mother told me. And, despite her warnings to keep the secret to myself, I enlisted a friend to help me. We were so close, I couldn't imagine keeping something like this, something so huge and magical, from this person. I talked to my mother, no, I *pleaded* with her. She, in turn, talked to Z. Time was beginning to run short for the mers and Z knew it. Now thinking back those 50 some-odd years ago, time was nothing as short as it is now." Nana's gaze drifted to the rolling waves, her eyes reflected the light of the retreating day and her mind drifted back to the place where memories are kept.

"Z came to me one night, we sat on this very porch and she warned me of the danger inherent with knowledge, inherent with the mixing of our kinds. But I was young and like most teenagers, I had the belief in my own immortality. It's an immortality of mind, however, given to us humans at a certain age unlike the immortality of body such as you have inherited. We only think we are immortal and unstoppable which makes us act brave and foolhardy. In the end though, our bodies are frail and subject to all the hardships just like the very young and the very old. Teenagers, God bless them, are the dumbest creatures propelled by their belief that they are unstoppable and all knowing."

Nana paused and took another slow sip from her perspiring glass. She let it linger in her mouth as if drawing some kind of internal strength from the pale liquid. Eventually she swallowed and her eyes closed to mere slits, lost in her own thoughts and memories. I was afraid she wasn't going to keep telling her story. I waited patiently for a minute, but that turned into two and finally at three I could no longer risk that being the end. I thought I might explode.

She looked at me suddenly, grey eyes shining like brushed steel in the afternoon light. "You must be dying of thirst. There's some Ginger Beer for you in the fridge. Go get yourself some. No protesting, get up and get yourself your drink and then come back and join me," Nana said.

Reluctantly, I went inside and got a Ginger Beer from the fridge. The first sip burned my throat as usual but in that burning, the dryness disappeared. Ginger Beer always helped the burning, not as well as Pearl's Salt ale, but better than nothing. I hadn't realized how thirsty I was until that first sip which was immediately followed by a large gulp. *Ahh.* I sighed as the liquid rejuvenated my limbs and the subtle headache I had been dealing with without being conscious of it, evaporated. *How does she always know?*

Maybe Nana was right, maybe teenagers, human *and* mer, aren't that bright.

She didn't rush right into the story as I curled myself back up in the chair. She watched the ocean and cupped her glass with the tips of her slim fingertips.

Oh Nana, you look like you've aged. Perhaps I am *being selfish. You've struggled all these years protecting me, losing time in your search in order to focus on mine...*

"So, as I was saying," she cleared her throat, "we had the charge of finding Pearl's braid. We were included in the secrets of the mers, we thought of them as friends, as allies, on this quest. But what we didn't know in our foolishness, was that not all mers are to be trusted. Not all mers wanted the braid found for the same reasons. Not all mers cared much about using a few humans to reach their ultimate goal. We are but tiny blinks of an eye to them, barely visible on their...your time scale."

I dropped my face and examined my legs. I felt ashamed when Nana related me to mers that didn't respect human life. *Will I ever lose my human-ness? Will I ever take human life for granted?*

"My careless actions caused the death of an innocent young girl, Storm. Winning always has a cost," Nana whispered, "the question is, what is the price that we...or you...are willing to pay?"

When our kinds mix it doesn't end well' were the words Rowan used, I thought.

"I think I understand," I said.

"Yes, I think you do. This choice will be yours to make. Sometimes the greatest burdens are the ones of choice. Take it seriously and choose wisely."

"Hey, Nana?"

"Yes?"

"I'm sorry."

"Thank you."

"I love you."

"I love you, too."

We sat back in our chairs and watched the clouds drift in the sky. As the sun moved behind our backs, the sea breeze picked up. The soft wind tickled my skin and made my hair dance around my head. My braid, allowed to hang loose while I was on the security of the deck, sang its beautiful melody to the sea.

Chapter Eighteen

"No really, it's *fine*," I told Jon for the millionth time in the past five minutes.

"I'm sorry, it's just a friend of my dad said we could use it if we just drove around a bit first," he replied for the millionth time in those same five minutes. "And well, it's better than riding bikes." He attempted a smile but it sort of looked more like a painful grimace.

"Really, it's okay." It truly was, it was actually pretty funny.

"Right, every girl wants their date to pick them up in a giant black hearse with *GhostAugustine Ghost Tours* printed on the side doors."

"At least you make a statement. I just wish I knew ahead of time so I could have worn black." I smiled.

"Ugh." Jon sunk lower in the huge, black leather bench seat.

Jon's dad was asked by his friend to drive the ghost tour hearse around town to do a little promotion and drum up some business. The deal was, Jon could take the hearse for the evening if he did the driving around part, too. He was mortified. I kind of liked it because it made everything seem less serious.

"So tell me about this car, er, hearse."

Jon looked at me out of the corner of his eye. "Well she's a '74 Cadillac. Her name is Tariqua. It means Lady of the Night. She really was a working girl until the owner of the tour company bought her and had her modified to fit the business."

"A working girl? You mean..."

"Yup, she actually was an ambulance that served as a real hearse driving around real dead bodies."

"Yikes, that's sort a creepy." I shuttered and made a quick glance to the back of the hearse.

He started to apologize again but I held up my hand to stop him and smiled. "No, really, it's fine," I said but silently decided to keep my gaze forward.

"This just isn't exactly how I pictured tonight going, you know, you and me, a date..."

"Well, I think it's fun." I wasn't sure if this was the human side or the mer side talking, but suddenly small life events like this really did seem pretty insignificant. I mean, I would rather laugh than worry so much. Even the Jon thing seemed not as big of a deal. I mean, so he liked me, it didn't mean I had to "like" him back, being friends was still an option.

"We just have to drive around for thirty minutes or so and then I can park this beast and we are free to enjoy the rest of the evening."

"Sounds great to me. You know, Saint Augustine keeps me on my toes. If you asked me a few months ago if I could imagine driving downtown in a hearse, I would have thought you were crazy. But here we are. When will this town stop with its surprises?"

Jon laughed. He was slowly relaxing. *I wonder how he'd take it if I told him the truth about me...one more of Saint Augustine's little surprises.*

"You look really pretty tonight. I forgot to tell you before. It looks like your skin has really taken to the Florida sun, it's almost glowing!"

"Thanks."

I watched him concentrate on the road. His sandy blond hair, his white shirt hanging loosely around him. He looked so young...so human. Nana's words came back to me...*humans are fragile.*

I was different now; I was more immortal than mortal and I even had a scar to prove it. But he was cute in his own way. In another life, I think the two of us would have made a great pair, a team. Not lovers, but something closer to brother and sister.

He caught me looking at him.

The heat rose in my cheeks.

I smiled.

He smiled.

We sat quietly with our own thoughts as he drove over the Bridge of Lions. The lights of downtown welcomed us.

"Hey, it's a Hearse!"

"Can we take your picture?"

"I want to get in!"

"What do you guys do?"

"Is there a dead body in there?"

"Wait, let me get my boyfriend for a picture!"

I smiled and waved and posed for pictures while Jon answered questions and handed out brochures to all of the inquisitive tourists. About a quarter of the way into our PR session, Jon finally smiled a genuine smile! We were back to being the two of us again, before the awkward part when hanging out was labeled *a date*. Jon was my friend and I was his. Who knew we needed a hearse to bring the two of us back to where we needed to be. By the end of the thirty minutes, I knew that I wanted to tell him...no, I *needed* to tell him the truth about me, about what I was. He was my friend and he deserved to know who I was. Or maybe I just really needed a friend's understanding. For either or both reasons, I mustered up the courage as we made one final loop around downtown.

"Umm, Jon?"

"Yeah," he said and looked over at me. His eyes widened. The color abruptly drained from his face and he nearly lost control of the hearse as he rounded the corner from Charlotte onto Hypolita.

"HOLY SH...!" He began to exclaim but stopped mid explicative as he struggled to regain control of the car. He nearly hit a fire hydrant but straightened out in time to avoid it. He drove slowly along the narrow street until we came to another narrow road. He turned right and pulled over. The engine rumbled beneath us.

"Oh my God, Jon, you okay? You look like you just saw a ghost or something," I said as my hands clutched the dashboard. Ignoring the endless jokes and puns bouncing in my head from my last statement, I just sat silently until Jon's breathing returned to normal.

"Yikes, Storm. I swear, when I just looked at you, your eyes glowed in the dark. I must be seeing things," he said and put the car in park and rubbed his eyes vigorously.

"No turning back now," I mumbled. "Jon?" The sweet tone of my voice surprised even me. I paused to let the ring hover gracefully in the air around us. "I need to tell you something." I looked down at my knees so he couldn't see my eyes. "Let's turn into this parking lot first. I need to tell you something important and I don't want you driving when I tell you."

Jon nodded slowly and pulled back onto the road. He drove to the old Toques place parking and pulled into an open spot.

"Okay, what?" He asked. His voice sounded still on edge.

"Umm..." 'choose wisely' Nana's voice rang in my head. *I know, Nana, I thought, I'm not planning on dragging him out to sea to his death, I just think he should know who or at least what I am and I need him to listen.*

I figured since he had parked the hearse, the danger was minimal. *Now or never.* I told myself. I took the chance and looked him straight in the eyes.

"Oh lord! Oh my GOD! Storm, what the..." He sputtered and pushed at his door trying to get away from me. But the door wouldn't open. "Damn it, let me out you stupid car!"

I lifted one eyebrow. My eyes widened ever so slightly. *Calm down,* I thought as I visualized a blue haze draping on his body.

He froze and slumped slightly in his seat.

Dear God I am *a monster.* One look, barely pleading from me, one thought barely a command and he was powerless.

"Jon," I spoke sweetly and softly, "I need you to relax and listen for a moment, 'kay?"

"Uh huh." He nodded his head slowly, a slight grin formed on his lips.

Boys, I thought. *How can Sara find this sporting? It isn't even challenging to control him. He's no more than a marionette to which I hold all the strings.*

"Okay, Jon, look...I need to tell you about who I am. Do you understand?"

Another nod.

Do it quick, Storm, like ripping off a band-aid, I told myself.

"Jon...I'm a mermaid."

The ring of my voice dissipated and we were left in the dark, black hearse with nothing but our own quiet breathing and the thumping of our hearts.

"Right, you're a..." He still seemed confused so I turned my eyes away. I glanced sideways at him and saw his face regain its composure.

"You're a what?! Okay seriously Storm, what's going on?"

"Jon, I'm telling you the truth." I looked at him again. I saw his eyes take in mine, then his eyes wandered to my bare arms, across to my full breasts and down to my slim waist and finally to my bare legs which extended well beyond the hem of my skirt; my skin shimmered even in the night. I sat very still so as not to scare him.

"You're a mermaid?" He asked.

"Technically, half mermaid, but yeah. That's why my body changed so fast after I got here, remember how I looked when I first arrived? My hair, my body, my face? That all changed to *this*, I motioned to my body...that's why you became attracted to me." The words made my stomach feel nauseous to say. He only liked me because I was a mermaid. I swallowed too loudly and continued. "And all these nights I've been training and learning how to be a mermaid. That's why I'm exhausted in class. I only just found out myself a short time ago.".

"You're a fish." He looked straight ahead and nodded to himself, his hands held the large, black steering wheel firmly at ten and two.

"Well, you don't have to be mean about it," I said.

"HA! You're kidding, right? Are you trying to get back at me for the stupid hearse?" He turned suddenly to me.

I deliberately stared at him. I saw him take me in again, the hair, the eyes, the body.

"But you were scared of the water!" He burst out; his arms flew wide in exasperation.

"I know...weird, right?" I said and gave a shy shrug.

He took a deep breath with his eyes closed. He slowly opened them and looked at me again.

"But..." He started to speak but decided against it.

"Take your time," I said.

"So, aren't you supposed to lure me to my death now?" His mouth curled into a smirk.

I exhaled. *Is he actually accepting this? More importantly, is he actually accepting me?*

"Well, I can if you want me to." I smiled.

"Hmm, maybe later." He laughed.

"Seriously? I mean, you aren't mad or scared or freaked out?" I asked.

"No, I'm actually a bit relieved. It explains a lot. Mermaids are pretty ditsy, right?" He asked.

"Hey!" I punched him in the shoulder.

"Ouch. And strong." He rubbed his shoulder. "Okay, okay, but there is one thing you got wrong."

"What's that?" I asked.

"I liked you from the moment I saw you, not just since you've changed."

"Awe, Jon." I leaned over and gave him a hug. I felt him inhale deeply.

"That's the smell!" He exclaimed.

"What?" I asked, pulling away in embarrassment. I was sure to put on extra lotion tonight to mask my scent.

"The one I kept smelling in the class and outside when we ate lunch! It was salty and oaty and repulsive and addictive all at the same time!"

"Gee, thanks."

"No, I mean, it's like a scent that grows on you. You don't realize you like it at first until it disappears and then you wish it would come back!"

"Really?"

"Really. So the others?"

"Yeah, Rowan, Sara and Pearl, too."

"You know, I actually feel better because there was no way I could compete with Rowan. Now at least I know that it wasn't just me. I mean, seriously, how could a human compete with a merman, right?"

At the mention of Rowan, I felt guilty again and as if Jon read my mind, he said, "Awe Storm, I thought I wanted us to be more than friends but it all got so weird after I asked you out. I kind of wished we could just go back to the way we were. Like the other night working on the paper and reading Humpphrey's book. That was fun! That's the way I want it to be."

"Oh my God! Me too!" I exclaimed.

"So, friends?" He asked.

"No, best friends," I said with a smile.

"Fish breath," he said mockingly.

"Hey, who you callin' fish breath monkey boy."

We both laughed in the front seat of the hearse, human and mermaid, until our bellies hurt.

"I think it's time to ditch the hearse," Jon announced. "Unless there's anything else you need to tell me, like is your Nana's a werewolf or are our professors really here to find Loch Ness?"

"No, that's all I got," I said.

Unless you count the search for Pearl's braid, the impending clan war, and my supposed unveiling at the Solstice Party, I thought. *But I suppose those little items can wait till later.*

We walked hand in hand down Saint George Street. I was so happy to have my friend back!

"So do you grow a tail in the water like in the movies?" He asked as we strolled past lighted store fronts.

"No." I laughed.

"No?! How can you be a mermaid without a tail?"

"I don't know, I guess that's just Hollywood. I don't need one, my legs kick like a tail. It's kind of weird actually, like I don't really control it, it just sort of happens."

"Huh. Do you talk to sharks and stuff?"

"No, I'm not Flipper," I said as I laughed. I punched him in the arm lightly. He nearly fell over.

"Oops. Sorry," I said as I grabbed his arm to balance him.

"So, I guess along with the good looks comes a bit of muscle?"

"I guess so. I'm sorta still figuring all this out myself."

"Well, add muscle to your list," he said with a laugh as he rubbed his arm. "And remind me not to piss you off."

"I can hear lots underwater, too. We, the others and I, can also hear each others' thoughts underwater. Kind of cool, but then again, some thoughts I wished wouldn't be heard. Oh and this," I reached under my hair and quickly showed him my braid being sure no one else was nearby, "this is called a braid of mar. Every female mer gets one when they turn sixteen. The royal braid, the one the book called the Mermaid's Knot, is special, it only goes to the heir to the territory."

"So that wasn't just a picture of rope?" He asked.

"Nope, hair. Mermaid hair."

"Wow!"

It was so nice to be able to talk to someone about this, someone who wasn't centuries old and treated me like a little kid.

Jon bought us some ice-cream, mint chip for him, pistachio for me. The streets were buzzing with activity of the evening. I sped up whenever people started crowding too close to us. Unlike Sara, I didn't welcome the added attention. I also checked often to make sure my braid was tucked well away. The memory of the ending to the shopping trip still hovered darkly in my mind.

We sat on the stone benches just outside the gardens on the corner of Hypolita Street to finish our ice-creams.

"Hey, you said you were *half* mermaid, Mom or Dad half? Your dad's not like Poseidon is he and he's goin' to strike me down with a thunderbolt or something?"

"First of all, that would be Zeus who uses lightning bolts, Poseidon has the Trident thing. But no, my dad is Matthew Harn, human all the way. My mom's a mermaid. But I don't know who she is." I couldn't completely hide my sadness.

"Oh, I'm sorry."

"S'okay. That was the other reason I wanted to talk to Mr. Humpphrey, with all of his knowledge, he was bound to know who my mom was. I mean, it would've been quite a scandal right? Mermaid gets together with a human and they have a baby. Doesn't happen everyday, ya know?"

"No, I guess it doesn't," Jon said. "Hey, what about Pearl?"

"What do you mean?"

"I mean, does she know your mom?"

"She does but she won't tell me. Mers have this weird sense of defining other people's truth. To be honest, I think she just doesn't want to tell me. I don't know. The most she said was that my mom would be at the Solstice Party."

"The what?"

"Oh, sorry, there's this party going on this weekend for the Summer Solstice. It happens every year. The northern clan and the southern clan get together and try to ignore their differences."

"Back up a bit, Storm, you're losing me," Jon said.

"Okay, there are these two Atlantic clans..." I said.

I explained the history of the division between the Sea Star Clan and the Lionfish Clan in a condensed version to Jon.

"Wow, that's crazy. And it's all been happening here?"

"Yeah."

"Wow," he said.

"Hey, are you any good at riddles?" I asked, suddenly remembering Pearl's assignment.

"Yeah! I love 'em."

"Well, how about this one, 'At night they come without being fetched. By day they are lost without being stolen. What are they?'"

"Seriously, you don't know?" He asked. "I thought you'd at least give me a hard one."

"What do you mean?" I asked, taken aback by his cavalier tone.

"Storm, what comes out at night but goes away in the day?"

"The moon?"

"Close...try again," he said.

"Stars?"

"Yeah, duh! Stars," Jon said and rolled his eyes. "Got any other ones?"

"Umm no. Thanks!" I said. *Huh, why would Tressman write a riddle about stars?*

"Well, now this is a surprise!" A beautiful voice rang high and clear.

Jon and I looked up. Sara and Paige walked toward us.

"Is she one, too?" Jon whispered motioning to Paige.

"Yeah," I replied.

"Out kind of late little Stormy, aren't you? Where's Rowan?" She looked at Jon.

"Oh, he's with Pearl setting up stuff for the party," I said. "Paige, this is my friend Jon."

"Pleasure." Paige's voice range smoothly in the night.

I bumped Jon to make his mouth close. I hated when mers messed with humans for no reason.

"So, what are you ladies doing tonight? I figured you'd be helping with the party, too." I asked.

"Nah, just wasting time." *And looking for trouble*, I thought.

"Want to join us?" Sara asked.

I looked over to Jon. He had already nodded his head.

"Brilliant!" Paige exclaimed. "Dinner and now dessert."

Sara and Paige laughed together. I was nervous about where this may lead. I absently rubbed my thumb on my middle finger where the moonstone ring had burned me Nothing but a small bit of raised skin remained but the memory of it was bright enough to keep my senses alert. Sara's behavior was far from predictable, but she seemed to be in one of her good moods and it was really hard to resist her.

The four of us roamed the streets of downtown for the next couple of hours. Sara and Paige seemed to have an *in* with somebody at every place we stopped. They drank Margaritas, Jon and I drank virgin ones. We danced at one place, we sang karaoke at another, and we listened to a mariachi band at another. It was an amazing night. We all laughed and talked and acted silly.

I suppose I overreacted, I thought, *Sara and Paige are being really cool.*

After the mariachi band finished, Sara pulled me aside and said, "Jon is a sweet little boy."

"Yeah," I replied.

"So you and Rowan..." she started.

"Oh, no...Jon and I are just friends," I said. I looked over and eyed Paige running her fingers through Jon's hair and giggling.

"Friends," she said, "that's so cute."

"Paige and I were thinking of heading out for a little midnight swim, care to join?" Sara asked me as we left A1A Aleworks.

"No thanks. I think Jon and I are just going to wander around a bit before we head home," I said. *I think it's time to get Jon away from the sirens*, I thought.

"Awe, it would be fun." Sara's voice was so seductive. Paige and Jon came over to join us. I felt heat emanate from Jon's body.

Quit it guys, I thought sternly. *He's just a boy! Leave him alone.* The air rippled in front of my eyes, like I looked through water...water that pushed both Paige and Sara back a step from Jon. Thunder rumbled through the tension charged air.

Their faces betrayed a momentary look of confusion, but as quickly as the expression appeared, it disappeared.

"Looks like our little orphan is growing up," Paige said after she regained her composure.

"Yeah, I guess so," Sara said with a smirk.

"Look guys, I just mean, I think we should go, that's all. Come on, Jon." I kept my voice as light as I could. The air surround me had lost the shimmer but I knew if I was pushed I could bring it back.

Paige giggled.

"Little sister, you really have to loosen up. We're just having some fun with our new friend," Sara said.

"Oh yeah?" I asked feeling defensive of Jon. "What ever happened to those two guys I saw you with on the beach yesterday?"

"Oops," Sara giggled. "Whatever, it wasn't my fault," she said with a wave of her hand. "Well, I'm sure it's nearly curfew, right?" Sara looked at me and smiled.

"Oh shame, we were just about to have some fun!" Paige said and then turned to Jon, "Maybe a rain check on that swim?" Her voice oozed seductiveness.

"Not to worry Paige," Sara said, "remember the surprise this year at the party?"

"Oh yes!" Paige looked between Jon and me. I had no idea what they were talking about and felt the hair on the back of my neck bristle in warning.

Sara and Paige laughed, winked at me and walked off arm in arm.

What are they talking about a surprise? Tonight had been akin to an emotional whiplash with those two. I watched the two gorgeous forms retreat into the crowd of an oncoming ghost tour. Their laughter could still be heard drifting along the street and it sounded eerily like wind chimes. I remembered the story of the Saint George Street angels. *Humpphrey and his legends sure seem to be right about a lot of things.*

Jon gave his head a little shake and took a deep breath of the night air. It probably no longer seemed as sweet now that the two additional mermaids left. But he appeared to have recovered his senses. "So what do you want to do now?" Jon asked.

"Let's walk for a bit," I said. I had a strange feeling my days of being and acting like a normal teenager were numbered and I just wanted this memory, me and Jon, two kids hanging out, to linger a bit longer.

"Okay!" He smiled, took my hand in his and we strolled along the seawall admiring the sailboats and talking about absolutely nothing important.

Chapter Nineteen

My window was opened wide to let in the evening's sea breeze. The blue silk gown caressed my body as I slipped it over my head. The night of the party had finally arrived and my heart beat with excitement, anticipation, fear, and nerves. I thought back to when I first arrived here. My first glimpse of Sara, Pearl, and Rowan, the mystery surrounding my true self, the revelations, the training, the near death experiences. All of it leading to tonight. I was about to be introduced to my extended family for the first time and inducted into the Sea Star Clan as an adult mer. *Whoa.*

I took one last look in the mirror. The fading light of the day created tiny reflections from my skin. My sun-highlighted curls fell loosely over my shoulders and my eyes just barely glowed. I usually forgot about my eyes, but their subtle glow was impressive and my ability to see in the dark was phenomenal.

Time to go. Ready or not, I thought.

******

"Why do we have to go by canoe again?" Jon's voice drifted from behind me as he paddled the aluminium two-seater canoe north from the boat ramp in Anastasia State Park.

"I don't know. Pearl said since you're a human, this was the only way we could arrive." I still wasn't sure why Jon was invited to the Solstice Party, but I didn't argue since it would be nice having someone there as clueless as I. I laughed at the memory of his response when I asked him to come, "Should I bring a mask and snorkel?"

Jon was barefoot like me and dressed in a white, linen, button down shirt and loose khaki pants that were rolled up above his ankles. His sandy blonde hair was in loose waves that floated around his head in the breeze. He gave little swishes of his head to move wayward curls from his eyes while he paddled.

I searched the distance for some sign of a party. So far, there was nothing but the dark, smooth waters of Salt Run and the moonless night sky. The full moon wasn't due to rise until just before midnight so the night was exceptionally dark.

"Everything okay back there?" I asked Jon after the canoe pitched and righted.

"Yeah, sorry, strange current running through here," he said. He sounded slightly out of breath.

Jon continued to paddle with increased effort. When I risked a quick glance back, I saw the beads of perspiration on his forehead and the wrinkles of concentration between his eyes. I quickly turned back foreword so he didn't get distracted by my glowing eyes; the near crash in the hearse was still fresh in my mind. The canoe seemed to be pulling to the right despite his best efforts to keep us in the middle of the channel.

A strong gust of cool air gave me goosebumps. Fog descended and blanketed our tiny craft.

"What the...?" Jon asked.

The canoe sped up toward the eastern bank. It swayed and shifted uncomfortably side to side.

"Hey, chill, Jon," I protested and turned to look at him, forgetting about hiding my eyes. His eyes were wide and confused as he sat with the paddle raised out of the water.

"I'm not doing anything. Whoa Storm, those eyes are freaky!"

"Thanks," I said sarcastically. "Would you mind trying to keep us on course?"

The canoe picked up more speed.

"I don't think it's up to me anymore. Hang on!" He shouted and I did. The canoe bucked and tipped. Water splashed over the sides.

"Is this some kind of mermaid joke?" Jon asked, his voice an octave higher than normal.

"I'm not sure, they are a pretty festive bunch!" I shouted back, too scared to turn around; my bright white knuckles clung to the boat's silver lip.

Our little canoe careened forward, I lost track of where we were in the foggy darkness. I clenched my jaw tightly to keep from screaming. The aluminium hull creaked under the strain of traveling so fast, the sides buckled inward.

One seam gave, then another. Water filled up the canoe beneath our seats. Then, suddenly and with a loud crunch, we came to a standstill. Or I should say, the *canoe* came to a standstill when it hit an embankment of sand. We, however, flew head over heals.

AHHHH! I screamed in my head but only a tiny squeak escaped from my tensed jaws.

I closed my eyes and prepared for the pain of impact. But rather than landing painfully on the sand, powerful arms wrapped around my waist and pulled me out of mid air. I ended up in a warm embrace, nestled into a broad chest that smelled of the sea.

"You sure know how to make an entrance don't you my little sea goddess," Rowan whispered playfully in my ear.

I opened my eyes and Rowan's face filled my gaze. He smiled and I smiled back. Then I remembered I wasn't the only one traveling in that canoe. I looked around just in time to see Jon cradled in Sara's arms. Apparently, she had caught Jon like Rowan caught me. Sara petted Jon's head like he was a puppy. Jon didn't seem too disturbed.

"I see our guest of honor has arrived. Looks like we can finally get this party started!" Sara's voice purred. Jon was completely entranced.

"Sara," Pearl said in a chiding tone.

"Oh fine," Sara replied with a roll of her eyes. "A mermaid can't have any fun anymore." And unlike Rowan's gentle placement of my feet on the sand, Sara just let go of Jon and he fell to the sand with a dull thud.

"Oops, sorry, Johnny," she said with a little shrug and walked over to the edge of the fog and joined Pearl.

As the mist dispersed, the expanse of the gathering became visible.

"Oh my God," I whispered when my eyes took in the scale.

Walking up next to Rowan and me, Jon brushed his pants and started to mumble something about guest treatment but I gave him a nudge with my arm and he stopped talking.

"What?" He asked. But I didn't have to answer because at that moment, he looked up and saw them...hundreds of them.

His jaw dropped with an audible clunk.

Surrounding us was the largest, most beautiful group of people, well, mers that I'd ever seen. Women in see-through gossamer dresses, others in bikinis, men in baggies, some in long flowing pants and still others in 15th century garb. Mers held guitars, sat beside djimbe drums and many had cats draped over their shoulders like living stoles.

A massive bon fire roared and sparked about ten yards away, a twenty-foot long table was adorned in crystal goblets filled with glowing liquid that seemed to be shift hues endlessly and another equally large table overflowed with food, both recognizable and foreign. Tall pillars of wood hung with flashing glass jars were standing proud. It was only on closer inspection of one of the jars that I realized the flashing was from fireflies caught within.

The smells were mouthwatering and all encompassing, the sights were overwhelming but the sound was very distinctly absent, save for the crackling of the fire.

Every single partygoer, even those by the drink and food tables, looked at us. Like a sea of LED party lights all facing the girl in the blue dress and the boy in a white shirt and khaki pants.

"Umm, hi?" I said feebly.

The thousands of glowing eyes blinked on and off as they stared back.

My hands were slippery and I rubbed them nervously along the side of my dress. Rowan put a comforting hand on my lower back and nudged my frozen legs forward toward Pearl.

She wore a thin white tank top and a long white skirt. Next to her, majestic as ever in one of two high-backed, ornately carved wooden chairs, sat Z in a dress of deep indigo. Her auburn hair cascaded around her shoulders and what could only be described as an inner light shone through her skin. Sara stood on the other side of Z. She wore a black, draping halter tank that shimmered with thousands of dark sequins and a short black skirt. Her wrists and ankles were adorned in dozens of sterling silver bangles. She held her arm high with of the glowing drinks in hand which set off a symphony of echoing chimes from the surrounding mers. "Welcome, Storm!" Sara announced in ringing tones.

I smiled, totally embarrassed.

"It's okay," Rowan reassured me. "Come on." His large hand still rested on my back, as much for support as for prevention of my escape. "We've been waiting a long time for you. No turning back now," he whispered. "Oh and take this to guide you. You might need it." He slipped the moonstone ring onto my middle finger.

"But," I hissed.

"It's okay, it won't hurt you anymore," he said with a wink and before I could protest further Z stood from her throne-like chair.

"To Storm!" Z proclaimed and raised her glowing glass high, hers shimmering like iced snow on a bright winter's day. Others followed in the toast and the beach turned to a sea of color, low and high.

There was thundering applause, laughter, music and the general sounds of a party returning to its gaiety. The awkward moment was over!

"You look beautiful!" Pearl said when I reached the trio. She softly brushed my long bangs from my eyes and then scooped up a black and white cat that hovered near my feet. It was Zelda from the house!

"She's been waiting for you, too," she smiled and stroked the cat.

"So, little Storm, are you ready for tonight?" Sara asked.

"I guess. This is quite a party. How can you call this a secret?"

"You'd be surprised how humans don't see what they believe not to be there," Z replied.

"Come I'll take you around," Pearl said.

I looked to make sure Jon was okay. He was surrounded by a handful of beautiful mermaids. They stroked his hair and his arms. He had an extremely stupid look on his face.

I guess he's okay without me for a few minutes.

Pearl and I walked arm in arm, little cricket-purr Zelda hung halfway over my shoulder. The soft sand gave way easily beneath my feet but I wasn't tiring.

Around the far side of the fire sat a young girl, or at least she looked young. Her skin was the shade of alabaster and she had white blonde hair. Her eyes glowed brightly as she watched us approach. They were cobalt or possibly purple, the dancing firelight made it difficult to tell.

"Oh my gosh, oh my gosh!" The girl started squealing with delight as she skipped over to us. "This is her, Pearl, isn't it?! I knew it! She's gorgeous. I can't believe you kept her from me. I mean, I could have helped train her and I totally would have kept it a secret. You know I'm super great at keeping secrets, well, sometimes. I mean, unless they're really too good to keep to yourself." Her voice was high but not squeaky. It was just a clear soprano sound like the music those tiny, silver chimes make. She spoke very fast, each sentence running into the next. "Is she all ready for tonight? Does she know yet? Can I help her? Please, please?"

"Storm, meet Lilli." Pearl said with a laugh.

Lilli's face lit up with an infectious smile. She stood up and wrapped me in her thin arms. Lilli was tiny compared to Pearl and me. Her head only came to my nose. The cat on my shoulders let out a disgruntled meow.

"Oops," she giggled. "I am soooo happy to meet you! I just know you and I are going to be BFF'S! We've all been waiting so anxiously for tonight!"

Lilli smiled and gave me another hug. "It's all just so exciting!" She said with a little bounce. "Well, there's the introduction ceremony and the challenge, but I know you'll do brilliantly and then the necklace ceremony. I think I may burst!"

"Huh? What challenge?" I asked.

"Oh, Pearl, haven't you told Storm about the challenge? I hope I haven't let the cat out of the bag so to speak." Lilli giggled at her own joke. "Not that we'd put cat's in bags, no, that wouldn't be nice at all...nor parachutes, definitely not."

"No, Lilli, all in time. She's just arrived, hasn't even had a drink yet," Pearl replied.

"Ooh, I'll get her some!" Lilli jumped with happiness. "Be back in a few!" And she skipped off. We heard her telling all the mers she passed that I was here. One by one heads turned our way.

"Wow, I've never met anybody quite so perky before."

"Yeah, that's a water sprite for you. They live in rivers and lakes. Quite a bubbly group, mischievous and wielders of very ancient and strong magic. But Lilli has a pure heart. She visits us quite often as she finds the action on the lake not always up to her level of activity. She enjoys a bit of fun and can get bored quite easily," Pearl said and we both looked to where she had bounded off. She was meant to be going to the drink table, but apparently got sidetracked along the way and now drummed away quite enthusiastically on a small bongo drum as others danced about her.

"Bored...and even more easily distracted than mers," Pearl said with a sigh. "It's probably best not to hold your breath for that drink. But even with her faults, she has a knack for showing up right when you need her. Loyalty is one thing not taken lightly by sprites. Revenge is another. Never...*ever* cross a water sprite."

I followed Pearl around the party and she introduced me to many more mers and a couple more sprites. The mers of the Sea Star Clan welcomed me warmly while the Lionfish Clan members were more reserved in their greetings.

"Is Jon okay?" I asked as Pearl handed me a drink that changed purple to green with each sip. It tasted like sweet tarts and made my throat warm. She called it Flicker Punch.

"Oh, he's fine. I asked Rowan to keep an eye on him," Pearl said and pulled me over to yet another group of mers playing guitars.

"What challenge was Lilli talking about?" I asked as we finally broke away from the group and their entrancing music.

"I'll explain later, we have to head back to Z. The ceremony is to begin soon."

"But what about my mom?" I blurted out before I could pull the words back in.

"Soon, love, very soon." Pearl's eyes twinkled and I thought I saw a tiny smirk on her lips.

Humph, I thought. *What if I walk right by mother and not even know it's her? She's somewhere at this party right now and I haven't a clue who she is.*

Pearl put her arm around my waist and led me back to Z. Now both chairs were occupied, one by Z and the other by a woman with an equally imposing presence. Next to them stood the largest hourglass I'd ever seen. It was at least three feet tall. The glass shimmered in the firelight and the sand inside the lower bowl was pink.

The woman next to Z eyed me with such intensity it made me feel very uncomfortable, kind of like when Paige stared at me in the shop. This woman's hair, also like Paige's, was black and shimmery like oil but the reflection of the bonfire made it seem as if it was also aflame. The uneven hem of her scarlet dress danced lightly in the breeze. The overall effect reminded me of a large jellyfish pulsing through the water...beautiful and deadly.

"Storm," Z spoke after I sat on the sand in front of her chair, "tonight, as you know, is one of our High Holidays. It's when Clan's put away their differences." Z looked to the woman on her left.

So that's Z's sister, I thought and suppressed a full body shiver.

"We come together in harmony and enjoy a night of eating, drinking, dancing, and of course, games!" Little shouts and hollers resounded around us by all of unseen mers just outside our intimate circle. "Each mer clan is identified by a kindred animal guide. Symbols of these guides, worn by each clan member, are a union of the purest silver, salt of the clan's sea and a tear from the clan's matriarch. The mighty Atlantic is home to two clans my dear Storm. Ours, the starfish, or sea star, symbolizes infinite divine love, guidance and intuition, and my sister Laverna's, the lion fish, symbolizes strength, speed, determination and the peril associated with beauty."

Lionfish. I know lionfish...why?

I struggled not to stare at the woman seated next to Z. To appear less obvious, I looked around at the group that was gathered. Sara and Pearl stood behind Z, Paige and a handsome man stood behind Laverna. The man was, of course, gorgeous. His dark, wavy hair was long, past his shoulders and his face looked like it was chiseled from a perfect piece of bronze-colored marble. There was something menacing, however, behind the chiseled mask of physical perfection. Paige smiled at me. *So Paige is the heir to Laverna's territory, she's Laverna's daughter! Wow.* The man, Paige's brother I guessed, scowled. This time the shiver won and tiny goosebumps erupted on my skin. *That's the guy! From downtown! The one that tried to stop Sara and me from leaving on the motorbike.*

"Pendants," Z continued, "are worn around the neck on a braid made of hair from the mer's mother and are given to the sons or daughters when they reach the age of transition. Tonight, Storm, is your final step in transition to mer adulthood."

Behind Z, Sara looked bored but Pearl gave me a nod of approval. I stole one more, brief glance at the man. His eyes glowed with a deep, golden hue and the lionfish pendant reflected the firelight and sent out random explosions of light.

Yikes, I thought. *What was that about peril hidden behind beauty?* I shuttered again.

"But before the ceremony begins officially, let me introduce you to your entire Atlantic family!" Z announced.

"Children!" Z's voice boomed. Mers all around stopped in mid action and turned their full attention to our small gathering in the sand.

"Come and join us!" Laverna called. Her voice resonated like a deep, cold, brass chime.

Mers sauntered toward our little circle; some sat on the sand around us while others stood arm in arm. The bonfire crackled in the distance. All eyes turned to Z and her sister, each seated in their beautiful chairs. Royal family, indeed.

Two faces, however, were distinctly absent. *Where is Jon?* I wondered as I searched the ever growing sea of faces but couldn't find him...or Rowan.

"I'd like to welcome all of you to this year's Solstice Gathering of Clans when we put our differences aside and the sea star and lionfish unite as one just as the mighty Atlantic is one," Z announced in a beautiful and bold voice. Cheers filled the night air and goblets clinked.

"Now tonight is a very special night as it is also in honor of the induction of our newest daughter, Storm! Welcome home, Storm!" Z said and raised her glass to me. All of the other mers mimicked her.

"Welcome!" They shouted in near unison. I'd never heard so many mer voices all at once. It sounded like a cacophony of wind chimes that ranged from low brass tones to the highest silver tinkles.

"Storm will be presented with her pendant..." Z started but was interrupted.

"*If* she completes the challenge," Laverna finished in a voice equally bold, but which lacked all warmth; the beauty in it was more due to its sheer smoothness, like a newly forged sword blade. Her face contorted into a subtle grin. The happy chatter of the crowd slowly died away.

My heart sunk. *What challenge do they keep talking about?*

"Yes, of course, sister," Z said. "As I was saying, Storm will be presented her pendant after she completes her challenge. Now as per tradition for coming of age," Z spoke directly to me, "the young mer must solve a series of riddles and then end with a show of skill. First, you will be given a riddle to solve. That riddle will lead you to a location and a person. Once you get there, you will ask that person for your clue. After you solve your clue, a new riddle will lead you to the next location. It's a combination scavenger hunt, skills test, and riddle game."

"Mers are, after all, known for their quick wit and strength," Laverna chimed in. "I hope you, dear, are the same. And I'm sure we are all excited to see who claims you if you make it through."

Z gave me a reassuring smile then turned to face her sister. "I have no doubt Storm is up for whatever is presented her."

Pearl, in a soft, sweet voice whispered, "I know this sounds daunting..."

"But the prize will be totally worth it little one," Sara interrupted. Mers all around giggled like they knew the punch line to a joke I was never told.

"Children." Z brought the party back into focus. "Storm, you will have one hour to complete the challenge. The final object must be returned here by midnight, when the moon is at its highest point. Do you understand?" Z asked. She smiled. I looked around and all the mers smiled and chatted excitedly among themselves. They apparently thought this was the greatest game ever and were excited to get it underway.

"I guess so," I said in barely more than a whisper.

"Do you have any questions child?" Laverna asked.

"What happens if I don't finish in time?" I asked.

The crowd of mers erupted in laughter. If it wasn't me they were laughing at, it would have been a really beautiful sound. But as it happened, it was me they were laughing at, and I didn't like it one bit.

"Best not make that even an option," Laverna replied. "But let's just say that something you care about will be lost."

"But..." I protested.

"Shh, you're okay," Pearl said as she leaned down to me. "Why do you think we've been training with you all these weeks?"

"Can I get help?" I asked. I scanned the crowd for Jon. He was so good at solving riddles.

"Of course, my child," Laverna spoke. Again her words were kind but the intonation sounded anything but. "You may choose one to assist but he or she cannot be Mer or mortal and the chosen one may not give you the answer, merely guide you!"

This was already some sort of riddle and we hadn't even started yet!

"Let me help her choose!" Lilli chimed.

Her eyes sparkled with the light of the fire.

Z nodded her head in approval.

"Okay Storm here you go. I'm going to make it easy for you! What do you get if you combine these two: Something that runs but never gets tired and a drink that is considered soft."

"Lilli, if this is helping me, I'm scared to think about when it might get tricky."

"Come on, Storm," Sara snapped, "we haven't got all night."

Other murmurs from the gathered crowd mumbled in agreement. They were restless for the game to begin.

"Let me think a sec," I said defensively.

"Come on Storm this is easy!" Lilli chirped. She looked like she was about to burst with trying to keep the answer a secret. Water Sprites were really funny and impatient.

Dozens of glowing eyes stared at me, equally impatient and not nearly as funny. Even Pearl had a hard time keeping a straight face.

"Something that runs. Is it an animal?" I asked.

"No," Lilli chirped.

"Is it a thing?" I asked. My brain spun.

"YES!" Lilli jumped up and down and clapped her delicate hands together excitedly.

"Okay, okay, I said. Calm down," I said. *I wish I had half of the excitement Lilli has.*

"A thing that runs and never gets tired. This sounds like something my primary school teachers would tell me. Like a kiddie joke," I said.

A mixture of expectant and bored eyes stared back at me.

I thought back to 3rd grade when Mr. Barry used to tell us jokes before recess. He was a funny looking teacher, short and round and he always wore blue sweaters. We used to call him Mr. Blue Barry behind his back. I chuckled at the memory.

"You got something?" Lilli asked.

"Oh, umm, well, I was just thinking about, oh, well never mind."

"Maybe you want some water?" She asked.

"Water? I don't think..."

"Water! She said water!!" Lilli exclaimed and jumped up and down again.

"That shouldn't count," a mer from the crowd called.

"Totally counts," Lilli insisted. "Okay Storm, you have the first half, water. Now do the second half!"

"Oh, yeah, right, water, of course. Okay, a drink that's considered soft. Like a soft drink? A soda."

Lilli nodded in encouragement.

What is she talking about?? Water-Soda?

Lilli began miming something. She pointed at herself.

"Water lily?" I asked.

"Oh for Pete's sake if this is all she has there is no way she is going to win this game." Sara mumbled.

Lilli ran to the drink table and back again. She looked like a ghostly blur. *Water Sprites move really fast* I thought.

"I thought you may prefer this to water." With a pop, she opened a can of soda. "It's not a coke."

"I can see that, Lilli. Thanks but I really don't like Sprite."

When I said the word Sprite she squealed with delight.

"What about the Sprite?" I asked. And then it all clicked. *Sprite...water...water Sprite. WATER SPRITE! The answer is,* "WATER SPRITE!" I shouted.

"She said it!" Lilli exclaimed and then bounced around the circle while she sang, "She got it! She said Water Sprite! She got it! She said Water Sprite!"

After a few rounds, she came over and leapt up to give me a hug. "I knew you could do it!"

"Yeah, thanks." I wasn't quite sure I had actually done anything.

"So, you are neither mer nor human. So you can help me," I said.

"Lilli, at your service madam." She said with a giggle and a formal bow.

"Okay Storm, ready to begin?" Z asked.

"Umm..."

"Enough already from the child!" Laverna called out. "The first riddle is this: *When young, I am sweet in the sun. When middle aged, I make you smile. When old, I am valued more than ever. What am I?*" Laverna then flipped over the giant Hour Glass.

Murmurs resounded in the crowd. There were giggles and hushed discussions and then the crowds dispersed. All of the mers went back to enjoying the party. Alone with Lilli, I sat in the sand with absolutely no clue as to how to answer this riddle. I was going to fail before I even began.

Tears welled in my eyes.

"Don't look so sad, young one," Lilli said. Her eyes still twinkled; this time with a lilac tint.

"I don't know what to do," I said. "I've never been good at riddles."

"Oh I find them extremely fun!" Lilli giggled. "I mean most of the time they tell you the answer, but you don't know they're telling you, but it's really all right there in front of you. I mean, everything you need to know is there." She stopped and listened with a slight cock of her head. She smiled, apparently she was pleased with the sound of her words.

"Yeah, I guess, but what if I can't figure it out?" I said.

"Oh, Storm, of course you will as long as you decide to. I mean, maybe you don't want to figure it out so then I suppose you won't figure it out, but since you had decided to not figure it out you did exactly what you wanted to do!" Lilli spoke quickly and excitedly while she bounced slightly from side to side.

"What?"

Lilli continued, ignoring my obvious confusion,"but if you decide to figure it out then you will figure it out because you decided to figure it out! Get it?"

"Yeah... no. Well, sort of. Pearl said something like that, but not in quite so many words." I remembered during training when she said, 'whether you think you can or you can't, you're right.' "Okay, well, whatever, either way, we have to get serious about this puzzle. The answer is right in front of me, I just have to see it, right?"

But without answering, Lilli darted off.

"Hey," I shouted, "I thought you were going to help me!"

"Hang on!" She called.

"Hang on...sure, I'll hang on. It's not like I've got anything to do, like solve riddles and complete transition and try to make it into a mer clan or anything." I mumbled. I sat alone in the sand and questioned my choice of partners until she bounded back excitedly with a drum in her arms.

"What are you doing?" I asked.

"I think better with music...don't you?"

"I don't know," I whined.

Lilli just sat next to me humming softly, tapping her drum and staring out at the calm water rolling in to shore. The moon had just peeked above the horizon and shimmery speckles danced on the water's surface. Lilli's tune was catchy, something my dad used to play. Despite my sour mood, I hummed along with her.

"Lilli," I said when I realized my mind was nowhere near the task at hand but rather melting into the rhythmic swells of the water and humming Red Red Wine with Lilli, "I can't concentrate.

She stopped and looked at me with her violet eyes gleaming.

"What?" I asked.

She hummed the refrain one more time.

"Yeah, I know the song Lilli, my dad used to play it when he worked at night on his writing. He..." I stopped in mid sentence. Ripe in the sun...makes you happy...highly valued! "WINE?" I shouted. It was my turn to tackle Lilli. She giggled beneath me, pinned to the sand.

"Lilli, you're a genius!"

"I know," she said with a wink and a flash of tiny, pointed teeth.

We both gave a nervous glance back at the hourglass, then jumped up and ran over to the drink table. A mer with bright red, curly hair greeted us with an alluring smile. Her dress was green with gold sequins and her bare arms looked as white as the sand under the newly risen, giant moon.

"Now Storm," her voice rang sweetly, "you know I can't serve you this wine, Z would have my tail! The Flicker Punch is at the other table."

"No, no I have the answer to the location. It's Wine! And that means you have the next clue, right?"

With another smile and a wink, she tossed a parchment envelope decorated with silver stars into the air where it hovered, seemingly caught on a lifting breeze.

"Hey!" I shouted in protest. The mer only giggled.

"You have to get it young one," she whispered with a quick look around to make sure nobody heard her helping me. She wore a sea star pendant. *I guess she's on my side,* I thought with a little flutter of hope.

"But how?" I asked as I tried to jump up after it to no avail. It floated at least four feet above my highest jump.

The red haired mer winked and as she did the envelope floated even higher.

Wind control, I thought. *Alright, I get it. This is the skill part.*

I furrowed my brow and pictured the wind like Pearl taught me. I tried to give it the color of my emotions, the color of my desires, light blue for gentle gusts, yellowish for stronger puffs and red for knock-you-off-your-feet gales. Red would be too hard, blue too little as it was now a good ten feet above me. Yellow should do the trick.

I closed my eyes and pictured the air, I saw it tinge with light which was golden, warm and bright. I opened my eyes and saw a pocket of my yellow light close to the envelope.

Okay, now to move it, gently, closer, closer, not too hard, just enough to push the envelope. That's right!

The envelope made a distinct shift to the left.

Okay, now to get on top.

I shifted the glowing air around, the envelope momentarily took a turn skyward but I corrected my mistake and within a moment the envelope fluttered lower and lower. I reached my hand high over my head and the envelope floated lightly into my palm. With a squeeze of my fingers, I had it crumpled safely in my hand.

"GOT IT!" I exclaimed.

A few of the mers that had been watching gave little claps of support. Lilli jumped up and down and smiled brightly.

Feeling very proud, I smiled back and triumphantly took hold of the envelope in both hands. I tore it to shreds to get at the contents and ignored the obvious beauty of the paper. A small slip of translucent silvery paper revealed itself and had the next riddle written on it in perfect calligraphy in gold ink.

"What is the next letter in this sequence-J F MA M J.." I read the words aloud.

"Huh." Moment of elation evaporated, I was back to self doubt and despair.

"Come on Storm, you got this one. You're smart despite the half human part," Lilli chirped.

"Gee thanks, Lilli," I answered, not quite sure if I was being insulted or complimented.

We both moved off to the side and sat down. Time ticked away and I wasn't even half way through the challenge. The round moon was over the dune line and rose steadily. Z said the moon would be at its highest at midnight, and that was when I had to finish or else something I cared about would be lost forever. I held my head in my hands. A headache was forming behind my eyes and my heart beat uncomfortably behind my temples.

"Hey." Lilli gave me a nudge on my shoulder. "Don't look so glum."

"But I don't know how to answer this, those letters don't make any sense. I mean as far as a pattern goes, I guess it could be starting over with the J so F would be next."

"I guess that could be right," Lilli said but she didn't smile or clap.

"Hmm." I walked over to the red haired siren. "Is the answer F?" I asked, fingers crossed.

She shook her head.

"Oh," I said, disheartened and shuffled back to Lilli.

"It's not..." I started to say but Lilli interrupted.

"You know, sometimes when I get stumped I just go back to the beginning."

"The beginning of what?"

"The beginning of whatever I need to go back to." She smiled as she spoke and her eyes seemed to be looking for something far away in the sky. "It is quite cool for a June night, don't ya think? I mean you may expect this in January and possibly February, but not June."

"I guess, I never really thought about the weather," I said. "But, okay."
What is she talking about?

"Oh no? You should. I mean January here is often quite nice, February can be a bit tricky but March and April are delightful." Then she started singing a song about the months in the year. It was a catchy little tune and like when she hummed Red Red Wine I started to sing along in my head, despite myself.

Ugh, focus on the riddle, Storm, I scolded myself. *Jingle From My All...no, Jump Find Man...no... Jump Forward Macaroni... ugh. This is supposed to be a party and I am supposed to be having fun. I'm not! This is so unfair! Why can't I be dancing with Rowan instead of solving this silly word game!*

"Lilli, please, singing January February, March and April, May and June and July is hardly helping me," I said.

And then she did it, just like with the last riddle. She smiled and her eyes glowed brighter, this time yellow.

"What?" I asked.

She hummed the same tune I had just scolded her for.

"All I said was to please stop singing about the months...the months? THE MONTHS!" I exclaimed. All of the mers around us stopped talking and looked at me. I laughed uncomfortably.

"Sorry," I said.

"Lilli, is that it? The months?" I asked in a quieter voice.

Her eyes widened with excitement.

"J for January, F for February." I went through the list and found that the letter to complete the riddle was J for July. I ran over to the red haired mer and told her J. This time she simply handed me another envelope with a smile. I raced back to Lilli.

"I am always hungry. I must be fed. The finger I touch will soon turn red." I read the location riddle aloud. "My stomach?" I asked.

Lilli laughed.

"No, really, I'm starving." My stomach agreed and gave a very vocal growl.

"We can grab something to eat as soon as you finish," Lilli said.

"No, really, Lilli I *am* hungry! I haven't had anything to eat since breakfast. I think better on a full stomach! Pleeeeeease," I begged.

"Fine, stop whining. I'll go get some food while you work on the location. We already have one letter down. You're doing great!" she patted me on the back and skipped into the shadows.

"Hey," I called. "Can you see if Jon is around? I haven't seen him since before the big speech. I just want to make sure he hasn't been dragged to his death by some beguiling mermaid."

"Sure," Lilli said and gave a reluctant giggle. She turned quickly and disappeared.

That's weird. Maybe water sprites don't like humans much, I thought.

I stared at the blazing bon fire. Dozens of silhouetted bodies danced happily around it. *I wish I could dance around the fire,* I thought.

Lilli returned with some small sandwich wraps. "Did you figure it out?" She asked as she handed me one and took a bite from hers.

"A baby is always hungry and must be fed," I announced. "But there's no baby at the party."

"Seriously Storm? All you've come up with so far is *baby*?" Lilli rolled her eyes. "What *besides* you or a baby is always hungry and needs to be fed?" Lilli glanced to the hourglass, I couldn't help but peek as well. *Uh oh! The lower bulb is already half full of sand.*

"Okay Okay! Hang on a sec." I squeezed my eyes shut and rubbed my temples to help me think.

"They were just kidding before, right?" I asked suddenly. Lilli looked at me with surprise.

"Kidding about what?"

"About the part with losing something I care about if I can't do this. That was a mer joke, right?"

Lilli's face grew serious and honestly looked sorta scary. I remembered Pearl's advice from earlier and I agree that wouldn't want to get on the wrong side of a water sprite.

"I think it's best for everyone if you finished the task." Her face morphed back into the playful, sweet look again. "Got anything else yet?"

I thought about my dad. I wished he could be here right now. I missed him. I really needed a hug right now. I remembered the smell of his clothes in the winter...how his scent mixed with the smell of burning wood from the furnace. He used to joke about feeding the beast in the basement. I was scared to go down, worried that it would eat me like some monster, a real beast. *Wait. Feeding the beast.*

"Hey, feeding the beast!" I said to Lilli.

"That's not very nice, I only had one sandwich." Lilli's mouth turned into a pout and her eyes darkened into the color of hot coals.

"No, silly, the *beast*. It's what my dad used to call our wood burning fireplace. The answer is fire!"

"Yay Storm! The fire pit!"

We ran together to the crackling bon fire.

As we reached the edge of the flames, Sara walked towards us with a smile. With the way the fire light and shadows danced on her features, I couldn't tell if her smile was sincere or cynical.

"I've been waiting for you, Stormy! I wasn't sure you'd make it this far! But, good for you! The prize is so worth it." She winked and then held her hand to me. In it was another envelope covered in the same silver stars as the previous ones. But before I could reach for it, she tossed it behind her where it fluttered helpless toward the roaring flames.

"NO!" I shouted and ran closer to the raging inferno but was instantly repelled by the wall of heat.

Think Storm, I scolded myself. I saw the defenseless envelope drifting lower, where the edges began to sear, the paper wrinkled from the heat and flames lapping at its delicate edges. I was so angry, I needed that clue. My heart beat fast, my temper rocketed way past anger and thunder boomed above us while lightening streaked across the cloudless sky. A large rain drop fell on my head, then another, then a third. I heard the angry hiss from the fire as rain fell on the flames. Smoke billowed up from where roaring flames once danced.

RAIN! I thought. *Yes, more, more, faster*!

And faster it came. A downpour so sudden that no one even had time to think about finding cover. Within seconds, the flames were completely extinguished and the partially seared envelope lay on a half charred log; the paper was obviously wet, but fortunately still intact.

I retrieved it quickly and turned to see a dozen dripping faces staring at me.

"Umm, oops," I said as I pushed wet hair from my face. My gown hung heavily around my soaking body. Smiles soon replaced the stares and conversations began again. Some very strong looking mermen took on the task of rebuilding the fire, carrying armloads of new logs toward the ruined pile.

"Well, that was effective," Lilli said as she wrung out her skirt.

"Yeah, I guess it was," I said with a shrug. Kind of like Rowan, I wasn't really very good at *subtle*.

I opened it. This time Lilli took it from my hand and read: "Two in a room, one in a house, none in a shelter but one in a mouse."

Puzzled as usual, Sara just laughed.

"Good luck little sister. Better be quick as there's less than half an hour left."

Lilli tugged at my arm and we sat down near the fire. I looked at the clue again and read it over slowly.

"I have no idea."

"Doors?" I asked.

"Remember, this should be a letter clue."

"Oh right." We already had the letter J.

"Well, two in a room, one in a house? Letters!" I said excitedly.

Lilli's eyes sparkled. The renewed fire light made them switch from lavender to orange.

"Lilli it's the letter O!"

She smiled triumphantly.

I ran over to Sara. "It's the letter O!" She pulled another envelope out of her pocket. "Here you go Stormy. Tick tock, tick tock."

"Three lives have I," I read. "Gentle enough to sooth the skin, light enough to caress the sky and hard enough to crack rocks. Honestly Lilli I don't even know where to start on this one."

"Well let's break it down together. What's the first thing you think of when I say *Light enough to caress the sky?*"

"The moon, the stars, the sun..." I ran out of things to list.

Lilli tapped lightly on her drum. "What about soothing skin?" She asked, still tapping on her drum.

"Fingers, hair..." My mind drifted to Rowan, his fingers, his hair, his skin...swimming together in the night sea, just the two of us...

"Ahem," Lilli cleared her throat loudly.

I looked up, flushed. "Sorry." I smiled. "I was just thinking about...eh, that I hadn't seen Rowan all night."

"Right, well, I'm sure he's just fine."

"What are you playing?" I asked

"Nothing special, just thinking." Her fingers tapped tapped tapped. Rhythmically, sequentially, like rain drops on a metal roof.

*Rain drops...*I thought of Rowan again when we stood on the beach in the rain and tried to catch the falling water in our mouths.

*Rain from the sky...Water on our skin...three lives have I...*liquid, gas, solid!

"WATER!!! It's WATER!"

Lilli squealed with delight. "Come on, we have to hurry!" She grabbed my hand and nearly dragged me to the water's edge.

A carnival atmosphere filled the air. Mers paid more interest to Lilli and me now, like they knew the game was soon to be at a climax.

Pearl stood at the water smiling, but only with her mouth, not her eyes. Her eyes were slightly pinched at the corners.

Without a word, she removed an envelope from her pocket and handed it to me.

"What, no skill test?"

She didn't answer. She just looked at me and then back out toward the water.

I tore the paper open and read, "What is in seconds, minutes, seasons and centuries but not in days years or decades?"

I smiled. *This was easy! It was like the clue I had earlier. It was one of those letter riddles.*

I examined it closely to see what the first set of words had in common. I paused and caught Pearl's eye. She glanced nervously toward the sky. The moon was nearly overhead. It shone brilliantly on the calm water.

"I totally got this! It's the letter N," I said proudly.

A cheer and loud applause went through the crowd. Pearl nodded her head.

"So, what now? I don't really get what..." Something clicked at that moment in my head. The letters appeared before my eyes one at a time. J...O...N...JON.

"JON? What does Jon have to do with this game?" The color drained from my face. Lilli squeezed my hand.

Pearl spoke in a quiet voice. "Storm, there was no other option. It was Laverna's choice for the final test."

"What? No choice for what?" I nearly shouted. Lightning streaked through the sky, ripples on water appeared in response to my angry gust of wind.

"Storm you must control your temper, it won't help you right now, in fact, it could be the end. Please." Pearl's eyes pleaded with her voice.

I took a long, slow breath. "Okay. I'm fine." The wind calmed, the surface of the water returned to its flat, reflective surface.

"This is your final clue," Pearl said in barely more than a whisper. "You saw me where I never was and where I couldn't be and yet within that very place my face is often seen."

"A mirror?"

Pearl shook her head. The mers were now gathered in a large circle around Pearl, Lilli, and myself.

"Looks like half a mer isn't quite enough, eh?" It was Paige's brother who spoke. His teeth shimmered in the darkness like a predator about to devour his prey. His voice haunted my ears. It was strangely familiar.

I looked at Lilli for help but she simply shook her head slowly. I stared up to the moon. It was so full, at what had to be its highest point.

I refuse to fail now. I've spent this entire friggin' night chasing my own tail and I'll be damned if I don't win this idiotic game.

"Reflection!" I burst out before I even realized the answer had popped into my head.

There was another cheer from the group, even louder than the first. I looked around frantically and that's when my eye caught it. The moon's light showed a bright reflection on the water's flat surface. I looked harder and then saw it; the outline of a face just below the surface of the water, just below the moon's beacon.

A hissing sound emanated from my throat. It was nearly a growl, inhuman and full of venom. The face under the water was Jon and he was held there by familiar arms.

"What the hell!" I shouted and darted into the water but I got no farther than waist deep when I hit an invisible barrier. It felt like I ran into a brick wall. I rebounded and landed on my back with a splash. My face hurt from hitting whatever invisible obstacle blocked my way and my bum hurt from landing so hard on the sandy bottom.

"I need to get to him!" I shouted as I scrambled to my knees.

"No, you need to get him to *you*." Paige's brother answered coldly.

"What?" I had no idea what to do and the moon was nearly to its zenith.

"Help!" I shouted.

"Think, Storm," Lilli spoke. "You can't get *to* him, but you can make him come to *you* somehow."

"JON!" I called. Nothing happened.

I heard a snicker behind me.

"Hush, Daniel," Pearl hissed. Part of my brain registered the connection between Daniel and the voice I knew. *He was the man that stood behind Laverna...Paige's brother was Daniel.*

Focused back on Jon there was still no sign of movement. *Please come here,* I thought to the pale face underwater.

Then it clicked. It wasn't Jon I needed to control, it was his handler, it was Rowan. This was a test of mind control.

I seethed with anger but fought my emotions so the water would remain calm. I needed a clear view of Rowan's eyes.

I tried my best to give Jon the 'it'll be okay' look and then I turned my focus on Rowan, on his glowing sapphire orbs that stared intently at me. To him I thought only of how I would punish him when this was all over.

You, I thought. *How dare you do this to Jon...to me. Bring him here this instant.*

I thought I saw a momentary flicker in his eyes, a second of indecision, but then they stared back with a solid resolve. Their bodies remained unmoved.

Bring him to me now, I thought directly to Rowan's eyes. He didn't blink and he didn't move any closer. In fact, he winked.

My first thought was a horrifying one. *I'm not strong enough. My will isn't stronger than Rowan's. I can't*...but that's where those thoughts stopped because at that moment, I looked into Jon's eyes. He stared back at me with something that could only be described as trust. He had no doubt that I'd save him. Jon believed in me. The least I could do was believe in myself. *I can and I WILL save you, Jon. Hang on.*

So, Rowan, I thought. *That's how you want to play?* I felt my energy draw in, toward my chest. My pulse slowed rather than raced. An inexplicable calm fell over me. I exhaled my breath and on the inhale I felt it, a palpable energy, nearly an entity unto itself, drew into me with my breath. All sounds disappeared; all distractions were now gone. It was only Rowan and myself. Our wills colliding viscerally. His will was strong, really strong. But, my will was now beyond strong. My will was unstoppable. My will spoke loud and clear the following 5 words, BRING. JON. TO. ME. NOW!

Rowan's eyes grew round with surprise. His body jerked forward against his own will. And with Rowan came Jon toward shore; toward me. I watched the painfully slow progress of the two of them, my energy pulling and Rowan resisting, it was like isometric exercise and was physically exhausting. My breaths came is short hisses through clenched teeth. I panted with every foot of progress.

Three feet, then two...*come on!* One foot, now within reach and HA! I had Jon's arm and pulled him out of the water to me. Rowan released him immediately and the three of us exploded from the waist deep water.

Jon gasped for air. I dragged him the rest of the way out of the water, felt his pulse, then pulled him to me as we sunk to the sand.

It was then that I noticed something strange. There was no noise. There was no laughter or chatter or snide comments or music or munching of food. There was absolute silence. I looked up over Jon's head to the crowd. The mers were all still there, but not one made a sound. In fact, no one moved an inch. My eyes drifted over the startled faces until I found two that I knew, Pearl and Sara.

"Storm," Pearl whispered. "It's okay, you can stop now. You won. Jon's okay."

Stop what? I thought. And then looked to Sara who's mouth was in a sly grin.

"Now that, Stormy, was impressive," Sara said.

"What?" I croaked.

Pearl looked behind her to the rest of the mers and then took tentative steps toward me and knelt down. "You just manipulated every mer's will to get what you wanted." She gave a slight nod toward Jon. "It was pretty amazing, and if I may say so, a bit scary. Well done. You seem to be able to draw on the strengths of others when in need. That's a skill no one else has. Remember I told you that once a mer is mature, her strength is pretty much set. Well, yours may be set, but apparently you can get more by tapping into the strength of others. Not even Laverna could have predicted that when she thought of this part of the game."

"Game? Is that what you call it? You horrible creatures!" I sneered. Then I looked back to the crowd which now shifted on its feet and blinked and smiled and whispered back and forth. A few started laughing nervously. "You could have killed him!" I shouted.

I was in tears of rage and adrenalin pumped full force through my veins. "STOP LAUGHING! So this was my prize? Jon's LIFE?" The words spit from my mouth. I stood over Jon like a mother bear. I had no doubt that if anyone tried to come close to him it would be the last thing they ever did.

"I'm...o-o-okay," Jon said between coughs.

I spun in a fury. "AND YOU!" I growled at Rowan.

Rowan froze in mid stride. His face was full of innocence and something else...*is that amusement?* I thought incredulously.

"AHHHHH!" I screamed at him. "I trusted you. I thought you and I...you and he....but you're no better than the rest of them. You *filthy fish!*" Lightning lit the night sky like the fourth of July and bursts of wind tore through the party. Sparks from the fire danced every which way while the ocean churned behind us.

"Storm, please, listen," his voice was low and soothing. He took one step closer but froze again when I made a guttural sound, like a growl. I crouched slightly lower over Jon, in a full protective stance.

I heard whispers and hushed giggles and one mer mentioned something about *amazing*.

"Storm," spoke Jon's voice from below me.

"Not now, Jon, I'm so sorry. I'll get you out of here," I said.

"No, Storm, I'm okay. It was okay. Rowan was there to help me. He explained it all to me."

"What?" I looked down at Jon's wide-eyed expression. "You call nearly drowning you helping you?" I wasn't sure who to be more mad at, the mers for their cruel game or Jon for his stupidity.

"Really, Storm," Rowan spoke again. He had inched closer, within an arm's length away.

I glared back at him with scathing eyes but didn't make a move or sound so he continued his cautious approach.

"The game was meant as a challenge to you. Jon was never in danger, really, at least as long as he was with a mer to guide him back through the wall."

My mind spun and as the adrenalin slowly left my veins and confusion infused them, I felt sick to my stomach.

"Humans can be underwater safely when in touch with a mer. I volunteered to be the one to remain with him to make sure he stayed safe until you willed me back through the surface shield created by Z and Laverna." Rowan's eyes pleaded his innocence.

I looked back toward Jon who now sat below me and looked fully recovered. *Would he pardon or condemn Rowan?*

"I was fine with Rowan, Storm. They told me about it, about what you had to do. I agreed but when Daniel said he would stay with me, Rowan refused and said he would instead." Jon smiled broadly. "It was really pretty cool to stay underwater like that. I mean I was a little nervous since I couldn't just pop up with that weird invisible thing stopping me but I knew you'd do it."

Rowan, vindicated by Jon's own admission, dared to speak again. "See, Love, I was there to make sure he was okay until you arrived," he said in a voice barely louder than a whisper.

I looked between Jon and Rowan. Both smiled, one broadly, one weakly. *These boys are going to be the death of me*, I thought.

"And what if I didn't make it?" I asked.

"I knew you would," Rowan said.

I hit Jon on his shoulder and he nearly toppled over.

"Hey, what was that for?"

"That's for you being stupid," I said.

"What happened to *poor Jon* and all that stuff?"

"Yeah, that was before I knew you AGREED to this damn game."

Despite my intention to remain angry, I sunk to the sand next to Jon and looked up to Rowan. "You really wouldn't let anyone else stay with him?"

"Are you kidding? Knowing how pissed you'd be when you found him, imagine how pissed you'd be if someone had left him and he drowned? I didn't trust that charge with any mer knowing how attention spans aren't one of our strong suits. Which, by the way, you did cut it pretty close there, Stormy."

He must have seen the venom return to my expression because he quickly sat in the sand in front of me and threw his arms around me in a tight embrace.

"You were awesome," he whispered into my ear. Chills ran down my arms at the tickle of his breath. He cradled my face in his large hands. "I love you AND your temper."

"Humph," I grunted. But I knew it was over. The adrenalin was gone, Jon was okay, I had succeeded in the game and mad or not, I loved Rowan with every ounce of my being. His lips touched mine and I surrendered.

"No regrets," he whispered.

"No regrets," I answered.

A tiny cough next to us broke into the tender moment.

"Come on," Pearl said, "it's time to bring your prize back to Z and Laverna."

I looked up at her angelic face. Lilli stood next to her and handed Jon a large, thin cloth, like a sarong.

"Thanks," he said as she helped him up. She only came up to his collar bones. He wrapped himself in the fabric.

I stood with Rowan and noticed the faces still stared at me. There were smiles and couples holding hands and other exchanging small trinkets most likely bets paid for those who wagered on my success or failure during tonight's test.

Z and her sister sat elegantly in their chairs. Z's face was serene but clearly proud and her sister's face slightly concerned. The others slid into the background and left me alone, as if I were on trial. Z's face glowed beautifully. I avoided looking at Laverna.

Z took a small velvet pouch from her pocket and poured what looked like liquid silver into her hand. It was my sea star!

"Congratulations my youngest child. It's time you wear the talisman and take your place among your family and clan," Z said.

Only one mystery remained tonight and that is who's braid of hair would my sea star hang from? I wondered. My heart beat quickly with anticipation.

"Z! Stop!" Daniel's voice thundered. *I know that voice,* my mind raged.

Rowan appeared silently at my side and clutched my hand in his. He stepped slightly in front of me in a defensive posture.

"Ah, Daniel. I wondered if you were going to make a scene tonight," Z said calmly.

*And then the light bulb lit. It was Daniel's voice from that day I was dragged to the ocean depths. The riddle, the answer D... Pearl mentioned Daniel as the one the water souls spoke of, of course! The Lionfish Pendant...*Heat rose inside of me. The wind picked up and a small ball of it became red. Mers looked around in confusion, Daniel's eyes grew bigger.

"I wouldn't do that little freak," he snarled.

"Now, now, temper, my son," Laverna chimed in. "What Daniel means dear sister is you can't simply adopt this unknown child, Z. You know that. Although she has, just barely, passed the tests, unfortunately, and I mean that with all sincerity little one, no mother has come forward to claim her. She has no rights to the symbol of the clan." She looked at Z calmly, victory in her eyes. Pearl moved closer to stand right behind Z's chair.

Confused, I looked at Z. Pearl stepped out from behind Z's chair. Her eyes were soft and there was a glimmer of a smile on her lips, as if she didn't totally disagree with my burst of temper. She stepped forward deliberately, and took the sea star from Z's palm. She threaded a braided rope through it and stood in front of me.

"Welcome home, Storm," she said, kissed my forehead, and then each cheek. She then whispered a word I didn't recognize and placed the necklace around my neck. It glowed brightly for a moment, like a ring of fire. I felt its heat, but it didn't burn me, it was more like being snuggled in a warm blanket on a cold night. The warmth started at my neck but seemed to travel inward and then radiate through my limbs until it drew itself back in and warmed the deepest part of my core. Then the sensation disappeared, slowly cooling within me but leaving behind a memory of its warmth, a strength that I hadn't had before. I took a deep inhale and as I exhaled, I knew that I was no longer an average teenager or a changeling. I was an adult mer. The glowing silver sea star likewise dimmed and then lay quite inert and cool on my chest.

I looked into Pearl's eyes. Sara's description from our very first meeting rang in my memory, *the green is bright, sea glass and the little flecks of gold look like tiny islands.* That description matched Pearl's eyes perfectly. Her eyes...identical to my own.

Before I had to even question, Pearl said, "Welcome home, my daughter." And she wrapped me in a giant hug.

"NO! Pearl is not this halfling's mother!"

"And why do you say so, sister?" Z asked.

"Because the ring she wears is sparked."

The crowed went silent.

I looked over to Z who's face had gone pale. "You dare to use the Enfiar Spark on one of my children?"

"Don't you see that she's a fake? She's not one of us," Laverna answered. "I told Paige to give her the ring to make sure she belonged here. And obviously she doesn't. With both of our clans present not once did she cry in pain as she came close to her heart's deepest desire, which for all orphans is, of course, to find their mother. Dear sister, I'm afraid one day, your belief that all are as good and honest as you will be your demise. The Pacific waters churn with Auntie's agitation. The Spark may be harsh, but we had to be sure she belonged here and not, perhaps, a distraction sent from across the seas."

"But look!" Lilli exclaimed.

All eyes turned to my hand where the ring rested. The stone, which had been a milky white was now deep crimson.

Gasps resounded all around. Murmurs and voices talked at once.

"Your heart's desire, Stormy, is being answered," Pearl said.

"My heart's desire? Well, Laverna is right, it has always been to have a mother...to find my mother! The first time the ring burned me whenever you were near. It knew that you were the answer to my heart? But now it's just turning red, it isn't burning me."

"Yes," Pearl said. "The Luvyen Flame. Also for identifying hearts' desires, but much less painful." She glanced behind me, "Well done Rowan."

"My pleasure." He smiled. "An old trick my mum taught me."

Daniel's voice roared through the other voices. "You mean to tell us that this little half-ling freak IS your daughter?"

Pearl smiled and while she still held me in a tight embrace, answered Daniel's ravings, "Well, yes and also my *daughter*, Daniel, will now receive the royal braid and take her place as the rightful heir to the territory."

"WHAT?" Laverna gasped!

"What?" I gasped and pulled back from Pearl.

Heir? Royal braid? Royal family? ME???

My breath came too quickly. To realize you're a mermaid is one pretty crazy thing, to be accepted into a clan is another, but to realize you're a mermaid of royal blood and the resolution to a century old territory dispute is quite a different kettle of fish all together!

"Pearl is quite right," Z said. "Laverna, Daniel, Paige, please welcome Storm, my granddaughter and heir to my territory."

Applause erupted. I looked around and realized that most of those gathered were happy for me and Pearl. I smiled despite my nerves and overly active heart, which threatened to beat itself nearly out of my own chest.

"This is NOT right," Daniel's voice boomed once again. I heard thunder rumble in a not-so-distant sky.

Daniel isn't going to let me enjoy this moment? Seriously? This guy is really getting on my nerves. Back off! I thought with all of my might.

Suddenly sand kicked up and formed into a solid ball. It flew at Daniel's chest, and hit him square on. He was knocked solidly to the ground with a dull thud.

Mers all around scattered. Paige looked at him with interest but stayed where she was, drink still in hand.

Rowan laughed. "'Atta girl, Storm."

"You little BRAT!" Daniel yelled. A ball of red flame shot across the crowd. Rowan pushed Pearl and me to the ground. The fire missed my head by only a few inches. In an instant, Rowan sprang back to his feet and before I knew what was happening, he sat on top of Daniel and punched his face. Then Rowan was pushed backward by an unseen force and it was Daniel's turn to be on top and throw the punches. Loud cracks of thunder peeled across the sky. Bones crunched beneath angry fists and the sand turned red with blood around the two fighters.

"STOP!" Z's voice thundered.

All the mers froze, including Daniel and Rowan. The two fighters staggered away from each other, drawn to standing by invisible strings. I couldn't have moved if I wanted to, but then just as suddenly as the weight of immobility trapped me, it was gone and I was free to sit back up.

"Storm is one of us," Rowan hissed.

Pearl put her arm on Rowan's.

"This is NOT over," growled Daniel. "When we claim what is rightfully ours, you can be sure a thorough housecleaning will be in order." His voice oozed with vengeance. And he spat on the ground to clear the blood from his mouth.

I stood next to Pearl and Rowan and faced Daniel, unafraid. Sara and Z stood behind us.

"I think it may be best, Daniel, if you took some time to calm yourself," Z said.

"Yes, Daniel," Laverna spoke. "Let's walk together. Now's not the time."

Her words again sounded kind but they felt more like a threat.

Laverna took Daniel by the arm and disappeared together into the shadows beyond the reach of the bonfire's glow.

Z clapped her hands and said, "Okay my friends, the drama is over. Let's get back to the festivities!"

The music started up again and laughter once again rang through the air. Mers dispersed into various groupings. I felt a light touch on my shoulder.

"I hope you can forgive me," Pearl's voice chimed.

I didn't have any words. My emotions were already well past overload and the adrenalin had begun to leave my veins for the second time tonight. I felt nauseous, confused, elated, and tired. One tear slid down my cheek, it took the course of my nose and hung off the tip for a moment before it fell to the sand by my feet.

Pearl stayed quiet and allowed me to gather my thoughts, whatever they may be. Finally I had one.

"Mom," I said in barely more than a whisper.

Pearl nodded with a smile.

With no more thoughts to follow, I lunged forward and wrapped my arms around Pearl and we twirled in delirious circles.

Chapter Twenty

It was still dark, but the feeling in the air had changed and I knew dawn was soon to be upon us. I sat with Rowan, Pearl, Sara, Lilli and Jon next to the ebbing bonfire. My fingers absently twirled the rope of hair that my sea star pendant hung from making the solid silver pendant twist and turn on my chest. My lips curved into a grin. *I have a mother, I have a clan! I have...serious responsibility.* My smile slacked as I remembered the Royal Braid which now hung heavily down from the left side of my head. It marked me as an heir. And it was heavy all right, both in its physical weight and in its mental burden. *Heir to the Sea Star Clan, me, Storm. Unbelievable. No wonder everyone was working so hard to keep me safe.* By me making it successfully through transition, the clan has one less worry. Now the missing Mermaid's Knot means that only Pearl is in trouble of not surviving, rather than the entire clan.

The process to put it in this new braid had been wonderful and painful all at the same time. It was kind of a combination movie star treatment, wedding preparation, hair appointment, and torture session.

First came the procession of mers to welcome me as their heir. My cheeks hurt from smiling at so many people and the back of my hand was numb from being kissed so many times. I was then led to Z's ornate chair and Pearl sat next to me in Laverna's chair. The other mers sat in the sand in a semi circle surrounding us. Rowan and Jon were in the very front. Lilli kept flitting in and out. I didn't think sitting still was a strong suit of hers. Sara drifted to the back of the group and I only occasionally saw flashes of her black sequined outfit in the darkness. Once all the mers were assembled,

Z removed the Braid of Mar and placed the beads in a shimmery shell filled with sea water.

"Abalone," Z said, answering my unasked question about the shell. "This particular shell is from the southern waters of the Atlantic, off the coast of South Africa. It belonged to my mother.

Three women then approached our chairs. They walked side by side, holding hands. They looked older than time. *And for a mer to look that old they really could have been older than time*, I reasoned. They murmured in a language I couldn't understand. Their hands moved in harmony around my head to locate the perfect place for the braid's placement. One was dressed in a long gown of shimmery green silk, another in a gown of gold and another in a gown with tiny silver beads which covered the entire length. All three gowns were thin and nearly falling apart. The gold and green ones were threadbare, barely held together by their very fabric and the beaded one was missing most of its beads. If I hadn't felt and observed the deference given these women by all the mers, including Z, I would have pegged them as homeless old people. They were another reminder that looks really can be deceiving in the mer world.

I closed my eyes and melted into the sensations of the gentle and sometimes not so gentle manipulation of my hair, eventually losing track of whose fingers belonged to which woman. They seemed to move as one entity pulling, separating, and twisting my hair in countless ways. Their continuous chanting lulled me while the strands of hair that didn't make the cut were yanked painfully from my head. It was an interesting balance between relaxation and excruciating pain. Apparently a common theme of being a mermaid. I opened my eyes in time to see the woman in gold pull a long thread from her gown, then the woman in green did the same. *That's why their gowns are so thin*, I thought. They used strands from them to make the braid. And the beaded dress? Same. No wonder so many were missing.

I was told later that only these three mers could put in a royal braid.

Their presence at the solstice party tonight was an event in itself, having arrived together after the talisman ceremony. They were summoned by Z following my successful completion of the challenge. I asked what would happen when they eventually died. The answer? That would be the end of all royal lines and the cycle of divisions would being anew.

The tiny, delicate sound of bells rang through the clear night air. The abalone shell held by Pearl was now empty and a new weight hung from the left side of my head. I looked down to my chest and saw the completed masterpiece.

"The Mermaid's Knot," I whispered. It was even more amazing and intricate than the drawing made it out to be. I looked up to Pearl. A single tear rolled down her cheek and when it met her lips, she smiled. A tear of happiness. Her mouth shaped three words. The best three words in the entire world. "I love you." The warmth that radiated within me at that moment was infinite.

******

"This was the best Solstice Party ever!" Lilli exclaimed. Her perky voice brought me back to the present moment. I still held my necklace between my fingers.

Lilli sipped her Flicker Punch and stared dreamily into the fire. She sat on the sand straddled by Jon's bent knees and one of her thin arms rested on his leg.

"Awe," she suddenly chirped and bent down to the sand. When she sat back up she held a lifeless, bright yellow butterfly in her palm. "Now that's not right, poor thing."

She leaned over the tiny body and dropped a single tear onto its closed wings. The little body responded with a shutter in her palm. Then cautiously, slowly, its wings opened and closed and opened again. It stood on its thin legs, still pumping its wings. Then with one great flap it rose off of Lilli's palm and skittered into the night sky. I could have been mistaken, but I think it did little spins as it fluttered higher and higher. *What was that Pearl mentioned earlier about Water Sprites and old magic?*

"Lilli?" Jon asked. "Was that butterfly sleeping or did you just do what I think you did?"

Lilli giggled. "Well, it was just so sad to see the poor thing dead like that. I mean the world can always use more beauty, right?"

"So you can bring things back to life?" I asked, eyes wide.

"Some things, not everything. Little is easier, like that little pun'kin and they have to be still considering life to make it work."

"Considering life?" Jon interrupted.

"Well, yes," she said with a grin. "Souls have choices you know, at least they have a moment when they choose to leave their body or stay. If a body is to die and stay dead it is a good choice, I think, for the soul to leave and move on. But there are instances where the soul may find that with some effort the body can be mended, those are what humans call *near-death experiences*. The darker side of that choice is if the soul clings out of fear and the body is not recovered, well, those souls are trapped here, unable to stay with the body and unable to move on. But that little guy still had a chance, I felt his energy, he just needed a little help."

"And your tears are the key?" I asked.

"Yes. But Sprites must be careful because to bring something back is to give a bit of yourself away."

"So that butterfly really was spinning, like you do?"

She giggled. "Yes, he will most likely fly a bit, umm, over-enthusiastically from now on and I will be a bit less."

"You said little things are easier, what's the biggest thing you've ever, er, helped?" I asked.

Lilli sat back against Jon's chest and put her finger to her chin in thought. Jon's expression showed he was in heaven. "Hmm, I believe that would have been Smokey, the Lighthouse cat."

"The what?" I asked.

"No way!" Jon exclaimed and looked down to Lilli. "*You* saved that cat? I knew a cat couldn't have survived a drop like that. Man, unbelievable!"

"Guys, what cat?" I asked again while Jon still muttered things like, amazing and crazy. Rowan and Pearl laughed.

"There was this cat, Storm. His name was Smokey and he lived at the Lighthouse," Jon said. "Remember the picture when we climbed the lighthouse with Nana?"

"You mean on one of those landings when I was desperately trying to catch my breath? No, I guess I wasn't paying that much attention. That was Smokey?" I asked.

"Yeah. The one and only flying cat," Jon replied.

"He belonged to one of the children at the time," Lilli continued the story. "Those kids were well behaved, but tended to experiment. The older boy liked to make model airplanes and send them flying from the top of the lighthouse."

"Yeah," Jon said. "And one day he decided to test a new idea; a parachute. And the rider was none other than Smokey the cat."

"No way," I said. I felt Rowan's chest vibrate with a chuckle. I looked up to his face, "It's not funny, that's really mean to throw a cat off the lighthouse."

"Well, it had a parachute," Rowan stated in defense. I huffed.

"Go on," I told Jon and Lilli.

"So, the day came to test out the invention," Jon said. "The story goes that a very unwilling Smokey was tied to the sheet and unceremoniously tossed from the top of the tower."

I gasped.

"And?"

"And cats can't fly," Lilli answered.

At this Rowan broke into true fits of laughter, I had to sit up to stop getting bounced around. Even I couldn't contain a chuckle. Pearl and Sara also giggled, obviously they already knew this story.

"The legend that they tell at the lighthouse," Jon said, regaining control of his own laughter, "is that the cat miraculously landed and disappeared into the forest. It only returned about a month later, skittish around people, but otherwise unharmed."

"But really that poor cat never stood a chance," Lilli said. "I saw it fall, it landed alright, with a slight bounce and then a thud. I dragged it and its homemade parachute into the woods and worked on it until it came back to life. Healing its bones took patience and a lot of care. That drained me for quite sometime and," Lilli giggled, "I noticed that after he was healed, the tip of his tail would disappear when it was scared." She shrugged her shoulders and smiled, her tiny perfect teeth glittered like opals.

"Oh!" I said. "Like you can disappear. So it took a part of that trait from you."

"Yes. And I took its pain. For months I felt the poor creature's fear and felt like I had broken nearly every bone in my body. I also had a distinct fear toward heights for a few years. But it was worth it. Smokey deserved more time here."

"Wow," Jon and I said simultaneously.

"Jinx!" Sara, Pearl, Rowan, and Lilli exclaimed.

We laughed and continued enjoying the crackle of the settling bonfire. After a shift of the last intact log sent sparks fluttering into the sky, Rowan kissed my cheek. "Nice job tonight, Love. I knew you'd do it!" He gave me a little squeeze.

"Yeah," Jon said. "I never doubted it." He looked quite content and even somewhat proud of himself.

"Awe Jon, I couldn't have done it without you!" I said sarcastically.

"Dang right fish breath. Or is it your highness, or princess or your princess of high fishness?" He said.

In a very unprincess-like fashion, I stuck my tongue out and threw a shell at him which plunked him right in the forehead.

"Ouch," he said and mock rubbed his head. "What is up with royalty these days."

Amid our laughter he added, "Perhaps some etiquette training should be added to her lessons, Pearl."

"You really okay?" I asked.

"Other than being lured to the sea by sirens and trapped underwater with my only hope being you, the worst riddle solver in the world, for a rescuer, well, yeah!" He said. He looked up to one of the mermaids that had been with him earlier. He winked. She winked back.

"This party rocks!" He exclaimed.

Then he caught Lilli's gaze. He quickly turned his attention back to our circle and muttered something about that mer not meaning a thing. He put his arms around Lilli's petite frame in a full embrace.

"So, you really went with Jon just to make sure he stayed safe?" I asked Rowan. Somehow, I thought there must be something else to his apparent act of selflessness.

"Well, if you must know, I was also kind of curious just how strong you were." He smiled his impish smile.

"And?" I asked, my eyebrows rose in curiosity.

"You beat me, Storm and that's sayin' something." He winked. "I know that I definitely want you on my side during a fight!" He leaned down and gave me a kiss.

"I love you Storm, more than anything," he whispered.

"I love you, too," I said.

We sat together in silence watching the fire dance within itself.

"What the hell was up with *Spaniel*?" Rowan asked after a bit.

Pearl laughed.

"Spaniel?" I asked, as I gazed up to Rowan, whose head was right above mine as I nestled against his chest.

"Yeah, Spaniel, what Daniel should've been called 'cause he's such a dog. And always hiding behind *mummy*."

"He's always been like that," Sara said. She tossed little bits of shells into the fire and watched them spark. "Remember when he used to hang around with us back in the day?"

"Oh God, don't remind me," Pearl said, looking up from a tiny sand castle she worked on. "He was always bugging us when we were taking care of the children, trying to get us in trouble by luring the children away. I told him to get lost plenty of times."

"When was this?" I asked.

"Back when Sara and I watched the children of the workers at the lighthouse. He was always stalking around. I didn't trust him around the kids. Or around me," Pearl said with a snide laugh.

"He tried everything to get you to choose him," Sara said.

"Yeah, he tried everything, including some very unbecoming forceful attempts," Pearl said. She gave a slight shiver at the memory.

"You mean he attacked you?" I asked.

"Sort of. At least he tried," she laughed. "You should have seen his face when he ended up face down in the horse stables!

"Anyway, he left me alone well enough after that, but didn't leave completely. He started hanging around Tressman, the other bad seed from that time. God those two were made for each other, Daniel's slimy eel personality and Tressman's wolf in sheep's clothing personality. Two spoiled peas in a pod," Pearl said.

"I wish I had been there," Rowan said, "I would have taken care of both of them!"

"Ha!" Pearl laughed. "I think a sudden tidal wave would have been a bit conspicuous, Rowan." As she spoke, she placed her flat palm atop her castle and giggled when it collapsed under her pressing fingers.

Rowan laughed. "Conspicuous but effective!"

"Well, that high tide was pretty close," Sara chimed.

"Yeah, those waters even flooded the basement in the Keeper's house. I remember Kate being so angry because Tressman had been holed up in the basement for weeks telling everyone to stay out because he was working to improve its structure and at the end of it all it totally flooded!" Pearl said to Sara.

"I miss Kate. She was a good woman," Pearl added.

"Wow," Jon said, "That must have been some tide. The new building is hundreds of yards from the water and thirteen feet above sea level. One of the great tides then?"

"Yeah, only happens every 15-30 years or so."

"What do you think Daniel meant by 'he'll be back to claim what's his'?" Jon asked.

"My guess is he thinks he can find my braid," Pearl said. "Storm is able to take my place as rightful heir, but if he were to find my braid before the time expires at the next new moon, then he would be my controller and in turn, joint heir with me."

"Well, how would he be able to find it if you guys haven't after all this time?" Jon asked.

"I don't know," Pearl sighed. "But I'll tell you that I sure don't trust him. I wish we could find that braid or at least, now that the clan's future is safe, make sure at least he *doesn't* find it before the time limit expires."

My thoughts refused to organize, there was something important about what Pearl, umm, my mom, said, but my tired mind couldn't pull the necessary pieces together. Everything seemed connected somehow. The stories about Daniel hanging with Tressman, always being a pain around the kids, Tressman working by the old lighthouse and then the flooding of the basement. I had all of the information I needed to solve the mystery, I just didn't know how to put it all together. I leaned my head on Rowan's lap and closed my eyes.

"Okay sleeping beauty, time to get you home," Rowan said after the conversation died away.

"What? No, I'm fiiiIII..." My protest was cut short by another yawn. The fire had died down to no more than a glowing pile of embers and the sky had begun its transition from night to dawn and I sensed the day promised to be a hot one. "Okay, maybe. But where's Jon?" I asked and looked around.

"Over there!" Sara said as she pointed her finger toward the ocean where Jon and Lilli sat together.

"He seems to be quite fine!" Sara said with a giggle.

"Come on, my love," Rowan cooed. He led me by my hand to the water.

Pearl and Sara followed, still chatting about antics from years passed.

"How are we getting home?" I asked.

"The old fashioned way," Rowan said and motioned to the water. "The currents have been removed so we can all head back through Salt Run without difficulty.

"What about Jon?"

"He looks okay to me."

"Rowan..."

"What?"

"How is Jon getting back? Swimming's fine for us, but he may have a bit of difficulty."

"He can hold his breath, right?" Rowan's face contorted into a big bubble shape as he puffed out his cheeks holding his breath. He deflated after I punched his arm.

"Ouch," he said, mock rubbing where I hit him.

"I'm serious, I can't just leave him here and he can't swim that far."

"You *could* leave him here but if you insist."

"I insist."

"Fine. I'll go get him." Rowan broke off and went to retrieve Jon from the arms of his sprite.

******

I swam slowly and effortlessly. The water soothed my tired limbs.

Where did everyone go? I wondered.

This dream was very different from my old dreams. For one, I wasn't scared, for another I swam happily and for a third, I was headed somewhere I didn't recognize but I had a purpose. I observed my dreaming self in third person for awhile wondering with excitement and anticipation what was to happen next.

Then I saw the cloudy water ahead.

Oh, I thought, *don't go in there!*

But without hesitation, the person representing me swam into the cloud. Third person switched to first and I felt my limbs grow heavy; I sank slowly to soft sand.

Great Storm, now what?

Then the giggles filled my head. The little girls come to play.

Except they weren't playing with me, they danced with some kind of doll...no, not a doll, oh my God, it was Jon! Like a drowned marionette puppet, his limbs were pulled in awkward positions and his body swung in grotesque circles. *Hey,* I tried to scream, *Let him go!* But I was so tired, so heavy...he danced morbidly with his head flopping side to side and his hair billowing languidly about in the water. I couldn't move, all I could do was watch, frozen by the draining cloud. His eyes opened during one of the spins and locked on mine, they glowed bright yellow. He smiled and held out a long shimmering braid with one arm. His lips moved and words echoed in my head, *Little freak.*

I was horrified. I was hurt. I opened my eyes. The bright room made them water. The sun hung bright and hot outside my window. My body was drenched with sweat and the room smelled thickly of brine. "Oh my God!" My mind raced as pieces of the puzzle flew into place at warp speed.

Daniel and Tressman working together, attacking Pearl rather than Sara, the building he built, the partially submerged riprap we almost hit in the boat, the same pile I hit trying to find Sara. Everybody looking to the old lighthouse for treasure. Misdirection by Tressman. The treasure had nothing to do with the old lighthouse. It had to do with that natural looking rock structure, the pile of riprap. It wasn't a natural feature at all. It was built! Built to hide in plain sight! The braid's in there! But to get in to the braid a super high tide is needed. That's what Tressman was testing. Humpphrey said that the final clue to get into Tressman's safe rooms was only given when the final payment was made. Daniel would have hired Tressman and then Tressman died before he gave the final clue. The riddle about the stars!!! Pearl knew the final clue but not the location. Daniel knew the location but not the final clue. He knows the tide is important and he's just waiting to see what happens hoping he'll catch a break and using the girls to keep the rest of the mers away.

'At night they come without being fetched. By day they are lost without being stolen.' The stars...what could that mean? And why was Jon in my dream? What does Jon have to do with it? C'mon Storm, think!

But thinking more didn't award me with any new insights. *Damn. So close.* Jon's ghastly dream image filled my head.

"Jon?" I said anxiously into the phone.

"Hmm mmm." A groggy sounding voice answered.

"Jon? It's Storm. Everything okay?"

"Hmm mmm." Still groggy.

"Oh, did I wake you?"

"Hmm, mmm."

"Wanna come over later? I thought of something that may be important."

"Hmm mmm."

"Okay then. Bye."

"Bye," he mumbled and the receiver clunked down heavily.

I guess I'm on my own for a bit.

"Hiya!" Chimed Pearl as she walked into my room.

Hmm, or maybe not! I still hadn't got used to the idea that Pearl was my mother. Every time I thought of it I smiled and reflexively touched my pendant.

"Whatcha doin'?" She sat at the foot of my bed with her legs crossed.

"Nothing," I said hesitantly, not sure what she had up her sleeve.

It had been a week since the party. Pearl, Rowan, Jon and Lilli and I hung out nearly every night which seemed to be taking a toll on Jon's body. He could barely keep his eyes open in class, a feeling I remembered quite well before my body finished its transition. And today, he was apparently still asleep at half past nine. Sara flitted in and out of our wanderings. She always seemed to have one date or another with a handsome tourist.

St. Augustine shown brightly in my new light of knowledge. I recognized faces belonging to the Atlantic clans. Silver sea stars and lionfishes hung on the necks of shop owners, surf instructors, beach wanderers, yoga teachers, artists, and many others. Those faces also recognized mine with a smile, a wave, or a wink full of mischief.

"Pleasant sleep?" Pearl asked me which brought my nightmare back to the forefront of my thoughts.

"Actually, no," I frowned and tried to recall the details. "I dreamed of the girls and the structure by the ruins." I purposely stopped short of saying I thought the braid was in the structure because I really didn't have any real evidence other than a hunch and I still didn't understand the star clue.

"We've looked all over there but have never found a way in, although the girls don't make it easy to spend quality time," Pearl sighed. She seemed inclined to drop the subject of her braid in favor of whatever more exciting event she had planned for the day.

"But I really think..." Even as I spoke, however, whatever epiphany I had during the dream retreated away to the shadows of my memory.

"I think we need some breakfast!" Pearl chirped. "Rean was getting some ready when I came in."

Sure enough, the smell of bacon wafted into my room and my stomach responded with an embarrassingly loud and clear signal. Pearl and I giggled. I stretched and changed into my green bathing suit and tossed a cotton dress on over it. I pulled my hair back as we walked downstairs.

"Good morning, my darlings," Nana greeted us with two plates of food. "I'm meeting with a friend later this morning, I trust the two of you will stay out of trouble?" She winked.

Pearl laughed. "Oh, Rean, have you any doubts?"

"Plenty, my dear. Some things never change. Now Stormy," Nana changed her focus on me, "we do have a few things to talk about."

Uh oh, what did I do?

Reading my expression she added, "You didn't do anything wrong, but your father will be expecting us home at the end of this month."

A knot formed in my chest. In all of the changes over the past month, I hadn't even thought about what was going to happen next. I mean I couldn't leave here now, surely. First of all, I wouldn't be able to return to my high school looking like this. Secondly, I couldn't leave my new family and my MOM! Third, I had a life here now, a clan, I had Rowan, I had...

My face once again betrayed my thoughts, Nana's thin, small hand rested on my shoulders. "Relax. We'll figure something out, Stormy. To be honest, I don't want to leave either. This has always been my home. And I think that with the danger passed, we can stay here." She smiled lovingly at me.

"Will Dad come here, too?" I asked. "I mean then we can all be together!" I looked between Pearl and Nana.

"Honey," Pearl spoke, "your dad can't come here. It isn't safe for him unless we find my braid."

"What? So it's like either I can be with you guys or him? That's totally not fair!" I said.

Pearl's eyes, filled to the brim with moisture, told me she totally agreed, but her pursed lips also told me there was nothing that could be done. She looked tired. I suppose I wasn't the first person to wish we could all be together.

"This sucks," I said feeling extremely human and exactly my age. I got up from the table and stormed back up to my room. The phone rang but I ignored it. It was probably Jon calling back.

Nana's voice grew louder downstairs. She talked very strongly to somebody. I was actually quite relieved she wasn't talking to me, that tone meant something very serious was going on.

A loud slam was followed by heavy footsteps.

Yikes, she's coming up here. Maybe I am in trouble.

I quickly reviewed all the things I had done or not done recently. There was that little incident with Rowan, Pearl and the fountain. But the bubbles were really harmless and they were pretty funny. Imagine going to church Sunday morning and the wishing fountain outside is overflowing with beautiful bubbles. I giggled at the memory.

*But that was harmless fun. That was...*my door burst open and a furious Nana stormed in.

"Stubborn, thick headed, obstinate, selfish..." Nana sputtered insult after insult.

"Nana, it was just a joke, the fountain..." I squeaked. My voice seemed to have abandoned me.

"We're so damn close..." She spoke in a hiss through her clenched jaws.

"The bubbles were just..." I tried again, but she didn't seem to hear me.

"And I swear if the mers don't kill him, I WILL!" She sat heavily down on the bed next to me.

Him? I closed my mouth and tried to make myself invisible. Maybe this wasn't about the fountain after all.

Nana faced me and exhaled in a giant huff. Her shoulders slouched and she seemed to take on a stance of surrender.

"Your father, Storm," she spoke each word slowly as if forcing them from her, "is at the airport. He has come here to take us home."

"WHAT?" I shrieked. "Take us home? Why? Right now?" *This is horrible, why would he, how could he, Pearl's braid, Rowan, the mers, me!*

"*Why?*" Nana repeated my question with obvious disdain. "Because he's a stubborn fool. *Now* because apparently he received a call from someone claiming to be your class instructor who said you were homesick and wasting away. Would he believe me when I told him it wasn't so? No, because he's a stubborn ox and now he's going to put us all in jeopardy and..." Nana kept on muttering. I think she forgot I was in the room.

Strangely, despite my knowledge of danger, I felt a warming in my body at the thought of seeing Dad again. Maybe I was the selfish one. I felt in over my head right now and I really wanted to curl up in Dad's lap and feel his big, warm hands on my back, holding me and making everything okay like when I was little.

"But..." I took a risk at interrupting Nana, "maybe he could help us." My voice was still tiny.

Nana stopped ranting and her eyes brimmed with tears. "We haven't a choice now, have we?"

Nana eyes caught mine and in an instant I understood what I never had before. She had sacrificed her life to protect her child just as much as my mother did for me. I felt Nana's fear, her mortality, and saw a glimpse of the drive behind maternal protection. *What would I do if I lost her...or him...or them...oh God.*

Nana reached out and held my hands in hers. "We will be just fine Stormy. This is our time, *your* time. I believe in you *and* Pearl *and* Z. And your dad and I will be at your side where we should be, together, as a family. We will finish this thing once and for all."

We sat in silence for a few breaths. The waves crashed outside and the seagulls called excitedly.

"Now," Nana spoke, her resolute exterior recovered, "I suppose I'll be off to the airport to fetch your father." She looked me up and down. I was still wearing the thin cotton dress I had tossed over my bathing suit. I didn't do much to hide my new curves. "Perhaps you could put on something a touch less revealing so he doesn't have a heart attack first thing." She sighed.

"Sure Nana." I smiled.

Nana stopped at the door. "What was that about bubbles and the fountain?"

"Oh, nothing." I smiled my most innocent smile.

Nana eyed me suspiciously for a moment then shook her head slightly and walked out the door.

Daddy...I thought with warmth expanding within me.

Chapter Twenty-One

"Come on, Zelda, let's go practice with the wind." I walked and talked with the cat as I went out to the beach to distract my impatience for Nana to return from the airport with Dad.

Wind manipulation was my stronger skill, at least compared to wave manipulation and weather, which were two skills still obstinately tied into my erratic emotions.

"Mrow." Zelda tended to be a cat of few words, but I took her company as support of my decision. We sat a few yards from the house, hidden partially by some mid-beach dunes with their waving sea oats. Just as Pearl taught me, I smoothed a small spot in front of me, then I collected some different sized shells and lay them out on the smooth patch. Zelda chased fire ants in the dunes.

As Pearl and Rowan had taught me, mers don't create wind, weather, or waves. They simply manipulate the existing energy into something they want using the charge within. It's like how magnets can push magnetic objects around without physically touching them. It's a force we create from inside of us. While my strength is set since I completed transition, my control is something that can be continuously improved.

This morning, I wanted to move only the far right shell, an orange and black clam, the largest of the four I had set out. My eyes saw the wind as I gathered it. It was blue and shimmery. I lowered it over the shell, but like a paper streamer, it had no effect on the shell. I squinted my eyes a bit and gathered more of the shimmering wind. The more I gathered, the richer and darker the color became.

The other part of manipulation is total concentration. You can't let your mind wander. Unfortunately, before I could catch it, my mind drifted to Dad's arrival and the impossible task with an impossible deadline and even more impossible consequences if we failed. The wind, gathered but no longer under control, spun into a tiny tornado and scattered all of the shells and the surrounding sand.

Zelda crouched low in the dune and gave me an indignant look as she stood to shake off the dusting of sand from her fur.

"Oops, sorry, Zel."

She sat back down with her back to me and licked herself clean with obvious discontent.

"She'll get over it, ma'love."

"How long have you been here?" I asked without turning around.

"Long enough my little selkie." Rowan's large arms wrapped around me. I leaned back into this chest and inhaled. By the feel of his wet body, he'd just returned from surfing.

"How'd the lessons go today?" I asked breaking the silence.

"Oh, you know, the same. Little girls screaming and squealing, lots of splashing, a fair amount of laughing and very little catching waves." He kissed me on the cheek.

"When you say little girls, do you mean actual children or mortal women?" I asked.

"Is there a difference?" His voice sounding innocent. I could tell he smiled with his words even without looking at him.

"Only so much as the latter tends to be overly affectionate to you." Now I turned to him and with my eyes dared him to go on.

He chuckled. "Yes, well, one has to have a job, no? Sometimes that job demands a bit of extra effort on one's part."

"Yeah, job. I am well aware how you handle your jobs."

"Well, some jobs are more special than others. And one in particular required lots of extra effort and some of my best tricks."

"Oh, so now I was simply being tricked. I see. You know how little control I have over my emotions and their consequences, it would be a shame if one of your students was knocked off of her *wittle* board right along with her *handsome* instructor."

He hugged me tighter. "A shame indeed. But tell me, when she gets knocked off her board, does her suit stay in place or is it lost in the chaos? And would said student need mouth to mouth resuscitation?"

"You!" I tried to elbow him in the gut, but he held my arms too tightly, obviously anticipating my retaliation. I was then tickled by merciless fingers. Of all the changes my body went through in the past months, my ticklishness hadn't disappeared.

"Hiya guys!" Pearl's chirpy voice broke through Rowan's laughter and my squeals.

"Hey Pearl!" I managed to say, gasping for breath. "Stop, stop...okay, you win," I squealed at his new attack. He released me and we both sat up. Pearl smiled, but her eyes were distant.

"What's the matter?" I asked.

"Oh, nothing, really. I think I may be just...what's the word...*nervous*?" She seemed surprised at her own assessment.

"What could you be nervous about?" Rowan asked. "You're the most fearless mer ever created. *I'm* actually scared of you half the time." Pearl gave a genuine smile back.

"Oh, I don't know. Just the thought of seeing Matthew again. It makes my stomach jump."

"Dad? You're nervous to see Dad?" I asked.

"Well, it's been such a long time and I don't know how he'll, how I'll...if he..." She stumbled over her words then gave up and fell silent.

I put my arm on hers. "He's always loved you Pe...Mom," I whispered. "We both have."

Her face glowed with unbridled radiance at my words.

"Really?"

"Really."

"Oh, this is all so surreal," Pearl said. She sounded very much like an excited little girl.

Did Pearl just say that her *life was surreal? What the heck does that make mine then?* I wondered.

"Nana should be back any minute, you wanna come back to the house and wait?" I offered.

"Perhaps I should let you two have some time before I intrude."

I smiled. "Sure. I guess he's in for more than one shock tonight." I made a mock presentation of my new and improved body.

Rowan laughed. "You best not do that in front of him, the poor man is already having a rough day. Seeing his little girl transformed into a blindingly beautiful siren may just be the end of him."

"I guess I should find something bulky to put on."

Rowan nodded and leaned in for a kiss.

"I will see you both later, though, right?" I asked.

"Wouldn't miss it, Love." Rowan gave me another tender kiss on the lips.

"Of course, Stormy." Pearl gave me a hug but her eyes were looking inward, perhaps at a memory.

******

I heard his familiar voice and heavy steps on the porch before I saw him. My heart raced with excitement. Whether I was five years old missing him after a long day at Kindergarten, seven years old needing comfort after a scary dream, or sixteen, a half mermaid in a strange place, faced with an impossible task and feeling way in over my head, I knew Dad could help make it alright!

"DADDY!" I called as the front door squeaked open. I raced from my room down the stairs. I barreled into his arms and buried my face in his warm, moist tee shirt.

"*Oomph...*" His voice was pinched from the tightness of my hold. I relaxed a bit, remembering my strength. "Sorry, I just missed you," I said to his chest.

"Well, those are pretty nice words for an old man to hear!" He replied with an extra squeeze. He smelled of the same comforting smell, Old Spice and a hint of Whiskey which he probably had during his flight.

"Now, let's have a look at you." I stepped back and stood still, unsure what his reaction would be. Thank goodness it was still bright enough that my eyes wouldn't look strange. Apparently my eyes weren't his concern. He turned quickly to Nana and she gave a small nod. His complexion faded a few shades.

"Storm," he spoke in barely more than a whisper. "You're..." He closed his eyes and pinched the bridge of his nose. His exhale came slowly. He then opened his eyes, wordlessly picked up his bag and walked with heavy steps to the back bedroom.

"Nana?" I whispered.

"Give him a moment," she said with a slight shrug of her shoulders. "Being told something and seeing it are very different things."

He came back to the room, passed by us without a word and went into the kitchen. I heard cabinets open and close, ice cubes clinking and liquid being poured. Returning for the second time, whiskey on the rocks in hand, he sat heavily down on the couch with his forearms on his thighs and his glass cradled in both hands. Nana finally broke the tension.

"I told you Storm was different now. You knew and now you're making her feel bad. Stop this nonsense." Nana's voice was stern with accusation.

"I know, I know." He shook his head slowly. "You said, I heard, but I didn't listen. I mean, I didn't expect the resemblance to...to..." He took a prolonged sip of his drink. When he finally looked up, his eyes were rimmed with red.

"Stormy, it isn't you. It's just that your mom, well, you look...I thought I..."

"Yeah, I know," I spoke softly. "I look a lot more like Pearl now than when I left."

At the mention of her name he hung his head back down. I walked cautiously over to the couch. I wasn't sure what he would do, but I knew I couldn't have handled it if he shuttered or moved away at my touch.

"I understand now why you guys had to keep this all a secret from me. I'm not mad...anymore." I stole a quick glance at Nana, she smiled. "And Pearl told me..."

Dad's head jerked up. His expression turned from sorrow to confusion to anger in the span of one breath. "Pearl... told... you?" He repeated my words, slowly, as if trying to make sense of them.

"Yeah, she..."

"She's *alive*?" His eyes were big and his posture became slightly menacing. I fought the urge to retreat from him. Instead, I nervously held my ground.

"Yes." I tried to sound strong, but my heart fluttered like a bird's and my palms sweated through my dress. "She didn't die that night. She's been searching for her braid ever since. She said it isn't safe for you to be here unless she finds it. We've been looking..."

"*We've*?" He repeated again, his voice rose. "Meaning you, meaning you've been helping *them*." He nearly spat the word *them*. "And *you*, Mom." He turned on Nana now. "Hasn't enough been sacrificed already? Haven't we all suffered enough for these *things*?"

At his use of the word 'things' I cringed and my face began to burn with anger.

"They give us nothing but sorrow, pain, hurt and for what? Half the time it's just games, just playing with toys to them. Well, I'm not a toy! Not anymore," Dad shouted. "And I'll not have my family a part of their problems any longer. We are leaving here at once and come hell or high water never turning back!"

"What?" I said. "No."

"Oh yes, Stormy. They don't care about us. They don't care about anyone but themselves."

"That's not true," I shouted back. "Mom loves you and me and she always has. Why do you think she sacrificed herself for us? And those *things* you keep talking about? I'm one of them in case you haven't noticed! Do you love me less now? Do I love you less? No. You can help us, help save *Mom's* life this time. Unless it's you who were playing games and attracted only to the long eyelashes and the perfect body!" The door burst open with a gust of wind. It hit dad like a punch to the chest. He fell back onto the couch.

His face was full of confusion as he tried to figure out who or what had just hit him. I stood tall, my gaze steady. Part daughter and part monster; which part would he choose to see?

"Like it or not Dad, I'm half you and half Mom and I love both of you with every ounce of my being but I won't let you insult us like that."

It was the first time I used *us* to separate myself from humans.

"You don't remember," he whispered. "You were just a baby; a newborn. I've spent the last 16 years trying to forget, trying to move on, trying and failing. You are all I have left and I refuse to let you be used as some kind of pawn or cannon fodder for whatever battle is about to take place."

"I'm not a pawn. And I AM going to help Mom. We're so close to finishing this thing. I know where the braid is...I think. I just need help to get to it. To figure out the last piece of the puzzle. Please. Help us. I know you can."

"Stormy, you don't understand." He looked tired now that the rage had left him. I knew that feeling very well. "I nearly lost you both that night. I learned my lesson. We...I can't hang with them without serious consequences. Humans are too frail, we're... ugh, I can't do a thing if Mom chooses to help, but I can do something about you. I can try to protect you. I promised your mother and God help me, I will keep that promise, even if that means...she's really alive?"

I nodded. "You did keep me safe until I was able to protect myself. But I...we can protect *you* now. We need your help. SHE needs your help. Pearl, I mean Mom, needs to know you love her, too. She's sad, she's lost, she's running out of time. She needs to know the battle is worth fighting, you know?" He looked up at me with confused eyes. I exhaled and took a step closer to him, my arms slightly open in an effort to make peace.

"Please," I said. "For me, for her, for *us*." My rage was gone as was Dad's. The wind was quiet outside although the door still stood open.

Dad exhaled long and slow with his eyes closed and his lips pinched tightly together. When his eyes reopened, they were softer, loving. He motioned for me to sit next to him. This time he held his gaze on my eyes, as if he were drawing strength from the familiar. He reached gently with one hand and stroked my hair lightly and then he gently picked up the sea star that hung from my neck and let it lay in his palm.

"You look just like her, you know," he whispered.

Nana joined us on the couch and put her hand on Dad's shoulder. "We'll be okay. This time, Matthew, we'll make it work. Storm says she's onto something and I think she may be able to finally solve this and set us all free."

A soft knock made us all turn toward the front door. In the frame of the open door stood Pearl and Rowan, two perfect forms, as breathtaking as ever. Pearl opened her mouth as if to speak but then closed it again. Rowan took a small step forward. Dad's arm tensed on my leg.

Dad wasn't looking at me or even at Rowan. His eyes were fixed on Pearl. One tear ran silently down his cheek and what little color had returned to his face during our argument was gone again.

"Pearl," he whispered.

"Matthew," she answered tentatively in return.

He spoke like he was talking to a ghost. She spoke like she was in confession, begging for forgiveness.

I wished I could have melted away and left Dad and Pearl alone.

"I..." They both started at once.

Pearl giggled nervously. Dad cleared his throat.

"You first," Pearl chimed quietly.

Dad steadied himself with a deep breath and then stood up.

"Pearl, I've thought about what I would say to you if I had one more chance to see you. I've gone over thousands of scenes in my head, dialogue, witty banter, heartfelt murmurs and the foulest curses. And now here I am and feel at a loss for words. You forced me and our daughter away sixteen years ago. I begged to let me stay and help you, I pleaded for you to come away with us, I loved you with everything I had but you chose to surrender, to give in, to give up, to force me away!"

This doesn't seem to be going in a very good direction...

Pearl's head shook slowly side to side as if trying to deny the accusations.

"No," her voice came out nearly too soft to be heard. "No," she said more firmly. "I did it to save you. It was the only way you both would be allowed to live. If they had killed you and Storm, or even threatened to kill you, that would have been the end of me...and us." Her head still shook slowly side to side. Her eyes weren't as bright as usual and her skin looked as if it were coated with matte powder. The sun had headed toward the western horizon unnoticed and now the room dimmed in the twilight.

"You had to think I was gone forever or else you would have stayed, you would have tried to fight and then you and Storm could have been lost or used against me." Pearl stopped talking. She seemed gathered her thoughts and her painful memories from that long ago night.

"Matthew," Pearl's voice rang lightly in the air. She took a step toward him but he immediately retreated the same distance. She stopped and looked as if she had been punched in the stomach. It was the same reaction, that look of repulsion, rejection, I had feared earlier.

"This is too much," Dad said. "You, me, Storm, here now. I prayed for the longest time to see you just one more time. Praying that you'd come back to me somehow. Loving you till it hurt to breathe. But..."

NO, I thought. *Don't say but. Dad, it's Mom. Please...*I begged in my head. I looked at Pearl, her skin looked pale, barely a sparkle to be seen and her eyes dimmed. Her head bowed slightly down and her shoulders slumped. Her emotions were clear...but there seemed to be something else, something deeper fading within her.

"No," Pearl said again, calm but firm. "I've been fighting every day since you left to free myself. I've searched, I've struggled. Why fight so hard? For you, Matthew. For what we had, for what I want." Her eyes now glowed fiercely as she spoke and a sudden gust of wind through the doorway blew her hair forward. The curtains ballooned up and dust and sand fluttered into the room.

Dad was unfazed by her outburst. "Pearl, I've gone over this, it can't work, you and me. We tried, we failed. Look at me, I'm an old man now. We were stupid kids who thought we could beat the odds."

"Then we try again!" Pearl nearly shouted. "If you won't have me then why the hell am I fighting? I *should* have died that night. The clan no longer needs me to live. Storm is their savior. The only reason I'm still fighting is to be together with you once more! If you don't want me, then who cares anymore what happens to me. I love you. I've always loved you."

They stared at each other not talking for the longest time.

"Damn Pearl. I don't know whether to say I love you or I hate you. You've caused me so much pain...so much hurt."

Pearl sagged, her eyes dimmed further. Her short outburst seemed to have weakened her.

The clock on the mantle ticked out the heartbreaking seconds.

"But," Dad continued, "no matter how hard I try to be mad at you and wish you out of my mind, I can't let go. I can't stop loving you. You're the face that comes to me in my dreams...you're my Pearl, my love." The side of his mouth twitched into a partial smile and the entire room exhaled their collective breath.

He opened his arms and without hesitation Pearl fell into them. He picked her up and cradled her and then they kissed.

My mom and dad, together. *Impossible*, once again, seemed to take on less and less of a meaning. *Magic*, meanwhile, took on more.

He set her down slowly to her feet, but they never lost contact. She leaned on his side and smiled at me. I walked over and together, for the first time in sixteen years, we hugged one another all at the same time. They both kissed me on my head and I wished that this moment would last forever.

"Ahem," Rowan cleared his throat.

"Oh my God!" I said, pulling away slightly from Mom and Dad. "Dad, this is Rowan."

Dad looked over my head at the figure still standing in the door. He was obviously a mer and I could see Dad tried to figure out this man's place in all things. *Wait for it*, I thought. *Wait*...and then click! Dad looked at me and then back at Rowan and then back to me.

"Oh no," he said shaking his head. "No, no, no."

I think this may just put the poor man over the edge.

"Dad," I whined, feeling less mer and more sixteen.

Pearl smiled. "Matthew, it's okay."

"There's no use fighting it," Nana said. "I tried that once and learned quickly the powers that drive this kind of bond are not ones that can be stopped."

Dad looked to Pearl.

I walked over to Rowan and took his hand in mine. I guided him over to Dad and Pearl.

"Be nice," I hissed to Dad when we got by his side.

Dad thought a moment and then put out his hand for a greeting. When Rowan met it with his own, Dad tightened his grip. "I suppose a welcome to the family is in order, then."

"Thanks," Rowan said.

"She looks happy," Dad said. "Thank you for that."

"You're welcome," Rowan said.

"Oh, one more thing," Dad said, still holding Rowan's hand in his, "don't screw it up."

******

Rowan and I sat together on the floor in the living room. He leaned against one of the chairs and I leaned against him. Nana sat on one couch, Dad and Pearl sat on the other. My family was together. My cheeks hurt from smiling so much.

After drinks were served and memories revisited and the summer recapped, I showed Dad my braid. He smiled, but his eyes still held hesitation.

"My favorite girlfriend," he whispered to me. I blushed at his reference to how he always greeted me when I was little as he came from work. He'd walk in the door, briefcase in hand, and I would run up and jump into his arms. He would spin me in circles and give me a kiss and ask, "So, how's my favorite girlfriend?" I laughed every time. I smiled now, the laughter long retreated to just my head but it was still there nonetheless.

"...is growing up," Nana said, "into quite a beautiful and strong wom...uh, mermaid."

With a room bright with smiles and laughter, I felt magical for the first time, not because I was a mermaid, but because I was surrounded by so much love. I thought about everything that my parents and Nana had been through just to keep me alive. And then how much Rowan loved me and I loved him. His strong arms wrapped around me and I stroked his hands with mine. This was magic alright, this was power beyond anything I'd ever experienced or witnessed above or below the water.

As the night ticked away toward dawn, conversations turned to Pearl's braid and I finally revealed my thoughts on the Tressman structure and my tentative conclusions about the significance of the high tide. It must be the key to getting into his secret structure.

"Daniel knows of his structure, but I don't think he knows how to get in and until I showed up to fill in as heir, all he needed to do was keep you all away from it, so he used the children."

"Daniel can be very convincing when he wants to be," Nana whispered. "But now, he needs the braid to take over the territory, it won't help to just let the time expire."

"But what about the tide?" Rowan asked.

"I don't know, but based on Kate's accounts, Tressman made a point of putting his structure where it was," I replied.

"You all know that a Proxigean tide is meant to happen next week, at the new moon," Dad said.

"What? A *new* moon. I thought the highest tides occurred during full moons," I said.

"According to Dr. Trouseau at Purdue, you remember him, Stormy? I'm working with him on the new book. Anyway, he was all excited about this year's Proxigean tide as it's supposed to be one of the legendary extreme tides."

"Well, I suppose that solves two mysteries, answering the questions of when and where," Nana said. "If what you think is true, Storm, the time to get into the underwater room will be next week, coinciding with the running out of the time span allowed to recover the braid. Unfortunately, we're still left with the big question of how to get in."

"Why can't we just break the thing down?" Rowan asked.

"Too risky," Nana replied. "Accounts of Tressman's other safe rooms all included rather extensive traps and devices that would destroy the contents if someone entered without using the proper techniques."

"What happens if nobody finds it?" Dad asked. "Like say, Daniel doesn't get it but neither do you and the calendar rounds conclude with the braid still left unattached?"

Up to this point, Pearl had sat silently, her face paler than usual and her eyes still lacking her usual twinkle. She cleared her throat. "Well, thanks to Stormy, there won't be an affect on the territory, she will be the next in line to rule. But as for me, well, I'm afraid that will be the end."

"I just got you back, there is no way in hell I'm going to lose you now!" I exclaimed.

"Look, Stormy, I know it doesn't seem fair, but that is just the way it is for mers. Please my baby..." She took me in her arms and held me. Her skin was covered in tiny salt crystals. The past few days I thought she was just nervous about the braid and then today, I thought her appearance was due to the arrival of Dad...but she's been slowly dying...fading...

"No, I won't let that happen. We will find that braid," I said.

"Not finding your braid was never an option. That's why we're all here," Nana chimed in.

"So we only have one week to figure out what Daniel knows about the structure?" Rowan asked. "He obviously knows the braid is in there, but we still have a chance to beat him to it since if he knew how to get in, he would have already done it."

"Yeah," I said. "One week to find out what he knows and then beat him to the entrance and the braid if it turns out he knows more than us."

******

Time has a very unique sense of humor. Whenever you wish it go faster, it crawls, and whenever you wish it to slow down it flies. The days of this particular week left nothing but a blur in their wake. The moon taunted us with its ever thinning crooked smile and on this night it wouldn't be around at all. Today was the day...time had run out.

"OHMYGOD!" I exclaimed. "I have to talk with the water souls," I declared as Pearl and I sat on the deck, the robin's egg colored afternoon sky had hints of storms to come in the billowing clouds. A perspiring margarita sat forgotten on the table. She looked tired, drained...resigned. Her energy waned exponentially with the moon this past week, the smaller it became the less space she appeared to take up. It was now or never for us to save her.

"They'll attack you," Pearl replied.

"Not if I hide my star. Remember when I told you about them before? They wanted to play with me, it was only because Daniel told them to keep away from the ones with the stars that they chased you all. They even mentioned missing Sara."

"'allo ladies! What'd I miss?" Rowan bounded up the stairs two at a time. He gave me a kiss and then frowned after looking over to Pearl. He picked up the margarita glass and put it in her hands. "Drink," he said flatly.

Her eyes looked up to his towering form but no other part of her moved from her fetal position on the lounge chair. "What's the point?"

"The point is, you can't give up. I won't let you and if I heard Storm correctly on my way up here, she's planning to pay a wee visit to the water souls and most likely kill herself in the process which won't help our little heir issue one bit. So, you," he looked at Pearl, "need to stay alive until we get your braid back tonight and you," he looked at me, "will have nothing to do with those souls."

"But..." Pearl and I both responded.

"No buts." He gave us both stern looks and then headed inside.

Pearl stuck out her tongue to his back. I giggled quietly. "You're going to go, aren't you," she whispered.

I nodded. The corner of her pale, dry lips curled into a hint of a smirk. It was the first sign of amusement I had seen from her for the past few days when even the tiniest movement looked effort-full. "My girl."

"They like me, remember?" I said. "I'm the nice lady they want to play with," I imitated their child voices. I have a very important question to ask them. I can't believe I didn't figure this out sooner! It had finally clicked. Like putting the final piece of a 5000 piece jigsaw puzzle in place. The remaining mixed up parts that had been running in random directions in my head since the Solstice finally fell into place. I saw the entire picture, clear as a photograph, in my head. I knew the connection between Daniel, the girls, Tressman, and the braid.

The brief smile disappeared from Pearl's lips and she took a slow sip of the drink and swallowed; not bothering to hide the grimace of pain.

"It's the only way." I smiled. "Not to worry, I have a plan!"

******

"When will you ever listen to me, Storm?" Rowan said with a stern face.

"Hmm, never," I responded with a smile and quick kiss.

"That's what I figured."

My family, both human and mer stood facing me in front of the light-house. The sun dropped below the western tree line and the air was heavy. The clouds from earlier hung low and thick with rain.

"You meet us right back here in exactly one hour. Even if your plan doesn't work, come back in what?"

"One hour," I repeated. "Don't worry, it'll work."

I forced myself to sound more confident than I felt. I had refused to tell anyone my plan which helped in the secrecy department, but the truth really was that I sort of didn't have a plan. Well, unless you call trying-to-have-a-conversation-with-water-spirits-that-could-kill-me-and-hoping-to-learn-the-secrets-they-knew-without-letting-them-know-I-was-now-one-of-the-creatures-they-were-supposed-to-destroy a *plan*. Hmm, no, I didn't really call that a plan either. But I did know that this was something only I could do. For so long I doubted my strength, I doubted my purpose...but tonight, it was crystal clear. It had to be me.

I heard them before I saw the clouded water.

I told him it was rising beyond the line he marked. He'll be here soon to play.

What will he bring us?

Ooh, I can't wait to play. He said this time he'd stay because we did such a good job!

Hey, who's that?

Look! It's the lady! Hi lady!

Hi girls. I thought back and tried to keep a safe distance from the opaque swirls of energy draining water I knew belonged to them.

Whatcha doin'? Despite my relaxed tone, my heart pounded furiously behind the confines of my ribs.

Oh, we're waiting for the man of course. He's so nice.

Ahh, I see. What's he coming here for? I poked around in the sand a bit with my finger and pretended to be distracted by a shell, still consciously keeping my distance.

He's...

Shh, don't say anything.

Why not?

Because he said not to tell.

But it's just the lady.

He said.

I don't think he meant her, *he meant the ones with the stars. She doesn't have a star, right lady?*

Right. I said. I fortunately had drawn my sea star behind me and tied it up with my hair. So far so good.

Yeah, I won't tell anybody. I promise. I said.

Oh, okay. He coming here because the waters are really high and he wants to get into the room and see the pretty things.

What pretty things?

Oh, all sorts of shiny things in tiny glass jars.

Really, has he ever been in before?

No, he tried before, but he couldn't.

Oh, that's sad. But you've been in?

Oh yeah, all the time. Walls don't mean much to us. We told him he should try the tunnel, but he couldn't find it.

Tunnel? What tunnel? Despite my best efforts at remaining calm, my thoughts rose in octave and my pulse pounded behind my temples.

You know, the tunnel. It fills up with water when the room does. We like to play in it, too. But it only goes a little bit and then we have to leave.

A little bit where?

I don't know, but we can't go so we just play in a little bit of it.

Yeah the part that goes into the room.

Ooh, I bet tonight we could go in more!

Yeah, the water will fill it up!

Yay!

Then we could show him how to get in so he can play, too.

Oh, yeah!

My mind spun with this information. They didn't specifically mention the braid, but it had to be there. And the tunnel, of course Tressman built a tunnel. Part one of my plan was a success. I couldn't wait to get back to tell everyone! Now for part two...

You wouldn't by chance be talking to a stranger would you? Daniel's voice resonated deep and powerful in my head. *Uh oh,* I thought.

No! They all chimed.

She's just the nice lady who likes to play with us. One said.

Really. If she's so nice why is she trying to trick you? His voice oozed with false concern.

No, she's not. Are you lady?

No, of course not. I still couldn't see Daniel, but I felt a disturbance in the water and before I could react, I tasted the scent of spice and cedar.

Ouch! I cried out as my sea star was yanked unceremoniously from the bundle of my hair. I struggled against his hold on me as he pulled me toward the mist.

Look girls, a liar! She's one of the star people I warned you about. You remember, don't you, the horrible girls that doomed you to these waters?

There were gasps and shrieks and angry cries. The girls and the mist closed in on me and within moments I was trapped on the sand with barely enough energy to breathe.

Don't listen to him. I'm not tricking you. He's the one. I closed my eyes. The darkness was soothing. It would be so much easier if I just let go. But Daniel's laughter rang in my head and brought my focus back.

You filthy half breed. Neither fully human nor fully mer. Did you really think you had a chance against me? I got Pearl's braid once and I'll do it again. Tonight's the night it all ends.

So it was you. I thought thickly through the encroaching blackness of my mind.

Yeah, it was me. She thought she was too good for me? Well, hardly. She can suffer for all eternity now for having scorned me. And you, well, you were never more than an accident anyway so I can't say I'm too sorry for how things are turning out.

And if you can't get in? I mean, it doesn't seem like your plans have been working out all that well. I laughed darkly. No reason not to push my luck. It was nearly all I had left in me to pull it off but the angry results from Daniel were well worth it.

You nasty little muck of a creature. I felt him close in. I heard his deep chime resonate through the water. My chest constricted. My limbs no longer had sensation. My head felt as if it would explode with a sudden pressure.

My plans are just fine and even if I don't get in to destroy the braid, Pearl won't have it either so if she doesn't want to live under my control she won't live at all and I can live with that. Daniel growled.

Except when I tell Z where the braid is... It took a lot of effort to string my thoughts together, the pressure was so intense.

Daniel's laughter peeled through my head. *Too bad you won't be around to share that bit of news and oh dear, Z without an heir once again...tsk, tsk...*

Heeeyyy giiiirrrls? A sweet voice broke through the water. *Did anyone ever ask you to play a game?*

I know that voice. I thought through the haze in my brain.

There was confusion between the girls and Daniel. The girls, despite Daniel's protests to ignore the strange voice, couldn't resist an invitation.

Yeah! We love games.

Girls, focus! Daniel's voice boomed. *Or I may not give you your presents.*

Yoo, hoo, girls! The same chipper voice broke in. This time it sounded like it came from a different direction. *I bet you like hide and seek.*

Yeah! They all chimed in unison.

Well, the voice chirped from yet another direction, *come find me!*

The mist faded slightly around me.

Ooh, so close, but still cold. The voice chimed.

The girls' giggles filled my head. If I wasn't battling unconsciousness and the very real potential of death, it would have been a really sweet sound to hear.

Sara told me you loved this game! The voice cooed.

It's Lilli's voice! I thought. *This little Sprite really does have the most perfect timing! How did she know I'd be here?*

Feeling returned in my limbs and the pounding in my head chilled as the girls slowly moved away from me.

Yeah, Sara! We loved Sara, she was the best seeker. She always found us.

My head cleared slightly as the girls moved away. I was able to continue my plan. *Really, always? She told me one day you hid without telling her*, I added.

Girls, get back here! Daniel roared.

Oh, is he always this cranky? The voice laughed.

The girls giggled. *Only sometimes.*

Who are you? Daniel roared.

Who am I? Oh, nobody of interest really. As she spoke to Daniel her voice took on more of a menacing tone rather than a sweet one.

My strength fully returned; *thank God for Sprites!* Now, despite my lingering headache, it was time to prove my theory about who was really responsible for the girls' deaths. I wasn't sure how much time Lilli could keep the girls distracted from Daniel's rantings so I got right to the point. *Remember girls that day by the lighthouse? Sara wasn't around and you wanted to find the perfect hiding place!* I said.

We never beat her. One girl said.

He told us this would win for sure! Another girl said.

Daniel, I thought loud and clear, *I believe you owe these girls an explanation and an apology.*

What explanation? The third girl asked.

Oh, I think Daniel should tell you about the game that day, when he told you to hide...where was it Daniel?

I don't know what you're talking about. Don't listen to her, girls. His deep voice sounded nearly soothing, hypnotic. And clearly farther from me than before. Lilli's distraction was totally working!

Wait, I remember! He told us Sara would never find us if we hid in the old supply lift. He said we would win the game!

Yeah! More voices chimed in.

But then the lift started rolling and we couldn't stop it. We screamed but nobody came.

Then we crashed into the water and everybody was crying. Our parents came in and we tried to tell them we were okay but it was like nobody could see us.

And when we saw Sara, she was crying, too. Then we swam closer but she swam away.

Did you do this to us, Mister? One girl asked.

No, I, never, I... His chime faded as he fled, but he wasn't alone. The girls kept after him, their voices overlapping with questions from that day. The hum was deafening. Daniel left and they followed.

Hey girl, we'd better go. Lilli floated next to me on the sand. If she hadn't shown up, I never would have been able to tell the girls the truth.

How'd you know? She asked.

I didn't. But I figured he'd want to have someone keep watch over his prize and what better watchers than water souls and little girls to fawn over him to boot?

He killed them on purpose? She asked.

Yeah, sounds like it. I answered quietly.

I never really understood humans, but I don't see a point in killing them, either. She replied.

We swam to the surface and climbed out of the water. I felt so sad for those girls as I crawled onto the sand. Their lives cut short simply for being in the wrong place at the wrong time and trusting the wrong person.

"Lilli! Thank you. I would have been dead right now if you hadn't shown up," I said as I wrapped the little Sprite in my arms.

"Well, to me, it looked like you were doing a fine job, but when Pearl mentioned your plan, I thought that maybe I could be of some assistance. Especially since I'm one of the best hide and seekers ever!" She winked. "Undefeated."

I smiled. "Thanks. Oh my God! There's a tunnel, Lilli! The girls told me! Come on, we have to tell the others! That's the way in! We can save Pearl if we hurry!"

The two of us scrambled up the sand, arm in arm, toward the lighthouse and the group anxiously awaiting our return.

Chapter Twenty-Two

There was too much talking all at once. Even with the extended daylight of summertime, twilight had cloaked the sky by the time Lilli and I returned. Our deadline loomed just a few hours away.

"How did you get away?" Dad asked again. I was wrapped in one of his arms and one of Pearl's. We sat on the grass in front of the keeper's house. Nana spoke in a hushed voice with Lilli and I retold the story of the girls and Daniel and of Lilli's great timing.

"So it wasn't Sara?" Pearl asked quietly. "All these years she blamed herself. Hell, I was blamed by Tressman. This was all Daniel. His plan all along. That's why Tressman attacked me!" Wind picked up around us. I gave a worried look at Pearl, she played absently with a piece of her hair, most likely where her braid once hung and her sunken eyes glowed with a faint, cold, ominous light. She looked quite frightening. Before I could say anything I saw Dad rub her hand and give it a little squeeze. She exhaled and her face smoothed.

"So, Pearl, where is this tunnel?" I asked after the fury had fully dissipated from her face.

"I have no idea. I never knew of any tunnel. Tressman must have built it in secret when he constructed the new lighthouse."

We all instinctively looked up to the silhouetted tower behind us.

"Miles and I searched every inch of these grounds over the decades of our youth and we never found an entrance to a tunnel," Nana said.

"Miles?" I asked.

"Yes, Dear, Mr. Humpphrey."

"Miles is Mr. Humpphrey? Seriously?" I felt so stupid for not connecting these things before. "So he was the friend you worked with back when you were young?"

She nodded.

"But you said an innocent girl died in that storm, I thought she was your friend."

"No," she replied softly, "Sophie was Miles' three-year-old daughter."

The sound of an approaching car broke into our conversation. Still in shock from Nana's disclosure, I gawked blankly at the black, vintage Cadillac. It had a skull on the front tag and looked almost exactly like...

"The hearse?" I questioned. The immense car made a wide, spinning turn into the parking lot. Sand and stones scattered in the air.

The tinted window rolled down on the driver's side, and Sara's bright smile greeted us! Jon looked strained in the passenger seat. His knuckles were white and appeared glued to the dash.

"Get me the hell out of this thing," Mr. Humpphrey mumbled from the back seat, his hand groping blindly for the door handle.

Sara laughed. "Oh, you crazy old bugger. Like you didn't have a blast on that last corner. Just like the old days!" She turned off the ignition and flipped the keys over to Jon. "Thanks for letting me drive kid. Told ya I'd get here in under two minutes."

"Yeah, umm, thanks," Jon said. His voice sounded shaky and slightly higher than normal.

"What are you guys doing here?" I asked. The others had joined me now by the hearse and everybody was busy giving hugs, greetings and introductions.

"Well," Jon began, "Lilli found me earlier and said she had a feeling that you were into something over your head..."

"Literally!" Lilli interrupted with a giggle.

Jon looked at Lilli and smiled. "She said I needed to come here with Mr. Humphrey as soon as possible. And when I went to his house, Sara was there."

"Yeah," Sara chimed, "This guy I was with downtown said..." Sara stopped talking, lost in a thought. "Oh oh..." she said.

"What?" Rowan asked.

"I left the guy at the bar after he told me. Oops. I meant to go back, but then I knew I had to find you and when I left to make a call, you know it's so rude to call from the table, anyway I left to make a call, but then I saw Melody and she said that..."

"Uh, Sara, what did the guy tell you?" Pearl interrupted, her voice barely above a whisper..

"Oh yes, well, he was a biologist, or an ecologist, or maybe a geologist, anyway he was some kind of ologist and he was talking about this crazy high tide coming tonight. That's why he was in town. Anyway, I remembered Stormy here talking about a tide and I remembered Tressman always noting the tides. He used to try to talk to me about it, absolutely boring if you ask me. But, I thought maybe Miles here would have some of Tressman's old journals. Thought it may help to find out what he was going on about."

"Yeah," Jon broke back in, "so when I got there, Sara and Mr. Humpphrey were together and I told them about what Lilli said and we all came here as fast as we could." Jon and Mr. Humpphrey shuddered.

"What?" I asked noticing their odd reaction.

"I drove," Sara said. "Well, they said they wanted to get here fast!"

I couldn't help but smile. *We're all here now. We're going to solve this! We're going to win!*

"So, what's the tale?" Sara asked me.

Everyone looked at me expectantly. I looked back unsure exactly where to start, the girls, Daniel's confession, the tunnel...

"Umm, well, there's a tunnel."

"Where?" Sara asked.

"I've never read of one," Mr. Humpphrey said. He stood next to Nana. She beamed with excitement and I think with Mr. Humpphrey's presence. "Are you sure?"

All eyes turned to me. "Well, that's what the girls, umm, the water souls said. They like to play in it when the water gets high enough. Daniel could never figure out how to get into it. And I think his plan was to have the high tide fill the tunnel and allow the girls to direct him to the entrance."

"So at least one more question is solved because it looks like we know as much as he does," Nana said.

"Where's Daniel now?" Pearl asked.

"Playing with the girls," Lilli answered. "He owed them a game of hide and seek. I think he's losing." She giggled and leaned against Jon's body. He wrapped an arm around her and smiled.

"So, we need to find this tunnel. Let's spread out," Dad said.

"There's one more thing, Sara." I touched her on the arm lightly.

"Yes?" She asked.

"Daniel told me about the day the girls died from that accident."

Her expression darkened. I swallowed nervously and had to fight the urge to take a step back from her menacing glare. Peril disguised by beauty...

"I told them that railcar was dangerous and they shouldn't play in it unless I was around. It wasn't my fault, I went to..."

"No, no, Sara, listen. It wasn't you, it was Daniel. He told them to climb in there. He tricked them into thinking they could beat you at hide and seek. He disabled the brake and he pushed them." I paused to let my words sink in. "He killed them, not you."

Sara stared at me in silence. Her face still as stone as her eyes burned brightly with the tragic memory of that day.

"Why?" Her voice suddenly sounded small...childlike.

"I think he wanted the children to guard Tressman's building. There was no other way to make sure you all didn't get in there. He needed help, so he made some. And as an added bonus he got to create bad feelings between you and Pearl. Sisters divided, like Z and Laverna."

"I loved them," Sara whispered.

I looked at her, unsure what to say.

"I loved them so much. They were like my own children. I wanted them to be mine, I wanted them to be with me forever," Sara's voice was still small and clear. I let her words resonate in the still air.

Losing the children hurt her like losing Dad hurt Pearl, like losing Rowan would hurt me. Sara loved those children so much and losing them tore her apart. *This explains why she acts so callous now*, I thought. She's not going to risk any further attachments because it hurts too much. The flip side of love...excruciating pain. Her defense? To be shallow.

"Thank you," she said and turned toward Dad and Pearl who talked together a few yards away. The three of them then headed off toward the tower. Even weakened as Pearl was, she put a comforting arm around her little sister. I heard Pearl whisper, "sorry."

Nana and Mr. Humpphrey went toward the south end of the Keeper's house which left Lilli, Jon, Rowan and I to scout out the North end.

"Maybe the entrance is in the kitchen," Rowan said as he eyed the detached little building.

With no better ideas of where to start, we made our way toward the small, one room brick building. I remembered Jon telling me it was detached from the rest of the house because in case it caught on fire, the main building wouldn't be destroyed.

We hopped easily over the low picket fence and entered the kitchen. Everything seemed quite solid to me. No trap doors, no downstairs, not even a pantry. Strike one.

"Hey, do you guys feel that?" Lilli asked as we wandered to the front of the keeper's house.

"Feel what?" I asked.

"The hum, like a little buzzy vibration," she replied and started to drift around the grounds, first a little left, then right, then a tiny bit back to the left.

"Right here!" She exclaimed. "Come here and stand in front of me." She giggled. "It tickles."

We went to where she was and stood in silence. I looked at Rowan who looked at me and Jon looked at both of us. It was unanimous. Lilli lost it. She stood between us still giggling.

"Oh come on! You don't feel it? Look it goes this way!" She walked away from the keeper's building in nearly a straight line.

"Hey, what do you feel again?" I asked.

"It's like a little tickle in the ground," she said and giggled again. She obviously enjoyed the sensations.

"Is it over here?" I pointed to the left.

She walked in the direction my finger pointed and her face dropped. "No." She pouted. She skipped back to where she was and giggled again.

"How about there?" I pointed in the opposite direction from my first question, toward an old oak tree.

She flitted over and had the same reaction as the other side. "Nope!" She flitted back.

"What about this way?" I pointed toward the Keeper's house.

This time she followed a nearly straight line all the way to the low wall. She nodded and smiled the entire way.

"Jon, do you think she's feeling..."

"Ley lines," Jon whispered. "She's feeling a source of underground energy."

We looked at the path she made. Then we made her walk that same line five more times.

"You remember what Dr. Ross said that day in class about ley lines when we discussed whether or not they existed?" I asked.

"Yeah, he said people who support their existence say that water follows them."

"And Z mentioned them when she talked about why the party was held where it was each year, 'at the crossing of the ley lines'! A ley line runs along here!" I exclaimed. "And if it's true that water follows them, then we have an underground water source running from the Keeper's house in a line toward the inlet...toward Tressman's secret building!"

"The tunnel," Jon and I said simultaneously.

"JINX!" Rowan and Lilli said simultaneously.

"Right," I said and got control back over the group.

"The water souls said the tunnel fills with water!" Rowan said as looked down to his feet. "Well, if the tunnel's down there," he pointed below him, "where the hell's the entrance?"

All four of us looked back to the Keeper's house.

"Oh my God! Storm, what was that riddle you asked me downtown that night? Something about stars?" Jon asked me.

"Yeah, it was the one Pearl said she saw Tressman write. It was, at night they come without being fetched. By day they are lost without being stolen."

"You guys, look," Jon pointed to the North wall of the keeper's house. And there for all to see were four large stars. Presumably to indicate where the beams were, and in fact there were matching stars on the south wall; I remembered the first time Jon showed them to me. But that meant that there were two possible sides for an entrance to our tunnel and with Lilli's perception of energy, I was pretty confident the answer lay beneath the North wall.

"Come on, let's go!" Rowan called. In a blur of skin and clothes we were all over the stone wall. Next stop, the basement of the Keeper's house.

I remembered touring the basement with Jon those many weeks ago. I found it creepy in broad daylight with other people wandering around. The moonless night didn't improve my perception of the place. Add to that, breaking in and the possibility of a secret tunnel that water souls played in and you had the vibe of a bad horror movie.

Relax Storm, I told myself, *you're a mermaid. You are the creature others fear. Or at least that's what everyone tells you. I wonder who would win in a battle between a mermaid and a vampire? Okay, stop. Focus. Right, find the secret tunnel and forget about possibly being attacked by the man in blue or ghost children or cranky cigar smoking captains or whatever else lurks down in this creepy basement.*

"Storm."

"AHHHHHH!" I screamed.

"Chill," Jon said. "I just wanted to give you a flashlight." He thrust a heavy and cold metal tube into my hand.

"Oh, right. Thanks." Luckily he couldn't see me blush in the dark.

I hadn't even noticed how dimly lit it was down in the basement until he brought it to my attention. Thanks to my mer eyes, I could see quite well even without the flashlight.

"Wow, you guys look freaky," Jon said when we were all gathered in the dark basement. He turned his flashlight off and looked at us.

"What?" I asked.

"Your eyes, they all glow. That's so cool."

I forgot about how we must look to him. Three dark shapes with bright orbs where our eyes should be.

"Hey what'd ya'll find?" Mr. Humpphrey's gentle voice joined us in the dark. Dad, Pearl, Sara and Nana followed him down the spiral stairs toward us. Dad held Pearl securely around her waist. Jon turned his flashlight back on.

I handed Mr. Humpphrey my flashlight. As he took it, I caught hold of his arm and drew him close to me. "I'm so sorry about your daughter. I had no idea."

"Thank you. It is for her I am here tonight...and for Rean. I'm afraid I haven't been a very good friend for a very long time. A lot was lost the night of Hurricane Dora...Saint Augustine and its many innocent lives were put at risk because of two, stupid people driven by the need to feel important."

"What do you mean Hurricane Dora?"

"I thought Rean would have told you about Hurricane Dora; the only direct hit of a hurricane on Saint Augustine. It was our fault it happened, we betrayed Z, albeit unknowingly, but because of our foolish actions," his voice seized in his throat and he cleared it roughly, "because of our foolish actions, my daughter died and Saint Augustine was put in peril."

"How could you guys possibly be at fault for that?"

"We moved the Hurricane Lady to a new location. We thought Z was behind the request, but when we arrived at the new chapel, Z was there. Mermaids can't be near the Hurricane Lady, she drains them of life."

"I've heard that."

"And with Z weakened to the point of near death, Hurricane Dora bore into our town with an unabashed fury."

"But who told you to move it?"

"Laverna's son, Daniel."

I was shocked into silence. *Would the twists and turns never end?*

"But why..."

"Over here!" Jon called from the North room making Mr. Humphrey and myself jump. I wanted to talk to him more but he had already started along the narrow passage, the glow of his flashlight dancing with the shadows on the damp coquina walls.

"The stars are right above us," Jon said as we all crowded into the small room.

"Jon, we were here weeks ago! How could I have been so close to the answer and never put it together?" I asked.

"Storm, relax. We've been working on this riddle for over a hundred years. You've been brilliant if you ask me," Pearl whispered. Her eyes barely glowed as she leaned against the rough wall.

I started walking toward her but before I could get more than a step, I tripped.

"Damn," I cursed under my breath as I fell for the second time over the same stupid uneven crack.

"You okay?" Rowan knelt beside me.

"Yeah, I tripped last time I was down here, really hurts too. Stupid floor," I said and kicked it hard with my foot. The crack widened.

"Huh?" I kicked it again and the edge of the cracked cement splintered. Tiny splashes echoed from somewhere below us.

"Storm, I do believe you've found a clue," Jon said in an extremely poor Sherlock Holmes impression.

Crouched around the crack, we dug, pried, pounded and pulled at it in turns. It finally gave to one of Rowan's heavy handed punches and a chunk of cement the size of a silver dollar fell though and landed somewhere below us with a rather loud kerplunk.

"Is that water?" Nana asked. She was out of breath.

Rowan's teeth gleamed brightly as he smiled, "We have a floor to break."

One finger tapped lightly on his chin while his glowing eyes scanned our surroundings for resources. "Ah, HA!" He walked over to the cannon and stepped lightly over the velvet rope with the hanging Do Not Touch sign. "Hey Jon, don't tell your dad," he said as he picked up the canon and walked it back to the hole.

"Right, I'm sure it's no biggie, you know with the breaking in and damaging of the keeper's house and all. What's a little abuse of the artifacts gonna do, right?" Jon laughed nervously.

"Get ready kids, on three." Rowan held the cannon vertically over the small hole.

"One..." Rowan said as he lifted the cannon higher.

"Two..."

"THREE!" The canon landed with a dull thud. Small bits of debris slid down the hole to the invisible cavern below our feet. Tiny little splashes reverberated back to us. Again Rowan sent the cannon down to the cement with a sickening thud. Twice more and then the floor cracked apart. Three more blows and the hole had grown to nearly a foot wide and the cracks spread laterally. The cement fell with heavy splashes into the water below.

One final blow and the hole was wide enough for one person at a time to slip down below.

We peered into the cavern of darkness. The water was only about a foot beneath and pulsed with an obvious swell proving it's connection to a much larger body of water. We had found Tressman's tunnel!

"This must have been what Kate complained about," Pearl said.

"Oh yeah!" Sara chimed. "She was so mad with Tressman because after he finished building this floor, it flooded after an unusually high tide. Remember? We were talking about that at the party! Kate was furious and stormed around with rags and mops complaining about his incompetence. She said the water appeared to just seep up through the cement."

"Incompetence or genius?" Nana said. "He hid this in plain sight. In front of everyone, a passage so secret that not even his partner in crime, Daniel, knew of the entrance."

"Well, 'allo all, isn't this a sweet family reunion?" Daniel's deep voice reverberated through the basement. I looked up in time to see two sets of amber eyes in the passageway. Laverna was with him.

"Pearl, Dear," she said coldly, "you are looking rather unwell. Such a shame it all had to come down to this. If you had simply accepted Daniel's proposal, all of this nonsense could have been avoided. It's not entirely too late, you know, I'm sure Daniel would be more than willing to retrieve your braid."

"Don't you dare!" Dad shouted and charged at the glowing eyes.

Daniel's laughter rang out and a burst of wind blew through the room pushing my dad off his feet and into the wall. He fell heavily to the ground.

"Matthew!" Pearl called.

"Dad!" I called.

The air turned red around me, my energy pulsed from within me and I shot like a rubber band released from its tension at the silhouetted figures by the hall. Somewhere before I reached my intended destination, I hit a wall of resistance as solid as brick and collapsed at Daniel's feet. Laverna picked me up roughly by the shoulder, "Oh, little one, you think you would ever have a chance against us?"

"Leave her," Pearl cried.

"Oh Pearl, so upset. You really shouldn't waste your energy. Perhaps you'd be willing to trade this Halfling, your heir, for your braid? Hmm? I'll send Daniel down..."

"No need, dear sister."

"Z!" Pearl sighed, her eyes were half shut. I wiggled around under Laverna's vice-like clamp on my shoulder to see the welcomed sight of Z's bright, flame-colored eyes drift down the spiral stairs like two bodiless orbs in the darkness.

"Let my granddaughter go." Z's voice was calm. Too calm. As soon as the words were spoken, the vice was released and I tumbled back to the ground. My shoulder throbbed as blood returned.

Nobody moved. It was a moment of breathless stillness, the calm before the storm, like the air had been sucked away and we all held our collective breath.

"Tsk tsk," Laverna's cold voice hissed. "Nearly midnight isn't it precious Pearl. You do like salt in your wine, don't you, *dear sister?*"

And that was it; the final straw that broke Z's reserved presence. It was like a sonic boom hit the building. Hurricane force winds screamed outside, ghastly squalls blew through the narrow passageway. Walls shook, pictures fell from their hooks, glass cases shattered and the ground beneath us rumbled.

Z flew at Laverna and they crashed together with an echo like the surf against a rocky coast. In the confusion and deafening roar, I was vaguely aware of Daniel leaping over my prone body.

"Not so fast," Rowan growled launched himself square into Daniel's chest, another explosion like a crashing wave against rock. I crawled over to Lilli and Jon who sat protectively around Pearl. My dad crawled over to join us, his forehead bleeding from when he hit the wall.

"GO!" Lilli said and pushed Jon into the hole. "Go," she said to me. "We'll guard the hole. You two get that braid!" I looked to my dad who nodded. Reluctantly, I lowered down and heard Lilli giggle. She said something about 'having fun' but before I heard more, a large crash overhead made me duck under.

I found Jon just ahead with his head pressed to the top of the tunnel and his feet kicked frantically to keep him afloat. The tide wasn't yet at its maximum so the tunnel was not completely filled. It became clear that Jon wouldn't be able to swim the entire length having to breath every few feet so I grabbed hold of his leg and pulled him down. He struggled against me.

Jon, stop. It's me. Relax, you can stay under now, like with you and Rowan at the party. You'll be fine as long as I don't let go.

Whoa, Storm, that's you? In my head?

I laughed. *Yeah, it's me.*

This is so cool!

Yeah, it's a hoot, can you swim a bit faster please we have a braid to recover.

Oh, right, sorry.

Every minute that passed I worried. The quiet of the tunnel was in such contrast to the scene we left behind. The journey with Jon was slow and after nearly fifteen minutes, the water ahead brightened.

The narrow tunnel widened around us and we floated side by side and looked up through the water. We were definitely in an underwater structure, surrounded by rounded walls that curved outward and gave an impression of more space than there actually was and the ceiling of the cave reflected dimly through the water's surface. I gasped in awe when I realized what caused the water to glow.

Tressman had made dozens of little biospheres, little glass balls which contained, in essence, mini ecosystems. They were designed to house and grow phosphorescent plankton. *How many generations of these plankton had lived and died and been born behind the walls of the thick, wavy glass?*

I stared at them in awe and they glowed happily back. It was like hundreds of underwater fireflies.

Beautiful, I thought

AIR! Jon's thought exclaimed as he burst away from my hand and up to the surface.

The cavern, as it turned out, was only about two-thirds full with water. Even though it was most likely completely or at least nearly completely submerged on the outside thanks to the still rising super tide, the water seeped leisurely through the coquina walls. It looked like it would be at least another thirty minutes before it was completely filled. And although Jon put up with his second experience as a merman, he seemed rather pleased to have air back in his lungs.

The biospheres' inhabitants gave the air and water an eerie green tinge. The dim light reflected on the uneven walls and shadow and light danced in time to the ripples we made on the water's surface.

"Wow," I said out loud when I surfaced. "This place is unreal!" My voice reverberated around the small space. We hovered at the surface since there was nowhere to stand. Effortless for me, a bit more of a challenge for Jon.

"Look at these!" Jon exclaimed.

We both cowered from the booming return of his voice.

"Sorry," he whispered. "Look at these," he repeated, this time much more quietly.

He pointed at a beautiful double strand of salt pearls, each slightly different in shape and hue. The tiny pearls were all strung together with more dangling pearls which hung down in between. It was quite stunning. The pearls were encased behind glass right at our current eye level. "And these!" He paddled over to tiny jewel encrusted mirrors, each the size of my palm, also enclosed in glass. "They must be worth a fortune."

"What about that?" I pointed up. Overhead, attached to the apex of the cave was a rusted, iron chandelier. It was draped with more strands of small pearls mixed with dangling periwinkle shells. Stubs of white candles with hard melted wax were stuck in each of the twenty-four holders. It gave me chills thinking about Tressman in this room with all of his odd treasures.

Innumerable glass cases surrounded us. Some with jewelry, some with intricately carved pieces of coral, others with gold statues, mirrors and diamond-encrusted silk bags.

"Wow. It's like a museum," I whispered.

"Or a mausoleum," Jon whispered.

We floated silently another minute.

"Oh," I said in shock. I pointed to another case which contained a glass etching of a girl with long hair and penetrating eyes. It was a portrait of Pearl. This was Tressman's private place to fawn over the woman he loved and to keep his collections. But thanks to the Keeper's request of a safe room and Daniel's information about Pearl, Tressman was able to build this in plain sight so to speak, seemingly with approval of both human and mer! The water around me rippled, echoing my shivers of disgust.

Each treasure had its own protective glass case and had its own carved shelf with a leather wrap across the front to prevent free floating objects. It would have been absolutely, breathtakingly beautiful if it wasn't completely disturbing. Time and the elements had left this grotto and its unique collections untouched, just like his most prized treasure, the one he never succeeded in getting...Pearl.

He, Tressman, made all of this, the structure, the tunnel, the collections, for himself. This was supposed to become Pearl's little grotto where she would live under the control of her master, the keeper of her braid. The thought of Pearl being held against her will in this underground fortress made me cry. It was not only about taking her braid but taking away her free will. She could live without her braid, but without her free will, she'd die. Did Tressman know this? Probably not, but Daniel sure did. He, Daniel, probably planned to be her savior, after all, what would her choice have been then? Die or go with him? I'd probably have given the options some pretty serious thought, myself.

"Slime," I spat the word into the cave as I thought of Tressman's intentions and then felt sick as I thought of Daniel's. No wonder mer's were tentative to let humans know of their existence and no wonder human's feared mers. I mean if this is the kind of treatment and deception both parties can expect, GAH! My skin crawled with heebee geebees.

"Let's find her braid and get out of here," I whispered.

Jon nodded. We swam in circles and examined all of the artifacts. The braid had to be here somewhere.

Maybe it's in something else, I thought as I looked at some of the small, intricately carved wooded boxes. *Maybe, but no, I think Tressman would want to see the braid. But then again, what if he didn't put it here? No, I can't let myself think it isn't in here. This is our last chance. It has to be here, I know it's here. It's...*

"It's not here!" Jon called.

"It has to be. What other secret cave could there be?" I swam in circles around the tiny room and looked at every object again. I mentally crossed each shelf off after examining it as not having the braid. *Crap, it isn't here.*

"Hey, Storm, what's that?" Jon called.

"What?" I was ready to cry.

"That, up there." He pointed to a dark shadowed area near the ceiling, next to the chandelier. His legs flailed with the effort to stay afloat.

"Umm, I don't know." I squinted at it but the light was so dim and the ceiling was at least seven feet above our current water line that I couldn't make it out. Although the water still rose, it would be some time before we could reach it, whatever it was.

"How can we get up there to see what it is? It looks like it could be some sort of hole or something." He kicked with his feet making an echo of splashes like at an indoor pool. He fell far short of the mysterious shadow and scratched his hand on the rough coquina on the way down.

"Ouch," he said as he rubbed his sore hand. I swam to him and made him hold his hand out to show me the scrapes. It was covered in tiny scratches, like little razors had sliced through the softened, wet skin of his palm. Small drops of blood oozed from each slice and mixed with the saltwater. It became at once more diffuse and worse looking than it was. He dunked it under water and clenched his hand into a tight fist.

"I'm okay, it's just a few scratches."

"I'm sorry," I said. I hated him getting hurt, even if it was just a few scrapes.

"Can't you jump? You're half fish," Jon said looking at me, his right hand still closed tightly.

"Nice, Jon, real nice." Indignant at being called at fish, I still knew that he was right. I'd leapt much higher than that before.

I swam over and eyed my target. I sank below the surface, took in a gulp of water and surged upward like a rocket. So fast, so high...too high, way too high.

"OUCH!" I yelped after I crashed into the ceiling of the cave and fell ungracefully back into the water with a loud splash. I resurfaced and rubbed my head. The walls of the cave swayed and tilted at odd angles.

"Great flipper, what can you do for your next trick?" Jon asked.

"Shut up, that really hurt," I moaned.

"Well, shake it off, try again," Jon said while he doggy paddled to stay afloat.

"Thanks for the sympathy Mr. Manistar," I said.

"Come on, get on with it, there'll be time for sympathy later," he winked.

I eyed my target and dipped below the surface again. My head still throbbed a little.

Okay, now, not so hard, I told myself. Pearl's voice from our trainings spoke in my head, *'It's easy to do things to your greatest ability, the real talent comes with deliberately being able to do less.'*

Deliberately do less, I repeated her words to myself.

I gulped and pushed subtly with my legs. I rose out of the water gracefully, hovered a few feet up, then slid back down.

"7.5," Jon said.

I scowled at him.

"I almost had it," I said.

"Third time's the charm, Storm," Jon said.

I set myself up, leapt higher, but not too high and this time could see right into the shadowed area. *It's a hole! It's totally an entrance to a second tunnel! The problem? We won't be able to get into it until the water rises higher unless we don't mind getting sliced and diced to pieces by the razor-sharp walls. Nice, Tressman.*

"So?" Jon asked after I resurfaced from my landing back into the water.

"It's a tunnel alright, but we're going to have some time to kill before the water rises enough for us to get into it."

"I guess that's also why the tide was important," Jon said. "Daniel needed the girls to show him the tunnel entrance, but he also needed it to reach that!" His gaze shifted to the shadowed spot near the ceiling.

"Yeah, it would take a huge tide to make the water in here rise high enough to get in there without shredding yourself on the coquina."

"So Tressman already had his entrance cleverly hidden but then he used his knowledge of tides to make the braid inaccessible except on very rare occasions. So even if someone had figured out how to get into the first grotto, chances are, they wouldn't have been able to get to the braid," I answered.

"So what do we do now?" Jon asked.

"We wait," I said with a sigh. *Please let the others be okay,* I prayed silently to any and all that would listen.

Minutes passed, the water rose steadily, but unbearably slowly. The air was thick and the walls of the cavern dripped with perspiration.

"What do you call a kitten drinking lemonade?" Jon broke the silence.

He was on his back, floating around the room.

"Huh?" I had been looking at a set of tiny silver mirr   a   a bronze pocket watch set atop an old, worn leather book behind o   the glass cases.

"A kitten drinking lemonade, what do you call it?" H asked again while he stared at the chandelier.

"Umm, what..."

"A riddle Storm, to pass the time. So do you know?"

"A riddle." I exhaled slowly. We held the life f my mother in our hands, we waited in a cave nobody had been in for over a hundred years, there's a battle going on not a half mile away and Jon is asking me a riddle. "Sourpuss," I answered.

"Wow, you've gotten better." He smiled toward the cavern's ceiling.

I splashed him with water. It landed right on his face and he rolled over with a cough. Floating upright now, he splashed me back. Then an all out splashing war began. Water went everywhere; not a single case was spared. We darted and ducked and swam. We laughed and for a few brief moments forgot about the weight on our shoulders. The wars, the battles, the betrayals, the fear all took a back seat to good old fashioned goofing around.

Finally exhausted we floated together on our backs.

"You're really cool Storm," Jon said. "I'm glad you decided to come back to Saint Augustine."

"Really?" I said.

"Yeah, this sure beats giving tours of the lighthouse."

I laughed. "Glad I could help liven up your summer." I gave him a playful shove.

"Hey, look!" He exclaimed.

Without asking at what, being that we had been waiting for only one thing for nearly an hour, I looked to the hole. If we had more time, we could have just waited until the cave filled, but time, to quote Z, was not on our side. We had to make a move now or we wouldn't be able to get back before midnight.

"You think?" He asked.

"Yeah, I think."

He smiled. "Okay, you give me a boost then follow." We had devised a plan earlier while waiting. We figured when the water got close enough, we could close the gap a bit quicker. It was similar to a trick used at the Shamu show at Seaworld. I played the part of Shamu and Jon was the trainer.

We both dove down to the bottom of the cave, Jon stood on my shoulders and then I pushed off. We leapt from the water. I kept my eye on the target and with perfect grace and timing, deposited Jon at the lip of the hole. He held on and then climbed in. Then I leapt a second time and thankfully he grabbed my hands and saved me from some nasty scrapes.

"We made it!" I exclaimed and Jon and I hi-fived. "Okay, lead the way." We crawled through the pitch black, narrow tunnel. I bumped into Jon when he stopped suddenly. I leaned next to Jon in the tunnel and looked over the edge he had reached. It was a second cave, only half as big as the first and unlit! The water seemed to be at the same level as in the first cave. And across the small expanse, on the wall opposite the tunnel entrance, was a single case. I gasped.

Protected behind the wavy glass was the most beautiful golden hair, shimmering and sparkling on its own and then enhanced even further, if that was even possible, by luminescent strands of green and gold thread strung with tiny silver bells weaved intricately throughout the impossibly elaborate 100 strand braid. It was perfect except for the end that had been attached to Pearl's head. On that end, having been ripped unceremoniously from her scalp, the hair was frayed, broken and tangled. I felt a sharp, searing pain on my own scalp and I instinctively reached for my own braid, which was tied back safely with the rest of my hair.

"Oh Pearl," I whispered.

"Looks like you have one more leap to perform, Flipper," Jon whispered. I smiled brightly. We found the braid!

"Come on!" He said and we both dropped into the water and swam to the opposite side. Jon swam cautiously as he couldn't see a thing. I lined up below the case, steadied myself and pushed up and out of the water. I slipped back into the water with my prize in hand.

The walls echoed with my joyful calls when my head broke above the surface.

"Let's go! We have to get this back!" I said. "What time do you have?"

He looked down at the glowing green hands of his watch. "Yikes, it's ten minutes till midnight."

The water, still on the rise, made our return trip to the first tunnel easier It wouldn't be long before both caves and their connecting tunnel were filled with water.

We slipped down into the first cave but Jon pulled away from me and resurfaced.

"What?" I asked.

"We won't make it, I can't swim that fast."

"Well, I can't leave you here, the water's still rising, there won't be air in either cave for much longer."

I looked at Jon. I was torn between getting the braid to my mom and making sure he was safe.

He answered my indecision. "I'll be fine. You go! Just be sure to come back for me."

"Jon."

"Go."

"I'll be right back, I promise. Don't go anywhere."

"Yeah, I'll just hang hang here. Maybe practice my backstroke a bit." He laughed.

"Jon." I didn't want to leave him.

"Go. I'll be fine."

Reluctantly, I dove beneath the surface and swam into the narrow tunnel. I turned one time to see Jon's legs treading water.

I made it to the entrance in just under five minutes but deliberately stopped short of the hole. The last thing I needed was to pop up and get knocked out by a flying brass bell or something. I peered up through the water. It seemed calm. I rose to eye level and made a slow revolution. *What happened here?*

Broken glass and artifacts littered the floor, puddles of water pooled in places, piles of sand and rubble mounded in others and large coquina chunks were missing from the walls. But as for action, there wasn't any. In fact, there was nobody around.

I lifted higher and pulled myself slowly from the hole and crouched onto the basement floor. With dripping steps, I made my way cautiously toward what was left of the spiral stairs. The humid night air greeted me and the stars shown brightly in the moonless sky. The storm was gone, replaced with the drone and chatter of insects. Muted voices made me freeze. And there, huddled by the base of the lighthouse tower sat familiar shapes, some hunched over others. "Hey!" I called with a hoarse voice. I hadn't gotten all of the water out of my throat yet.

Glowing eyes as well as shadowed faces turned in my direction. The tension was as thick as the air. Rowan's broad form strode to me with outstretched arms and electric blue eyes. His hair was disheveled, his shirt was torn and some blood had dried on his lower lip. He looked like an ancient warrior with his chiseled face and the muscles of his exposed chest emphasized by his sweaty, iridescent skin. He surrounded me in his warm embrace.

"Am I in time?" I asked as the two of us walked quickly to the tower.

"Do you have it?" Rowan asked.

"Yes!" I held out the small glass case. I noticed as I approached the small figure resting on dad's lap, the hair in the case shimmered brighter. Pearl's eyes opened, faded torches of green light. The others drew in closer to us and murmured softly.

I knelt into the sopping grass and placed the case in her hands. She took hold with her thin fingers and in one moment of a simple squeeze, the glass shattered and the braid fell softly into her palms.

The smile on Pearl's face could have lit an entire city. She absolutely glowed from every pore. She looked at me, tears raced down her cheeks.

"My love, my daughter, my soul. You saved me when I couldn't save myself. Thank you."

"Just like you did for me," I said with a smile.

The bells of the braid in her hand chimed lightly in a breeze that whispered through the palmettos. She brought it closer to her face and I watched her light return, dim at first, but then brighter and effervescent. Her eyes reopened with their full power and I was nearly blinded. I had never known Pearl with the full power of her braid. Strong didn't begin to describe her.

"Where's Jon?" Lilli asked.

"Still in the cave. I have to get back to get him," I said as I darted back toward the building. *Hang on, Jon. I'm coming!*

I dove in and swam as hard as I could.

I'm on my way! I thought as intently as possibly when I got back in the water.

Jon? Can you hear me?

Nothing.

I swam through the entire tunnel without a sight of him. He would surely be waiting, although anxiously, for me to arrive. The water was rising faster as the cave top was smaller than the base, but there should have been enough time...*there should have, crap...I'm coming!* I thought and pushed my speed.

The walls widened and the green glow lit the water. I looked around, nothing. The light from the bioluminescence that had once looked beautiful to me took on a sinister glare. I looked up. The cave was now completely full of water.

Oh God. I saw him. He floated like a rag doll, effortlessly buoyed by the salty water, pushed to the top of the cave. I swam up, past the second tunnel entrance that only a short time before held the key to our success. I heard Jon's mocking voice in my head, *'you're half fish...great flipper'...We had won, we had beaten Daniel and Tressman. We had solved the riddles, we had fought and we had succeeded. JON!* I called in my mind. There was no response.

No Jon. No! I swam up to him.

This is all my fault! I screamed in my head and reached out for his bare leg. It felt cold. I caught a glimpse of his glazed, unseeing eyes. *NO!* I screamed again and tucked his lifeless body behind me. I swam us back toward the tunnel.

As I swam through the dark, narrow space to the hole, I calculated how much time he would have been underwater. It couldn't have been too long, there was bound to be a bit of air for him when he got back to the cave. I remembered taking my CPR class, I saw people revived in movies. *He'll be okay, we just need to get him back.* I thought.

After what felt like eternity we reached the hole, Rowan and the others sat waiting for us. I pushed Jon up to Rowan's waiting arms with great effort. He was limp and heavy and his limbs splayed and were uncooperative.

I climbed up after. Rowan dragged Jon so he lay flat on a space he made on the floor. I leapt onto Jon's drenched body. I felt for a pulse, I listened for breathing. Nothing. I began with two rescue breaths in his mouth and then compressions.

"One-one thousand, two-one thousand, three-one thousand, four-one thousand," I counted the numbers aloud.

I did more breaths, more compressions. *Why isn't anybody helping me?*

More breaths, more compressions.

I looked up with wild eyes and saw only sympathetic stares.

"What?" I yelled.

"Baby," my dad spoke, "he's...he's gone." His voice cracked with emotion.

"No! No, he's not!" I squealed.

More compressions; my arms ached.

Nana knelt next to me and tried to make me stop. I pushed her aside. One-one thousand, two-one thousand...

"Come on, Jon. Wake up! WAKE UP!" I yelled. His face had a grayish tint, the skin around his lips and eyes were a sickly blue.

It was Z who finally pulled me off of Jon's drenched, inert body. She wrapped me in her arms and we sat curled together on the floor next to Jon. We rocked slowly as she held me tightly to her chest.

Jon is gone. No, it can't be. Wake up Storm. This is just another bad dream. WAKE UP!

But I didn't wake up. I heard Nana say something about calling Greg. Lilli sat next me on the wet ground. She touched Jon's shoulder lightly with one hand and closed her eyes.

*NO! Not possible. Jon's my friend. Jon...*Behind my closed eyelids I saw his smile, I saw his wink, his stupid looks, the way he used his hands while he talked...*Jon. Not Jon. JON!!!!!* My mind screamed in torture.

Tears ran from my eyes. *'Us mortals can't keep up with your kind for long'*...Nana's prophetic voice spoke in my head.

I'm a monster, I told myself. I'm a witch...a horrible, monstrous, sea witch. It's all my fault. I killed him. Why did I have to get him involved. I...

Z's hand rubbed my back, "Storm,"

"No." A voice I barely recognized croaked. The voice was my own and yet somehow I was no longer the girl I knew.

"No." My voice spoke with more emphasis.

"NO!" I screamed to everyone and no one. The silence following pulsed in my head.

"NO!" I spoke again as if that simple word could reverse the reality of the nightmare in which I found myself wide awake in. *My mother was alive, my best friend was dead. Can't everyone and everything just stop for a second. This was a carousel ride I no longer wanted to be on.*

I rose slowly to my feet. Eyes glowed in rainbow hues around me. My gaze turned down to the soaked cement floor where the lifeless body of my best friend still lay. Lilli's petite frame curled against Jon's side. Her eyes shimmered like mercury as one hand rested on Jon's arm.

"Storm," Nana spoke now, her voice thick from pushing back tears.

"No." The word this time came out like a low growl directed very specifically at those surrounding me, like a warning when a panther feels threatened. *I didn't ask for this. I didn't want this. Jon didn't want this. Be good, do what you're told. For what? This?* NO! My mind spun with thoughts as I stole one more glance at him. My legs trembled with anger, my limbs ached to move, to run, to escape.

I looked at them all in turn. They surrounded me; trapped me. I had to get out.

I can't breathe. My mind screamed for air. Looking wildly around me, I finally saw it, a speck of light reflecting off the twisted metal remnants of the spiral stairs. *Light. If there was light, maybe there was space. If there was space, there was bound to be air. And I needed air. Now.*

Nobody tried to stop me as I pushed passed them. I burst up the spiral stairs and out into the still raging night air. My feet ran and my voice screamed. I leapt over the stone wall of the Keeper's house. I flew across the gravel parking lot, onto the paved road and followed it into the State Park.

"NO!" I kept screaming. Louder each time. My voice matched the decibel level of the thunder above me. I made it to the old coquina quarry and by now my screams blended into one another until the beginning and ending were unrecognizable. My voice seemed to reach out to the sky. It was as if the sound itself was electrically charged. I felt it from my core. The energy rose up and out. A burst of lightning flashed from the sky. Actually, it flashed from me to the sky and then back down again. *Energy. Me. Pearl had mentioned something about mers and energy and ions and...NO! NO!*

"NO!" I screamed again, lightning flashed again, thunder roared again.

I ran through the park, the landscape morphing from oak canopy to exposed sand dunes. Over the rolling dunes I scampered and then finally collapsed as I reached the shoreline directly opposite the lighthouse. I fell to my knees and then my side and then wrapped my arms protectively around my body as if by holding tight enough I could keep myself from splitting apart.

I don't know how long I lay curled on the sandy bank. A warm touch brought me back to the present.

"Stormy," his deep voice whispered. It wasn't threatening or demanding. I didn't answer.

"Babe. Open your eyes."

I did. Rowan's face was invisible but his eyes glowed electric blue. I had nothing to say so I just blinked.

"Sit up." His voice was still patient but I understood that ignoring him wasn't an option. I sat up. "Good. Feel better?"

"No."

"Hmm." He sat down next to me and gazed toward the lighthouse. "Babe, tonight you saved Pearl."

"Jon," I croaked.

"Yes, he made the biggest sacrifice a human can make for us. He will be remembered fondly."

That's it? Remembered fondly? Human sacrifice? I thought bitterly.

"You have to accept you're a mer, Storm. Accidents happen when we mix with humans."

"I don't want to," I whispered.

"I don't care," Rowan said. "You have to, you're Storm."

"Stop saying that! Everybody keeps saying that. I'm Storm. What the hell does that even mean? All I've managed to do so far is get my friend killed."

"And save Pearl."

I exhaled slowly. *Of course he would have to remind me of that.*

"And save our clan."

And that.

"And..."

"Okay. Stop already." I looked at his silhouetted face inches from my own. "I can't do this anymore. I don't want to be responsible for people's lives. For their deaths."

"Well, you can't change who you are, Storm. None of us can. We just do the best we can, you know? And I am really sorry about Jon. He was a good kid."

"He's not coming back is he?" A hot tear slid down to my lips.

"No. Lilli said she 'couldn't find him'."

We sat together in silence and stared at the slow spin of the lighthouse's beacon light across the still choppy ink colored waters inlet. Rowan put his arm around me and I leaned my head on his damp shoulder. His shirt was torn and his skin felt slick and hot beneath my cheek. My breathing slowed and the tears dried in sticky streaks on my cheek.

"You know something else?" Rowan nudged me lightly.

"What?"

"You're damn hot when you're mad."

"What?"

"Seriously my little sea nymph. And you have got some speed! I nearly had to jog to keep up!" Bright teeth glowed in the darkness behind his grin.

"Ugh!" I shoved him and he fell sideways. But I couldn't stop a grin from forming briefly on my own lips.

"Ouch. Careful Stormy. I'm very delicate you know."

I didn't even see his arm coming at me but I somehow landed in a pile on top of him. He didn't stop there, though. Fingers multiplied until he had me in a tickling frenzy.

"Okay, Okay. I give up," I finally managed to gasp. My breath came in spurts and gasps.

Our sandy bodies lay in a crumpled heap on the shore line. My energy, both positive and negative, was spent. A smile lingered on my lips. A smile. *A smile? How could I smile when my friend just died? I guess my transition really was complete...I really am a sea witch.*

"Storm, no you aren't." Rowan replied to my unspoken realization. Our feet were touching the water's edge. My thoughts weren't my own.

"Yeah. Right." The light moment from a moment ago dissipated. *Was I becoming more a cold-hearted mer than a human?*

"Hey. We aren't cold-hearted, Storm. We just have a different scale to go by, that's all. And tonight you and Jon saved thousands. Unfortunately in any battle there is a price to pay. We are lucky it was only one soul. We have not always been as lucky."

"I guess so," I said aloud this time.

Rowan slowly sat up, cradling me on his lap. I didn't resist. "It gets easier with time. The first one is always the hardest."

"Yeah. Okay," I mumbled. *More mer than human*, I thought again. *The first one. Meaning there will be more. My mind spun to Nana and Dad. There will be more. Time to face reality. I needed to let go of the things that were fragile, things I could harm just be circumstance...things that were human. I let out a sigh of resignation and resolution. I am Storm. A mer. Better to cut ties now than to cause more senseless tragedy.*

"Yeah," I said again. This time more forcefully.

"Wanna race back?" Rowan winked and glanced across the inlet to the lighthouse grounds. "I could give you a head start," he said with a playful shove.

"Whatever," I replied. "I could beat you if you started yesterday."

"Sounds like a challenge, ma'dear."

I smiled, this time for real. I had been trying to balance two lives for too long. I was a mer. No longer would I be held accountable to those horrible human emotions of guilt and sorrow. I lived in a different world with different rules and different accounting.

"On your mark," I said.

"Ready or not," he smiled.

Ready, I thought.

"GO!" We shouted in unison and launched ourselves into the night water of the inlet.

Rowan's sleek form was just to my left as my body cut effortlessly through the murk. But I didn't need to see him. I could smell him and hear him and I was going to beat him.

In your dreams, my darling minnow. His voice resounded in my head and I felt a pulse of water, with the force of a small explosion, hit my head. He had obviously just given a giant kick. No worries, a quick kick of my own and...

Storm? An utterly familiar voice cut through the darkness. It stopped me short. While intentions of being less human are easily stated, the soul is not one to be easily tricked. So despite my convincing speech of moving on, the human parts of me, the guilt, the sorrow, the anguish, and the worry were still, apparently, very much there. And all it took to have those parts rush back to the forefront was one voice. Jon's voice.

Storm? Is that you? Where am I? His voice spoke again. I floundered in the water, treading in place looking with useless eyes, searching with all of my keen senses. *Nothing.* Rowan was long gone. *How long until he figures out I stopped racing? How am I hearing that voice? Why am I hearing that voice?*

Hey, look it's the lady! Lady, did you see? We have a new friend to play with us! The girls all chimed in high pitched unison unable to contain their excitement.

No. I thought. *No, no, no.* I shook my head in the water and my hair danced weightlessly around my face. *The girls, the water souls...a new playmate...his voice...no.*

Jon? I asked the voice in my head, part of me praying that it wasn't true and part of me praying that it was.

Storm! Yes, it's me. Where the hell am I? And who are these little girls that keep asking me to play? Jon's voice asked.

Oh God. I slowly sunk deeper in the still, dark water. *Jon. You're here! I need to...Lilli said that...I have to get...*my mind was thick and I couldn't think straight, *You're not gone*, was all I could solidly come up with in my brain. I smiled and settled onto the soft bottom as the cloudy water covered me like a blanket.

Yeah, I'm here, but where the heck is here?

Jeezus, I'm so sorry. I should be doing something, I just can't remember what it is. I felt so tired and it felt so good to rest. And Jon wasn't gone. That's so good. If only Lilli knew...

Sorry? Storm? What's going on. Am I...

Oh, Jon. We need to talk.

Acknowledgments

We are extremely grateful to a number of family, friends, and local St. Augustine attractions for their help and inspiration along the way. Early readers: Shannon Pitchford, Samantha Eide, Erin Kipps, Mary Williams, Lisa Burnett, Claudia Richards, Andy Nance, Terry Tranthom, Frank and Maureen Bolen; Editors: Nancy Moreland and David Bolen for not accepting "just because" as an explanation, and Owen and Jonathan Pitchford for help with "it's" and "its"; Lap warmers: Zelda and Mufasa; Local Mer Haunts: City of St. Augustine and St. Augustine Beach, The Beach Comber, Jacks BBQ, The Pit/Stir It Up, St. Augustine Lighthouse, GhostAugustine and the "yellow beach house"; ABC of St. Augustine: for maintaining their stock of champagne! Casey Toons: for including Storm in the map of St. Augustine; Facebook fans: for LIKEing us! Mandy Bolen for her wonderful article in the Citizen, Denise Kaminsky and Martin Olson: for showing us the power of social networking, Jim Strader and Jonathan Westover for showing us our potential and to The Tribe, The Yoga Chicks, Meg's husband, Dean Richardson, Tina's angel: Paul Archekto, Nick Archekto, Debbie Braden, Josh and Abbey Archekto, John and Andrea Bolen, and JP and Rachel Bolen: thank you all for your kind words, thoughts, and consistent encouragement. And also a huge debt of gratitude to David Bolen, who in addition to being mentioned above as an awesome editor, also helped make this Second Edition possible! Thank you for helping her (and us) accept the tale!

About the Authors

There is no tale...quite like this one!

So what would you do if there was a book you wanted to read but it didn't yet exist? Well, if you were Meghan and Tina, two close friends living in St. Augustine Florida who shared a desire for a book with adventure, strong female characters, magic, and, of course, mermaids, you'd probably share a glass of wine while sitting in Tina's lush garden and decide to write it. The rest, as it is often said, is history.

Tina, a proud cat mom, still lives in St. Augustine; having left her rather chillier origins of Iowa long behind her. Meghan, mother of 3 and wife to 1, currently lives aboard her sailboat in the Florida Keys. But don't let the distance fool you, Tina and Meg are still fast friends, co-authors busy with Storm's next adventures, and now as the fates would have it, business partners in their own publishing company, LunaSea Publishing.

When they aren't writing or promoting Storm, Meg teaches yoga, and Tina dives headfirst into her art. Interested in reading more about this awesome pair? Or even better, want to schedule a Storm book signing, or book club, school or library literacy event and have Meg and Tina come out to play?

Visit their website to schedule your event:

LunaSeaPublishing.com

-or-

Contact them by the Facebook Page:

Storm and the Mermaid's Knot-A Novel

Made in the USA
Columbia, SC
21 July 2017